Praise for

THE ARCANUM

"From some dark bridge between history and fiction, *The Arcanum* throws the reader into a midnight's maelstrom of mystery, thrills, and pure adrenaline fun. Hold your breath and enjoy the ride!" —Wes Craven, director of the *Scream* and *Nightmare on Elm Street* series

"Great fun . . . a fast-paced supernatural thriller." —*Rocky Mountain News*

"Wheeler does a good job bringing to life characters we've all at least heard of if we're not all that familiar with them. . . Enjoyable and a clever illustration of how the supernatural can be used to tell modern tales." —*Santa Fe New Mexican*

"A highly entertaining occult thriller." —*Register Pajaronian*

"A cinematic debut novel . . . with a wealth of well-researched period detail . . . Vividly written." —*Publishers Weekly*

"*The Arcanum* is a rare feat, a perfect blend of history, mystery pop culture, and class-act pulp-fiction. It's the sort of thing Lovecraft and Conan Doyle might have collaborated on . . if they weren't already characters in the novel." —Christopher Golden, author of *The Boys Are Back in Town*

"Entertains and thrills!" —*Deadly Pleasures*

"If a secret society involving Houdini, Conan Doyle, and Lovecraft isn't enough, add voodoo, the *Book of Enoch*, and a young girl with a world-shattering secret. A roaring tour of a secret history all of us wish was really true." —Alexander C. Irvine, author of the award-winning *A Scattering of Jades*

Thomas
Wheeler

THE ARCANUM

BANTAM BOOKS

THE ARCANUM
A Bantam Book

PUBLISHING HISTORY
Bantam hardcover edition published May 2004
Bantam trade paperback edition / July 2005

Published by
Bantam Dell
A Division of Random House, Inc.
New York, New York

All rights reserved.
Copyright © 2004 by Thomas Wheeler
Cover painting © Jules Elie Delaunay/The Bridgeman Art Library
Cover designed by Jamie S. Warren Youll

Library of Congress Catalog Card Number: 2003063571

Bantam Books and the rooster colophon are registered trademarks of Random House, Inc.

ISBN: 0-553-38199-7

Printed in the United States of America
Published simultaneously in Canada

www.bantamdell.com

BVG 10 9 8 7 6 5 4 3 2 1

FOR CHRISTINA

ACKNOWLEDGMENTS

LET US START at the beginning.

In addition to being a wonderful writer and storyteller, my father, Gerald Wheeler, also had a rich appreciation for history's misfits, mystics, and rogues. This novel is proof my father's enthusiasm was infectious.

The unconditional support of my mother, Judi Barton, and the creative example she set for her children has inspired me to view the world through a lens of adventure and infinite possibility. I love her and thank her.

My manager and friend, Warren Zide, has been a steadfast supporter of *The Arcanum* from its inception through its many generations. His partner, Craig Perry, one of the best story minds in Los Angeles, stretched, tested, challenged, and pushed *The Arcanum* at every turn, resulting in a vastly improved story and an often exasperated author.

My brother, William Wheeler, a formidable writing talent himself, could recite passages of this novel in his sleep. His patience alone has been heroic but his brilliant suggestions at critical junctures helped shape this story more than any other person save the author.

I would also like to thank my dear friends Bobby Cohen and Michelle Raimo for their early advocacy, outstanding advice, and steady guidance.

My researcher, Carolyn Chriss, and my assistant, Robbie Thompson, came to my aid late in the game but each had a lasting impact in defining this world and readying the manuscript for publication.

I'll always be indebted to Mel Berger, my agent at William Morris, for his enthusiasm and able stewardship.

My editor at Bantam Dell, Richard SanFilippo, along with being a superb collaborator has also proven to be an honest broker, a trusted ally, and a great friend.

And, lastly, before anything I write sees the light of day it passes under the exquisite brown eyes of my wife, Christina Malpero-Wheeler. Her truth, her fire, and her wisdom give me daily strength. She's taught me more than she'll ever know. I want to thank her for being the passion of my life and for bringing Luca Thomas Wheeler into the world.

1

LONDON—1919

A SEPTEMBER STORM battered a sleeping London. Barrage after barrage of gusting sheets drummed on the rooftops and loosened clapboards. Raindrops like silver dollars pelted the empty roads and forced families of pigeons into huddled clumps atop the gaslights.

Then it stopped.

The trees of Kensington Gardens swayed, and the city held its breath. It waited a few dripping moments, then relaxed.

Just as suddenly, a Model-T Ford swerved past Marble Arch in Hyde Park and buzzed around Speakers' Corner, peals of laughter following in its wake.

Inside the car, Daniel Bisbee held the steering wheel with one hand and patted Lizzie's plump thigh with the other. The five pints had done their work, strengthening his resolve. Lizzie was still wearing her shabby costume from the theater, and pretended not to notice Daniel's nudging fingers ruffling under her skirt. She was a notorious flirt but failed to realize the expectations that would arouse in her suitors.

As he inched his hand to her knee, she babbled on nervously. "And Quigley had the bloody nerve to give me notes right before

I'm about to go on, completely shattering my concentration. And you know his breath is simply dreadful. I've no idea what he eats but there's something unhealthy about the man. And where do they find these pitiful crowds? They didn't laugh at all."

Daniel smiled, giving the impression that he was listening, but his attention was focused on moving his fingers another five inches up her thigh. He crept like a spider into her skirts but she pulled him back with a shy "Danny," while another round of giggles erupted from the backseat.

In the back, Gulliver Lloyd pawed Celia West—a less pretty, less talented actress than Lizzie, but one who still drew the boys by offering the carnal treasures Lizzie so coyly protected.

What Gulliver lacked in height he more than compensated for with his unflagging persistence. Also, being rich didn't hurt. Celia fended off his pinches and pokes in a gentle wrestling match.

"You're horrible, stop it," Celia teased, then slapped Gulliver on the arm when he relented.

Gulliver snuck his hands around Celia's waist, then swiftly brought his lips to hers and kissed her before backing away.

Celia touched her lips. "You're terrible, Gully." And she dropped her chin, gazing up at him with eyes darkened by mascara.

Up front, Daniel Bisbee clenched his teeth.

The four actors were halfway through the run of *Purloin's Prophecy,* a new play at the Leicester Playhouse. Daniel and Lizzie played the lovers, yet somehow, Celia was Gulliver's fourth conquest of the run. And that wasn't right. Daniel's upbringing in the tenements on the East End had bred a competitiveness in him. Gully got everything he wanted because he was rich. Even Daniel's excitement at driving Gully's new car was dampened when he realized he'd become nothing more than an unpaid chauffeur.

Anxious breathing and rustling clothes replaced the giggles. Daniel looked over at Lizzie, who was blushing furiously.

He swigged from a cracked leather flask and pushed on the

accelerator, skidding onto Piccadilly. Lizzie grabbed the door handle.

"Slower, Danny, please."

Daniel spun another turn, thumping a curb in the process.

"Oi, Dano! A lighter foot, if you don't mind," Gulliver groused from the backseat. His hand was wedged between Celia's breast and her corset. This was a delicate moment and he wanted nothing to upset his venture.

"Drop me off. It's late," Lizzie said to the window, her breath fogging the glass.

THE MODEL-T skidded around the corner eighty meters from the museum gates. The British Museum was closed for the night, its windows darkened. It was a solid, squat building stretching three square blocks, guarded by towering firs. Its small windows were barred, its tall gates sharp. The only visitor at this late hour was a fog that rolled in from every intersection, peculiar ground clouds that surged forth like a massing army, wisping about the buildings, misting the windows, choking off the rain-glimmered air. Shreds seeped through the fence and seized the interior grounds.

Then, somewhere in the darkness, glass shattered and an alarm bell started clanging.

FOG SURROUNDED THE car. Beyond the windows, nothing was visible save tendrils of twisting air. Lizzie pushed her foot on an imaginary brake.

"Danny."

Daniel Bisbee tapped the low-speed pedal as the road disappeared before his eyes.

"What's all this, then?"

Lizzie later told the police that her first thought was "snow angel." Her wealthy grandparents once took her skiing in Switzerland with her two younger brothers, and they learned to make snow angels in the deep drifts. The gray blot in the fog was in the shape of an angel, with wings outstretched. But soon those beating wings made her think less of beauty and more of panic. And as the fog peeled away, the feathery wings melted into mere arms, waving frantically.

"D-Danny?" Lizzie said.

But there wasn't a chance.

A body erupted out of the fog. Lizzie's hands slammed the dashboard as she screamed. Daniel Bisbee crushed all three brake pedals with both feet and spun the wheel, but the body had already collided with the hood and was somersaulting over the windshield. The sounds of crunching metal blended with the snaps of human bone. The Model-T surged over the curb, skidded on the grass, and chimed off the steel fence, while the body slapped onto the wet pavement and rolled to a halt.

Lizzie buried her face in her hands and screamed.

"DAN, JESUS GOD—"

"Was it a man? Was it a man?"

Daniel couldn't think over Lizzie's screams.

Gulliver turned to the back window. "Oh, by Christ, Dano! He's in the road!"

"I didn't—" Daniel stared at the windshield, now crunched inward in the shape of a body. A clump of white hair had torn off on impact and was stuck to a crack in the glass.

Celia shook Gulliver's arm. "Is he dead?"

"Lizzie, open the door." Gulliver shoved at her seat.

"Oh-my-God-oh-my-God-oh-my-God—"

"Lizzie, for Christ's sake." Gulliver scrambled over Celia as Daniel stumbled out into the street. The two men sprinted toward the body, their path marked by a wide swath of blood.

The body was bent at impossible angles, a lumpy mound on the road.

Daniel and Gulliver circled it warily.

"By Christ, Dano. By bloody Christ." Gulliver ran his hands through his hair.

Daniel could tell, from the white hair and beard, that he had hit an old man, over six foot, with thick arms and a wide back, still fit. But now one arm seemed twice the length of the other due to a graphic dislocation. A shoulder blade erupted through the skin like a white shark's fin. And the old man's right knee had buckled in the wrong direction, making him appear like a blood-soaked marionette dropped from a player's hand.

Daniel's guilt brought him to his knees. He touched the old man's hand. His face was mashed into the pavement.

"S-s-sir?" Daniel gave the fingers a squeeze.

A groan emerged in reply.

"That was him, Dano. He's breathing!"

Daniel peeled the body away from the pavement. Half of a stripped face flopped in his lap.

Gulliver wheeled back.

Most of the old man's face was still on the pavement. His surviving eye blinked. Where the flesh was pulled off, Daniel could see the muscles of the old man's jaw working, dripping blood onto his beard. A large hand took hold of Daniel's biceps. Daniel attempted to back away, but the old man held him firm, lifting his head a few inches from the pavement.

"He's in—"

"Gully, get 'im off!" Daniel cried, trying to pry the old man's fingers from his arm. "Agh, Gully! He's—"

"He's in my mind," the old man shouted.

Gulliver tried to pull Daniel off, but stopped when he heard the words.

"What'd he say?"

The old man yanked Daniel closer. Daniel could smell blood and tobacco on his breath. And death. The old man hissed: ". . . warn . . ."

"Oh God—" Daniel again tried to pull away.

The old man suddenly let go and Daniel scuttled back into Gulliver's arms. The old man's head lolled to the side. The good eye stopped blinking. He stared at nothing.

His last word, "Arcanum," echoed through the silent streets, punctuated only by the girls' muffled sobs.

The clouds suddenly parted for the full moon, which cast a

white glow on the street and washed over the old man's ruined features.

Despite the light, no one noticed the glint of a blue monocle in the shadows. There was another witness. And in a swirl of a black topcoat he was gone, leaving behind only the hush of the retreating storm.

2

THE PAPER BEFORE him was blank. Sir Arthur Conan Doyle could not concentrate, distracted by the metronomic tick of his grandfather clock. He tapped his shoe on the snout of a Bengal tiger-skin rug splayed out at his feet and surveyed his surroundings, scanning the evidence of a life fully lived.

The billiards room of his Windlesham estate ran the length of the manor and substituted as a ballroom and Doyle's writing office. His wife, Lady Jean, kept a piano and a harpsichord in the corner by the redbrick fireplace. The lion-toed billiards table counterbalanced the room at the opposite end. The walls were ornamented with an eclectic array of Napoleonic weapons and a stag's head with an impressive six-foot rack. Doyle's gaze drifted past the bust of Sherlock Holmes in his deerstalker cap, and settled wistfully on a Sidney Paget portrait of young Kingsley Doyle in his Royal Air Force uniform. The boy's rounded face could have been a mirror of his own at that age. Doyle looked at his hands and counted the blotching age spots. He glanced back again at the portrait until he felt a chamber of welled-up sorrow creak open in his chest. Then he turned once more to the empty pad of paper.

The phone rang: a dull jangling that never failed to distract. He found Bell's contraption grossly intrusive. Not answering seemed boorish, but Doyle could never predict when a visitor might arrive unannounced into his office, demanding his attention even if he was writing. It was technological rudeness; a harbinger of things to come. Doyle glared at the phone from across the room, rapping his fountain pen on the arm of the chair.

Then the floorboards creaked as he crossed to the mantel and plucked the receiver from its post, holding the body of the phone in his other hand.

"Yes? Hello?" Doyle tended to shout into the telephone.

"Arthur?" The voice was deep, rich, and unmistakable even across the crackling phone lines: the Minister of Munitions, Winston Churchill—a friend of Doyle's since the Parliamentary elections of 1900.

"Winston?"

"There's news, I'm afraid. Bloody awful news." The phone lines were quiet save for static. "Konstantin Duvall is dead."

A single droplet of ink struck the floor. Doyle ran a hand over his walrus moustache and closed his eyes. His shoulders sagged. He placed the dripping pen back on the table. "When?"

"Last night, they say. Clipped by a motorcar. In the fog."

"My God." Conan Doyle felt his emotions hiss away into the recesses of his heart, leaving only nausea. But after sixty-plus years, this, he knew, was only a precursor of the tidal rush of grief to come.

"Did he have any family, Arthur? Of all of us, you knew him best."

"Honestly, I . . . I don't know."

"I'll have the Yard look into it, but I suspect they'll have no better luck than I will. We may have to put something together. Small, of course."

Doyle was reeling. Bits and shards, pictures, words, a rush of thoughts had broken free. He grasped for useful information. "He spoke once . . . of wanting to be cremated. From his days in the Orient."

"Eh? That's something, then. We can accomplish that. It seems unbelievable. Unbelievable . . ." Churchill allowed the silence to loom. He was clearly waiting for information he knew Doyle possessed. The good doctor, however, was lost, for the moment, to the past. Finally, Churchill pressed on. "What on earth was he doing at the British Museum? And at that absurd hour?"

Doyle hesitated, then lied, "I have no idea."

"Bollocks," Churchill answered. "There's much you've left unsaid of your business together, Arthur. Reams left unsaid. Now, I've been straight with you about Duvall, and I would appreciate a portion of the same courtesy in return. Someday quite soon, old boy, I want to know what you chaps were up to."

Doyle sighed. "Honestly, Winston, we've been over this—"

But Churchill cut him off. "Duvall was an important man, but only you seem to know how important. At some point, you've an obligation to your country, your king, and to me to tell us what you know. In the meantime," Churchill's voice softened, "I'm very sorry. I know he was important to you. He lived well. That's all we can ask in the end. To live well. I'll ring you later."

"Yes, Winston. Thank you for calling."

The line went dead. Doyle recradled the receiver, finding it difficult to swallow. It was the secrets, held for thirty years now, surging forth to overtake the present. But he held on to the mantel and fought them off, locking them back where they belonged.

LADY JEAN DOYLE was trimming the roses, in a white dress with long sleeves and a yellow hat. Her fair skin was susceptible to the sun but she enjoyed gardening—especially when she could watch their young daughter ride her horse along the green bluffs of Sussex Downs. The Doyles' estate at Windlesham was the picture of tasteful grandeur: a redbrick mansion of thirty-two rooms guarded by a ring of 300-year-old maple trees.

But moments of beauty like this had grown rarer of late, making Lady Jean doubly thankful for each one. The recent past had tested the Doyles' mettle with a harrowing string of deaths.

Aside from the loss of their adored Kingsley, Doyle's brother Innes had died of influenza. And Jean's brother, Malcolm, perished at the Battle of Mons. Recovery—if it was to happen at all—would be painfully slow.

Worse still, the Doyles' recent crusade on behalf of the Spiritualist Movement had sent unintended shock waves through the British press, and set off a firestorm of ridicule. Enemies and admirers alike had declared Doyle a rube, as gullible as Sherlock Holmes was skeptical. There seemed no reprieve from the insults and jibes, but Doyle soldiered on, watching his reputation crumble, like a man burdened with secret knowledge.

As indeed he was.

Yet, even knowing this, it had still shaken Lady Jean to see her dear Arthur—her robust champion—age before her eyes. Now even the natural escape of writing was lost to him. He would sit in his normal spot in the billiards room, in his creaking swivel chair—the birthplace of scores of novels—frozen like a statue, staring at the page. Grief had wrung him dry and Lady Jean feared the strain of it was killing him.

Now, as Doyle stumbled out onto the patio, he looked frail and drawn. Lady Jean dropped the clippers, and ran to him. "Arthur, what's wrong?"

"Duvall was killed by a motorcar last night. At the museum, of all places."

Lady Jean took him into her arms, his forehead resting on her shoulder like a child's. She stroked his hair and kissed his brow, not only out of love, but also so as not to betray her relief. It was not one of their children or immediate loved ones. And, to her, it meant that one of the worst and most frightening chapters of their lives had finally ended.

Or so she believed . . .

3

THE FUNERAL CAME and went, a puzzling and pathetic anticlimax to Duvall's life. The weather was typically English, a cold, steady drizzle leaking from the sky. Doyle knew how Duvall would rage at such a paltry display. The occasion called for hurricanes, tempests to flatten trees. After all, Duvall was the last of the great mystics, a remnant of the Middle Ages. He bore the likeness and courage of a Templar Knight, yet embraced the perversions of an Inquisitor priest. He was as burnt-fingered and secretive as an alchemist, yet spoke dozens of languages, wrote manuscripts in cipher, and traveled the world with different identities, in the tradition of a court spy.

And now his end was all too depressingly human. It seemed, in the end, that Duvall was just a man.

Doyle gazed at the other seven mourners lined up along an ivy-covered bridge—luminaries all, though scarcely a fraction of Duvall's vast network.

Even now, Doyle shook his head at the breadth of the man's influence. Duvall was among the most pivotal voices of his time. His friends and confidants had been the elite, not only of Europe, but of the Americas as well. Prime ministers, kings, archbishops, presidents, philosophers, and writers—all considered it necessary proof of their standing to know Konstantin Duvall, and to call him friend.

And he was still a paradox to Doyle, even throughout the many years of their acquaintance. No newspaper journalist had ever printed his name, he mused. Few publishers—Hearst being the exception—even knew he existed. Yet Duvall reigned supreme in the pantheon of Occult masters, straddling cultures and worlds: ever-present, enigmatic, ageless.

Doyle took note of a woman wrapped in black standing apart from the others. Her lashes beat like butterfly wings as tears dripped from the curve of her elegant nose. Doyle recognized her as a Spanish princess, and also the wife of one of the richest shipping magnates in Europe. It reminded him of the way women lost their senses in Duvall's presence. In his lifetime, Duvall had been challenged to eight pistol duels by cuckolded husbands and won them all.

But beyond the society gossip, the rumors were impossible to confirm, for Duvall was a man who made embellishment too tempting. Indeed, embellished stories of Duvall were the currency of social advancement amongst the European aristocracy. The stories of his international diplomacy were too widespread and inconceivable to be believed, but Doyle knew full well that Duvall was involved in the more crucial decisions of the last half of the nineteenth century, despite showing no allegiance to any one country or king.

Many feared him. There was a dark side to the stories, not so kind or easily dismissed; tales of political treachery, of spy-craft and assassination. There were even whispers of sorcery and Devil worship.

Supposedly, Pope Pius IX had placed a secret bounty on Duvall's head, though some found that to be more an act of self-preservation than of holy writ.

He never paid for a meal, Doyle remembered with a smile, and could be an oppressive braggart. But no one had any concept of the scope of his knowledge, or the depths of his experience.

And then there was that memorable accent, impossible to decipher. Russian? French? And that crisp laugh, like a rifle report.

The memories clogged Doyle's throat and fogged his sight. How distant it all felt. And yet . . . where grief had once barricaded the doors to the past, now the past wanted out.

For Montalvo Konstantin Duvall had chosen Doyle, and that one simple fact had been Doyle's seminal secret for the last thirty years. Duvall had brought them all together. It was his vision from the start. The Arcanum was the one thing Duvall called his own. But who took charge now?

Doyle watched the dust puff and scatter from the urn. Most of it hit the stream beneath their feet, but some swung back, peppering overcoats and bowler hats. Doyle released Lady Jean's hand and swept a bit of ash from his sleeve before realizing what Duvall had become. Just a smudge. Dismissed.

It was wrong. All of it was wrong. The act of brushing Konstantin Duvall off his sleeve confirmed it.

A rusted lever turned over in Doyle's mind. For a moment, he was more awake than he had been in four years. And he knew something was wrong about this. Very wrong.

To Doyle's left stood Churchill, his bulbous red nose protuberant beneath his bowler. Doyle took his elbow and spoke softly. "The Yard looked into this?"

Churchill whispered back, "Young actors drove the car. Actors in a play. They told the authorities that Duvall rushed at them out of the fog."

Doyle stared at Churchill, who tilted his head up, annoyed. "What?"

"You are not answering the obvious question, Winston. *Why* did Duvall rush at them out of the fog?"

"How am I supposed to know?" Churchill's voice rose, and he was shushed by someone down the line of black-clad mourners. "There's plenty about that man I never understood," he added in a whisper.

Doyle released Churchill's elbow and gazed over the bridge at the last of the dust melting into the streambed.

Churchill shot him a wary look, and lowered his voice even further. "What are you thinking, old boy?"

"Nothing of consequence."

"Call off the dogs, Arthur; it was an accident. That's all. No point mucking round in it."

"Don't be ridiculous."

"Let the boys at the Yard do their job. Splendid to see you still have the old fire, though." Churchill patted him on the back.

Doyle softly repeated the words. " 'The old fire,' yes." He smiled at Churchill. He knew better than anyone that nothing in Duvall's life had ever been an "accident." And now Doyle sensed the same would hold true in death.

LADY JEAN TURNED to her husband in the back of the Bentley limousine. She was not a psychic, but she could read her husband's mind better than most wives. She knew the meaning of every line, blanch, and color of his sturdy, handsome face. He ignored her gaze by studying a fly buzzing against the car window. She would have none of it. "What were you and Winston discussing?" she asked.

Doyle pretended to be lost in thought. "Yes, dear?"

But Lady Jean was not fooled. "There's a saying, isn't there, Arthur?" she said. "About sleeping dogs and where they lie?"

Her husband did not respond.

"It was a terrible accident."

Doyle turned, his eyes containing a certain steeliness that made her flinch. "Then there's no reason for concern, is there?" he answered.

4

THE FOLLOWING MORNING, Doyle took a carriage into the heart of Whitechapel on the east end of London. There was heavy foot traffic on the narrow streets, for motorcars were still rare in this part of town, and Doyle was jostled as vendors hawked cold cups of jellied eels and children played cricket using lampposts as wickets. A tribe of barefoot orphans latched on to his pant legs until he sprinkled them with small coins, and when the dust cleared he found himself deep in the labyrinth of tenement alleyways.

The gold knob of his walking stick tapped on the door of a row house.

A woman answered the door. "Yes?"

"Good day. Is Daniel Bisbee on the premises?"

The woman scowled, wiping wet hands on her apron. "You with Scotland Yard, then?"

A mother protecting her cub, he thought. "Most certainly not. My name is Arthur Conan Doyle, and I—"

"Jesus, Mary, and Joseph!" She pulled the door wide and ushered him through as he tipped his hat. "What an honor, sir.

What an honor! Such a fine man, and ye've come fer me Danny! It's a bloody mess—please, can I make you some tea, then, sir?"

"That would be lovely, yes."

Daniel's mother pounded hard on the wall of the tenement. "Danny! It's Arthur Conan Doyle, for God's sake. Get up, now!"

"Bugger off," came a muffled voice from behind the wall.

Daniel's mother flashed her guest an embarrassed grin, then turned and kicked the wall. As mother and son bellowed at each other between the walls, Doyle took a long look around the room and determined—in three days, fifteen hours, and forty-two minutes less than Scotland Yard—that Daniel Bisbee was innocent of murder. It was a level of observational acuity as basic to him as that of a master pianist playing scales. His mind allowed information to flow through a meticulous mental machinery that sorted, prescribed, rendered, annotated, and filed with photographic precision: yearbooks, family heirlooms, trinkets atop counters, the scent of fresh-baked scones, the quality of the carpets and furniture, the placement of keys on the coffee table, the brand of cigarettes smoked . . .

Doyle was the measure of his greatest literary invention, and more.

" 'Ave ye come to save 'im, then, my Danny?" Mrs. Bisbee was suddenly at Doyle's side, tugging at his sleeve. "I know what ye've done with that poor Indian fellow."

She spoke of George Edalji, an East Indian immigrant wrongfully accused of bizarre cattle mutilations across the moors of southern England some years previously. Many had seen Doyle's intervention as simple humanitarianism. But had the public—or the legal establishment—known what had truly mutilated the cattle of Cheltenham that year, the world would never have been the same. There would have been riots in the streets, capitals burned. For publicity purposes, it had been convenient to use Doyle both for disinforming the public and to preserve Edalji's innocence.

Doyle took Mrs. Bisbee's hand from his sleeve. "Madam, I trust Danny never meant for this to happen. The victim was a friend. I would like to ask your son some questions, that's all."

Daniel Bisbee appeared in the hallway. His brow was fur-rowed as he tucked a dirty T-shirt into his trousers.

Doyle offered his hand. "Daniel?"

"Are you really him, then?" Daniel asked, as they shook hands.

"Yes. And you are Daniel Bisbee?"

"The Yard sent you after me? To fox me out?"

Doyle squeezed Daniel's hand, then released it. "I know you did nothing wrong."

Daniel relaxed. "How'd you know that, then?"

Doyle smiled. "It is my business to know things. Perhaps I've trained myself to see what others overlook."

Mrs. Bisbee brought a tray of tea to the table and picked lint off her son's shoulder. Daniel shook her off. Doyle turned. "If you don't mind, Mrs. Bisbee, I'd prefer to speak with Daniel alone."

"I don't mind in the slightest, sir."

Daniel glared at his mother, who was gazing adoringly at Doyle. The doctor patted her hand and she backed away.

When she was gone, Daniel settled into his chair and eyed Doyle. "So you wrote them stories, then? Them Sherlock Holmes stories?"

"Have you read any?"

Daniel took a cigarette from his case and lit it. "A couple, yeah. Smart bugger, that Holmes. You as smart as him, then?"

"I'm only the humble creator," Doyle said, looking hard into Daniel's eyes and causing the actor to shift nervously.

"You knew the feller, then? I heard ye tell Ma . . ."

"He was an old friend."

Daniel spit a bit of tobacco off his tongue, and sucked on his cigarette. "I still see him, Mr. Doyle. Every night, I see him. In the fog."

"Go on, son."

Daniel told his story. And being an actor, he told it well, and Doyle found himself drawn into the tale. And when caught up in the memories, Daniel took Doyle's arm the way Duvall had grabbed his, and Doyle flinched. Then Doyle shut out everything but Daniel's voice, repeating Duvall's dying words, until . . .

"The Arcanum," Doyle finished.

Daniel blinked. "That's it exactly. 'The Arcanum,' just like you just said, sir. That's bloody unreal. You know what it is, then?"

Doyle stood, offered his hand. "You've been very brave, Mr. Bisbee. And very helpful."

Daniel shook Doyle's hand. "It was a pleasure to meet you, sir. You're the most famous person I ever met. A real honor, sir."

Doyle liked the boy. "Give Lizzie time, son. Nothing worth having ever comes easily."

Daniel frowned, confusion painting his face, "How did you—?"

"Of the two schools you're considering, I would always favor Oxford over an American college. The Queen's English is far preferable for stage work. American playwrights are just getting their footing, wouldn't you say?"

Daniel spluttered. "Did—"

"Ah yes. Your mother's arthritis, untreated, could become de-bilitating. Yet she's too proud to go to the doctor. There's a physician in Wellington I want you to telephone." Doyle scrib-bled a name and number on a sheet from his tiny notebook, then handed it to Daniel. "He's one of the best, and most cer-tainly will take some of the pain away. And for you, my boy, it's less midnight tea if you want to have a decent night's sleep again. You're too young to be an insomniac."

"You've got bloody magic, sir."

"Eyes and ears, son. Eyes and ears. Wish your mother good day." Then he squeezed the boy's shoulder and departed.

5

DOYLE TAPPED HIS stick against the spot where Duvall had died. It was dusk on Sunday. Traffic was light. Bicycles rolled by in the park, and a few motorcars filled with formally dressed families drove home from afternoon Mass. Doyle breathed in the autumn air and turned to face the British Museum, feeling like a venerable hound lured away from the barn by the scent of a fresh young rabbit.

A mystery beckoned.

He squeezed past a horde of tourists leaving the museum, run out by a stout, high-collared security guard with a deep bass voice. The man stood like Gibraltar between two enormous ancient Egyptian sculptures of Anubis.

"Five o'clock. Museum is closed. Don't forget purses, umbrellas, or packages. Please 'old small ones by the hand as you leave. Doors will close in two minutes." The security guard saw Doyle approach and announced at full volume, "Best turn right back around, sir. Museum's closed, and I've a sup waitin'."

Doyle smiled at his fellow Scotsman. "My name is Arthur Conan Doyle and—"

"I'm Little Miss Penny Maypole," the guard finished. "Now,

sir, please, the missus is preparin' her beef stew and I've a laxative to imbibe, so—"

Conan Doyle presented identification. The security guard glanced at it, then straightened with a start. "Bugger all." He did not look Doyle in the face as he spoke. "With all due respect, sir, I'm a boneheaded fool. My missus always tells me so, and now I've proven it true again. God help me. 'Ow can I be of service, now?"

"What's your name, man?"

"Welgerd, sir."

"Well, Mr. Welgerd, I've been sent on the orders of Lord Churchill to investigate the circumstances of the accident that took place the other night."

"The gentleman wot was struck by the motorcar?"

"Precisely. And if I'm not mistaken, there was also an attempted robbery here that same night?"

"Wouldn't call it so much a robbery, sir, but we did have a window broken, which set off the bells. But I've been over the premises backways to Sunday, and I assure you nothin's gone missin'."

"I've no doubt of the thoroughness of your search, but I hope it won't offend if I, myself, take a small tour of the building to satisfy my curiosity."

Welgerd wrinkled his nose. "After thirty years, sir, I've come to know this museum like it were a part of meself. I assure you nuthin's missin'."

"I'm not at liberty to divulge the particular sensitivities of my mission, Mr. Welgerd. Suffice it to say that your cooperation on this matter would mean a great deal to Lord Churchill. And I would be gravely mistaken not to mention your assistance in my report to his lordship. And, of course, to forward that report to your good lady wife, whose dinner may grow cold as a result of my unannounced visit."

At this, Welgerd seemed to weigh his loyalties. "That's kind of ye, Mr. Doyle, sir, but it won't spare me a whale of a hollerin'."

"You're a brave soul, Welgerd."

Welgerd nodded and corralled the remaining visitors out of

the main hall. The boom of the locks echoed through five miles of empty museum corridors, leaving a blanket of silence behind.

"Follow me, sir," Welgerd said, polished black shoes clicking on the floor as he marched off.

Doyle hurried to keep up.

The two men entered the Hall of the Dark Continent. Behind huge panes of glass stood some of the world's first frozen images of the many tribes and indigenous peoples of Africa. Visitors to the museum were particularly drawn to the wild masks and ceremonial skirts, which depicted demon faces and hinted at primal energies.

Welgerd pushed a lever, and electric lights blinked on down the length of the exhibit. With a fistful of keys, he unlocked the heavy cage door and rolled it into the ceiling.

"You were here that night?" Doyle asked as they strode down a long corridor lined with medieval suits of armor.

"At the other end of the buildin', sir. Then the alarms rang, and me and some of the other fellows went about searchin'. We weren't awares of the accident till much later. Far as I knew, the man wot got struck wasn't even dressed for the weather. Poor bugger likely lost his senses. It 'appens."

"And nothing else unusual occurred that evening?"

"Nuthin' that arises in memory."

Doyle drew to a halt. "I'm afraid this is where we part ways. Government business, you see."

Welgerd looked disappointed. "Oh, of course. Well . . . You know the museum well, do you?"

"Should I get lost, I'll shout your name."

"Right, then. No worries." Welgerd flushed in the cheeks and looked down at his hands, where he clutched a pad and pencil. His hands mangled the pad with indecision.

"I'd be honored." Doyle took the initiative and pried the pad from Welgerd's hands. The museum guard stood on his toes as Conan Doyle signed.

"I've, ah, penned a few stories myself, sir."

Conan Doyle continued to write. "Is that so? You've a literary bent, Welgerd?"

"No, nuthin' so stately, sir. Just cops-and-robbers-type scenarios. But my missus enjoys them and she adds suggestions and that type of thing."

"And the gentlemen from Scotland Yard, they searched the area?"

"With a fine-tooth comb, sir. Absolutely."

"Splendid." Doyle finished the autograph and handed back the pad. He had written: *To Welgerd, Well named and well done. Keep up the writing. Arthur Conan Doyle.*

Welgerd grunted with appreciation as he read it. Doyle tipped his hat, and strolled off down the corridor.

IN THE ARCHAEOLOGICAL exhibit, Doyle looked dwarfed beneath the colossal Assyrian reliefs. Yet for an investigator of a robbery, he scarcely glanced at the Rosetta Stone and ignored the Elgin Marbles from the Parthenon at Athens. Instead, he descended a flight of stairs and passed through another hall of ancient Greek pottery and textiles, looking neither left nor right.

His steps came to an abrupt halt at the door to the water closet, located in the farthest corner of the British Museum.

He entered. The paint on the walls was yellow and peeling above a stretch of green and white hexagonal tile. There were two stalls housing toilets flushable through the pull of a chain. The only notable aspect of the room was its history, for this was the very spot where they had broken ground on the present neoclassical structure imagined by Robert Smirke over the foundation of Montague House, the museum's home since 1759.

Doyle washed his hands and dried them on a towel folded atop the basin. Then he turned to the tiled wall across from the door. He touched one of the center tiles with his palm, then moved his hand to a spot two tiles above and did the same. His hand then glided across some five tiles and pressed again, then dropped down another four.

After a pause, there was a grinding, and an assortment of tiles receded into blackness, forming the jagged outline of a hidden doorway.

Doyle swung the door open, glancing briefly behind him, then stepped into the shadows. With a grinding of gears the tiles reattached to the door, leaving—for all intents and purposes—a perfectly uninteresting wall.

A flaring match illuminated Doyle's face as he touched the flame to a candle in a tin holder set by his feet. A stairwell curved down before him, consisting of twenty steps. The texture of the walls changed halfway down from smooth plaster to uneven rock and grit. At the bottom was a simple wooden door. Doyle turned the knob, and it opened.

The revealed office smelled of old paper and jasmine incense. It was not a large space, wide enough to accommodate a desk against one wall, a chair, a wardrobe, and a single shelf of books. Arabian silks stained plum and emerald shrouded the cracking walls, and draped low from the ceiling. The wardrobe in the corner contained a portion of Duvall's famous shoe collection: Thai slippers, Tibetan yak boots, German dancing clogs, a crumbling pair of Samurai two-toed socks . . .

Doyle turned to the coatrack. Resting there was Duvall's staff: a five-foot piece of wood, smooth and twisted. Burned into its surface were Druidic ogham. Sagging on posts were Duvall's beret and overcoat.

Doyle spoke in a whisper. "Gone walking in the rain, Konstantin? Without your staff? Without your hat?"

Doyle glanced at a chessboard beside the desk, its pieces arranged in mid-game.

He next turned to the bookcase stationed at the wall farthest from the door. It held a collection of occult texts. There were rows of interesting first editions: a 1619 folio of *Clavis Alchemiae* by Robert Fludd, a 1608 *Discourse des Sorciers* by Henri Boguet, Blavatsky's *Isis Unveiled,* and a 1555 *Les Propheties De M. Michel Nostradamus*—admirable titles for an adept of the occult, but child's play to a magus of Duvall's stature.

This brought Doyle's attention to a map. It was an eighteenth-century map of the world tacked above Duvall's desk, its face marred by hundreds of small handwritten scribblings: symbols, x's, and dates. Doyle withdrew a magnifying glass from his jacket pocket and held it close to the map, his finger tracing a line from Greece to Italy. Magnified by the lens, the notes read:

First record of lost tribe, Athens to Rome in 420. Consult Dee's journals for date of Enochian fragments. Tribe separates in Imperial Persia. Some to Buddhist India, others to Han China.

Conan Doyle freed a necklace from one of the nails holding the map to the wall. The charm hanging from the frayed leather band was a coin, the symbol of a soldier on horseback on its face. It appeared to be an antique Roman coin. Glancing back to the map, Doyle noted a thick circle drawn around Manhattan Island in the United States.

Spies and evidence suggest tribe reunited in New York City. Consult Lovecraft. New players. New dangers. Sacred Order of the Golden Dawn.

The last line was written in an almost manic scrawl and underlined several times:

PROTECT THE SECRETS OF ENOCH

"Where is it, then?" Doyle spoke aloud as he surveyed the otherwise empty walls. He checked under the antique ashtray lamp. His fingers frisked the sides of the bookshelf and poked among the books, searching for false bindings. He tossed the Persian rug aside and stamped on the wooden boards, listening for hollows. But in vain. Doyle's brow knit with frustration as his gaze drifted to the chessboard beside Duvall's desk.

He noted an obvious move on behalf of white, which had always been his color when playing Konstantin. But making the first move wasn't nearly advantage enough. Most of the time when they played, it felt to Doyle as if Duvall was simply humoring him, delaying the kill out of fear of boredom. In this case, however, Doyle spotted a nearing checkmate.

"Castle, of course," he muttered as he switched the positions of the rook and king.

At that moment, the bookcase clicked open. "Cagey bastard," Doyle whispered, with a grin. Duvall could best him even from beyond the grave.

Doyle pulled the bookcase away from the wall to reveal an elevator lift beyond. His heartbeat picked up. Trapping his cane under his arm and carrying the candle, he entered the lift. He forced the operating handle clockwise a half revolution. Machinery hummed as the cage door slammed shut, then Duvall's office lifted out of sight. The candle flame wavered in the suffocating blackness as the lift descended. Pipes banged. Thick wires slid against metal. The lift shook. After ten uneasy seconds, it came to a jarring halt.

Doyle braced himself against the walls. For a moment he stood there, listening to his own furtive breaths. Then he folded the cage door open and stepped onto a carpet of rich red velvet.

Candlelight flowed across the mustard-colored walls of a small salon, replete with mirrors and standing candelabras. On the walls were framed portraits—one of which bore a distinct likeness to Doyle himself. At the far end of the room were a set of French doors. He opened them, then reeled backward, stunned.

He had found the Hall of Relics.

The items were displayed on masterwork pedestals, protected by globes of Venetian glass. One of the first relics, a corpse, rested inside a glass-enclosed coffin. It was a woman, her decayed arms stretched taut at her sides, her face hollowed to a husk, eyes black sockets, hair splayed about the withering skull like so many spider legs.

Doyle knew the body, and recalled its discovery. He remembered the waves of a West African ocean rolling it forward in the sand.

His eyes traveled down the rest of the body, past the shriveled stomach, to where the legs would normally be—if she had been human. Instead, there was only a thick fishtail, scales flaking off the sides. The inscription on the coffin read:

**MADAGASCAR, 1905—PHYSICAL PROOF OF
MERMAID LIFE, POSSIBLE ATLANTEAN
DESCENDANCY**

Doyle moved on, holding up the candle to the next display. A shimmer of green met his eyes. It was a slate of emerald, carved with an ancient Phoenician script, circa 200 A.D. It was the grail of Alchemical scholarship, brief as a sonnet, yet fathomless in its truths.

THE EMERALD TABLET OF HERMES TRISMEGISTUS

The mere sight of the next relic raised the hairs on his arms. Doyle had led the investigation to its discovery, and bore witness to the exorcism that had quieted the demonic spirit. Yet evil still pulsed within its broken smile. For beneath the glass was a skull, belonging to the vilest man of an age, whose malice was so pure it survived his living body. The inscription read:

1766—THE CURSED SKULL OF "BLUEBEARD" GILLES DE LAVAL

Doyle quickly turned his attention to the objects on either side of the skull, counterbalancing the energies of the room.

One was a pile of brown rags: monks' robes. A rope belt was visible in the folds. The importance was the wearer, and the healing power bestowed upon those who touched its hem. The inscription read:

THE ROBES OF ST. FRANCIS OF ASSISI

Across from it, imprisoned also in glass, lay a slender piece of wood and a hunk of iron on a cushion. Once it was a weapon held by a Roman soldier. The blood it had spilled belonged to Jesus Christ as he hung on the cross.

THE SPEAR OF DESTINY

Doyle's weight shifted, and a chip of glass snapped under his foot. He lifted his shoe and stared at the glass. His eyes followed that piece to another, and another, and another lying at the base of the last pedestal in the hall. With growing apprehension, his eyes moved to the letters penned in Duvall's immaculate script. The inscription read:

AGE UNKNOWN—ABYSSINIA—THE BOOK OF ENOCH

The globe once protecting it was broken. A velvet pillow lay empty, except for the imprint of a heavy object in its center. Doyle let out a shuddering breath and straightened to his full six feet, his jaw clenched tight.

"So . . . it begins again," he said.

6

IT IS 1912.

THE CASTLE BELONGS to Wilhelm II, and towers atop a heath in the dark forests of the Bavarian highlands. Torchlight flickers on every parapet, and from the muddy roads the fortress resembles a looming jack-o'-lantern. Moaning winds swirl through the valley, swaying the pine treetops like sea grass.

Forks of lightning stab down as four black stallions muscle a royal carriage through the icy rain to join others waiting at the castle walls.

A butler with skin like parchment pulls open the mighty doors and gives way to Tsar Nicholas II of Russia, who sweeps rain from his sleeves as he enters, trailed by the mad monk: the black-cloaked and bearded Grigori Rasputin.

The guests gather in the dining hall, a cavernous room dominated by an enormous fireplace where a veritable forest of trees roar in flames.

Rasputin guides Nicholas to one of the four chairs at the long dining table. The only others present are Kaiser Wilhelm II of Germany, England's King George V, and lingering in the far corner—wrapped in a black cape and wearing huntsman's leather boots—Konstantin Duvall.

Sir Arthur Conan Doyle removes his glasses and looks up from his journal. His sits by a tall stained-glass window, far enough away from the others as to be inconspicuous. Or so he hopes.

The superstitious kaiser grumbles at the presence of Rasputin.

Nicholas snaps a retort.

Tensions are high between these two because of the Balkan situation. The kaiser sees Russia's formation of the Balkan League and the declaration of war on Turkey as an attempt to gain a European foothold.

Nicholas wonders aloud as to the exclusion of Prime Minister Asquith.

King George scoffs.

As the leaders bicker, Duvall strides over to Rasputin and whispers something in his ear. Whatever the contents, it goads a reluctant smile from the monk.

Kaiser Wilhelm curtly demands an answer to his summons.

Duvall offers a few more words to Rasputin, then backs away toward the fireplace, taking the measure of each leader. "I've asked Sir Arthur Conan Doyle to chronicle this meeting for my personal archives. I trust there are no objections?"

But Duvall doesn't wait for answers. Instead, he turns his back on the leaders. He is framed in fire. It licks around his shoulders, and casts a halo around his wavy white hair. "Gentlemen. There has been a discovery in Abyssinia. A discovery of enormous consequence. A discovery that with it brings the potential for great peace . . . or great war."

The kaiser leans forward in his chair.

Rasputin whispers in Nicholas's ear, his lips obscured by his shaggy beard.

King George sniffs, unimpressed. "You've created some marvelous suspense, Konstantin, as is your wont. Perhaps you'd care to tell us what was found?"

"A book," he answers.

"A book, you say?" The king's smile is cold and thin. He recognizes that Wilhelm and Nicholas, despite their associations with Duvall, consider him England's responsibility. The king is eager to avoid that which most terrifies him—embarrassment. Which now appears inevitable. "You've called us here, Konstantin, because

*someone in Abyssinia found a book?" George smoothes his mous-
tache with his finger. "Interesting."*

Meaning: You're moments from being shot.

*Duvall speaks to the fire: "It is the legendary scriptures of
Enoch—which, along with the New and Old Testaments, form
the Biblical triad."*

This tidbit is enough to knit frowns upon three brows.

Wilhelm's squeaky voice asks a question in German.

*Duvall answers, "Yes, Kaiser, the Enoch manuscripts were from
the original Bible. Yet their contents were incendiary enough to
be excised by the occult priests of Zoroaster in thirty A.D." Duvall
hesitates. A spot of pitch in one of the logs snaps, showering the
carpet with sparks. "Excised at the behest of Jesus Christ himself."*

*King George sits back on the divan, somewhat relieved. "Most
intriguing, Konstantin. Good show. But rather on the . . . esoteric
side, wouldn't you say?" George raises his eyebrows to the other
world leaders. "Certainly I have no immediate use for knowledge
better left to the students of the mysteries. What do the Brothers of
the Rosy Cross make of this? Hmm? Rather more in their field, I
should think."*

Rasputin and Duvall share a glance. Nicholas glares at George.

*"With due respect, my king," Duvall says, "the Rosicrucians are
a conflicted association—a group whose leaks I grow weary of
plugging. Once they were entrusted with the secret of the Grail.
That is more than enough, I think."*

*"Well, what about Roosevelt and his Masonic friends in Amer-
ica?" the king persists.*

The question is left unanswered.

Nicholas asks in English, "What is in the book, Konstantin?"

*Duvall turns around, a rare shadow of fear in his gray eyes.
"God's mistakes, Tsar Nicholas. God's mistakes."*

7

DOYLE STOOD AT his bedroom window and watched the mid-afternoon rain. That night, seven years earlier, Duvall had mis-calculated. He had underestimated the leaders' personalities, their egos, and their brewing enmities. The result had been a protracted negotiation for possession of the Book, resulting in its robbery and eventual resurfacing in the hands of Archduke Ferdinand of Serbia. Shortly thereafter, Ferdinand had been as-sassinated and the Great War had begun.

Doyle felt like a truant gardener returning to find ivy growing through the windows of his house—into his wife's dresses, the cupboards, the sheets, the mouths of his children. The Book of Enoch was missing again. And though he knew nothing of its contents apart from Duvall's cryptic words, he knew that it was—in part or in full—the cause of the worst conflict in the history of modern civilization.

And the reason for Duvall's death.

A short butler with the jowls of a mastiff appeared at the study door. "Your luggage is prepared, Master Doyle."

"Thank you, Phillip."

The sky had darkened to purple, heavy and pregnant with

rain. And stark against the brooding sky was Lady Jean's reflection in the window. She was standing at the door, as pale as a wraith.

"Wasn't it enough? Wasn't losing Kingsley enough?" The words fell between them like shards of glass.

Doyle sighed and spoke to her reflection. "I'm sorry."

"You're old, Arthur. You're an old man."

"There is no one else."

Lady Jean frowned. "And what makes you think they will join you? There's been too much anger . . . too much pain. You'll fight alone, Arthur."

"I'm prepared for that."

Lady Jean sighed deeply. Then, "No," she said, "you're not prepared. Not yet." She lifted a battered and cracked leather satchel, and he smiled ruefully. His Jean had always been the stronger one.

He took the satchel from her hands.

Jean touched his cheek. "Forgetful as always," she said.

Doyle undid the rusting buckles. "I thought I'd lost it," he replied.

"No, I hid it."

Doyle opened the case. The contents were as familiar to him as his own reflection in the mirror: an evidence-collection kit of small paper bags, evidence tags, string, paper coin envelopes, small vials and numerous glass containers, dental casting material and equipment, tweezers, scissors, rubber gloves, pencils, and a tape measure.

Of medical supplies there were forceps, a scalpel set, gauze bandages, a clinical thermometer, a vial of alcohol, hypodermic syringes, and a hand saw—beneath which were hidden a heavy leather sap and brass knuckles.

And, lastly, a crumpled deerstalker cap, frayed and weathered.

8

"LADIES AND GENTLEMEN, may I present to you the most sensuous, the most mysterious, and the most controversial talent of the Spiritualist age. Welcome, if you will, the infamous and extraordinary . . ." Barnabus Wilkie Tyson thrust his thick arms into the air, his massive body swelling in his seventy-five-dollar silk suit ". . . Madame Rose!"

Flash powder exploded, and a mob of skeptical reporters craned their necks to get a view of the medium as she ascended the four steps to the makeshift stage and stood beside Tyson, her promoter and manager. Her style was daring. She was wearing a sleeveless, black silk smoking suit and high heels. A long black scarf was tied around her hair, spilling down over her shoulders. A monocle was perched over her right eye, and a cigarette holder was clutched between her lips. That sealed it; she was a walking scandal.

Tyson set his own cigar stub on the table in order to light her cigarette, and breathed reassurances into her ear. But she only shifted away, her face belying the boldness of her dress. She didn't smile at the photographers. In fact, she seemed quite ill at ease with the attention.

Which was odd, since the rumor mill spun hot and heavy around Madame Rose. She broke the hearts and marriages of the richest men in town, and flaunted it all in the gossip pages. Toss into the mix a reputed talent for conversing with spirits and the only séance in America where ectoplasm was guaranteed, and you had the ingredients for bona fide celebrity.

And Tyson was, if nothing else, a great trend spotter—and the first promoter of his kind to discover the unified field theory of publicity: Sex plus violence plus scandal equals money. Sensing a slight decline in the draw of his vaudeville acts, Tyson had poured his energies into the burgeoning Spiritualist Movement. It was a fertile garden in which to plant his greedy seed. Ruthless, cruel, and ill-mannered to those close to him, Tyson was still capable of dispensing enormous charm. He settled his hand on Madame Rose's arm and savored the curious buzz that filled the Waldorf Astoria ballroom. Madame Rose was his phenomenon, and this rare press conference was an opportunity to squeeze even more ink out of the reporters.

"Now, let us be courteous in our questions," he said, "and show Madame Rose some of that old New York charm we're known for the world over."

"Why's she wearin' pajamas, Barnabus?" a lanky *Times* reporter asked.

"Do you believe in free love, Miss Rose?"

Both Madame Rose and Tyson ignored the question.

"In the back." Tyson pointed.

"Are you a home-wrecker?" someone shouted.

"That depends who you're asking," Madame Rose answered, to the amusement of the assembly. She took a long draw on her cigarette.

"Are the rumors true about you and Ivor Novello, the nightclub owner?" another reporter asked.

"Is he leaving his wife?"

Madame Rose smiled. "I didn't know that he was married."

Tyson grinned at the amused gasps and mutters from the crowd.

"What about Valentino?" someone asked testily, sounding as if they'd lost a bet.

"Please," Madame Rose said scornfully.

"We thought it was Dempsey."

"Who's he?"

"The boxer."

"Ugh, how appalling. Now, Douglas Fairbanks is a different story." And she vamped to the whistles and catcalls.

"Let's behave ourselves," Tyson said, loving every minute.

"Haven't we any real questions?" Madame Rose purred, warming to the audience.

"Is Mina Crandon a fake?" a *Gazette* writer shouted.

"I think a better question is: Why are we afraid? Why are we so obsessed with disproving this phenomenon?"

"Eileen Garrett says you're a fraud."

"Poor darling, she's just insecure." Madame Rose tapped ash on the tablecloth. "There have been seers since before ancient Egypt. Prophets and mystics have turned the tide of history at every crucial juncture. The dead speak. And it is our duty to listen, to learn from them."

Most of the reporters wrote her words down, if only to justify their presence. But in the silence that followed . . .

"Do you worship the Devil?" a voice demanded from the back.

Tyson made a face. "What sort of question is that?"

There was a sudden shift in the energy of the room, a pall of discomfort.

Madame Rose stiffened in her chair, her eyes searching the audience. "Of course not. What an absurd question! This goes to the heart of the ignorance I'm referring to."

"Perhaps I've mistaken you . . . for someone else." The voice belonged to a man standing near the back, far behind the cameras. His coat collar was pulled up, concealing his features, and the brim of an English cap shadowed a set of bulging eyes.

"Who are you?" Madame Rose demanded.

"A friend," he answered. "Of the family." The last word was uttered with bite.

Madame Rose paled.

"What paper are you from?" Tyson snarled.

The doors swung shut. The man was gone.

Hands shot up from the crowd.

"Who was that?" someone yelled.

"What'd he mean?"

"Are you a witch?"

The questions piled up.

Madame Rose whispered "I'm leaving" into Tyson's ear and stood, inadvertently knocking her chair backwards.

Flashbulbs popped.

"Okay, enough. That's all!"

Madame Rose swayed on the steps. Tyson took her arm, waving off the photographers.

"I said that's all, damn it," he barked.

The reporters surged forward, and Tyson found himself tangled in the curtains as his medium vanished backstage.

9

FROM THE GANGPLANK of the *Marie Celeste,* Doyle marveled at the monstrous growth of New York City since his last visit, only six years before. Overnight, it seemed the metropolis had blossomed into an electric, sky-scraping, man-made forest. It was humbling. Disturbing.

He stepped up onto a trembling running board and into a Dodge sedan taxi off Pier 14. "The Penn Hotel, please."

"Yes, sir. Welcome to New York, sir."

A confirmed car fanatic, Doyle had bought a capsulelike Wolsey for country drives in England. Now he leaned over the front seat to watch the driver use the self-starter, for the newer cars no longer required the drivers to jump out and crank. Suddenly, and with unexpected speed, the driver released his foot from the low-speed pedal and the sedan launched into a circus of traffic.

Trolleys rumbled down the streets like the mechanical invaders from an H. G. Wells novel, while the newer and faster Briscoe and Maxwell automobiles swerved wildly around the slower and rarer horse-drawn carriages.

Times Square was a sensory assault of light and sound. Gigantic banners, the size and the like of which Doyle had never seen, were rimmed with thousands of sparkling lights advertising Lucky Strikes and Fatima Turkish Cigarettes, B. F. Keith's Palace Theatre and the Million Dollar Mystery. There were crowded dance halls with recorders blaring "I'm Always Chasing Rainbows" and "I'll Say She Does."

The whole world, Doyle mused, rushed headlong into an industrialized age that transformed daily life—daily. First the steam engine, then the gas-engine automobiles, electric typewriters, paper clips, Quantum theory, silicones, animated cartoon film, the hydraulic centrifugal clutch, Relativity, Vitamin A, tear gas, stainless steel, tanks, and air-conditioning. It was a nonstop maelstrom of progress that left the whole world breathless.

The Futurists saw this galloping pace as the signature of an idealized age, just within reach. Others saw it as the beginning of The End.

Doyle eyed these changes with a distinct caution. He knew firsthand that scientific genius was no guarantor of morality. Quite often it could be a harbinger to madness. And such an age required greater vigilance over the occult world than ever before; magic and science were quarrelsome sisters ever entwined. Mankind was scraping the surface of the Mysteries and naming what it found. It made men proud to catalog and quantify their world. Command it. Bend it. Shape and dissect it. This was science. The Mysteries, however, were likely to recoil from this leeching curiosity. Recoil and strike.

Doyle remembered the words of a colleague.

"The most merciful thing in the world, I think, is the inability of the human mind to correlate all its contents. We live on a placid island of ignorance in the midst of black seas of infinity, and it was not meant that we should voyage far. The sciences, each straining in its own direction, have hitherto harmed us little; but someday the piecing together of dissociated knowledge will open up such terrifying vistas of reality, and of our frightful position therein, that we shall either go mad from the revelation or flee from the deadly light into the peace and safety of a dark new age . . ."

* * *

BANISHED AND FORBIDDEN knowledge, this was H. P. Lovecraft's food and drink, his very reason for existence. Nothing else mattered to him—certainly not friendships or loyalties.

He was an enigma from the very beginning—a dark prodigy gifted beyond fairness with a mind like a knife and a flawless recall. His scholarship at nineteen had shamed occult masters four times his age, and his arrogance had enraged the rest. He suffered no fools, and offered the bluntest of opinions without concern for emotions or feelings, for which he showed utter disdain.

But that was Lovecraft's paradox, for within his genius lay a boy on the verge of madness, completely isolated from the world. Doyle had never trusted him, but knew that he now needed him, more than ever.

As dusk spilled down the long walls of the Flatiron Building, Doyle warmed at the thought of his first trip to America: the most publicized literary tour since Oscar Wilde's in 1881. Now he was anonymous, as he meant to be; as he had to be.

ONLY A FEW blocks south of Doyle's taxi, Detective Sergeant Shaughnessy Mullin pinched his nose with a handkerchief to ward off the body's stench. The place reeked enough of fish without the rot of a human to make it worse. It was a hell of a scene. The rats had already taken their due.

Lanterns swung in the haze as more blue boys gathered on Pier 5, and a dense mist sat over the Hudson. Two officers tried to straighten out the body, but it was clenched like a fist.

Backwards.

It was a terrible death. The woman was naked, found curled around a buoy thirty feet off the pier. The parts of her face not eaten away showed an expression of agony unmatched in Mullin's experience.

And Mullin had plenty of experience. His consciousness was tattooed with the sort of images that, when witnessed at a young enough age, can shatter psyches. Mullin carried around a special one—one that asserted itself more than the others. A domestic dispute call two years before. A tenement building. The husband had fired a shotgun into his wife's face at close range. Mullin recalled marveling at the pieces of head scattered over the living room carpet. Red meat tossed with tufts of hair. An eye. A few teeth embedded in the wall. Bones and a tongue hung from the lampshade. Amazing what drunk husbands could do to wives.

Mullin had an ex-wife, and God knows he had a drunken fury. Many were the nights he'd waved a pistol in her face. She'd left him; no explanation had been necessary. Mullin was unfit for most of the demands of society. He kept that image, though, in his back pocket. He wasn't sure why. He just couldn't seem to shake it.

This one would linger awhile, too.

The corpse was bent from the lower back almost like a wagon wheel, her heels nearly touching the back of her head. Her hands were clenched into fists by her cheeks, like a child in a frozen tantrum. Mullin had only seen this sort of rigor with strychnine poisoning. While attempting to straighten her out, one of the blue boys had pulled too hard, and everyone winced at the loud crack of her snapping ribs.

Mullin scowled. "Leave 'er be."

The blue boys retreated. Mullin was pugnacious and fierce, thanks to a life lived hard. Born premature into a destitute and starving family in Cork, Mullin fought God's will at every turn. An early battle with diphtheria robbed him of hearing in his left ear. While siblings were killed by influenza, Mullin survived. And once they managed to cross the ocean, the trials didn't stop. One of Mullin's eyes was clouded thanks to a street-gang fight in Brooklyn's "Irish Town." He gained a reputation as a street fighter, making up for his short reach by getting inside on opponents and working the body. Though Mullin's father died soon after their arrival in America, his "Ma" was still an enormous influence in his life. He was devoted to her and she, in turn, still boxed his ears.

In 1919 Manhattan, the journey from street thug to police officer wasn't a long trip. Mullin had convenient ethics and few qualms over solving complicated problems with violence. He wasn't a champion of reform. He disdained idealists. Accepting a bribe now and again didn't hurt anybody. And though Mullin, like most other cops, treated poor people the same as criminals, he had a soft spot for mothers—especially those struggling to feed fatherless children.

His thick red moustache twitched as he gazed on the girl. "Where is her ma?" he wondered aloud. He squatted down and turned the body so the lantern could shine on her back. The damage was merciless. Some butcher had carved her like a pumpkin, torn out her spine. This was no drunken rape gone awry, no drug fiend robbing for a fix. Even the wharf rats of Fourth Ward were above such depravity.

No, this was the work of an intelligent maniac, operating out of some private belief system. There was a purpose to this crime, and messages on the body that Mullin wasn't yet able to read. And he was running out of time—because this wasn't the first.

Sweater Martha, a kind but senile old woman who wore a dozen sweaters at one time and sniffed out orphans in the dangerous haunts of Chinatown, the Bowery, and Chatham Square, had been found in a ditch, torn open like the young girl at Mullin's feet. At first, the police thought it might've been one of her troubled youths. Most if not all of them had prior records and severe emotional problems, but Mullin was beginning to think otherwise.

The similarities between the cases were disturbing, but this time, there was one difference.

This time there was a witness.

"I'll see 'er now," Mullin growled as he stood up.

He followed one of his boys down the pier to a medical wagon and rapped on the door.

A pale doctor, roused from sleep only one hour prior, stepped out of the wagon. Over the doctor's shoulder, Mullin saw a woman, a prostitute by the looks of her, seated upright with bandages over both eyes. Her lips quivered as words spilled out in a breathy whisper. The doctor shut the door.

"Can she talk?" Mullin asked.

"She could die of shock tonight," the doctor said as he ran a hand through his graying hair.

"That wasn't my question."

"Trust me, Detective, what she's saying doesn't make any sense. There's no reason to traumatize the poor woman further." The doctor glanced back at the wagon, then turned again to Mullin. "For goodness' sake, she gouged her own eyes out," the doctor said. "With her own hands; with her own nails. What in God's name could she have seen that would cause her to do such a thing?"

"That's what we'd like to know." Mullin nudged the doctor to one side and opened the carriage door. He climbed in and sat across from the woman.

Her straw-colored hair was dry and tangled, clotted with blood where she had torn it out. Her lime green dress was ripped up the leg. She seemed to be clasping her bloody hands together, maybe praying. Mullin strained to make out the gibberish still streaming from her lips.

"*Yaji-ash-shuthath . . . yaji-ash-shuthath . . . yaji-ash-shuthath . . .*"

Mullin patted the woman's knee, to no effect.

"*Yaji-ash-shuthath . . . yaji-ash-shuthath . . . yaji-ash-shuthath . . .*"

Mullin's hand fit easily around both of hers. He shook her gently. Something fell from her hands and landed on the floor of the wagon. Mullin picked it up. It was a pendant, on a long, leather thong. He twirled it before his cloudy eye.

A coin.

But it wasn't like any coin Mullin had ever seen. It looked old, for certain, and he dropped it in his shirt pocket for safekeeping. Then he leaned back and gazed at the woman, who continued to rock in her chair and mutter: "*Yaji-ash-shuthath . . . yaji-ash-shuthath . . . yaji-ash-shuthath . . .*"

The wagon door opened, and an out-of-breath deputy thrust his head inside, sweat streaming from under his helmet. "Detective, there's a lead on a suspect."

"From what?"

"Anonymous tip."

Lucky breaks and brave citizens were the stuff detectives depended upon far more than investigative wits, but as Mullin stepped out of the wagon and glanced back at the terror-stricken prostitute, something told him there would be nothing tidy or simple about this case.

10

FARNSWORTH WRIGHT, AN untidy man in once-expensive clothes, plucked a manuscript off a formidable pile and settled into his tilting chair. With his heels on the desk, he licked his forefinger and opened to page one. He read the first sentence. Frowned. The second sentence sealed it. Farnsworth heaved the manuscript across the office, where it struck a bookshelf. The pages swooped to the floor in company with dozens of similarly disposed of manuscripts. Farnsworth poured himself a generous Jim Beam and settled into another weighty tome. Then across the air it flew, striking the same spot on the shelves before plummeting to the floor. Farnsworth chugged his whiskey as a shadow crossed the frosted glass window of the office door, followed by a gentle knock. Farnsworth's eyes narrowed to slits. "Hell is it?"

The door opened and Doyle stepped inside. "Good evening."

"You write?" Farnsworth barked.

Doyle hesitated. "Well, yes, actually."

"Homicidal maniac story. Ten thousand words. On my desk Monday." And Farnsworth went back to his reading.

Conan Doyle stood there a moment, then double-checked the sign on the door, which revealed it to be the office of Farnsworth Wright, editor-in-chief of *Thrill Book*—a bimonthly journal of horror stories.

Farnsworth glanced up again, irritated. "I only pay you if I like the story. Got it? Three cents a page. No longhand. And don't try to be cute and throw in vampires or some crap like that. I got fifty-two hundred vampire stories, and I don't need another. I want straight maniacs. Nothing too spooky. Just murder. A chase. What? I gotta write it for you?" Farnsworth polished off the whiskey. "And for God's sake, grab me with the first sentence. Nobody knows how to start a damn story anymore. Boom, hit me. Get the damn thing going! I don't need the life story of the maniac. Kill the girl. Chase the maniac. Don't tell me how his grandpa lit his toys on fire. First sentence. Boom! Not enough writers listen to this kind of advice. I like you, pops. What'd you say your name was?"

Doyle brightened. "Ah—"

Farnsworth Wright slapped the table hard. "They don't understand I have to sell these magazines. This ain't art. Grab me. Shake me. Scare me. Wiggle me around. This isn't complicated. My God, these first sentences I'm reading, some of 'em go on half a page. You know how long it takes me to read half a page?" He stopped, fished his pocket watch from a gravy-stained vest, and flicked open the face. "Jesus, is that what time it is? You know how to get a guy going. Anyway, get me the story and we'll talk. I'll see what I can do. No promises." He plucked another manuscript from the dwindling pile and read the first sentence. "Jesus Christ!" Farnsworth's chair slammed back down on all four wheels as the manuscript came to a messy end on the second shelf of the *Thrill Book* library—narrowly missing Doyle, who had quickly dodged left.

Doyle rapped his walking stick hard against the floor. "That's quite enough of that," he declared.

Farnsworth looked up, confused. "So, what? Go on. Tell me your great idea. Thrill me. Drive me wild."

Doyle smiled. "My good fellow, in your wildest dreams you

couldn't afford me." He offered his hand. "Sir Arthur Conan Doyle."

THE WHEELS OF Farnsworth's chair slid out from under him and Farnsworth fell backwards in a heap. His earnest attempts to rise, halted by his head meeting his desktop with a *klonk,* stirred pity in Conan Doyle's heart, and he chastised himself for using his celebrity in that way.

Farnsworth rose up with a hop, the greasy panel of hair that normally covered his scalp lolling long across the left side of his face. He collected himself and marched across the office in a businesslike way. "Farnsworth Wright." He shook Doyle's hand with vigor. "I can't explain, sir, I can't. There are some . . . This is truly . . . You're why . . . You understand . . . I can't."

"That's fine. I do appreciate it."

Farnsworth continued to spew half thoughts as Doyle led him back to his desk. "I'm looking for an author you've worked with, or at least may have heard of. A gentleman named Lovecraft. Howard Phillips Lovecraft."

Farnsworth's neck swiveled. "You know H. P. Lovecraft?"

"As an acquaintance."

"I never . . . he never said anything. Nothing at all. Truly." Farnsworth began searching the office. "He never mentioned you. I would've. I certainly would've published him if I knew."

Doyle found himself in a snowstorm of manuscripts as Farnsworth tore the office apart. "I just need an address, Mr. Wright."

Farnsworth kicked one tower of books to the floor, and then another, before barking triumphantly and slamming a manuscript onto the desk. Its title was *At the Mountains of Madness.*

Doyle nodded. "That's the fellow."

"I can't believe he never told me. If I knew he shared such distinguished friendships . . . but it's the season, you know. His work. It's bleak. Terribly bleak. People want homicidal maniac stories. Redemptive stories. Not this. I mean, I don't know what to make of this. *Mountains of Madness*? It's just not anyone's cup of tea. Desolate alien cities hidden away in the Arctic?"

"Try seeing them in person," Doyle offered.

"Pardon?"

He smiled. "I'm not his literary advocate. I just need the address."

"Yes, of course." Farnsworth hastily provided it and turned back to his manuscripts, eager to end the meeting after his embarrassing introduction.

NIGHT CLOAKED THE city. Doyle stepped off an empty trolley onto Delancey Street on the Lower East Side of Manhattan. He turned to watch the creaking trolley rumble down the Bowery into Chinatown, and the lawless wards of Chatham and the Five Points. This was as far into the ghetto as he intended to go. And if atmosphere was the goal, Delancey possessed it in spades.

The streets were quiet, and barrel fires lit the darkness.

Electric lampposts had not yet been erected this far south. It was still the dark frontier of Manhattan, without a social safety net of any kind—where the bottom dwellers needed different sustenance and where nourishment came via thievery, drugs, and prostitution. Violent crime and murder were common, their numbers never tallied. The disappearances of immigrant children were never investigated, and when those same children's bodies washed up on the charnel shores of the Hudson, they were tossed onto wagons and forgotten.

Long ago, Doyle knew poverty—a result of his father's debilitating alcoholism and insanity. The family worked hard to support ten children in a tiny flat in Edinburgh. There, from the age of thirteen, Doyle had worked three jobs up to and through his university years, until he earned his physician's degree.

Yet this new world with all its plenty and promise was a different animal, and the helpless ones who crawled to her breast did not understand the nightmares that hid in the long shadows of liberty. The carrion of the occult lived here, and it was safest not to ask why the children vanished. Some nightmares do not end; some nightmares go on eternally. And in these sad ports of loneliness and suffering, certain organisms grew and thrived. Which was why Howard Phillips Lovecraft called it home.

Doyle stood outside a collapsing tenement. Only one meager light glowed from the top-floor window. In the wavering silence, a trash can lid fell to his left, and a figure in rags swayed into an alley, face obscured by darkness. Doyle turned to his right and felt more eyes upon him. They were in the alleyways and under the stoops. Quiet, watching. He could make out two faces filled with dull rage, lit by the glow of a dying barrel fire. Though tall and powerfully built, he was still sixty years old, and dressed in a thirty-dollar Worsted wool suit. This marked him as prey. But beneath the surface was strong fiber. Doyle reeked not of fear but of steel. He was a gentleman warrior, and knew how to out-think dull-witted predators like these. Perhaps because of this, they only waited while he crossed the street to Lovecraft's last known address.

A hobo slept on the stoop of 1414, cradling a bottle of scotch. Doyle stepped over him and passed through the unlocked front door. He was assailed by the heavy odor of excrement and urine; the floor of the corridor was shiny and slick with it. He put his monogrammed handkerchief to his lips and took shallow breaths. Twenty feet down the hall was the door to the first-floor apartment, and inside a woman moaned loud enough to vibrate the walls. There were men talking to her in rough, low voices. The moans spiked into sobs, which were swallowed up by laughter and slaps.

Doyle set his jaw and stepped past the door and onto the stairs. The banister shook as he grasped it and climbed to the second-floor landing.

Something cadaver-pale flashed in the corner. A man with wild, bloodshot eyes moved toward him. "Money. Give me money." Doyle stopped him with his stick, pinning him to the wall. The addict wriggled. Doyle swept past him and continued climbing to the third floor.

Lovecraft's door was ajar, and the apartment had been ransacked. Numerous shelves lay empty or facedown on the floor. Books were everywhere. The card table by the window had been upended. Jars of God-knows-what lay broken on the kitchen floor.

A .45 snub-nosed revolver pressed to Doyle's temple, and the wielder patted Doyle down expertly with his free hand. "Evenin', sir."

"Good evening," Doyle replied politely.

A heavyset officer emerged from the closet, holstering his weapon.

"Lookin' fer Mr. Lovecraft, are you, sir?" The man with the gun retrieved Doyle's wallet and perused the contents.

"I am, yes. Is there a problem, Officer—?"

"Detective, if you please. Mullin's my name. You, ah, English, then?" Mullin surveyed the travel visa. "Mr. Doyle?"

Doyle sensed this wasn't a plus in Mullin's eyes. "Scottish." He tried his usual, "I'm a writer, actually. Perhaps you may have heard—"

"I don't read." Mullin holstered his .45. " 'Ow d'ye know this Lovecraft feller, then, sir?"

Doyle watched as the uniformed officer picked up one of Lovecraft's paperweights—a gnarled, petrified human hand. "I don't know him well, Detective; hardly at all, really. We corresponded. Lovecraft's a bit of a fiction writer, and some pieces I found to show talent. I like to counsel young artists on their work, knowing what a lonely business writing can be . . ." He could see his rambling might pay off; Mullin's eyes were already glazing over. "After several letters back and forth, Mr. Lovecraft invited me, if I ever returned to the States, to stop in and have a tea, discuss writing and such. Turns out, I've some business here. I arrived only a day or two ago, and decided to take Mr. Lovecraft up on his offer. I do hope nothing's happened to him?"

" 'Appened to him? No, he's safe at the sanitarium fer the criminally insane. 'Acked up two persons in this past week, though."

Doyle flinched. "That's impossible!"

"Well, as you say, Mr. Doyle, you didn't know the man very well. In any of his letters, did Mr. Lovecraft express any sort of grudge against the Catholic Church?"

Doyle watched the uniformed officer wince as he paged through a seventeenth-century torture manual. The floor was littered with first-edition texts on demonology and necromancy. "Not that I'm aware of, no." The real answer was different. Lovecraft despised organized religions of all kinds. And yet, Doyle knew, something else was at work here. "What's the evidence against him?"

"I'm not at liberty to discuss that, sir." Mullin glanced at his officer, who was examining a broken jar containing what appeared to be a human organ. Mullin turned back to Doyle. "But it don't take a genius to conclude Mr. Lovecraft weren't no ordinary fellow."

Doyle inched toward the door. "Well, this is terribly shocking; I would never have guessed. He seemed rather harmless on the page. In his letters, you know."

Mullin did not seem averse to letting Doyle go. "Where might ye be stayin', sir, case we'd like to ask a few more questions?"

"Outside the city, actually. With friends."

"There an address, sir?"

"I'm sure there is, only I don't know it. I've forgotten." He turned to leave.

"Mr. Doyle, sir," Mullin barked.

Doyle turned back. Mullin walked toward him, slowly. He stopped and examined him. Then, "Your wallet, sir," Mullin said, handing him back his identification.

"Of course. Forgetful as always." Doyle smiled, parroting Jean's words. He dropped the wallet into his coat pocket, and the metal of his money clip clinked off something else.

Mullin heard this. His eyebrows arched.

"Oh." Doyle chuckled. "It's nothing." He produced the Roman coin on its leather rope that he'd found in Duvall's office.

Mullin's expression didn't shift, but suddenly Doyle sensed danger.

"Where'd ye get that, sir?" Mullin asked in a low, quiet voice.

Doyle kept his face equally passive. "A keepsake." He watched Mullin examine the coin. "From my daughter."

"Well, isn't that a lovely present?" Mullin turned and showed his partner the coin.

The officer wore the same blank expression as Mullin as he stared at Doyle. "Sure is."

Doyle could see Mullin's right hand sliding up his hip, toward the holster of his .45, as the detective turned back to him. "Now, then—"

There must have been something in Doyle's furtive glance that alerted Mullin, because his fist clenched fast over the author's wrist.

"Wally!" Mullin shouted.

Just as quickly, Doyle swung his cane across the back of Mullin's hand, bruising the bone.

Mullin screamed and released his grip as the officer lunged. But Doyle spun to meet him, driving the end of his cane deep into the officer's midsection. Then he spun a second time, hooking the officer behind the knees and dropping him like a sack of potatoes. The officer crashed down atop books and broken glass.

Mullin was still between Doyle and the door. The detective pulled out his pistol, but Doyle swung his cane again, swatting the .45 across the room then driving his shoulder deep into Mullin's sternum. The two men hit the wall hard, and before Mullin could get a handhold, Doyle drove his knee into the detective's belly. He wrestled himself free and flew out the door, down the stairs, and out into the streets.

MULLIN BURST THROUGH the doorway of the building moments later. His bowler was missing, and his bald head was beaded with sweat. He stumbled into the middle of the street, shaking with rage.

Wally trundled out behind him.

There was no sign of Doyle.

"Anonymous tip, eh, Wally?" Mullin growled.

"That old-timer sure can move," Wally said, rubbing his belly.

"This case stinks." Mullin stuffed his .45 back in its holster as Wally held up his bowler. Mullin snatched it out of his hands. "Bloody lot o' help you were," he snarled.

*   *   *

DOYLE JOGGED THE seven blocks to Broadway, where he grabbed the railing of one of the last trolleys headed uptown.

Seating himself in the back, he checked his pocket watch. The time was 12:33 A.M.

"Pardon me," Doyle asked a tired woman clutching a brown bag of vegetables, "but will this trolley take me to the Penn Hotel?"

The woman stared blankly at him and nodded.

Doyle sat back and examined the evening's events. The situation was deteriorating faster than he'd feared. Duvall's death, the theft of the Book, and Lovecraft's involvement in murders three thousand miles away—surely these were all connected. Yet Doyle felt he was seeing only a single thread of a vast and complex web of conspiracy.

Perhaps in the years since he had last seen Lovecraft, the man had undergone horrible changes. Knowing Lovecraft's mind, it wasn't beyond the realm of possibility. But Doyle dismissed the thought. Lovecraft had been framed. The man was many things, but not a murderer.

And the coin? Mullin recognized the coin, and had seen it as some proof of guilt or complicity. So much for anonymity. Doyle cursed. He had managed to blunder his way right onto the New York City Police Department's Most Wanted list. His younger self wouldn't have made such a miscalculation, wouldn't have carried I.D., wouldn't have produced the coin so casually. Wouldn't even have approached Lovecraft's apartment so cavalierly. He was long out of practice, and in this sort of game there were no second chances. Today, he'd done more damage than good. Perhaps tomorrow he could set it right—if he wasn't arrested in the meantime.

The Penn Hotel was a welcome sight by the time Doyle arrived. A doorman ushered him into the old-world charm of the lobby. Exhausted, Doyle retrieved his key from the desk and went up to his suite.

Once inside, he took off his jacket, loosened his tie, rolled up his sleeves, locked the door, and wedged a chair underneath the knob. Then, satisfied, he loaded his pipe and lit it, puffing sweet smoke while staring out of his fourth-story window.

After several minutes, he locked the window, too. He placed his trinkets, wallet, change, pocket watch, magnifying glass, pipe, and tobacco on the bureau. From his suitcase he retrieved a small framed photo of Kingsley in his Royal Air Force uniform. He placed it on the bed stand, and positioned it favorably in the light. He then removed the rest of his suit. In nightshirt and ankle straps, he sat on the bed and pulled the window table to him. Glasses balanced on his nose, Doyle dipped his pen and proceeded to write a letter to his wife, feeling her absence as strongly as the pull of the hunt.

11

HENRY THE KNOB swayed in the cool autumn air outside Chick Tricker's Fleabag on the Bowery and thought about throwing up. He wiped cold sweat from his deformed forehead—his namesake—and willed his stomach to settle. Then he straightened his crooked tie and stuffed his shirt back in his pants, and strolled down the avenue like a man trying very hard not to look drunk.

A drunk was a mark and, on this particular street, a mark was a bad thing to be. The Knob didn't need to worry, though; his Tammany connections kept him in the pink with the Five Pointers, and his gambling hall above the Harp House on Park Row made money for the right folks. Still, it was wise to be alert on a Friday night in the Bowery, when every cutpurse and thug was out blowing his earnings at various nightspots like McGuirk's Suicide Hall, the Plague, and the Dump.

The Knob wasn't quite ready for the evening to end, however. All that awaited him at home was a wife and twin sons who screamed themselves hoarse. No, the Knob wanted company, and had a wad of dollars in his vest that he was eager to spend.

He weaved his way onto Mott Street to sample the wares parading outside the Inferno club. But it was a sorry lot of toothless hags and he waved them off, disgusted.

In a few blocks, the Knob found his way to Chinatown, which bustled with traffic and stumble-bums trading time at the gambling parlors and opium dens set above the vegetable shops.

The Knob got lost in the twisting byways of Doyers Street until he found himself in front of the old Chinese Theatre—a once notorious and popular spot for gang-fights until it was shut down and handed over to the New York Rescue Society. The Knob gazed up at the upper-floor windows, and grimy orphans stared back at him.

His buzz now in full retreat, the Knob stumbled down Doyers in search of a taxi or rickshaw—or whatever sort of transport they offered in Chinatown.

Then, "Fancy comp'ny, stranger?" a voice asked from the shadows.

The Knob turned to survey a scruffy waif with huge green eyes leaning against the wall of an alley. Her dirty blond hair was bundled up under a man's top hat, and her small body hidden beneath a rough gray overcoat.

"How old are you?" the Knob asked.

"Old enough."

Unbathed though she was, the Knob saw promise. She had all her teeth and a pretty face. Couldn't be more than sixteen.

"How much?" he asked.

The waif hesitated, seeming to think it over. She wasn't a professional; the Knob could tell.

"What's the usual?" she asked.

The Knob's smile spread, displaying crooked yellow teeth. "A dollar a bump," he said, lowballing it.

The waif's brow knitted. "What's a bump?"

"I'll learn you, lovely," the Knob said. He glanced both ways, then pushed the waif into the alley. He backed her against the bricks, his right hand fumbling in his trousers as the waif lifted her chin to glare at him. "I'll learn you." He breathed heavily, pushing her coat open, showing off a dirty dress, nice young legs, and breasts pushed up in a bustier. "I'll learn you good," the Knob declared as he pushed his face into her chest and his damp hands grasped her buttocks.

"Aren't you a tiger?" the waif purred as her hands mussed the Knob's oiled, thinning hair. Her small fingers toyed with his ear-lobe. Then she took his ear in her teeth and, with a good hard yank, tore it off his head.

"Ow-gah! Agh!" Blood spurted through the Knob's fingers as he grabbed at the stump of his ear and reared back.

The waif turned to the blackness of the alley, snarling, "Matthew, you shit!"

A young dandy in a bowler hat, not old enough for a full beard, lunged out of the shadows and whipped a blackjack down across the Knob's face, bloodying his nose. The Knob grunted and landed on his backside.

The waif wiped the blood off her lips, her green eyes blazing as she drove her boot into the side of the Knob's head. He top-pled sideways into a pile of garbage. She whirled on Matthew, punched him hard in the stomach.

"What the hell, Abby?" Matthew complained.

"Get his billfold, you louse," Abby ordered as she rebuttoned her overcoat and straightened her top hat, giving the Knob an-other clean kick in the groin.

He groaned.

Suddenly, a figure in a long coat, carrying a rifle, appeared at the end of the alley. "Show yourselves!" he barked.

"Bloody hell, it's Dexter," Matthew hissed.

Abby ran in the opposite direction, down the alleyway.

"Abby? Matthew? That you? I'll hide yer asses if it is."

Dexter marched after them, a close-cropped black beard framing his sharp chin and lean features. He stopped and leaned over the Knob, who peered up at him, pleading. "Good Christ," he muttered. Then he turned to the shadows, where Abigail's and Matthew's escaping laughter echoed. "Have you lost your minds, you two?"

*   *   *

ABIGAIL AND MATTHEW exploded out the other side of a tenement building and paused for a kiss beneath an archway, exhilarated by the danger.

Abigail bit playfully at Matthew's bottom lip, and he cursed. "Damn you, girl!"

She laughed and jogged backwards, daring him to follow.

"I think you're cracked," he said.

"I think you're right," she answered, crossing her eyes and sticking out her tongue. "What were you gonna do back there? Let 'im stuff me like a turkey?"

"You could use it," Matthew teased.

Abigail grabbed his shirt collar and pulled Matthew into another long, lingering kiss. They stood there, in the middle of the street, lost to the moment. So much so, neither caught the glint of moonlight off blue glass and the flow of a cape as a stranger stepped into the shadows, eyes upon them—watching.

12

THE BELLEVUE HOSPITAL claimed thirty acres on the East River, and stretched some ten blocks north and south. Comprised of two redbrick structures on the southernmost tip of the twenty-building chain, the Institute for the Criminally Insane was walled off with high fences held together with a chain lock and rimmed with razor wire. Though empty of people, the grounds of the ward were attractive, with high trees, benches, and green grass. But those inside did not walk the grounds, a reassurance to the public, since monsters lived inside the walls—violent monsters that had to be chained, drugged, and often beaten to be kept under control. So a calm exterior masked the grotesqueries within.

It was a blustery day with a light charcoal sky, suggesting rain or snow; Doyle could not decide which. It was also bitingly cold, and he pulled his wool collar tightly around his neck as he approached the guard at the gate. After a few words, the gate opened and Doyle walked across the grounds.

The lobby was large, with high columns and a commanding reception desk stationed at the foot of a wide staircase. Doctors and nurses walked their rounds at a medical pace: a step or two faster than the rest of humanity.

It took some arm-twisting to gain access to Lovecraft. He was a suspect in a murder case, and likely a harm to himself or others. He was on a twenty-four-hour suicide watch, which meant he was being restrained and medicated in the most barbaric ways. His paperwork was also being readied for transfer to a more secure hospital upstate, pending trial.

Nobody had visited Lovecraft. And the years and distance had left room in Doyle's heart to feel some empathy for a man who lived his life with only demons for company.

Like most hospitals in Manhattan, Bellevue was overworked and understaffed. In some cases, there was only one physician for the whole wing, and it was always the insane who suffered the most. Since modern medicine was only beginning to come to terms with such afflictions, the patients often did nothing more than waste away behind bars.

Doyle used a false name on the sign-in sheet and lingered in the nearby corridors to avoid attracting the gaze of the two police officers stationed at the front stoop.

After an hour's wait, a gorilla-sized orderly with a sprout of wispy hair on his pointed head led Doyle down a set of stairs. A smooth club hung from the orderly's belt. It looked well used.

"Ten minutes. No more," the orderly grunted as they descended to the basement level.

Doyle felt a chill scuttle up his back. He did not like this place. He could feel his hands dampen through his leather gloves.

The orderly pulled open the door at the bottom of the stairs and a sickening waft of urine and ammonia stung Doyle's nostrils.

IT IS 1869. *Ten-year-old Arthur struggles to be brave. There are no electric lights in this corridor, only the fire of lanterns. He has never smelled anything like this place. It is what Hell must smell like. He looks down at his untied shoes. Papa will be upset if he sees. As Doyle kneels down to tie his shoes, voices call to him on both sides. They say foul words. They spit. They scream.*

Doyle's bottom lip vibrates, but he will not cry. He will not cry . . .

STILL FOLLOWING THE orderly, Doyle stepped into the corridor. The intermittent electric light gave it a ghostly hue. Sounds bubbled up: gentle laughter, weeping, frantic whispers, barks, shouts, blabbering screams, gibberish. All at once, bodies slammed into steel doors. Wide, staring eyes rolled in their sockets, struggling to glimpse Doyle through the tiny slats at the top of their doors. A lunatic symphony deafened him. His breathing quickened. The gorilla orderly, a few steps ahead, loosened the club from his belt. Everywhere, Doyle saw chattering mouths of yellow teeth, or bloodshot, glaring eyes. The sounds, the sights, reeked of desperation.

"Shaddup! Shaddup!" The orderly rapped his club on the door slats, sending the prisoners skittering away.

"Fuck you, motherfucker—"

"I hear Jesus—"

"They're in my mind—"

"I fuck you! I fuck you!"

Doyle winced.

DOYLE STANDS SHAKING outside a cage door. He is dressed in his church clothes and carries a single flower. A blue-capped guard with a long face and a longer beard scrapes a key in the lock. The door creaks as it opens. Doyle wants to run but his legs won't move. It is even darker inside the cell. A man moves from where he sits on the edge of a wooden cot nailed into the floor. His dirty bare foot pushes a slimy bedpan aside. He turns, embarrassed, to young Doyle. His face is unshaven.

Doyle raises his arm, presents the flower. "Hello, Papa."

His father's smile looks like a frown. His face, cheeks, and eyelids move on their own. He gestures hesitantly to some sketches leaning against the wall.

"I drew ye some pictures, Arthur."

The sketches are of woodland scenes: nymphs and faeries atop pebbles in streams; pixies peaking out from between rose petals.

"Don' stan' there like a fool, boy. C'mere, then."

Doyle swallows and steps inside the cage, and it slams shut with a thunderous clang.

THEY STOOD OUTSIDE the quietest cell on the block. The madness quieted, giving way to a milder din of muttering and weeping. Keys slid into the lock. The door groaned wide. Doyle took a deep breath and entered the cell.

Six delicate bands of light squeezed through a six-barred window, set twelve feet up the wall. Doyle could make out a curled body huddled at the end of an army cot. The door shut behind him. Again, the crawling silence. For all he knew, Lovecraft was dead, the body was so still.

Doyle whispered, "Howard?"

The body did not stir.

"Howard, it's Arthur. I'm here."

Still nothing. Doyle tried not to think of what the conditions in the asylum would do to Lovecraft's particular mental framework. The cells looked like they had never been cleaned. If Lovecraft had not been mad when he entered, surely he was now.

"Howard, I brought you something. I thought you might . . ." Doyle took a pair of clean white dress gloves from his jacket pocket. "Gloves, Howard. I know how you like to wear them." Doyle leaned over and dropped them by Lovecraft's inert body. "I thought they might . . . make things easier." Doyle felt a curdling in his stomach at the thought of doing this all without Lovecraft's aid. The man's intellect and knowledge of occult matters might help to put the pieces together. Without him . . .

"Thank you." The words hung in the air, childlike.

It was the first time Doyle had ever heard Lovecraft utter those words. "You're very welcome, Howard."

"I'm afraid . . ." Lovecraft shifted " . . . that they won't do me much good." He lurched out of the shadows, tied in a strait-jacket stained with vomit and food. His ink-black hair, normally pasted to his scalp and parted with razor precision, hung greasily into his deeply sunken eyes. Patchy stubble dotted his cheeks. He tilted his head, doglike, taking Doyle's measure. "Arthur."

"How . . . how are you feeling?"

"Marvelous. Can't complain."

Doyle could not determine the level of damage to Lovecraft's mind, nor could he interpret the peculiar expression on his face. "I've come here to help you, Howard. And in turn, I want you to help me."

"Really?" Lovecraft stared into Doyle's eyes as if keen to look through him.

"What I'm about to tell you may come as a shock, Howard. Duvall is dead."

Lovecraft's breathing quickened. "You're lying."

"I'm sorry."

Lovecraft worked his way back into the shadows, away from Doyle. "What the hell do you want?"

"I know it wasn't an accident. Something was taken from the Hall of Relics. A book. An important book."

"I don't know what you're talking about."

"Of course you do. This is your field—"

"Get out of here. Get away from me." Lovecraft scuttled farther back.

"Duvall was killed for this book, I know it."

"I don't know about any book. Guard," Lovecraft shouted. "Guard!"

Doyle took Lovecraft by the shoulders and shook him. "Duvall had a map in his office—"

"Don't touch me! Get away from me!"

Doyle shook him harder. "Howard, what are the secrets of Enoch?"

Lovecraft let loose a high-pitched shriek. He tore himself from Doyle's grasp and slammed his body against the door. Then he whirled around and stared at Doyle. "Who are you? Why are you using his face, damn you? Show yourself!" Lovecraft crumpled to the floor. "Why don't you kill me? Just kill me . . ."

"No, Howard, it's Arthur. Arthur Conan Doyle."

Lovecraft scrambled across the floor in a pathetic attempt to escape. "No, no."

Suddenly, Doyle understood. He crossed the room and turned Lovecraft's face toward him, holding it there.

Lovecraft moaned.

"No. Listen to me, Howard. Duvall's last words were: 'There's someone in my mind.' Howard, tell me. Who's after us? Who's framing you? Who stole the Book?"

Lovecraft suddenly looked as if a pinprick of light had pierced the end of his dark tunnel.

"You are H. P. Lovecraft," Doyle insisted. "And I am Arthur Conan Doyle. And you know what the truth is!"

"They're in my mind." It was almost a gasp of relief. Tears slid down Lovecraft's cheeks. "They're in my mind, Arthur. Help me!"

"They won't take you," Doyle said softly. "I'm here. They can't beat us. Your mind is your own. You are Howard Phillips Lovecraft. We've faced darker than this, you and I."

Lovecraft's teeth chattered, though his raging had subsided. "The Arcanum."

Doyle nodded. "Yes, the Arcanum."

Lovecraft shivered like a broken child. "Is this real? I don't know what's real."

Doyle slapped Lovecraft hard across the face. Lovecraft's head jerked, and a welt rose on his face. He turned back, furious, but his eyes were sane.

"That is real," Doyle offered.

"Arthur?"

"Yes, Howard?"

Lovecraft started to cry. Doyle patted his shoulder awkwardly. "You all left," he gasped, between sobs. "You all left me."

"I'm sorry." Doyle meant it, too. They'd all gone on to different lives, whereas their work had been Lovecraft's life. There was no family for him, nowhere else to turn.

"It's too late." Lovecraft's body no longer shook. "You're too late. They'll kill me in here."

"They who?" Doyle persisted.

"It's like nothing we've ever faced." Lovecraft lifted his tired eyes. "I know what's happening. That's why I'm here."

A club rapped on the door. "Ten minutes are up," the orderly declared.

Lovecraft panicked, "No! You can't leave. They're coming."

"Time's up." The door creaked open.

Doyle took Lovecraft by the arms. "So, these murders are related? To Duvall? To the Book?"

Lovecraft's eyes were windows onto the abyss. "It's a conspiracy, Arthur. Two thousand years in the making—"

"Out!" the orderly barked as he stepped inside.

Doyle glared at him, then turned back to Lovecraft. "Tell me."

Lovecraft stared over Doyle's shoulder. "Find the others, Arthur."

The orderly plucked at Doyle's jacket. "Now—"

Doyle shoved him off. "Manners, friend. Manners." He stepped into the corridor.

Lovecraft launched after him, only to be halted by the orderly's arm.

"Back, you loon," the orderly growled.

"They'll kill me now. They're watching all of us."

"I'll be back, Howard. I swear it."

As the door swung shut, Lovecraft's words hissed from the shadows. "Find the others! We're running out of time."

The orderly banged his club on the door and gave Doyle a push.

"Arthur!" Lovecraft's pleas echoed behind him. "Arthur!"

TEN-YEAR-OLD *Doyle sits in the asylum cage on the edge of his papa's wooden cot, watching as his papa sketches a picture with hands that shake.*

"They live in the grasses, see?" Papa is almost serene. On the page, an elfin creature peers mischievously from under an autumn oak leaf. It has pointed ears and slitted eyes, and long, tapered fingers. " 'E's smilin' at ye, Arthur."

For a moment Doyle forgets where he is. For a moment he is lost

in the picture, lost in the fantasy. He believes the elf exists, some-
where out in the wilderness. His papa makes him believe.

Then the pencil cracks in two with a snap and the makeshift
easel falls over.

Doyle turns to his father, who is stiff as a board, eyes rolled
back. Blood trickles between his lips, and his tongue is caught be-
tween clamped teeth. His hands are balled into fists at his sides.
Every vein in his neck swells to bursting. His head knocks back
and forth against the wall, though he utters no sound but a high-
pitched whining from the nostrils. More blood pours from be-
tween his teeth as his tongue severs.

Doyle sits and watches. He does not understand. He does not
know what to do.

DOYLE SLAMMED OPEN the stairwell door and braced himself on the banister. Epilepsy. There was a word for it, finally.
His father had had epilepsy. Doyle held his head in his hand,
feeling an almost insane desire to speak with Duvall. Things
were spiraling out of control, and he could not keep up. He was
an old man, and Duvall had always been the anchor. Duvall was
their leader.

But his first concern now was Lovecraft. He would be dead
unless Doyle found a way to get him out.

Out of the asylum.

Out of the cell.

Out of the straitjacket.

Not surprisingly, a name came to mind.

13

THE FERRY ACROSS the Hudson was too slow for Doyle's liking, though the sun was bright and the wind bracing. Seagulls cawed and circled the boat, then sailed away on the breeze. A family of German tourists—mother, father, and two little girls—joined Doyle at the railing and threw popcorn at the gulls. They were dressed in their Sunday finest for the ride. Doyle smiled; he always enjoyed the company of children. As the ferry rumbled into port, he patted the girls on their cheeks and tipped his hat to the parents.

Leaving the terminal, Doyle boarded a trolley for West Hoboken. Along the way, the car passed through a youthful neighborhood filled with a surge of new shops and cafés. The level of traffic still bothered Doyle. He winced every time a car swerved into the trolley's path, and at the pedestrians who dodged not only trolleys but wagons, carriages, taxis, Model-T's, and horses.

Ten minutes later, Doyle spied his destination—a nondescript three-story building sporting a sign that read: FDC—FILM DEVELOPMENT CORPORATION. He pulled on the wire running the length of the trolley car and disembarked.

A small crowd of autograph-seekers stood outside the door; mostly young men clutching magazines under their arms.

Sturdy boys, with their shirtsleeves rolled to the elbows, smoked cigarettes. They stood atop a line of wagons parked outside the building and guarded cumbersome film equipment: floodlights, cameras, and a large backdrop painted to resemble a tropical beach.

Doyle approached a harried young woman in an ankle-length black dress wearing a cloche hat and carrying a clipboard. Her eyes were dark with mascara, and she stood sentry outside the front door. When she saw Doyle, she snapped, "Are you on the list?"

"I'm a friend."

From the look on the woman's face, that wouldn't be enough. She scanned her sheet. "Name?"

Doyle sighed. "Arthur—"

"Knock me over with a feather, what are you doing here?" a cheerful voice called out from a window above.

Doyle looked up to see a pretty face with sleepy eyes and lustrous brown hair piled in a bun hanging out a second-story window. He smiled. "My dear Bess!"

"I'll meet you downstairs. Let him in, Sandra." And Bess vanished back inside.

Sandra raised her eyebrows, and opened the door.

Doyle entered, and found himself in near-total blackness. A wall stood before him, braced by wooden slats. Through its cracks streamed bright lights and movement.

A voice carried above the din. ". . . .the sincerest actor on the screen. Yes, and that's the Hollywood papers, mind you, and they know of what they speak. Those are their words, Mr. Baker, not mine. Right. Yes, I'll let you speak in a moment, but firstly your review—and I use that word reluctantly because 'skewering' might be the more appropriate one—your review obviously shows a sad lack of taste. But I wonder, sir, if you have any sense of fun?"

Doyle followed the sound of the voice around the walls, which he now realized were the backs of film sets. He crossed over to a table where three brawler types in whiteface ate pastries and chatted over coffee. The loud growl of an animal spun him around, and he found himself staring into the feral yellow eyes of a caged male lion. It stalked the tiny confines of its prison, a rumble stirring in its throat. Its handler sat by the cage door eating a grilled cheese sandwich. Dazed, Doyle turned back to the film set as the sound of high heels distracted him.

Bess emerged from the darkness, wearing a pink waistcoat and an ankle-length dress, smiling broadly. "Arthur."

Doyle took her gloved hands and kissed her cheek, to which she responded with a not-so-gentle punch to his belly.

"Why on earth didn't you tell us you were coming, silly man? We arrived back from California just two days ago. We're coming to England, did you hear?"

"Urgent business forced me here, I'm afraid. I hate to bother him . . ."

"No, not at all." Bess took his arm and led him toward the set. "He's in quite a mood today, though, so be warned." Bess led him through a thicket of technicians fiddling with the scorching floodlights, past the ever-moving crew members, and into a rush of sight and sound soon to be the site of the climax to *The Man From Beyond,* starring . . .

. . . Harry Houdini.

Doyle shook his head at the sight of his old friend. A coiled ball of energy, Houdini moved at double the speed of those around him. His face was smeared with white greasepaint and his wiry hair was flecked with gray at the temples, but he was as fit as ever. His linen shirt was unbuttoned to his sternum, showing off a muscular chest. A hapless aide ran alongside, carrying the base of a telephone, whose receiver was at Houdini's lips.

"By your standard, it's a good review, Mr. Baker, not mine. And since when does the star of the picture, let alone the generator of the idea—the conceptualizer, if you will—get such scarce mention, when every other worthy journal on the continent acknowledges my performance for what it is: magnificent?" Houdini glanced across the set. "Not like that!" He jogged across and snatched a hammer from a set designer's hand. The designer backed away. Houdini handed the phone to his aide, saying, "Keep Baker on there," then he studied a box laden with heavy anchor chains. He proceeded to hammer nails into the box, stopping when the heads were a half an inch from the wood. "I need all these nails to have a little breathing room," he said. Houdini assessed the effect, then flipped the hammer back into the arms of the designer. Then he grabbed the phone back from the aide and resumed his tirade. "Have you some bone to pick with me, sir? Because I assure you that Houdini is not a trifling enemy."

Bess glanced at Doyle, grinning.

"What's that?" Houdini paused. "Let me think about that. That might work. I don't want to appear too eager, you understand, but an interview that rementions the film . . . Maybe that might work. If it focuses on my acting. There are new worlds to conquer, Mr. Baker; surely, you understand. As long as it isn't another 'Handcuff King' article, then perhaps . . . well, that might work out, like I said. Let's do it in my library at 278, eh? I have the largest collection of books on magic in the world, you know. We should talk about that. Perhaps a Sunday piece."

Houdini began to wave angrily at two men setting a cardboard tree in place. He stalked over and pushed them away, righting the palm. Still into the phone, he said, "That might do fine. Good, then. I'll see you this week. Call Franz; he'll handle the details. We'll have lunch, talk about the pictures, see the library, and that will be fine. I'm glad we chatted. Perhaps you should have the wife and children come along. We'll tour the studio here. Yes? Marvelous. I'll send a car. Call Franz about that, too. Yes, fine, Mr. Baker. No, no, call me Houdini. My closest friends—even my wife—refer to me only as Houdini. That's right. Very good. Yes. Yes, I understand. You're most welcome." The phone snapped down on the receiver. Houdini looked around at a set filled with movement and asked, "What is everyone standing about for? There's a picture to be made!"

Houdini turned to Bess and gave her a wink. She, in turn, flipped a thumb in Doyle's direction.

It took Houdini a full five seconds to register Doyle's presence.

"My God." Houdini crossed the set; the man had unimpeachable posture. He held Doyle at arm's length, looked at him with those piercing blue eyes, and repeated, "My God," pulling him into an embrace, which surprised Doyle—until he recalled the man's endearing, if over-the-top, sentimentality.

"It's good to see you, old friend." Doyle managed to pat Houdini on the back with his cane. "Good to see you, yes."

Houdini released him in a rush and held him at arm's length once more. "My God, Doyle, why didn't you tell me you were here?"

"I—"

"We just arrived back from California."

"I told him—" Bess began.

Houdini cut her off. "Have you been? Marvelous place. The sun never stops shining. You must write for the movies, by the way. You see all this around you?" Houdini spread his arms to the film set.

One wouldn't know it, but there was a director, a somewhat forlorn gentleman wearing a black beret seated in the corner, face in his hands.

Houdini took Doyle by the arm, pointing out his favorite articles on the set. "What do you think? This is the medium of the century, I'm telling you! Get in on the ground floor. But we're heading to England. Don't you read the papers, man? We could have saved you the trip." Houdini laughed and swatted Doyle hard on both shoulders.

"Houdini—"

"Wait. Ladies and gentlemen!" Houdini dragged Doyle into the center of the room. "May I present my dearest friend, and the creator of the world's greatest detective, Sherlock Holmes—the one and only Sir Arthur Conan Doyle." There was applause. Doyle raised a hand to the crew. A photographer appeared out of nowhere and popped a picture. Houdini took Doyle's hand like a politician.

"I must speak with you."

"Of course." Houdini was already nodding to another visitor on the set.

"Alone," Doyle insisted.

A haze of irritation passed across Houdini's features. "Certainly, yes. Head up to my dressing room, Arthur. I'll be there shortly."

DOYLE WAS ABOUT to read the *New York Daily News* for the second time running when Houdini burst through the dressing room door. He threw off his shirt, grabbed a robe, and started digging through a cardboard box. "Here. Wait. Sit. I insist. Down. Before you say another word, I must show you something. My God! It's impossible to find anything around here. Ah, yes, here it is." Houdini brandished a film reel and handed it to Doyle, who was seated at the makeup table. "For you. The very first print of *Terror Island*, the next box-office hit. Have you a screen? I'll get you one; never you mind. Call Franz; he'll arrange it. You're at Windlesham, of course? I'll send it there. Oh! Perhaps we can watch it together?" Houdini was at the sink, running the water and soaping his hands. "The ideas are all mine, you'll see. Sensational! Some other fellow penned the words, of course—fine fellow, you should meet him, Ted somebody." Houdini washed the makeup from his face. "Anyway, we shot the stunts dead-on, see? There's no way to fake that. Just marvelous footage. But these son-of-a-bitch critics, excuse me, sons-of-bitches keep going after me. What can it be but jealousy? They don't want me to cross over, see? Some don't. Most do. Sold out most theaters in the last run. Did you see that picture? Damn good." Houdini scrubbed himself dry with a towel. "Chaplin's quite the fan. He's a good chap. You should meet him. English, like yourself—"

"Houdini, enough!"

Houdini looked startled. "I beg your pardon?"

Doyle stood, deposited the reel on Houdini's desk, went to the door, and shut it. He turned back. "Sit down, please."

"Doyle—"

"Sit down!"

Houdini sat.

Doyle settled both hands on the desk. "Duvall is dead."

"I know," Houdini answered.

This surprised Doyle. He hesitated.

"I am president of the American Society of Magicians; they have an adequate network, keep me apprised. It's sad news." Houdini's words were an unspoken warning for Doyle to tread carefully.

"He was murdered. Did you know that as well?"

"Doyle—"

"Did you know that as well?" Doyle felt the press of time, felt Lovecraft's panic and terror.

"He was struck by a motorcar," Houdini said.

Doyle's voice lowered to a growl. "Allow me to remind you who stands before you now. If I tell you he was murdered, then he was murdered. I've been known to smell a crime out. Upon occasion."

"And what business is it of mine, I ask you?"

"The game's afoot," Doyle replied.

"No longer my game, sir."

"But it was."

"And will never be again."

"A book is missing from the Hall of Relics. Duvall was killed for it. And now Lovecraft has been charged with murder—"

"That has nothing to do with me," Houdini said.

"You and I, Houdini, we were Arcanum before it all—"

"That is not true. It was a distraction, an idling of time that grew out of control. A swerve into madness—"

"We saw phenomena that defied explanation, and yet you go about crusading against all you know to be true."

"Rubbish. What? These psychic mediums? These charlatans?"

Doyle's anger was getting the better of him. "But it's earning you wonderful press coverage, isn't it? And that's really what matters, I suppose."

"And you support them! You with this Spiritualist nonsense."

"That nonsense happens to be my deep conviction."

"They're reporting you the fool, Doyle. Don't you see? That's what they're saying. And why shouldn't I reveal these psychics for what they are, hah? Why not? They take people's money and prey on their grief, give them false hope. It sickens me. Let one—just one—do something I cannot explain, and I'll believe. Christ, I want to believe! You don't think I want to talk with Mother?" Sentimental as he was, the mere mention of the woman choked him up.

This tempered the heat of Doyle's anger. "You can't erase the past, no matter how hard you try."

"I don't want to hear its name spoken, Doyle. Not in my presence."

"It was all a lie, then?"

"Duvall is dead." Houdini turned away. "Let it die with him."

"You owe him more than that."

"I owe?" Houdini whirled around. "I owe? I'm Houdini! I was known around the world before I was twenty-two years old—"

"That's all you bloody care about, isn't it?"

"Mind your tongue. You lose yourself, Arthur."

"Your world of fakery and illusion. That's all, is it? Cheat death all you like, Harry Houdini; I know the cowardice you hide."

"Were you not an old man, I'd teach you a lesson . . ."

"Don't let age be your excuse, Harry; have a go. I insist on it."

"I'm a gentleman—"

"You're a fraud."

"Damn your audacity!" The walls shook from the volume. All activity on the set below ceased. Then footsteps were heard, coming toward the stairs.

"People are dying," Doyle insisted. "And Lovecraft's in the bloody sanitarium. He's next!"

"They knew the risks," was Houdini's curt reply.

Doyle sighed. "Perhaps I've gone senile. My wife believes so. But of late . . . for the first time in fifty years, I've found I cannot write. Not a word. There is only sadness where inspiration used to be. Now, interpret this as you may, but Duvall . . . his death . . . it's as though he's drawing us back one last time, to finish what we started. There's been so much pain and distrust. But still, the fact remains that we've seen beyond the veil, and once you've done that, nothing ever feels the same. Why is it you rush headlong into one venture after another with scarcely a second to breathe? I'll tell you why. Because you've never experienced anything since that even touches what we saw, what we did, together. The world idolizes you, Houdini. Your fame is beyond measure. Nothing can enhance it. The decision you make now is not about what they see, it's about what you see. When you look inside yourself."

Franz Kukol, Houdini's executive assistant, swung open the door. "Boss? There was yelling?"

Houdini did not answer right away. He was staring at Doyle.

"Boss? Everything okay?"

"Mr. Doyle was just leaving," Houdini answered.

Doyle scowled. "I'll show myself out." He flashed a disparaging glance at Houdini, then approached Kukol. "Pardon."

Kukol stepped aside.

Doyle stopped in the doorway. "They've locked Howard away at Bellevue. Unless something is done, I doubt he will live to see the morning."

Houdini's face was unreadable. Doyle shook his head, disgusted, before exiting into the hall.

14

"AND MAY GOD'S righteous sword of justice lead us to truth and wisdom and mercy and charity in all our hearts and actions . . . amen."

"Amen."

Paul Caleb, the young district attorney of New York City, having said his prayer, unclasped the hands of the chief of police and the captain of Fourth Ward.

"To business, then, gentlemen." Caleb unbuttoned his suit jacket and hung it on the coatrack.

Chief McDuff sat behind his desk, looking uneasy. Everyone seemed more conscious of their shortcomings in the presence of the young D.A., who was living up to his billing as a dueling stew of piety and ambition. But still, the realities of how Tammany Hall worked would temper the boy in time.

Captain Bartleby of Fourth Ward—the most notorious of the five boroughs—felt inadequate, too, and winced through the burn of his ulcer; a thousand troubles, both personal and professional, claimed the lion's share of his attention. He was a saggy man in his fifties, kept alive by coffee, neither principled nor corrupt. His one desire in life was to have a decent bowel movement. Caleb's assessment of Fourth Ward was not high on his list of concerns.

Caleb smoothed his hair and leaned back on the sofa. "Congratulations are in order, Captain. I'm happy to see the apprehension of a suspect in those murders in Chatham."

"Yes, Mr. Caleb. Detective Mullin's one of our best, sir." Bartleby removed his finger from his ear and examined it.

"I should like to meet this man," Caleb added.

"He's on his way, sir."

Caleb raised his eyebrows at McDuff. "If only all our wards showed such commitment."

McDuff didn't react. "There are budgetary issues involved, Mr. Caleb. Of course we'd like to solve every crime, but it's complicated."

Caleb's expression was blank. "I see. You're speaking of priorities?"

"Of course, sir." McDuff clipped the tip off a cigar.

"Applying values to certain crimes over others?"

"Exactly." McDuff smiled cynically and sampled his cigar.

"In other words: A dead poor person simply isn't as important as a dead wealthy person."

McDuff frowned. "Look, Mr. Caleb—"

" 'And the meek shall inherit the earth,' Chief McDuff," Caleb reminded him. "It's time this police force served all the people and not just the political hand that feeds it."

"Now, wait just a minute—"

"There will be changes, I promise you that. And this case . . ." Caleb pointed at Captain Bartleby ". . . is a good first step."

Detective Mullin knocked, then stepped inside. "You called for me?" he asked Captain Bartleby.

"Yes. Come in, Detective." Caleb rose to his feet and shook hands with Mullin, who glanced at the others with apprehension. "Job well done. Well done."

Mullin looked to his captain. "Sir?"

"The Chatham slashings, Shaughnessy," Bartleby reminded him.

Mullin turned back to Caleb: "We haven't closed that investigation yet, sir."

Caleb blinked. "I was told we have a suspect in custody. That the evidence is overwhelming."

"You've been misinformed, sir."

"What's this hogwash, Bartleby?" the chief grumbled.

The captain squirmed. "Eh, Shaughnessy's just explainin', weren't you, Shaughnessy?"

"Who's the man at Bellevue, Detective?" the chief asked.

"This Lovecraft fellow? 'E's an odd duck, fer certain. But there's others involved. They may be settin' up this Lovecraft to take the fall. The boy's not all at home upstairs, if y'understand my meanin', sir."

"But you had evidence," Caleb insisted.

"Nuthin' tyin' 'im directly to the crimes, sir."

"Demonological tracts? Blasphemous writings? Occult literature? Am I mistaken, or were these not found in Mr. Lovecraft's apartment?"

"As I said, Lovecraft's an odd duck, sir."

"I'd say it's quite a bit more than that; I'd say it's proof of a diseased mind spilling over into bloody action." Caleb turned on Chief McDuff. "I'd say these are just the sort of crimes—and just the sort of criminals—we should be applying all our might to stopping." Caleb addressed Mullin directly. "Mr. Lovecraft is the symptom—the tumor, if you will—of a cancerous society. This man cut the spine out of an old woman whose sole reason for living was to save orphans from the streets. And we're supposed to do nothing?"

"Not nuthin', sir. I just think there might be others involved."

"Who, Shaughnessy?" Bartleby asked. "Have you got a name?"

"Doyle, sir. Arthur Conan Doyle."

Caleb frowned and looked at McDuff.

Captain Bartleby scratched his ear. "Name sounds familiar . . ."

"Older fellow," Mullin went on. "Said he was a writer. Showed up at Lovecraft's apartment the night he was arrested."

"He didn't . . . he wasn't English, was he?" Caleb inquired.

"Scottish, sir."

" 'Sir' Arthur Conan Doyle?" Caleb repeated.

"He might've said that, yeah."

"The author of the Sherlock Holmes stories?" Caleb continued, incredulous. "British war hero?"

"Well, now, he didn't say as such . . ."

"Did he look wealthy?"

"I suppose," Mullin answered reluctantly.

"Just so I'm clear, Detective." Caleb gestured to the chief and
the captain, who were both a little paler than usual. "Just so
we're all clear, are you suggesting that Sir Arthur Conan Doyle,
knight of the king of England, is murdering old women and
young girls downtown?"

Mullin seemed flustered. "I just said, sir, that not all roads led
to Mr. Lovecraft. I, ah—"

"Because that will make wonderful news. And not just in New
York, but around the world. We'll make all the front pages. I'll
be famous, indeed." Caleb rose to his full six feet and looked
down at Mullin. "As the biggest ass of the twentieth century!
Are you trying to make a fool of me, Detective Mullin?"

"No, sir."

"Is this some attempt to sabotage me? Humiliate me?"

"Frankly, it has nuthin' to do with you, sir. I'm just statin' what
I saw—"

"That's the stupidest thing I've ever heard. Either you're a
complete incompetent or a bald-faced liar. And neither, I assure
you, bodes well for your career, Detective." Caleb spun on the
chief and waved a finger at him. "If anyone breathes a word of
this, heads will roll."

Chief McDuff simply nodded.

"And I see my praise of Fourth Ward was premature, Captain
Bartleby. That's all right. I'll save you from yourselves, if I
must." Caleb took his hat off the chair and swung back to
Mullin. "Well, Detective, you've managed to snatch defeat from
the jaws of victory. Congratulations." Caleb walked past him
and grabbed his suit jacket off the rack. "We will prosecute Mr.
Lovecraft to the fullest extent of the law, and I expect full support from everyone in this room. I know how I'm viewed by the

rank-and-file," Caleb continued as he shrugged into his jacket. "I know how my beliefs are mocked behind my back, but make no mistake: Cross me at your peril."

Caleb slammed the door as he left.

There was a moment of silence.

"Bartleby?" the chief began.

"Yes, Chief?"

"Give me a few minutes with Detective Mullin."

Bartleby stood hesitantly. "Yes, Chief."

Mullin pulled on his ear as the door closed behind him. He turned to Chief McDuff, who took his cigar in both hands and slowly mashed it in his fists until pulp squeezed out of his hands like toothpaste onto the desktop.

15

DEXTER'S LONG COAT flowed behind him like a sheet of black rainwater; a twelve-gauge single barrel shotgun in his hands. It was 2:30 A.M., and he was walking his usual route, corralling the older orphans from the Chatham hellholes, but he was keenest on finding Abigail and Matthew. It seemed his life's work had been nothing more than running herd on those two, and he had thankless little to show for it. They'd become thieves and alley cats and seemed to thrive on danger. And it wasn't only Dexter who had grown weary of their adventures. They'd exhausted the patience of the police, the Rescue Society, and near everyone else who knew them.

But none of that mattered. Tonight was different. No one should be out on the streets tonight. Not after what happened to poor Martha. How perverse that a woman so gentle could die so viciously. Dexter tried to shake the memory off, but another just rose up to take its place. Audrey. There would be no more of her silly songs, no more of her mischievous little tricks, her ways of calming colicky babies.

Dexter couldn't let himself feel the full impact of their loss;

not yet. Instead, he just pressed on. Protecting the others, that's what mattered.

Dexter spotted a local thief, Chops Connelly, catching a cig outside a brothel on Mott Street.

Chops spoke first. "Whaddya say, Dex? Goin' huntin'?"

Dexter never smiled. "Seen Abby or Matthew?"

"Seen 'em? I wish! The little shits owe me fi' dollars on a dice game. They ran off, o' course, 'fore payin' what they lost. I can't allow that to happen, see?"

"You'll get your money." Dexter always looked men directly in the eyes as he spoke, which won him respect even from thugs like Chops.

"I don't know why ya don't tie a brick round their ankles and drop 'em off a dock."

Dexter calmly lifted the shotgun and touched the muzzle to Chops's chin.

"Ay, ay, easy, Dex. I ain't sayin' I'm doin' nuthin'; the kids is trouble's, all. Don't be like that."

"Anything happens to them and I'll hold you personally responsible. Do you understand?"

"Whaddya takin' everythin' so personal fer?" Chops backed away and flicked his cigarette into the street. He rubbed his throat. "You shouldn't a done that, Dex. That weren't smart. Them kids owes me fi' dollars." And Chops stalked off into the night.

Dexter watched him go with steady black eyes. He'd been dealing with men like Chops for so long, and in so many different cities, that their threats meant nothing to him.

For the next hour he searched all the way to City Hall Park, but in vain. He combed the usual hideouts—the Doctor's and the Billy Goat and the dance halls—but none of the regulars had seen them. Although by Dexter's calculation, Abigail and Matthew owed half the city approximately fifty dollars and change.

By now most of the riffraff had retired for the evening. The streets were canyons, empty save for the stray bottle rolling in the wind.

Dexter's anger gave way to worry. Regardless of their age he still thought of Abigail and Matthew as children—and of him-

self as their guardian. And, silly as it was, he felt like he was letting them down, leaving them open to danger.

Suddenly, Dexter spun into a low crouch, the rifle locked and
loaded. He knelt there in the middle of the street, aiming into
the darkness of a tenement alley. He wasn't sure what he had
seen, but his peripheral vision was legendary. And something
that had moved caught his eye.

Steel scraped off steel, and Dexter sprang to his feet, dashing
across the street to a small children's playground.

A child's swing squeaked on rusting hinges.

Dexter pressed his back to one of the trees, then turned and
aimed into the darkness again, eyes searching for movement.

A gurgling squeal echoed through the air. Dexter tried to
place the sound. It was like phlegm rolling in a long throat; like
a pig's squeal on the chopping block.

Dexter heard the steel-scraping sound again, and ducked
down. It came from the opposite direction as the squealing, and
sounded farther away this time.

Another round of squealing erupted, closer now. Dexter's gaze
darted up and down the streets. His heart swelled in his throat.
He could smell something in the air—something fetid, decaying.

Then there was a blur of movement behind him. Dexter
whirled around. There was nothing there, but this time the
squeal he heard was the loudest yet. It rang off the buildings,
and goose bumps rose on Dexter's arms.

His only thoughts now were of escape. He was outnumbered,
and he knew it. They were hunting him like pack animals, trying
to lure him out of hiding. Old instincts took over: old senses, old
skills that had been dulled over time by city life.

Dexter concentrated on the wind, and when it flowed his way,
he tried to read the scents upon it. But the moon caught on
something steel in the playground, between the trees. Dexter
feinted left then rolled right, rising up fast, ready to shoot.

Then he spun southward again as a new volley of squeals
threw his senses off. He couldn't count the numbers. Three?
Ten? He began to sense movement all around now, in every
shadow, in every alley and doorway. A gleam of ruby eyes.

There was movement behind him again.

Dexter spun about and caught a glimpse of brown robes snaking up a tenement stairwell.

More waited all around him.

Dexter walked in a small circle, listening to them breathe.

A twig snapped.

Dexter swung his rifle around as two silver axes sliced the air.

"Yaji-ash-shuthath," his attacker hissed as one of the axes bit through his coat sleeve, taking with it a chunk of flesh.

Dexter fired wildly into the trees, sending dozens of pigeons fleeing across the moon.

With his attacker too close now to shoot, Dexter used the rifle as a cudgel. The ax blades rang off the forged frame of the shotgun, striking sparks with every blow. Dexter spun around, throwing off his opponent's balance, and caught him in the side of the head with the walnut stock. A shard of blue glass dropped from the attacker's face and he stumbled away. Dexter's hands were shaking as he searched for a shell in his pockets. He saw his opponent steadying himself, readying for another attack, and Dexter was suddenly aware of his own blood dripping from his fingers; he felt its stickiness beneath his coat sleeve. The wound was deep.

He turned to run, but they were already upon him.

They swayed forth from the stygian darkness, lithe robed bodies with drooping hoods concealing long faces with glowing red rubies instead of eyes. Thin stalks of wood, like beaks, substituted for noses. Clutched in their gloved fists were enormous scythes gleaming silver. Their heads bobbed, crowlike, and they seemed to communicate without language, though their breath gurgled through lungs thick with mucus.

Dexter roared as they closed around him, the air hissing with the passing of blades. He heard three sickening thunks and a wet gasp.

The creatures yanked their blades free of his torso, spraying the air with blood, then swooped in again like raptors. Dexter's hands went to his punctured throat as his knees buckled. His eyes turned skyward, but the heavens were obscured by bloody hooks and staring ruby eyes.

16

DOYLE LEFT THE Manhattan Club on Fourth and Madison Square in an ill humor. His breath stank of cigars and his chest burned from gulping several brandies. He wavered in the cold autumn air and tried to gather himself.

"Need a car, mistah?"

He turned to an unsmiling black man with penetrating eyes and a tilted top hat. Something was strung around the brim of the hat, something white. Doyle could not make it out. He stepped into the back of the Lexington sedan.

"I'm headed to the—" He jolted back as the car lurched forward. "The Penn Hotel, please, and no rush."

The coachman ignored him. Doyle leaned forward, and saw that the objects strung about the brim of his top hat were small animal bones. A severed chicken foot dangled from the front mirror.

Doyle frowned at the voodoo ornaments; his history with that religion was fraught. Among its highest priests and priestesses, he could name both hated opponents and beloved allies. And he feared it. He knew that voodoo was more than just religion. It was instead some mystical transmitter to a lawless universe of primal, passionate spirits, both beautiful and ugly.

Doyle settled back into the seat and turned his thoughts instead to the matter of Lovecraft. Houdini's refusal made his task all the more difficult, and Doyle's response had been to retreat into drink. Everything was different now. Houdini had become a caricature of himself. Even Lovecraft, the youngest of them, was outmatched by this new breed of conspirator.

The Penn Hotel rose in the front windshield. Doyle gathered his walking stick and long coat, but the taxi showed no sign of slowing.

"This is it. Right here."

The taxi picked up speed.

"Driver, this is the hotel."

Doyle watched as the doorman and the glowing stoop of the Penn Hotel rushed by his window. He banged his stick on the back of the driver's seat.

"I say, you've missed the stop."

The driver pressed down on the accelerator, throwing Doyle forward then back.

"Stop the car!" His hand went to the door handle. He pulled on it, but to no avail.

The driver kept going.

"I'm ordering you to stop this car!" But even before he spoke, Doyle recognized that he was in no position to give orders. And even if the door were to open, a dive out would most likely kill him.

The taxi careened around a corner, missing a pedestrian by inches and throwing Doyle across the seat. His head cracked the window glass. He was sobering fast as the taxi sped up Central Park West, past the Museum of Natural History. Central Park whizzed by on the right. Doyle had at first assumed that the police had found him, but the situation suggested otherwise. It seemed he'd blundered into the hands of Duvall's killer.

He cursed himself. "Old fool." He still knew how to fight, though. This would be one victim his captors would not forget.

✳   ✳   ✳

THE STREETS OF Harlem pulsed with activity as motorcars honked and jockeyed for position on the packed streets. The sidewalks were clotted with ticket lines and laughing couples. Club lights sparkled. The Novelty Fire played across from Wilbur Sweatman's Jazz Band. Even through the closed car window, Doyle could hear the wail of jazz trumpets. There was a refreshing mix of whites and blacks together on the streets, all dressed in tuxedoes and evening gowns.

The assault on the senses was such that, for a moment, Doyle did not realize that the taxi had taken a sharp left into an alley, then screeched to a halt.

Bodies converged on the car. The back doors swung open. Doyle thrust his cane at the groping hands that reached for him, but he was dragged out from behind by the scruff of his neck. He landed on his back on the pavement. Legs shuffled in the gloom. He expected a volley of blows but none came. Instead, he was wrenched to his feet and his arms pinned behind his back. Doyle weighed two-hundred-plus pounds, yet he scarcely touched the ground as he was ushered through a rusted back door.

"Tell me what this is about! Tell me—"

The bwwaaaaap of a horn solo greeted him, and his words were lost in the music. The nightclub stench of cigar smoke and sweating bodies made his eyes water. He was pushed through the mob.

Doyle felt faint by the time they reached the velvet staircase. The soft carpet muted the sounds of the music. And, like Alice hurtling down the rabbit hole, he entered another world beneath the jazz club. Beaded curtains gave way to warm, candlelit corridors, where the dark eyes of suspicious children peeked out from behind cracked doors. There was a delicious combination of kitchen smells: baking breads, spicy soups, and fried meats. An attractive black girl with a jeweled necklace pulled red curtains aside as the men forced Doyle into a voodoo parlor. Circulation returned to his arms as the well-dressed black men set him free and departed.

Only the driver remained. He circled Doyle aggressively, bare-chested beneath his suit jacket. Doyle flinched as the man patted him down for a weapon. As the driver's rough hands swept down each pant leg, Doyle surveyed the room. Hundreds of dripping candles warmed the chamber. Ornate chaises lined the walls, reminding him of French New Orleans. A rooster clucked in a small cage atop a table decorated with human skulls.

Then, without a word, the driver was gone. Doyle's heartbeat increased. Then from behind came a rustling of skirts and a tinkling of bells. A perfume of gardenias and raspberries filled him with longing, then memory . . .

. . . then terror.

Doyle spun around.

A beautiful young woman with chocolate-cream skin stood before the red curtains, her hair tied in a tignon. She batted her long lashes. "Been a while, *non*?"

Doyle held up his hands to ward her off. "Are you real?"

The woman lifted her chin, the light flowing off high cheekbones. She was in no rush to dispel the mystery. "What you think, *chère*?"

"I think you're dead, drowned in a river five years ago—or so I was led to believe." His voice shook.

"Two graveyards in New Orleans got headstones wit' my name on 'em. Lot of folk want Marie Laveau dead." Her hand touched Doyle's pale cheek. "Sometimes I oblige."

Doyle didn't know what to feel: rage, horror, bitterness, or relief. Marie Laveau, the famed and feared voodoo priestess of New Orleans, was a living tempest. The fact that she had once allied herself with the Arcanum did nothing to allay his fears. For her loyalties were as mercurial as Duvall's, and her influence almost as sweeping. Her power over Louisiana culture and politics was unprecedented. The mere threat of one of her curses could force judges to commute death sentences and drive adultering husbands back to their wives. A living enigma, she was a saint to many, and a demon to more. And it only enhanced her legend that there were, in fact, two Marie Laveaus. Marie Laveau the First gave birth to fifteen children, one of whom went on to carry her mother's name and mantle.

And Marie Laveau the Second invited even more controversy than her mother, if that was possible.

And this was the woman Doyle knew, feared, and had briefly loved.

Where her mother had balanced the darker aspects of the voodoo by showing a charitable, more humanitarian side, her daughter was content to be feared as a sorceress and a witch. This earned her enemies by the legion. Corrupt politicians, racist police, rival voodoo cults—all wanted her dead. But was her magic real, as her followers swore? Or were she and her mother merely accomplished fakes, preying on the public's fears and superstitions?

Doyle thought he knew the answer, but as he touched a face unlined by age, his thoughts turned to trickery. "You're a daughter. Another Marie Laveau. You're not the woman I knew."

She took his hand, held it to her cheek. *"Non. C'est moi."*

Doyle pulled his hand away. "You expect me to believe you're eighty years old? Look at you. You're a young girl."

Marie cocked an eyebrow.

His head swam. "But Duvall told me . . ." He rubbed his eyes, feeling confused and betrayed.

"I lied to him, too," she said.

He rubbed his shoulder, still sore from the rough handling. "So why all this? Why treat me like an enemy?"

"Enemies are what I protected you from, *chère*. You were followed. And we are in danger, all of us. All who knew Konstantin."

THE LOOK IN her brother's eyes tells her something is wrong. He is quiet, but has always had a sense about spiritual matters.

"Something evil," he hisses, "in the forest."

Marie steps past her younger sibling and onto the porch, where she is bathed in the light of the bonfire. She knows something is wrong; her stomach tells her. Something has twisted in her belly all day. Now she watches her dancers framed against the fire, naked and sweating, their voices trilling, their pupils rolled back in the sockets. They are keeping the evil at bay. But Marie senses it just beyond the lick of the flames, hiding in the trees, waiting.

She pulls up her skirts and walks down the porch steps.

"Marie, non!" her brother calls.

Marie passes the dancers and the raging fire, and stops to pull a torch free. Then she crosses into the high grasses, toward the trees. She will meet this spirit in her forest.

The moment she crosses the border of the woods, a quiet falls. She hears the dancers in the background, but nothing else. No mosquitoes. No frogs. Not even a wind rustles the leaves. She walks deeper into the forest's heart, until the ground is muddy and the willows bend in grotesque shapes.

Flap, flap, flap, flap, flap, flap.

Marie whirls in the direction of the sound.

Flap, flap, flap, flap, flap, flap.

Marie pushes through underbrush, her flame skimming the ground until she finds it.

It's a dying owl. It writhes on the ground, wings thumping.

Above her, something snaps small branches and plunges to the earth. She hears it behind her now, flapping.

Another owl dies in front of her. They fall out of the trees. She hears their soft bodies collide with the ground. Some plague has struck them.

Marie walks over to one of the birds, kneels beside it. She still hears the fluttering around her, but softer now. She strokes the owl's broken neck. There is no pulse. Marie covers her face and cries over the owl. Her shaking hands cradle the body, press it to her breast and throat.

"Konstantin," she cries. "What did they do to you, my Konstantin?"

MARIE WALKS PAST *the bonfire. The dancers have stopped. Their chests heave from exhaustion. They watch the priestess climb the steps of the house with a bloody owl clutched to her chest.*

She enters. Her younger brother sees her tearstained cheeks, but knows better than to ask. Marie goes to the kitchen and places a wooden bowl on the cutting board. Then, displaying little emotion, she takes a carving knife and guts the owl, groin to throat. She pulls the organs free and slaps them into the bowl.

"Tell me, my love." Marie stirs the organs with her bloody hand. "Tell me who do this."

Her eyes scrutinize the deep purples of the arteries, the brownish hues of the lungs. She sees patterns in the viscera. Her eyes are dry, the tears replaced by horror. "Oh God . . . oh God."

Marie leaves her body.

When she opens her eyes, she is in England, floating above the British Museum. She hears guttural screams. Her attention floats to the road, to a car on the grass by the museum fence. Young men pull themselves free of the car to run to a broken body in the road.

Marie hurtles down to Konstantin Duvall as he gasps, "He's in my mind!"

The boys kneel by the body, but Duvall's eyes are locked on the incorporeal Marie.

"Warn them . . ." he says, ". . . warn the Arcanum."

Marie sobs and reaches for him through the ether, but her cries are lost in a vacuum. Life ebbs from Duvall's body like seeping gas. It rises like steam away from the shell of Duvall and dissipates in the cool London night.

Then Marie feels a sub-aural hum and turns her attention to the pulsing energy near the trees of the museum park. A figure in a top hat stands in the shadows, watching. He shifts, and the moonlight glints off a blue monocle. There's something in his arms, a book.

She cannot see his face.

He whispers to Marie through the ether. "Yaji-ash-shuthath," he says, and chuckles.

Marie recoils, hurtling away from Duvall's shattered body. She hovers above the world. The Earth turns before her eyes. Then suddenly she speeds into the clouds, until she floats above white feathers in a puddle of human blood. The blood becomes a fire. Now she is in a corridor of fire. Long bodies sway in the flames, and gaze at her with ruby eyes.

Their squeals become screams.
They see her.

DOYLE STROKED HIS moustache as he listened.

"The owl was Konstantin's animal spirit," Marie told him. "It was his message. His warning."

"What message?"

"A man with the blue eye. I saw New York City, and blood. And a book . . ."

"The Book of Enoch," Doyle finished. "What do we know about this killer?"

Marie paused. "He is not as powerful as he thinks. He's in danger, too."

It was a moment of consequence. They allowed it to linger.

"So, he's brought us together again, hasn't he? Even in death."

"You are still angry?" Marie asked.

Doyle's jaw tightened.

"*C'est fou.* What was I to do, Arthur?"

"Nothing."

"You want to discuss it?"

"What is there to discuss? I was a fool. Duvall was my friend for thirty years and . . ." Doyle faltered as he met her gaze.

"And what choice did you give me? To follow you to England?"

"No, of course not—"

"Meet your wife, perhaps? Your family?"

"Stop it."

"I'm no man's secret save I choose to be." Marie's voice was sharp.

"I was selfish."

"Spoiled," Marie added, with emphasis.

Color rose in Doyle's cheeks. "Is this why you went to all the trouble of dragging me here? To tear the dressing from old wounds? There was enough injury done on all sides, my dear. None of us was innocent—least of all you."

Marie stiffened. "I was the cause, then?"

"Let us put the matter to rest," he growled. "I've lost a dear friend; you, a lover. In his memory, let us try to heal the breach."

Marie's expression softened. "I was never good enough for either of you, was I?"

Their eyes locked. Doyle swallowed. The left side of her lip curled in a question mark, an enticement.

He broke the spell, not trusting himself further. "Howard's in prison."

"*Oui.* I know."

"He's in terrible shape. His mind. Someone's gotten to him."

"Howard, he's been courting the fire too long."

"He wouldn't . . . he couldn't tell me everything. He believes he's being watched." Doyle acknowledged Marie's smile. "Yes, I know he always thinks that, but this Book of Enoch is different. We need him."

"So, how we s'posed to get him outta that jail?"

Doyle did not answer. His eyes said it all.

"You went to see him?" Marie demanded.

"I had no choice."

"*Encore, c'est fou!* Why? You know what he say."

"I had hoped he'd changed."

"Better chance of a thousand sparrows flyin' out of my behind. We better off without that magician."

"Then how do you propose we free Lovecraft?"

Marie stretched her arms over her head and arched her back. Her breasts strained against the low-cut bodice of her dress. "We all have certain powers of . . . persuasion."

Doyle cleared his throat. "So it appears."

17

THE BURST OF flash powder turned Detective Mullin's head. The alley lit up briefly with daylight.

"Got a smoke, Detective?" Rags asked. She was a rail-thin prostitute with the face of a horse and only a tattered shawl to protect her from the cold.

Mullin offered her a cigarette as more flash powder burst in the alley. Police officers milled on the sidewalk, their breath steaming in the wet, chill night.

"You were sayin'?" Mullin turned back to Rags.

"So, Jimmy, he's a regular, an' he likes to do it standin', but he felt all strange about the playground. He's got two daughters, y'know. So I took 'im in the alley, an' that's . . ." She trailed off.

"Anyone touch 'im?"

"No, Detective," Rags answered. Mullin noticed a tremor in her hand as she brought the cigarette to her lips. Rags was one of the tougher girls. She'd seen bodies before. She'd even cut a john's throat with a piece of broken glass, and that was one of the bloodiest messes Mullin had ever seen. Now her lips were pursed as though she might cry.

"Dexter was a special person." Her voice broke.

"Go on home, Rags. Get warm," Mullin suggested.

"Thanks, Detective."

Mullin rubbed his bruised hand through his black leather glove. The cold throbbed in the bones. Flecks of icy rain added to his misery as he left the playground near City Hall and trudged over to the alley in question. The officers hunched their shoulders to stay warm and stepped aside, making a path.

The police photographer knelt in the middle of the alley, his fedora tilted back as he pointed his camera at a windswept drift of garbage and newspapers against the wall. His finger compressed a button connecting to a wire.

Mullin was blinded for a moment, dazzling suns looping behind his eyes.

He waved the photographer off. "That's enough for now. Go on."

The photographer rose and straightened his hat. "Just a couple more, Detective. This one's a beauty."

"Get lost," Mullin ordered.

The photographer grabbed his light stand and marched out of the alley in a huff.

Mullin took his time on the short walk to the middle of the alley, perhaps unnerved by the tremor in Rags's hand.

Dexter Collins was no senile old woman or young maid. Mullin had known Dex and thought him a decent egg. The boy had a toughness that wasn't faked or forced, and Mullin had seen him intimidate gangsters twice his size. Dexter knew how to take care of himself.

But not this time, apparently. Blood vessels had burst in Dexter's eyes, which, in the cold, had swelled and turned a milky blue. His close-cropped beard was caked with blood, as were his ears. Mullin counted at least a dozen puncture wounds, deep and gouging. His body was flat gray in pallor. Stranger still, intricate pathways of blue veins had risen to the surface of the skin, extending from the forehead, across the torso, to the bottoms of Dexter's feet.

Mullin heard the officers shuffle in behind him.

"Turn 'im," Mullin told them as he stood up and got out of the way. The officers positioned themselves at the head and foot of Dexter's body, then lifted and turned him. Newspaper pages stuck to the frozen blood on Dexter's thighs and shoulders as they set him facedown on the pavement.

Mullin tore aside the newspapers, revealing what he already knew. Dexter's spine, like the others, was missing. But because of the frozen condition of the body, Mullin couldn't tell if the body had been killed last night, or a week before. Which meant Lovecraft was still the prime suspect. But regardless of the evidence, Mullin knew that Dexter, even one-handed, could snap Lovecraft like a toothpick. It made no sense. None of it did.

Dexter had been killed by multiple assailants. And more than one meant a conspiracy, whether Paul Caleb liked it or not.

But what Mullin couldn't determine was the reason. The victims weren't rich, they weren't famous, they weren't special in any way. Except to their mothers, perhaps.

And this brought Mullin's thinking back to Doyle. He had also found it hard to imagine the old dog as a murderer, though he swung his cane like a man half his age. But if he wasn't the murderer, what the hell did he want with Lovecraft? And why bother lying about letters?

And who had thrown Lovecraft's name into the ring in the first place?

THIS TRAIN OF thought was what led to Mullin freezing his ass off in a parked police car outside the Bellevue asylum next to a snoring Wally. A great many questions converged upon Mr. Lovecraft, and Mullin assumed he wasn't the only one looking for answers. Lovecraft had only had one visitor, a Mr. Watkins, but Mullin figured it was a false name. So, was Lovecraft a killer or a convenient pawn? A man swept up by events, or an intelligent psychotic? And if he was a puppet, who pulled the strings?

"I'll be buggered," Mullin whispered, and whapped Wally awake with a fist to the chest.

Wally blinked. "What did you do that fer?"

"Shut yer trap," Mullin snarled, and pointed to the sidewalk outside the Bellevue asylum building. "Three o'clock. Mr. Doyle."

Beneath a lantern, several car lengths ahead, he could make out Doyle and some woman in quiet conference. Every few seconds, they looked about in search of observers.

"Who's he wit'?" Wally asked.

"Hooker, looks like." Mullin scowled, puzzling over the new turn of events.

"Likes 'em dark, then." Wally lifted a flask to his mouth and drank. "Well, you was right, boss. Let's do this thing."

Wally reached for the door handle but Mullin stopped him. "No. Let's wait and see what they—"

A hairy face suddenly blocked the passenger window. "Pardon, gents! I'm bone cold out 'ere, fellas, and couldn't 'elp observin' some spirits in that bottle there. I'm jus' lookin' fer somethin' to heal the cold, the winds just fiercely goin'—"

"Shut yer hole, ya mutt," Wally muttered.

"Get 'im outta here," Mullin growled, his gaze still fixed on Doyle.

" 'Ave I interrupted a rendezvous? That weren't me intention, boys." The vagrant pressed his nose to the glass.

"What'd that clown say?" Wally fought with the door handle. "I'll show 'im!"

"You wanna blow our cover?" Mullin hissed, yanking Wally back.

"Gimme a drink. A drink." The vagrant's voice echoed off the buildings.

Mullin had had enough. He wrestled his .45 out of its holster.

Wally flashed his badge at the window. "Police business. Go on. Get lost."

"Police?" The vagrant shouted loud enough to be heard in Newark. "Why didn't ye say so in the first place?" And he licked the window in thick strokes.

"Jesus!" Wally exclaimed, disgusted.

"Goddamn it!" Mullin punched the dashboard, for Doyle and the woman were nowhere to be seen.

"Motherless son-of-a . . ." Mullin was out of the car and rounding the hood as the vagrant scuttled around the back, circling his fists in the air like a pugilist.

"No call fer violence—"

"I'll give ya some drinks, you stinkin'—"

The vagrant scampered into the shadows, cackling. Mullin fumed for a moment, then returned his .45 to its holster and got back in the car. The engine sputtered and they rolled off down the street, their cover blown.

DOYLE HELD MARIE by her exposed shoulders. They were both pressed to the alley wall. The growl of Mullin's car drifted into the distance.

"Have they gone?" Marie asked.

"I believe so." With the danger passed he released her, suddenly aware of their closeness. He cleared his throat and crossed the alley. "Aren't you cold?"

She smiled. "Not anymore."

"Marie—"

Her hand went up. "Ssh!"

Footsteps approached.

Doyle wrapped his hands around his walking stick and stepped in front of Marie.

"*Non*, Arthur. Pretend we embrace," she whispered, and pushed the cane down. She took him by the arms and pulled him to her, pushing his head into the curve of her neck and cooing like a prostitute. Doyle's hands went to her hips as the vagrant stumbled into the alley, muttering, "Threaten me to tell you something or other rat bastard mixing me up all I ever wanted to tell you . . ."

Doyle and Marie broke their hold.

"Spare a penny for a sinner, Cap'n?" And the vagrant grinned.

Marie winced. "My lord, he smell."

"Shove off, friend," Doyle advised.

"Get a load of them bubbies." The vagrant widened his eyes and advanced on Marie.

Doyle placed the tip of his cane against the man's chest. "Watch yourself," he threatened.

"Aye, I'll watch meself. But in the meantime, who's watchin' you, eh?" The vagrant's blue eyes twinkled. "Ye've got the police on yer tracks, boyo. 'Ave you been a bad boy, then?"

Doyle scowled. "Who are you?"

"I'm me, myself, and mine. But who's in that buildin' over there, isn't that the key question? They're sayin' it's the Occult Killer, that one who's doin' away with all them nice Mission folk, eh?"

Doyle snatched him by the collar, ignoring the smell. "Who sent you?"

"Who sent me? Oh, ye' don't want to cross her if I tell ye. She's feared by anyone with any good sense."

"Who, then? Out with it!"

The vagrant's eyes glanced left, then right. "They call her . . . Bess."

"Bess?"

Marie sighed. "He had to make his grand entrance, *n'est ce pas?*"

The vagrant's head turned sharply. "The papers said you were dead, Marie, but I never doubted you for a second."

"Nor shed a tear, I'm sure . . . Herry."

"Houdini, please."

"Bollocks!" Doyle pushed Houdini off.

The magician spat the fake gums from his mouth and smiled. He sniffed his coat. "Goodness, I do need a bath."

"What in the bloody hell are you up to?"

"Only saving your clumsy behinds, Doyle. You've got detectives following you; you've bungled everything, of course." Houdini pulled the wig and beard off in one movement. "I won't get a moment's rest while you're in this city, of that I am certain. In the meantime, what's a friend to do? Let you flop along until I have to bail you out? I'm here to talk some sense into you."

"You can't be serious. After everything I told you?"

"Times have changed, for God's sake. We're public figures. The scrutiny is too great. Howard made his bargain with the Devil. Fine; that's his problem. Now he's reaping the rewards."

"What did I tell you?" Marie said.

Houdini turned to her. "If I were less of a gentleman, I'd have plenty to say to you. I finished with you many years ago."

"*Va t'en!*" Marie shot back, then spit on the ground. Her hand made the sign of Devil horns.

Doyle frowned. "You've wasted your time, Houdini. And you've wasted ours."

Houdini unbuttoned his soiled coat. "There's no talking you out of this, then?"

"No," Doyle avowed.

Houdini's breath puffed in the cold air as he emerged from his costume, wearing only a tattered jacket, a white T-shirt, and trousers. He shook his head. "Well, then, let's get this over with."

SEAMUS AND PARKS, two uniformed police officers, lingered at the chain-locked front gates of Bellevue, huddled against the cold. Their beat for the evening required them to provide extra security—against what, Detective Mullin had not said.

"Some kind of vampire's what I heard." Parks slapped his gloved hands together to warm himself.

"Whaddya mean?" Seamus feigned skepticism. In truth, he'd always been scared of vampires.

"You didn't hear? The bodies they found was blood-drained. And he took the spines out."

"The spines?" Seamus glanced at the quiet sanitarium.

"Callin' him the Occult Killer in Fourth Ward." Parks's eyes always glowed with a hint of paranoia; in this case it added to the suspense. "They say this Lovecraft had body parts in his ice-box, frozen up like steaks."

"C'mon."

"What, you don't believe me?"

"I don't want my dinner comin' up, is all. You been talkin' all night. Give it a rest."

"But I ain't got to the best part yet—"

Just then, the sanitarium gates creaked open and something lumbered in their direction.

"Jesus," Parks whispered. "Is he a guard or an inmate?"

"I hope to hell he's a guard," Seamus answered, feeling small even at two-hundred-plus.

The man didn't bother with a coat. His breath steamed out of his nostrils like dragon breath. He wore black rubber gloves up to the elbows, handled a rolled cigarette clumsily, and stuck it between his lips. His dull eyes blinked with crocodile boredom as he towered in front of Seamus and Parks.

"Evenin'," Seamus offered with a nod.

"Match," the gorilla said.

"Sure, sure." Parks fumbled in his pocket, produced a matchbook, and threw it at him. The man, dressed like an orderly, turned like a swaying tree and headed back into the grounds of the asylum.

"Yeah, keep 'em," Parks offered, like it was his idea.

Seamus swatted Parks's arm. "That was the last of 'em, you bozo."

"So go ask fer 'em back," Parks suggested.

Seamus watched the hulking figure retreat into the gloom. "Ah, screw it."

DISEMBODIED WORDS BIT at Morris the orderly's ear like tiny fish. With a growl, he sucked the smoke from his crumbling butt, extinguished it between his rubber-gloved thumb and forefinger, then flicked it against a tree. He swayed on the stoop of Bellevue's main entrance and clenched his fists. His knuckles popped. Disembodied voices in his head raged at him. Women's voices. A grandmother with hands knotted from arthritis. She would strike Morris on the forehead with those bony fists and tell him he was stupid. Morris couldn't learn the lessons at school, and the other children called him "Morris Doris" because his grandmother wouldn't cut his hair. He wasn't allowed to go back to school after he pulled a little girl's arms out of their sockets. Didn't matter; he couldn't remember the lessons anyway. But Morris remembered the girl crying, thinking she looked funny with stretched-out arms like a character in a funny book. He got beat on the head plenty for that. The things he liked to do always got him beat on the head. He'd figured he'd just have to get used to it.

As a child, Morris had also discovered he had an aptitude for strangling cats. Cats frightened him, so he killed them. Hunted them. Yanked their heads so hard, their necks broke. Morris then collected the dead cats under his grandmother's house, but eventually the smell gave it away. Morris's nose was blocked from a childhood injury; he couldn't smell. That was the problem. And it was too bad, because Morris loved his collection. He'd crawl under the house and lie in the cold dirt, petting the cats. They couldn't run away like this, so Morris could pet them for hours. When his grandmother finally discovered his treasures, there were forty-eight cat bodies melting under the house. That brought him many more blows and considerable trouble with the neighbors. That was the first time he got sent away.

Morris spoke on a monthly basis with a Bellevue intern about "violent urges," but he kept his job just fine. Morris knew they let him alone because he was the only one who could wrestle down the bad ones. They wriggled just like the cats had. It didn't matter if Morris accidentally broke one of them, because there were always more coming in off the white trucks. Different faces but the same eyes, the same voices. Nobody ever punched Morris on the head for breaking these. They were not in short supply.

The one down there now with the whiny voice and dark eyes—he was a skinny cat, all bones. It hurt to wrestle with bones; he liked the fat ones better. But the Man with the Blue Eye had told Morris to make sure he broke him good. And it was funny, but Morris wanted to please the Man with the Blue Eye. He didn't know why. He knew he'd get in trouble like he did with the cat collection, but the Man with the Blue Eye made it seem just fine. And he had promised Morris all kinds of work—the kind he was good at.

Morris glanced at the wad of twenties in his palm, enough to buy plenty of warm buttered rolls. Then he stuffed the wad in his shirt pocket, turned, and lurched into the empty lobby. He headed straight for the stairwell door, snatching a fire ax off the wall as he went.

18

HOUDINI KNELT BEFORE a rusting security door, squinting into a keyhole. "You'll never learn, will you, Doyle?"

Doyle bristled. "She wants to know what happened to Duvall, just like we all do."

"They deserved each other, you know," Houdini scoffed. "Neither one could be trusted."

"Does your suspicion never tire?"

"We were played for fools once. Never again. I'm sick of this whole business. This one favor and then I'm through." Houdini fingered dozens of keys on an oversized ring. "I need a double tube. Don't have it here."

Doyle frowned. "You need a key? What on earth for?"

Houdini turned around. "Am I expected to dematerialize through it, perhaps?"

"No. I just thought . . . Well, you are Houdini, after all."

Stung, Houdini stood up and removed his coat, as a man might before a bar brawl. "Hold this, won't you?"

"Of course."

Houdini examined the tall, imposing wall before him. They were at the back of the asylum, amidst stinking barrels of trash.

A barred window was the only break in the wall, and it was fifteen feet above the ground. Houdini backed up and spit on his hands. He clapped twice, took four long strides, and then leaped. He looked like a giant cockroach as he scuttled up the wall, gripping the tiny grooves and divots with incredibly strong fingertips. He reached the barred window in seconds.

Houdini gripped the bars and tried to wrench them out. The muscles in his back and shoulders strained, but the bars refused to budge.

He managed to slide open the window by pressing his hand to the glass and lifting. But the problem remained the bars.

It was time for Plan B.

Houdini studied the bars and the space between them, roughly six or seven inches, his eyes making precise measurements. Then he took several long, deep breaths.

Suddenly, he thrust his head between the bars. His shoes scrabbled against the wall for leverage, and were his arms to tire he would choke. By pushing all the breath out of his lungs, he was able to shrink his torso enough to force it between the bars. The process was agony; Houdini grunted from the compression on his bones and the lack of air. His head, his chest, and one arm were through, and he dangled precariously, half in and half out.

Then he forced his other shoulder against the bars, once, twice, three times, and his arm dislocated, giving him all the slack he needed. He wiggled his second arm through. Then all it took were a few snakelike movements before Houdini's feet vanished through the window.

LOVECRAFT'S HEAD LAY in a puddle of his own urine, his eyes glassy and unblinking. Deep down in the turbulence of his mind, his sanity bobbed and tossed like a toy boat in a hurricane. His panic and dread, coupled with an already fragile mental circuitry, taxed him to the edge of madness. Yet he clung by a thread to reality, his ears attuned to every sound. In the next cell, a lunatic masturbated to the hiss of his own breathy whispers. Somewhere else down the hall, another inmate sobbed into his pillow.

Lovecraft thought of Angell Street and East Providence, his beloved home. He thought of the silence of those streets at two A.M., when he would leave the smothering bleakness of his bedroom in the house he shared with his aunts and taste the chill wetness of the Rhode Island air. Walking that desolate village, Lovecraft would meditate on the stars and their secrets—secrets he would spend a lifetime struggling to decipher. He thought of Mother—her pretty, questioning eyes and her nervous dotings; those small, shaking hands with their bitten, bloody fingernails. His syphilitic father was only a grim ogre lost to precognitive memory, a presence in Lovecraft's life only as the gibbering terror of his fitful dreams.

Lovecraft blinked. Something had forced his mind back to the present. He listened. There. Nothing. No sound. That was the problem. Even the masturbator had stopped. They were all waiting. It was like a forest when the bugs ceased buzzing. That was how you detected the monsters, when the buzzing stopped.

Lovecraft heard it then. A footstep. Then another. Something heavy. Lovecraft's mouth opened, but only a hoarse gasp escaped. The footsteps grew closer. Lovecraft's lip quivered. He was ill prepared for death. And certainly not a violent death, the kind this would surely be. He grit his teeth as the footsteps rang louder, then stopped outside his door.

Keys jangled against each other, and one scraped into the lock. Lovecraft's eyes widened. The bolt clanged back, and rusted hinges moaned.

Morris stepped inside.

The orderly's gait was casual, disinterested even. He turned and shut the door, the ax dangling at his side. He sniffed the air and grimaced, snorting something into his mouth then spitting it to the stone floor. Lovecraft flinched, and Morris adjusted his grip on the ax.

Cellular instincts took over as Lovecraft squirmed into the corner and curled into a ball. Every muscle tensed for what he assumed would be several rending, tearing blows.

Morris swung the ax back in a wide arc and Lovecraft screamed.

But the blow never landed.

Morris looked at his empty hands. He turned around.

Houdini held the ax. "I'm sorry. This is yours?" Houdini then whipped the flat end of the ax blade up and under Morris's jaw. Morris's head snapped back, and he went spinning into the corner of the cell.

Then Lovecraft giggled. The giggle became a chuckle. Then the chuckle rose to chortles and the chortles to hysterical laughter.

Houdini stood there a moment, watching Lovecraft curl and roll on the ground in a cackling fit. He sighed. "About what I expected." He snatched Lovecraft off the ground by the strait-jacket straps and plopped him on the bed.

Lovecraft continued to laugh, though tears rolled down his cheeks.

Houdini fought quickly with the straps of the jacket. "Nice to see we're of good cheer."

OUTSIDE THE ASYLUM, Parks whistled as a curvaceous black woman sauntered toward them, a shawl wrapped over her bare arms and shoulders.

Seamus puffed out his chest. "Y'ain't workin', is ya, kitty-cat?"

"Jus' takin' a walk, suh. I don't mean nuthin'." The woman stopped and placed a foot on the fence, then hiked up her skirt and rubbed her calf. "Mmm, my legs sure is tired." With a sleepy glance, she took in the men before her. "I sure do like those uniforms y'all is wearin'. I don't wanna get in trouble, Officers."

Parks looked at Seamus, knowingly. "There's prolly a way to avoid any kind of unpleasantness."

"Who needs the paperwork?" Seamus added.

"On such a cold night?" Parks leered at the woman. "Throw the boys a free warm-up, and we might see to lettin' ya slide by this time round."

"I sure don't wanna go to no jail tonight." The hooker strolled by Parks and tickled a finger under his bony chin. "Let's go across the street where the light ain't so bright, hmm?"

Parks pulled his trousers higher and smirked at Seamus. "Man the fort, buddy."

Seamus pouted.

"No, no. Bring your friend with you." The woman smiled at Seamus, sending his pulse soaring. "C'mon, chubby. It's cold tonight."

Then she crossed the street ahead of the officers, swinging her hips.

Parks poked Seamus, laughing. "Yeah, c'mon, chubby."

"Shaddup," Seamus shot back as he sucked in his gut and followed behind them.

Suddenly, gunshots froze them to the spot. Windows shattered somewhere in the asylum.

Parks's hand went to his .38.

Seamus freed his pistol and ran toward the gate, dropping the keys to the lock. "I got it!" He fumbled, retrieved the keys, and jabbed them in the padlocks with shaking hands. The locks opened. Parks shoved Seamus aside and kicked open the gates.

Neither of them noticed that the prostitute had vanished, cursing bitterly.

HOUDINI SLAMMED INTO the stairwell door as gunshots pinged off the steel and punctured the glass.

The lobby was occupied by three New York police officers, and an elderly security guard armed with a shotgun. Using the lobby reception desk as cover, they unleashed a hail of bullets against the stairwell door.

Lovecraft was useless, slumped against the wall, giggling into his hand.

"How is this happening?" Houdini demanded rhetorically.

Footsteps thundered behind him. Morris was coming.

Houdini studied the door. He pulled the long pin from the bottom hinge. "Okay . . . yes . . ."

Morris's shadow fell across the wall.

Houdini yanked the pin from the top hinge. The door jostled.

Houdini lifted Lovecraft to his feet by his shirt collar. "Pay attention, you nitwit."

Tears of amusement rolled down Lovecraft's cheeks. His mouth was open, but he had no breath left.

"When I tell you, run to the stairwell across the lobby. Don't stop. Go up. Do you understand?"

Lovecraft did not answer.

"Fine, then. You stay here and get shot, for all I care. But I'm going." Houdini turned and wrestled the door off its hinges. Bullets pounded into it. "Now," Houdini cried, and exploded into the lobby, carrying the door.

Houdini flipped across the marble floor, holding the door handle, and it seemed that Lovecraft had enough sense to use it for cover. He ran for the staircase as ordered.

Houdini's door blocked the bullets. Then he swung the door in the direction of the reception desk.

The guards stopped shooting, waiting for his next move.

In the pause, Houdini charged and leaped onto the desk, ramming the bottom of the door at the policemen's feet. He then jumped off the desk and seesawed the door so that it knocked the policemen's guns skyward, causing them to fire at the overhanging chandelier.

The hail of bullets broke the clasp attaching the chandelier to the ceiling, bringing two hundred pounds of glass and steel hurtling down.

The police scattered as Houdini back-flipped to the stairs and sprinted to the second floor. Bullets pinged off the marble banister in counterpoint to the click of Houdini's shoes.

THE METAL DOOR to the roof buckled and burst open. Houdini shoved Lovecraft forward and leaped gamely up on the ledge. The treetops were too far away for a leap. Thick telephone wires, however, reached from the asylum roof across the fenced grounds to the next pole on Twenty-third Street.

"Oh mercy," Houdini whispered as he took in the length of the wires. He turned back to Lovecraft, who sat helpless on the ground.

A look back at the fire escape showed several police officers climbing fast. A revolver flashed and cracked. Houdini spun away as a bullet ricocheted off the metal rail.

Mind made up, Houdini launched back across the roof and lifted Lovecraft to his feet. "You will do as I say when I say it," he hissed. "Understand? No hesitation. We hesitate, we die."

In his peripheral vision, Houdini saw Morris materialize from the shadows of the staircase, the ax blade propped on his shoulder.

Houdini swatted Lovecraft on the back. "Run to the ledge. Go!" Lovecraft staggered toward the ledge as Houdini ran toward the stairwell door. Morris lurched up the steps, pulling back his arm to swing. Houdini grabbed the steel door and slammed it in Morris's face as the ax blade plunged through, stopping inches from Houdini's nose. He backed away quickly, kicking off his shoes. Morris struggled to wrench his ax from the door as Houdini spun around and darted toward the ledge.

He took Lovecraft by the scruff of the neck, wrapped an arm around his stomach, and moved him nearer to the telephone wires.

"Walk," Houdini growled as he shadowed Lovecraft from behind. "Walk onto the wires. I'll guide us." Lovecraft grunted and made a feeble attempt to wriggle free of Houdini's grasp, but Houdini seized him tighter. "Walk, or I'll pitch you from this roof myself."

Morris lumbered toward them, huffing. The ax blade scraped along the gravel.

"No," Lovecraft wailed as Houdini used his foot and knee to thrust Lovecraft's foot onto the telephone wire.

"I'll move you. Relax your body." Houdini slid Lovecraft's foot farther out. "Struggle, and you'll kill us both. Put your feet on mine."

Morris raised the ax for another blow. The blade crossed the stars, a silhouette against the half-moon.

Houdini craned his neck, paled at Morris's approach, then nudged them completely onto the wire. "I have you, Howard, I have you."

Lovecraft whimpered. But the seed of self-preservation still grew somewhere in the crawling thicket of his mind—enough to let him follow Houdini's orders.

"Good, Howard. Very good. That's it . . . gently."

Houdini's leg nudged Lovecraft's in a wide circle to touch down on the wire, high above the trees.

"We are not stopping, Howard. Just close your eyes. I do the walking. That's it. That's it."

Houdini and Lovecraft walked farther out, over a hundred feet of concrete. Animal moans trailed from Lovecraft's lips.

Morris's ax sunk deep into the telephone wires, spewing fireworks. His heavy rubber gloves insulated him from the shocks.

Two strands of the bundle zipped out from under Houdini and Lovecraft's feet.

"Mother, Mother," Lovecraft whimpered.

Houdini bent his knees to try and still the shuddering wires. They were barely a third of the way across. Worse, a cluster of police had gathered by the fence of the asylum in a grassy clearing beyond the ring of birch trees, guns out, waiting for Houdini to enter their range of fire.

Houdini, though, mused upon the usefulness of this stunt in one of his next performances—presuming they survived, of course. Having reachieved balance, he circled left legs around right legs, fusing himself to Lovecraft, holding Lovecraft's wrists out wide to balance them both. Midnight winds buffeted them. "Very good, Howard. We're nearly there now. Keep the eyes shut. We're doing fine."

Morris swung wildly with the ax. The blade chewed up more strands. Sparks showered the lawn.

Wires fluttered away into the breeze, lazily swinging across the lawn. The police ran to escape the stream of spewing electricity.

"Aaaah! God! Agh!" Lovecraft's foot stepped off Houdini's foot and searched for the wires, instead finding air. His body lurched right.

Houdini grabbed Lovecraft's wrist and leaned his whole body in the opposite direction. They hung there a moment, like some bizarre sculpture of improvised chaos: Lovecraft dangling one way, Houdini the other. Again, Houdini righted their course.

But there was less of a path now. Only a few slender wires remained of the original bundle.

More police officers had arrived on the roof. They positioned themselves, their .38s levered over their forearms. Muzzles flashed.

Bullets whipped by Houdini's head; one scorched his shirt-sleeve. Houdini just roared with triumph. "Outstanding! Ha-ha. Surely this rivals the barrel over Niagara Falls, eh? Surely?" Houdini took Lovecraft by the shoulders.

"Don't shake," Lovecraft pleaded.

"Did you see *Man of Mystery,* Howard? Remember the barrel over the falls?" Houdini rotated their legs, gliding their feet along the wobbling wires.

"Will you shut up, man, and concentrate?"

As Houdini and Lovecraft crossed the tree line, halfway to their goal, the police below opened fire.

"Aaaah! Put me back. Just put me back where you found me." Lovecraft jerked his head to avoid the hissing bullets.

"Balls, man. And ruin a perfectly nice stroll? Full speed ahead, ha-ha!" Houdini turned back and saw Morris heft the ax into the air for one last swing. "Hmm." He glanced down at the two remaining wires. "Hmm."

"Help me," Lovecraft shouted to the police.

Houdini frowned. "Now, that's not being a good sport." It wasn't clear what gave him more pleasure: Lovecraft's torment, or staring death squarely in the eye. "You know, we really should spend more time together, Howard. Ha-ha!"

"They locked me up, and you're the mad one," Lovecraft gasped.

"Indeed, yes."

A wire exploded ten feet in front of them, cleaved by a bullet.

Houdini waved his arms to balance them. Lovecraft screamed at a deafening pitch.

Down on the grass, the elderly security guard paused to reload his shotgun. As he dug in his pockets for shells, his head turned to the sound of galloping horses and squeaking wheels. Closer. Getting closer. The security guard's eyes widened and he dove out of the way. "Oh Lord!"

With a driver's "Yah! Yah!" the Bellevue fences swung open under the fury of stampeding horses pulling a taxi carriage. Doyle whipped the reins with one arm and brandished his walking stick with the other. Wielding the cane like a polo mallet, he knocked the gold sphere into the heads of dumbfounded policemen. Guns fired and bodies fell. The horses kicked up dirt as the carriage pulled a wide turn and rumbled toward the last of the police.

Up above, Morris's ax sliced through the last of the telephone wires.

Houdini wrapped his arm around Lovecraft's waist and snatched the wire as it plummeted away from their feet. Their bodies plunged toward the ground, accompanied by Lovecraft's shriek. Houdini held fast to the wire as Doyle wrenched the carriage around to parallel their fall. Their legs skimmed the ground, then the wire yanked them back up. Houdini released it. They soared through the air before crashing through the thin roof of the hijacked carriage, landing beside a terrified couple clearly on their first date.

The man's moustache twitched and he lifted a finger to Houdini. "Aren't you—?"

OUTSIDE, DOYLE SLOWED the carriage and extended an arm to Marie, who vaulted onto the driver's seat. "To Crow's Head, then?" he said.

The doors opened, and the man and woman were ejected. And in a spray of mud and galloping hooves, the carriage stormed into the night.

19

CROW'S HEAD—KONSTANTIN Duvall's North American estate—was located on a wooded hill in Tarrytown, only forty minutes outside Manhattan. It was more a castle than a house—a
magnificent gothic Victorian of quarried marble designed to rival Walpole's house in Strawberry Hill. Set against the night sky,
all one could see were the soaring medieval towers, and the
gleam of moonlight reflecting off leaded glass windows.

Paved roads in Tarrytown were the exception rather than the
rule, and everyone in the carriage was bruised and aching by the
time the horses reached the vine-swallowed gates of the estate.

For the first time in twelve years, the Arcanum again stood at
the threshold of Crow's Head. There was an unexpected sanc-
tity to the moment, and no one spoke as the double doors
groaned open.

Doyle thought he could hear the excited whispers of ghosts as
he took the first step inside, with the others following his lead.
He lit a match and the spark ignited a spider's web. They all
watched the ember burn up to the high ceiling like a tiny orange
comet.

As Doyle turned, the light spilled over a clawing raptor. He flinched, but it was only a bronze statue of a predatory owl, descending upon a rabbit whose eyes bulged with fear.

In the entry hall, grand staircases flowed east and west like terraced waterfalls, inviting the brave onto the gloomy upper floors, where a ballroom waited silent as a tomb, and bedrooms numbering in the dozens lay empty.

In the downstairs dining room and parlor, hidden within the shadows, the hand-carved rosewood chairs and tables were set for company beneath Tiffany chandeliers.

No living thing but the prolific spiders had walked the halls in years, and their handiwork hung in musty folds from every corner and crevice. In the vast library, a sheet of cobwebs reached, unbroken, the length of the room, while a blanket of dust the color of dirty snow, a quarter of an inch thick, coated both shelves, book jackets, and floors.

Lovecraft wobbled, but Doyle caught hold of him. To the others, he said, "Try to light a fire. I'll attend to Howard. There's a well out back. Perhaps we can draw a bath for him."

Two hours later, the Arcanum gathered in the library, though Lovecraft had not yet joined them. A roaring fire provided a tiny circle of light. They huddled within it, feeling dwarfed by the gigantic curtain of webs reaching floor to ceiling, and the towering bookshelves.

Doyle puffed on his pipe, finishing his story. "In the press of time, I realize I may have only made matters worse."

Marie stared into the shadows, listening intently. Houdini, meanwhile, gazed up thirty feet of shelving, an envious look plain on his face. Nevertheless, he said, "No, you've done wonderfully, Doyle. I especially liked the fact that you assaulted the police officers after making sure they knew your name. That's splendid. No point working the boys too hard."

"He know what he did. Now, hush up," Marie scolded.

Doyle ignored Houdini and dangled the Roman coin before the flickering fire. "They were about to let me go, but this seemed to change their minds. I wonder why."

"Who would want to frame Howard?" Marie demanded.

"Enemies of Duvall, perhaps, or the Arcanum?" Doyle answered.

"Or maybe," Houdini said, "Howard finally went off. We all know it's possible. Maybe the wheels came off the wagon. Maybe the pigeons flew the coop." Houdini rounded on Doyle. "And, just maybe, Duvall died in an accident, after all."

"But what about the Book?" Doyle demanded.

"What about it? Who knows? And who cares?"

"And what about Marie's vision?"

"Marie sees things all the time. She thinks evil spirits live in the telephone, for goodness' sake."

Marie raised her eyebrows and shrugged.

Doyle smiled. "Must you always be the skeptic, Houdini?"

"In this crowd, I'd say it's essential."

"Herry could be right," Marie said, to Doyle's surprise. "Of course, he isn't, but I just wanted to say it's within the realm of possibility."

"Thank you," Houdini deadpanned.

"See, even if Howard is crazy as a swamp rat," Marie continued, "he ain't got the power to kill people when he locked up in jail. An' thas jus' what happened. Somebody else got killed. And it weren't no Howard Lovecraft that did it."

"How do you know this?" Doyle asked, relighting his pipe.

Marie chuckled. "You be surprised how many people practice wit' the spirits, Arthur. People you'd never expect. And word spreads."

"Well, if it is some specter from our past, why don't they simply show themselves and be done with it?" Houdini groused.

"Be careful what you wish for," a voice said.

They all turned to the door.

Lovecraft stood under the archway, wearing glasses with oval lenses. A towel was draped over his head and tied into a knot under his chin. His usually pale face was patched pink where he had scrubbed at his skin with steel wool, bleach, and soap. After a moment, he added, "I feel better now."

A log snapped in the fireplace.

Doyle glanced uneasily at the others. "That's splendid, Howard."

"And no matter what you might think of me, I'm no murderer," Lovecraft added defensively.

Houdini crossed his arms. "I was merely theorizing, Howard. Don't take everything so personally."

Marie chuckled.

"We know that, my boy. But what we don't know is why. Why were you accused?" Doyle gestured for Lovecraft to join them.

Lovecraft walked stiffly to one of the rosewood chairs. The last few days—the last few hours, in particular—had clearly taken their toll. He untied the towel from his head, folded it slowly, and draped it over the arm of the chair. Then he tried to flatten his mussed hair into its familiar part.

Doyle tapped his pipe ash into the fireplace as they all waited for Lovecraft to speak.

"I don't know who," Lovecraft said at last. "But I think I know why."

"We're adrift, Howard, without your insight. Help us to understand." Doyle crossed from the fireplace and laid a hand on Lovecraft's shoulder.

"Just get to it," Houdini said tartly.

Lovecraft bit a fingernail. "Where to start? I suppose the beginning is as good a place as any. In this case, however, we must journey far back in time, to the days of Enoch the prophet." Lovecraft encountered nothing but blank stares. He went on, patiently. "Enoch was the great-great-great-great-grandchild of Seth, and the father of Noah. He was also specially chosen by God to interpret His Word. The result of their collaboration was a book—a very controversial book. A book that, for some time, formed the third testament in the Biblical triad. In numerology, three—the triangle—is quite potent, indeed. And three and three equals nine, of course, which is the most—"

"Don't start with the numbers. I can't bear it," Houdini snapped.

"Mathematics is the universal language," Lovecraft countered.

"Yes, well, none of us speak it, so try English."

"Houdini, please," Doyle said. "Howard, we know the Book is important. We know it was instrumental in provoking the Great

War, and I think we're all convinced that Duvall was killed for it. What we still don't know is why."

"I'm not a scholar on the subject," Lovecraft stammered. "There are gaps in my knowledge, but . . . On its surface, you see, the Book of Enoch documents the Fall of Lucifer. The War of Darkness and Light. A show of hands now for the cause of this war?"

Houdini looked at Doyle, who turned to Lovecraft. "Pride?"

"Yes, pride, vanity, and all that—but I'm speaking as literally as one can about such things." For all his youth, Lovecraft suddenly looked like a man of eighty, hardened and aged by the weight of his knowledge. "When God created man, according to early scripture, he required armies of angels to guide and teach mankind how to live, how to interact with our new world. Yet the closer these angels grew to the material world, the more they were tempted by it. Until, eventually—quite unexpectedly—they succumbed to their desires."

Lovecraft placed a chewed-off fingernail on the arm of the chair for safekeeping. "The angels succumbed to human lusts, and this merging of the spiritual and the material was seen as an abomination in the eyes of God. And to these parents were born offspring of a most hideous nature: grotesque giants given the name of Nephilim. In the story of David and Goliath, for example, Goliath was of the Nephilim. But perhaps even worse were the secrets imparted to mankind by these . . . let's call them falling angels. Secrets of technology. And magic. And weaponscraft. And war-making. And leading this charge was Lucifer, God's most trusted servant. The betrayal was just too great. God's great experiment was being destroyed, and he chose to set it right. Armies of angels were sent to destroy the Nephilim and Lucifer's corrupted legion, and the world descended into chaos. Yet Lucifer's forces were strong, and Lucifer decided that he— and he alone—should rule the kingdom of Heaven. God realized there could be no negotiation, no peaceful surrender, for his beloved Lucifer. No return to the fold. And in that realization Satan was born." Lovecraft paused, and the only sound that filled the room was the crackling of the fire.

Finally, Lovecraft sighed. "You see, Lucifer was winning the war. He had temptation on his side. And the closer the armies of angels came to earth, the more they hungered for it. For the spirit longed for the material just as the material did for the spirit. God's creation was spinning out of control. Free will was ruining everything. Now God had to reckon with His mistakes."

Doyle remembered the phrase from that fateful night in Bavaria. "God's mistakes," he whispered.

"As long as Lucifer was an angel," Lovecraft continued, "he threatened the throne of God. As long as he possessed a connection to the spiritual plane, he was a danger. So God, in His fury, cast him out. In a sense, cut his cord to the divine, and henceforth Lucifer was known as the Great Adversary—Satan. The same fate was visited upon the other fallen angels, for fear they would return to corrupt the Heavenly Host and challenge God's kingdom. But even with Lucifer sent away, there were still problems left for God to contend with. As we all know, temptation is a disease, and it was spreading. The Nephilim were multiplying, threatening to overwhelm mankind. The entire experiment of Creation was threatened. A single, terrible remedy was called for." A thin smile curved Lovecraft's lips. "But in that fog of war, even God could not see all the dangers."

"By what means were Lucifer and his fallen legion cast out?" Doyle asked.

"It's a mystery," Lovecraft answered, having anticipated the question. "The exact mechanism is unclear."

"And you said Enoch was the father of Noah?" Doyle asked.

Houdini slumped on the sofa beside Marie. "Wake me up when it's over," he said.

Lovecraft ignored him. "Enoch was the favorite prophet, privy, in some cases, to God's decisions. That is how Enoch was able to warn his son, Noah, that God was preparing a flood to cleanse the earth of His aberrations. And so Noah built a big ship for all the pretty animals."

"And the Nephilim were destroyed," Doyle concluded.

"Yes, they were. Oh, a few may have wiggled through the cracks, but the Israelites dispatched them a few hundred years later." Lovecraft fell silent again, but that little smile still curved his lips.

Doyle was not fooled. He knew there were meanings in all Lovecraft's silences. "I trust you realize that you've completely avoided answering our questions."

"Have I?" Lovecraft asked innocently. "Well, maybe you're not asking the right questions, then."

"Let's take him back to Bellevue," Houdini suggested, his eyes still closed.

"You unsettlin' all the spirits in this room, Howard, wit' all your talk of evil. Wrap this up, *chère*, 'less you want to hear them, too."

Lovecraft frowned. "What is it you want me to say? The Book of Enoch is extremely dangerous. I told you I didn't have all the answers."

"But what is it, man? Is it the value of the Book itself? Or is there some hidden meaning in it that you're not telling us?" Doyle said.

Lovecraft dabbed spittle from the corners of his lips with the corner of the towel. "The actual text disappeared around the death of Christ and stayed hidden until 1765, when James Bruce—"

"Yes, the Scotsman."

"—journeyed into North Africa in search of the fabled Ark of the Covenant. What he ended up discovering in Ethiopia, known as Abyssinia at the time, was the Book of Enoch—far more powerful, and far more dangerous."

Houdini opened his eyes. "Seventeen sixty-five?"

Lovecraft ignored him. "Reportedly, Bruce then gave the Book to a venerable translator, who adapted Enoch's words into English from Hebrew. The Book of Enoch was then distributed in some elite occult circles. The Masons had a copy. Their quarrelsome brethren, the Rosicrucians, also had the information."

"But Howard," Doyle said, "that time line doesn't follow. Duvall told me—"

"Ah, yes, Duvall. He got his hands on the Book of Enoch at some point, didn't he? I wonder how that happened?"

"This doesn't make sense." Houdini, no longer feigning boredom, was actively scowling.

"Of course, there's always the possibility—and I'm just

supposing here—but maybe the Book never left Duvall's hands at all," Lovecraft added.

"Talk in circle and never say anyt'ing, that's what he does. Like the Devil talk," Marie said in disgust.

"Quit your squawking." Lovecraft rose and crossed the room. He took hold of an ancient ladder, which had rusted into place, and, with a hard yank, dislodged it. Then he rolled the ladder some forty feet across the wall and climbed to the topmost shelf. He blew the dust from the books, then coughed and nearly slipped off the ladder.

"What the hell is he doing now?" Houdini muttered.

Doyle gave Lovecraft the benefit of the doubt. "So, if there were translations of the Book of Enoch . . ."

"Then what's so damn special about it?" Houdini concluded.

Lovecraft pulled out a quarto-sized book and examined it. "Decent Grolier binding." Lovecraft descended the ladder, talking as he went. "Oh, there were translations; dozens, at least. Very hard to come by. Of course, an elite group like the Arcanum had their own copy." When his feet touched on the floor, he swept the dust off his sleeves and collar, coughing a little. Then he held up the Book. "Here it is. First edition. Fetch a pretty penny." He offered it to Doyle. "Would you like to see?"

Doyle reached out, but Lovecraft just turned away and tossed the Book onto the fire.

"What are you doing?" Houdini exclaimed, lunging for the fireplace.

"Howard, have you taken leave of your senses?" Doyle spluttered.

"It's useless. All lies."

The Book burst into flames.

Houdini whirled on Lovecraft and shook him by the shoulders. "What the hell is wrong with you, man?"

Lovecraft sighed. "Konstantin Duvall was James Bruce, you imbeciles." He shook off the stunned Houdini. "Or Bruce was Duvall. Take your pick."

"But that's impossible," Doyle breathed. "That would make Duvall—"

"Very old, yes. Yet it doesn't seem to bother you that this

one"—Lovecraft gestured to Marie—"was supposedly born in 1827, does it? The Children of the Mysteries live by different rules, Arthur. You should know that now."

Houdini had regained his composure. "The translations were faked?"

Lovecraft nodded. "There is only one Book of Enoch. Think of it from Duvall's standpoint. For Heaven's sake, we all knew the man. He lusted for secrets. And here were the words of God, denied to civilization for millennia, and they were in his possession. But how could he take credit? How could he gloat if no one knew of his triumph? The answer: fakery. Give out enough information to whet appetites, but keep the real secrets to himself."

"And how do you know all this?" Houdini demanded.

"How do you free yourself from handcuffs?" Lovecraft parried.

"But Duvall went to the kaiser and the tsar and told them—" Doyle began.

"Yes, he did. The final, unutterable truths of the Enochian scriptures forced Duvall into action. For he understood at last what he held in his possession . . . and it horrified him."

Houdini approached Lovecraft, fists balled. "And that is?"

Lovecraft held up his hands. "We are now in the realm of conjecture—educated, of course, but still conjecture."

"Duly noted." Doyle's voice was grim.

"There is a school of Enochian magic based, in part, on the writings of the magician John Dee, court astrologer to Queen Elizabeth the First. Dee claimed to have been taught the language of the angels through his medium Edward Kelly. It is that school's contention that the Book of Enoch is a gigantic cipher, that its true contents lie hidden, encoded in a secret language."

"But what does it say?" Marie asked.

"I don't know. I'm not a student of Enochian magic."

"You're a magnificent piece of work, Howard, and I've missed you terribly. Please give a call while you're in town, if you're not in the booby hatch. Doyle, if you need me I'll be at home, sleeping." Houdini rose and vanished into the shadows.

"Hold," Doyle commanded.

Houdini paused halfway to the door. "I've heard quite enough, thank you."

Doyle stepped toward Lovecraft, who shrank back. "What did you mean by 'the fog of war,' Howard?"

"It's only a theory," he stammered, holding up his hands.

"It's anything but, and you know it. Now, Duvall had a map in his office, a detailed map of the world, charting the travels of a group he referred to only as the 'lost tribe.' Who are they?"

Lovecraft winced as he drew closer to the fire. "I told you. Armies of angels were dispatched to every corner of the Earth."

"Yes. And?" Doyle said grimly.

"Well, not all of them made it back to Heaven. Nor did every angel fall. That's what I'm saying." And Lovecraft folded his arms.

"Are you suggesting that this 'lost tribe' is actually a lost tribe of angels?" Doyle's voice grew softer as he finished.

"Every war has its refugees, Arthur," Lovecraft said, just as softly.

"What a load of spectacular bullshit," Houdini spat. He stalked back into the firelight. "Sunday school claptrap."

Lovecraft seemed to crumple in on himself.

"Here endeth the lesson, Howard?" Doyle asked.

"I've told you all I know . . . honestly. But my knowledge only scratches the surface. The Book of Enoch is one of the most potent relics in the world. As I said, an entire school of magic was built around its secrets."

"You've done well, Howard. You've taken us this far. Now, it seems, we need an expert in the field of Enochian magic. We need a name."

Lovecraft laughed, but the sound had a maniacal edge. "Oh, I'll give you a name, all right . . . but you won't like it."

"Try us," Doyle suggested.

"Short of John Dee himself, he's the unquestioned master. Maybe even better than Duvall."

"Who?" Houdini asked, now interested.

"Crowley."

Marie's eyes widened. "You got to be jokin', Howard!"

Doyle was aghast. "Aleister Crowley?" His lips could barely form the name.

"You honestly have gone mad," Houdini said, with grave seriousness.

"You wanted a name and I gave you one," Lovecraft retorted.

"I'd sooner trust a scorpion." Houdini shook his head, looking to Doyle for support. "Well, Arthur?"

"Where is he?" Doyle asked Lovecraft.

"Here," Lovecraft responded. "In New York."

"Don't tell me you're even considering this," Houdini barked at Doyle.

"Can we get to him?" Doyle pressed.

"I can," Lovecraft answered.

"Doyle! For all we know he's behind this entire thing," Houdini exclaimed.

"All the more reason we should go to him," Doyle said firmly. "Whoever the killer is believes he's working in a vacuum; that no authority exists to bring him to justice. Well, he's wrong." Doyle leveled his steely gaze on the others. "It's time for the important players in the game to know the Arcanum has returned."

20

As LOVECRAFT PULLED up his jacket's threadbare collar, he gritted his teeth against the bone-chilling wind. He recrossed his thin legs and shifted his position on the bench in Washington Square Park. Lovecraft hated the cold, and was unmoved by the dusky oranges of the turning leaves and the collage of autumn scents. His palate favored the dry musk of parchment and the stale stillness of library corridors. Were it not for the mysteries of the beckoning night sky, he would never leave his room. But these grousing thoughts fled in the rush of his building apprehension.

His eyes were fixed on a rust-colored building at 63 Washington Square South, the current address of the self-proclaimed Great Beast, Aleister Crowley.

Lovecraft half prayed that Crowley would fail to appear, or would dismiss Lovecraft on the spot. A prolonged interaction was what he dreaded most—not merely because of the obvious dangers it presented, but also for the temptations. For if there was an equator in Lovecraft's life, it was a line drawn by the influence of two men: Konstantin Duvall and Aleister Crowley. The Sun and the Moon. One a sage to kings, the other a pox on society. One fated to legend, the other doomed to infamy. Both tragically flawed, yet gifted beyond their time. And their saga was so intertwined, it seemed, from a distance, like a paradoxical love affair. But the contradictions only multiplied under closer examination.

In his time, Duvall sought to provide leadership and give structure to the occult world, gathering the world's secrets under a protective net.

Crowley, meanwhile, through vanity and a hunger for power, subverted and destroyed every mystical association to which he lent his name.

Publicly, Crowley was seen as a deviant poseur. Privately— and among the informed—he was feared. And the deeper one probed, the greater that fear grew, along with a grudging respect.

Crowley, like Duvall, had had his eye on Lovecraft from the start of the young demonologist's career, seeing in the boy a kindred seeker, an adept worthy of learning at the sorcerer's knee.

But Lovecraft chose Duvall and the Arcanum, and that choice had set like an undigested meal in Lovecraft's stomach ever since. Unlike the Arcanum with its rigid moral compass, Lovecraft approached the occult like a scientist, recognizing that the only truths worth acquiring came at a cost—be it of the mind, heart, or soul. This was an easy price to pay for a man with few, if any, close relations, but put him at odds with people like Houdini and Doyle: men with families, reputations, and a solid Judeo-Christian belief system. This philosophical prejudice nudged him nearer to Crowley, a man who had never met a social convention he didn't violate or revile. But Lovecraft suspected that was merely the outward consequence of a mind dedicated fully, perhaps madly, to the exploration of darkness in all its forms.

As Lovecraft mused on the road not taken, a tall man in a Chesterfield overcoat and a seal-skin cap exited 63 Washington Square South. He strolled into the park and headed north toward Fifth Avenue. His gait was deliberate, his posture erect. He carried an umbrella that he tapped on the ground with every third step.

Lovecraft was halfway to Crowley before he realized he'd left the bench at all. Crowley's influence over him was deeper than he'd expected, and Lovecraft's fear was matched by a perverse fascination. He tried to think of Duvall to dispel the gnawing doubts, but the weight of the moment pressed down on him like a stone.

When they were ten feet apart, Crowley stopped. So did Lovecraft.

"Brave of you to come alone," Crowley said, gazing north.

Lovecraft, too, dispensed with formalities. "We need your help."

Crowley turned to face him. His eyes were as black as ink and too large for his face, bulging from under wrinkled lids with froggish strain. There was a coldness to their gaze, like that of a dead man. "You certainly do," he answered, with a curl of his lip.

DOYLE HELD HIS hat in his hand as he stood in the center aisle of a hushed and empty St. Patrick's Cathedral. The smell of the stone brought him back to the Sunday mornings of his Roman Catholic upbringing, and he felt a twinge of guilt for turning his back on that religion. But until the Church changed its ways and opened to the mysteries of Spiritualism, Doyle would not return.

It was a Tuesday, and no Mass was in progress. Doyle was here for an appointment instead. Footsteps sounded in the distance, and a balding priest with spectacles emerged from the shadows of the sacristy to the right of the altar. "Sir Arthur?"

"Your Eminence. Congratulations are in order," Doyle said as he walked to meet Patrick J. Hayes, the newly anointed archbishop of New York City.

Hayes smiled. "Thank you, and it's a pleasure to meet you after all this time, the writer of my favorite sleuth."

Doyle smiled in return as they shook hands. "Thank you for your time."

"My pleasure, my pleasure. What can I do for you?" Hayes

pulled his round glasses down to the tip of his nose, and peered over their rims at Doyle. "Returning to the flock, I hope?"

"Sadly, no."

"Alas. That would've earned me high marks from the council." But Hayes's expression was easy and trusting.

"I hate to disappoint, Your Eminence."

"Eminence? Nonsense. Come." Hayes led him to a pew beneath the pulpit. They sat.

"I need your guidance on something," Doyle began, cautiously.

"A personal matter?"

"Religious, actually. And, in a way, historical, too."

"Oh." Hayes brightened. "Certainly. I do hope it's research for a new novel. I'd love to feel I'd played a part."

"In a way it is, yes. What is the Church's position on the Book of Enoch?" Doyle studied Hayes's expression.

Hayes frowned. "I don't know if I've heard of that. There was a prophet Enoch in the Old Testament."

"That's the one," Doyle responded. "According to some . . . scholars, I'm told this book formed the third testament of the original Bible."

"Well, I assure you that isn't the position of the Catholic Church. Fringe groups and amateur historians often claim possession of ancient writings or biblical secrets, but most are writings the original Church fathers dismissed centuries before as Apocrypha. In other words, it was material deemed unsuitable for the Holy Scripture."

"So what would have been the criteria for such exclusion?"

"Well, there were probably a variety of factors the Church fathers needed to contend with. Firstly, many early writings made outlandish claims about mythical beings still walking the Earth. Which is unsettling content for the laity."

"Creatures like the Nephilim?" Doyle queried.

"Am I being lured into some sort of debate on Spiritualism?" Hayes countered with a wry smile.

"Hardly."

"And if I answer, may I rely on your discretion?"

"Of course."

"Goliath was a Nephilim. And of course the Bible talks of miracles and magical creatures. It was mostly a question of discriminating between folklore and supportable history. The type of material that would ensure noninclusion, however, would be anything that suggested flaws in God's design. Fissures, if you will, in the fabric of Creation."

"The Fall of Lucifer," Doyle interjected.

"You presume that occurred without God's sanction," Hayes said.

"So why would God allow it?" Doyle asked, more bitterly than he had wished. It was a question that had plagued him throughout a lifetime of senseless loss.

"Yes, exactly. Why?" Hayes folded his hands in his lap. "I am of the belief that without free will there is no love. A father who dominates his children, who doesn't allow them to grow and choose their own way, is not a father but a dictator. But God wants us to join Him out of love, not fear. To do that, we must be allowed to choose our fate."

"My son, Kingsley, my eldest, who died at the Somme—"

"I'm so sorry," Hayes offered.

"Thank you. He used to ask me why God didn't show Himself, to give the faithful hope, a reassurance of His presence."

"That's a good question. My answer is this: were God to appear suddenly on Fifth Avenue, in all His Heavenly splendor, we would fall to our knees in awe. And, I believe, we would become slaves. For in the wake of such magnificence, how could we react in any other way? Again, choice. Free will. We are His children, and a loving father lets his children make their own decisions."

"And Satan?" Doyle asked. "What of his followers?"

"Earth is a battleground. It is the position of the Church that he must function through emissaries, that he has no special powers. He must influence others to do his bidding, just as God comes to our aid in the most unexpected ways."

"Your Eminence," Doyle said hesitantly, "do you believe in angels?"

"Certainly I do."

"Are they here? Among us?"

"Yes, of course."

"And who protects them?" Doyle asked, again with more emotion than he'd intended.

Hayes chuckled. "You have it turned around. They protect us, Sir Arthur."

Doyle rubbed the back of his neck and squeezed his eyes shut, fatigued.

"But what if they're lost? What if they've been lost for so long that they've forgotten the way home?"

"There are no lost angels, Sir Arthur. God wouldn't allow it."

"But if there were and Satan somehow knew this, could somehow find them . . ." Doyle faltered.

Hayes shook his head. "I don't understand."

"How would he take his vengeance on God?"

"Well, that was the point of banishment, you see, to deny Satan access to the spiritual. There is no way he could gain revenge."

"For the sake of argument, then," Doyle suggested.

Hayes frowned. "Angels are pure spirit. And Lucifer was damned to the material world. So I suppose you could argue that if he somehow had access to creatures of the spirit, then . . ." Hayes hesitated, thinking it through. "There might be some mechanism for corruption to take hold once more in Heaven. The material might overtake the spiritual, and we could see the second Fall of Man, as foretold in the Book of Revelations. But I wouldn't lose any sleep over it."

Doyle stood up and buttoned his jacket. He offered his hand again. "Thank you. And I hope you're right."

Archbishop Hayes rose as well, clasping hands with Doyle. "I hope so, too. Did you get what you needed?"

"You've been a great help, Your Eminence."

"Then, let me know if I can be of any further assistance."

"I shall," Doyle replied, suspecting he'd be calling upon the archbishop far sooner than he liked.

21

MARIE COULD SEE the fear in Antoine's eyes as he glanced at her in the rearview mirror of the Lexington sedan. The beads in his braids clicked together as he surveyed the desolate lots and tenements of Talman Street in Brooklyn. Blacks were gradually crowding out the Irish settlers, and the thin young men on the sidewalks, clad in moth-eaten jackets, surveyed the car with dead stares.

Antoine pulled his top hat down to shadow his eyes, absently fingering the cat bones that encircled the hat's brim as he searched for the building they wanted. Marie regretted involving him. But she was not the divine *mambo* here in New York, only a potential usurper to the powers already ensconced. This was the territory of the dreaded *houngan* Tito Beltran, a West African witch doctor of the Dogon. Her presence in the city would not have escaped him, and she could not rely on her reputation to protect her if Beltran perceived a challenge. Complicating matters were the political maneuvers to unseat her currently ongoing in New Orleans. A cabal of rival voodoo clans and crooked politicians had joined forces to drive her and her followers into hiding. And that was not to mention the many bounties on her head. No, if Beltran perceived Marie to be in a position of weakness and felt he could strike with impunity, she would be walking into the mouth of a crocodile. For it was not simply voodoo that Beltran parlayed, but thriving drug and prostitution rings: profit businesses that he protected with knife and bullet. And the young men on the street corners were not jobless hooligans, but soldiers and lookouts.

However, if there was a spyglass on the occult underbelly of the city, it belonged to Beltran—and for that Marie needed him. For all her ridicule of Lovecraft and his ways, his words mirrored her visions. A necrotic hand was enclosing the city, the spiritual oxygen being cut off. When she closed her eyes, Marie thought she could see the dying light, and the hopelessness of that vision overwhelmed her fears.

The Lexington pulled up to 154 Bridge Street, a four-story brick tenement with boarded windows. "Don't do this, Mam'zelle," Antoine said in Creole-French, turning to Marie in the backseat.

Two long-boned sentries stood on the stoop of the building, their hands in their jacket pockets.

"Stay and wait," she answered him, also in Creole, and reached for the door handle.

"No, I'll go first," Antoine insisted, and stepped out onto the sidewalk.

Marie watched as Antoine exchanged a few words with the sentries and allowed himself to be frisked. Then he was taken by the arm and led into the vast, condemned structure.

"You stupid woman," Marie muttered to herself as she stroked the gris-gris tied around her neck. It was a small red-flannel pouch filled with rock salt, a lock of her mother's hair, and the ground-up bones of a water moccasin. It was powerful protection—hopefully more powerful than the magic she was about to confront.

Minutes later, the sentries reappeared and descended to the sidewalk. One of them opened the car door and offered his hand. "Come, mam'zelle," he said.

Marie took the sentry's hand and allowed herself to be escorted into Beltran's lightless den.

The corridors were lined with slouching men in their twenties. Some held pistols in the bands of their trousers, and the strength of their hostility quickened Marie's pulse. Teen prostitutes smoked furtively, and ducked away at the sight of the voodoo priestess.

Marie was led into a large five-sided room with as many doors, and a large *vever* drawn in cornmeal on the floor. It was a symbol of power, indicating that the *houngan* was guarded by vengeful *loas*. The altar was immense, and took up two of the five walls at the back of the room. It was littered with dripping candles and hundreds of wax, wood, and clay fetishes, along with dozens of the Nkisi carvings of West Africa, each driven with hundreds of nails. Each nail was a curse—proof of the *houngan*'s liberal use of black magic for punishing his enemies.

The smell of the lamps hanging from the ceiling made her stomach churn: oil mixed with ground pepper and corpse powder and burned in coconuts to drive away enemies.

Beltran's ten prized fighting cocks strutted in their cages, steel spikes fitted over their beaks and foreclaws.

And seated in the center of the room, ringed by three muscular giants with pistols at their hips, was a small black man in white pants, a white Cuban shirt, and white shoes—Tito Beltran. He wore a talisman around his neck: a cobra skull painted with the blood of a dove. He held a handkerchief to his mouth and breathed in the vapors of crushed eucalyptus—medicine for his chronic asthma. His round face dripped with sweat, and Marie saw it had soaked through his clothing. It seemed that the air around Beltran was fifty degrees warmer than anywhere else.

At the sight of her, Beltran lowered the handkerchief and clapped his hands softly, singing with a raspy voice: *"Eh Yeye, Mam'zelle Marie, Ya, Yeye, li Konin tou, gris gris. Li te kouri lekal, aver vieux kokodril. Oh ouai, ye Mam'zelle Marie. Le knonin bien lie Grand Zombi."*

"Yeye" meant "esteemed mother," and the song was one sung by her mother's followers years ago in the Bayou. It was both a sign of respect and also one of subtle mockery. Marie did not smile as Beltran wheezed into his handkerchief, chuckling to

himself. It was at that moment Marie realized Antoine was nowhere to be seen.

"Where's my boy?" she asked Beltran, a bold question that went outside the bounds of normal voodoo etiquette.

The slight was not lost on Beltran, who rolled a lunk of spit in his mouth, "Best to show respect in my house, child. Dis ain't no swamp now." And Beltran pointed a stubby finger at the floor.

With her eyes locked on Beltran's, Marie swept her skirts aside and knelt. She bowed her head reluctantly, and spoke her words to the floorboards. "For your health, *houngan*." Marie placed a gris-gris of powdered sassafras and hummingbird bones by Beltran's white shoes.

"Rise, girl," Beltran wheezed. He had dropped all pretense of treating her as an equal, and his voice dripped with disdain.

Marie stood, flushed with anger. Beltran leered at her, his eyes deliberately lingering on her breasts and hips.

"Where is Antoine?" she asked again, her voice sharpened by fear.

"Why don't you tell me what make you so bold, Marie-girl? You t'ink de gris-gris don' make it no insult? You comin' here? Whut my boys to t'ink, eh?" Beltran coughed and cupped his mouth with the handkerchief.

"I want information 'bout the killins on the island. I'd like to find who's doin' such things. I 'spect you want the same, seein' it's a sheddin' o' blood on your sacred ground."

"People die all the time, Marie-girl. It's de nature of t'ings," Beltran answered, with a sneer.

"It's more than that and you know it, *houngan*. I 'spect you know a lot more than you tellin', an' I just say this: you in danger, too. His magic is powerful. We all in danger."

"Sorcerer he may be, child. But at least he know how to give de proper respect."

Marie's throat grew dry.

"He don't bring me no dried-up gris-gris as an offering." Beltran flicked the pouch across the floor with his shoe. "He bring money to Beltran. He tell me, '*Houngan*, if dat nigger hairdresser's daughter come to you, den you do de right t'ing.' He tell me you tryin' to steal his book of magic. He tell me, dat nigger queen spyin' on him like a spirit, seein' t'ings she ain't sposed to see."

"You a bigger fool than I thought," Marie hissed.

Beltran's guards moved to encircle her. Marie's hand went instinctively to the pouch around her neck.

Beltran leaned over in his chair. "Your mama's lock o' hair won't save you, girl." And Beltran snapped his fingers.

A vivant opened one of the five doors, revealing Antoine, tied to a chair. His top hat was upside down on the floor and a white sheet was held over his head by a guard. A painted skull dripped on his muscular chest. Marie could see the outline of Antoine's mouth beneath the sheet as he sucked for air.

"He can't breathe," Marie said.

"Let him breathe, Bobo," Beltran growled.

The bare-chested guard drew a knife from the pocket of his jeans and thrust it into Antoine's throat. A bright spurt of blood shot from the wound, and the boy's legs kicked furiously at the chair.

"*Non!*" Marie screamed as she lunged for him. But rough hands grabbed her and forced her to the floor. She tore the skin off her knees trying to fight Beltran's men, but she couldn't shake them. Her arms were drawn tightly behind her back.

Beltran slid his hands into heavy gloves and shuffled to his cages.

Tears slid down Marie's cheeks as she watched the life ebb from Antoine's body and rivulets of arterial blood pattered onto the floor by his bare feet.

Beltran freed a black-and-tan cockerel from its cage. Its wings beat furiously. "Dis is Monsieur Pepe." The rooster's steel claws ripped at the air. Its beak was open in a silent scream as it writhed in Beltran's grip. "My best fighter." Beltran shambled toward Marie, holding Pepe out.

One of Marie's captors yanked her head back, loosening the knots on her silk scarves. They spilled like water down her shoulders, freeing her hair.

"Pepe so smart 'cause he know de best way to win a fight is not to go for de throat; *non*. Best way is to blind your enemy. Go for de eyes first. Scratch dem out." Beltran brought the cock nearer to Marie's face. Its claws slashed and its steel beak snapped. Black feathers floated in the air.

Marie could feel the bursts of wind on her cheeks. "You don' want this, *houngan*," Marie warned, steeling herself for the first cuts of Pepe's claws.

"You won't die, girl; not yet. Not until I've tasted you. I jus' want your eyes, child."

Pepe snapped at her face, only inches away now.

Suddenly, a tremor shuttled up Marie's arm and across her chest. Her legs spasmed violently. Her throat swelled and her pupils rolled back, showing only bloodshot white. Her captors struggled to hold her down, such was the strength of her seizure. Marie's teeth were clenched, yet a deep groan erupted from her belly.

Pepe's flailing body abruptly buckled. The rooster's neck stiffened and its claws went rigid. Then it gasped and flailed weakly, its tongue stretching out of its mouth like a tiny purple finger.

Marie's captors exchanged nervous glances.

The voodoo priestess was still in the throes of a pitched frenzy. Her entire body shook with a force that threatened to dislocate her bones and tear her open. She bucked under their hands as Pepe thrashed from side to side. Beltran thrust Pepe closer to Marie's face, but in that instant, the bird's neck dangled, lifeless, over Beltran's fingers.

One of the guards released Marie's arm and backed away. In that moment, Marie freed a concealed ivory-handled knife from the folds of her skirts and drove it into Beltran's white leather shoe, through his foot, and into the wood of the floor.

Beltran howled and dropped Pepe, who landed with a soft thud. Beltran himself was overcome with a wet jag of coughing.

Marie tore herself free of the other guards. She pointed a rigid finger at the two men who'd held her, and the fury in her eyes sent them scrambling.

Antoine's killer also dropped his knife and bolted through one of the doors.

"Out!" she screamed, and the remaining vivants fled into the corridor.

Surprisingly, only the prostitutes remained, gazing through the doorway in mute fascination as the voodoo queen circled the coughing Beltran, who knelt on the ground, trying to free his foot from the blade. His lungs convulsed and stringy drool slung from his gasping lips.

But Marie didn't touch him. Instead, she walked to Antoine's still body and ripped the pillowcase off his head. The boy's face was rigid with terror.

"This man who paid you to kill me, what was his name?" Marie asked sweetly.

Beltran's breathing was labored, and he reached for his handkerchief with its dose of eucalyptus. But Marie slid a toe under the handkerchief and flung it across the room. Then she leaned down and whispered, "His name, *houngan*."

Beltran tried to wriggle away from her, but cried out as his foot twisted under the knife. He stared at her with fear, one hand clenched to his chest. "Da-Darian." Beltran was convulsed from coughing. When he could draw another breath, he added, "That's all I know, Ye-ye." But it was too late for respect now.

Marie loomed over him. His hands came together in a gesture of prayer and mercy, but there would be none. "Darian? That's his name?"

"*Oui, mam'zelle.*"

"*Merci.*" Marie smiled as she straddled Beltran's chest, pinning his arms with her thighs. She pulled the pillowcase, still fresh from Antoine's body, over his head. The old man thrashed as she twisted the pillowcase tighter, watching as the outline of Beltran's mouth vainly sucked for air.

In a few seconds, he was dead. Marie released him and swayed, wrung out by emotion. But then she felt eyes upon her, and turned to the teen prostitutes at the door. They neither smiled nor frowned; they merely stared at her impassively.

Marie lifted her chin and summoned what little strength she had left. "I got each one of dem faces o' yours locked in my mind now. So, get home to your mothers an' fathers an' don't ever come back here, 'less you want to see Marie Laveau in your nightmares." She took a step forward, and they scattered like frightened pigeons, pouring out the front door and into the street.

Marie, meanwhile, braced herself on the doorjamb and gave in to a warm flood of tears.

22

"NO ONE APPLAUDS the return of the Arcanum more than I do, Arthur. But I fear it may prove too little, too late." A. E. Waite sipped his Darjeeling as a tuxedoed waiter replaced the ashtray at their table.

Doyle had arranged the meeting with Waite—one of the premier cabbalistic scholars and renowned mystics of the day—at the Union League Club on Thirty-seventh and Park. Arthur Edward Waite had run the Isis-Urania Temple of the Golden Dawn in London. He had written dozens of occult books, and designed the most widely used Tarot deck in the world. The mystic had a bushy thicket of black hair swept up and to the left, and a curly moustache. His black topcoat and trousers were immaculately pressed.

"Duvall always spoke of you with respect," Doyle said.

Waite nodded at the compliment. "He'll be missed. And not only for his friendship. These are dangerous days, I fear. There is a terrible dissonance in the occult world. Blavatsky's dead, as are Westcott and Woodman. Duvall was one of the last with his finger in the dam. I'm certain that with his death comes anarchy. A cancer will rise in his place."

"Crowley," Doyle said without prompting.

"A venal monstrosity," Waite agreed, his lips pressed tight. "Whether or not he's personally responsible for Duvall's death, I don't know. But what I do know is, he did all in his power to weaken him, isolate him, and set him up for the killing blow." Waite placed a cigarette into his holder. "Now there are no institutions left to stop him. He's undone them all."

"Surely, the Freemasons—" Doyle began.

"They've no influence, Arthur; they're too exposed. The Rosicrucians are paralyzed with internal squabbles. And when that pillar falls, God knows what secrets will spill out. Laugh if you will, but part of me thinks Crowley planned it all along, over the course of years, so there would be no authority left to challenge him. The Golden Dawn is no more. And the O.T.O. is nothing but a breeding ground for Crowley's occult terrorists. I'm sorry, Arthur, but the Arcanum is all that's left between our world," Waite blew a smoke ring that folded into a half-moon "and his."

"And the Book of Enoch?" Doyle asked.

"That's what worries me most. It's Crowley's field of study, you know. My Lord, he thinks he's the reincarnation of Edward Kelly, Dee's medium. He sees himself as divinely chosen to interpret Enoch's words."

"But does even Crowley possess the audacity for such a brazen act? Surely he knows he's being watched."

"Does he? By whom? Duvall was Crowley's only rival."

"So, we're alone, then."

"I'm sorry, Arthur. I'm neither a warrior nor an investigator, only a humble student of the mysteries. However," Waite lifted a round object off the floor and placed it gently on the tabletop, "I can offer you this."

Waite pulled out a battered wooden case bound in red leather, with star imprints on its face. He lifted the fragile lid to reveal an object about the size and shape of a tennis racket without the handle. It was black, smooth, and featureless, though it didn't appear to be made of steel or stone.

Doyle looked up at Waite with questioning eyes.

Waite smiled. "The obsidian mirror of John Dee."

Doyle's eyes flashed, and he gazed at the object with renewed respect. "Duvall searched for years."

"Yes, but on the wrong continent. It was accidentally brought years ago to the Americas as expedition treasure, and traded to the Natives. Truth be told, I've yet to glean its secrets. But its powers are legendary. I hope you have better luck."

There was a gleam in Doyle's eyes as he took the case from Waite. "I know just the man."

LOVECRAFT FELT CONFINED. Proximity to Crowley was always unsettling. His chest was tight and his hands were wet. And Crowley seemed to relish the tension, using it against Lovecraft like a turning screw.

A mousy waitress came to the table. Crowley ordered for them, his eyes fixed on Lovecraft. "Two coffees, my dear."

The bookshop café on Church Street was warm and musty with old cigarette smoke. There were only a few scattered customers—New York University students, mostly, and a hobo or two. Cakes and pastries sat in a glass case, and a bean grinder chewed loudly while the girl fixed their coffees at the counter.

Finally, Crowley spoke. "My condolences, Howard. You must be suffering."

"Why waste your breath?"

"I'm not without feeling. The loss must be terrible." Crowley frowned and shook his head as though feeling it himself.

"No matter. He'll be avenged," Lovecraft said with a certainty that surprised him.

Crowley raised a mocking eyebrow. "Spoken like a true Duvallian acolyte, with all the accompanying bluster."

"Was it you?" Lovecraft asked.

"If it was, my boy, what could you possibly do about it?"

"It would be a mistake to underestimate me." Lovecraft chewed a fingernail as he made his threat.

Crowley laughed.

Lovecraft flushed. "Perhaps it was you who had me imprisoned as well, to cover your tracks?"

The waitress delivered the coffees to their table. When she had gone, Crowley sipped his with apparent amusement. "If I meant you harm, Howard, you'd know it." He tapped his sharpened nails on the cup. "And as entertaining as it would be to dance you about on my string, I'm a busy man with appointments to keep." Crowley paused. Lovecraft sensed he was reluctant to say what came next. "I didn't kill Duvall," Crowley added, eyes flashing, "though I certainly celebrated the news."

"Then who did?"

"I've no idea. But whoever did should be canonized."

"I think you're lying," Lovecraft insisted, though he knew he was playing a perilous game.

"And I think you've grown soft," Crowley answered with a sneer. "You could have been a true master, but you chose to serve that buffoon Duvall instead."

"Duvall was a magus," Lovecraft countered.

"Duvall was a collector," Crowley hissed. "A hoarder of treasures he could never hope to understand."

"Then why are you here? Why are you even speaking to me?"

"My reasons are my own."

Lovecraft suddenly realized the truth. "You're in danger, too," he said.

Crowley looked contemptuous. "Don't be ridiculous."

"No, you are. He perceives anyone with knowledge of Enoch as a threat. Duvall, myself, you . . ."

"You're reaching," Crowley growled.

"Am I?" Lovecraft leaned across the table. "You're afraid you're next."

Crowley exploded from his seat, upsetting his coffee, and loomed over the demonologist. "How long before they're all hunted down, eh? Are you such a virtuoso that you would presume to play me? You're smelling smoke while the forest burns!"

"Tell me who it is," Lovecraft persisted, though he shrank back in the face of Crowley's fury.

"You want your killer? I want the Book," Crowley snapped, baring his sharpened canines.

Lovecraft felt a sinking in his stomach. "You *do* know him."

"Perhaps." Crowley sat back down. "So, what'll it be? The choice is yours. Bargain with me. Betray your friends. Find a killer."

Lovecraft's thoughts raced as he struggled to keep up with the master tactician. It was no accident that Crowley was a grand master of chess. Lovecraft assumed for the moment that Crowley was being truthful and had nothing to do with the murders. So if he wasn't interested in the Lost Tribe, why did he want the Book of Enoch? What other secrets did it contain? The thought troubled him deeply.

"And why should I trust you?" Lovecraft asked, hating himself for his shaking voice.

"For the best reason. You haven't a choice."

"But you've given me no proof."

"And you've wasted quite enough of my time." Crowley got up again. He stalked past Lovecraft, who still wrestled with his thoughts.

Suddenly, Crowley's hand snaked around Lovecraft's throat, and the sorcerer hissed in his ear: "Just remember. While you agonize, the heavens scream." His nails dug into Lovecraft's skin.

"Tell me his name," Lovecraft gasped.

" 'What's in a name, the lookout cried'?" Crowley whispered, and in the next breath was gone.

23

THE CANDLES BURNED brightly behind the leaded windows of Crow's Head.

"You should never have gone alone," Doyle said, turning away from Marie to face the fire.

Marie was fresh from the bath, her hair in a thick ponytail that hung down between her shoulder blades. She wore a dress of green silk that tied with a blue ribbon beneath her breasts, and was wrapped in a red shawl. Were it not for the faraway look in her eyes, no one would take her for anything but a wayward teen at odds with an older parent. She said nothing to Doyle's tirade. His were old emotions reappearing on a new stage.

"She can take care of herself," Houdini reminded Doyle as he crossed behind the divan to place a towel filled with ice cubes on Marie's injured shoulder. "Is that too cold?"

"*Non. Merci*, Herry," Marie said as she repositioned the ice on the correct spot.

Houdini rolled up his shirtsleeves. "She got us a name, though. That's something."

Doyle frowned. "Yes. But we're still no closer than we were."

Houdini sighed. He turned to Lovecraft, who was sunk in a chair, half enveloped by the shadows, most of his attention fixed on the fathomless obsidian of Dee's mirror.

"And what about you?" Houdini asked him.

After a moment, Lovecraft looked up. "What?"

Houdini said bitterly to Doyle, "You know how he is when he gets a new toy."

"What about Crowley, Howard. Did you find him?" Doyle asked.

Lovecraft thought about his answer, eyes still fixed to the mirror. "I did."

"You met with him?" Houdini said.

"Yes."

"And?" Marie probed.

"What did he say?" Doyle added.

Lovecraft recounted some of his meeting with Crowley, leaving out the details of the suggested bargain for the Book of Enoch and Crowley's admitted knowledge of the killer's identity. When he was finished, Lovecraft added: "There was something strange that he said, near the end. 'What's in a name, the lookout cried.' "

"And that's everything?" Houdini asked, concern in his eyes.

"Of course," Lovecraft answered, a little too quickly. He turned his attention back to Dee's mirror.

"Good," Houdini said. "The less we have to deal with Crowley, the better." His eyes didn't leave the demonologist. Then he added, "What's that thing do anyway?"

"It doesn't come with instructions," Lovecraft answered, somewhat petulantly. "I need time to study it—alone."

"Houdini, have you today's newspaper?" Doyle asked, his voice distant, a sure sign he was deep in thought.

Houdini's suit jacket was slung over the back of the chair where Marie sat. He freed a folded newspaper from the inside pocket, and offered it to Doyle.

Doyle began to rifle through the paper. "Crowley's trying to tell us something." He scanned the pages. "Why a 'lookout'? What does he do?"

Houdini turned to Marie for encouragement. "Looks out?"

"He sees, yes?" Doyle continued to turn the pages. "He is, in fact, a seer. But a seer is also a medium, and if I'm not mistaken, 'a Rose' by any other name would smell as sweet!"

Doyle suddenly folded the paper in two and slammed it down on the coffee table for all to see, revealing a Barnabus Tyson advertisement for the spiritual medium Madame Rose.

24

THE VEINS SWELLED in Madame Rose's slender neck. Her head jerked from side to side, shaking her black mane of hair perilously close to the flickering candles. Her lips moved as breathy words poured out in a steady flow of inaudible gibberish. There was something erotic about the way her breasts heaved and her body squirmed in the trance.

Marissa Newlove felt a heat rise in her cheeks. She glanced at her husband, Patrick, who looked like a drooling sheepdog, his eyes locked on Madame Rose's bosom. It had taken Marissa weeks of persuasion to let them join the waiting list for a Rose séance—hands down, the hottest ticket in New York City. Marissa then waited six months and committed a season's clothing allowance for the privilege, and she aimed to get her money's worth.

The guest list confirmed her expectations. Marissa stole glances at the other attendees, pleased to be seen in such august company. To Patrick's left sat the portly Gerald William Balfour, the second earl of Balfour and a former president of the S.P.R., the Society for Psychical Research. Beside Gerald was his unattractive sister, Eleanor, also quite active in the Spiritualist Movement.

Holding hands with Eleanor was Sarah Winchester, the heiress to the Winchester rifle fortune. The deaths of her husband and baby daughter had launched Sarah on a lifelong quest for spiritual forgiveness. Believing herself the receptacle for spiritual vengeance from everyone killed by a Winchester rifle, Sarah had built a house in San Francisco that had already achieved national acclaim. In a constant state of renovation, the house covered six acres and possessed one hundred and seventy rooms, two thousand doors, and uncountable secret corridors. Stairways were built to lead into walls, and doors opened to nowhere. And Sarah's growing obsession with the number thirteen prompted her to insist that all rooms have thirteen windows, and thirteen chandeliers with thirteen lights. Her presence at a Rose séance was sure to raise the medium's popularity even higher.

The only sour note was the Man with the Cold, to whom Marissa had taken an immediate dislike. He had a mop of white hair and a tight, wrinkled face, and all his snuffling and coughing was a rude distraction. Twice his sneezes had blown out the nearest candles.

Rounding off the table were the British anthropologist Margaret Murray, and Rose Fitzgerald Kennedy, daughter of the mayor of Boston. Fine company indeed.

"Go away!"

Marissa whirled around at the fierce, rasping voice, lower than any man's.

"Mongrel bitch!"

Marissa gasped when she realized that the voice was coming from Madame Rose's throat. Rose, herself, was still lost in a trance.

The table jumped at least a foot in the air, eliciting startled yelps from the attendees. Madame Rose's chair banged on the floor, leg after leg, and she moaned, her head lolling.

Marissa dug her nails into Patrick's forearm, but he was too terrified to notice. A mist had begun to gather in the room.

Marissa felt sweat bead on the small of her back, and her breath strained against her corset.

"Who are you?" Sarah Winchester asked with urgency.

Madame Rose smiled. "Ah, Sarah, good of you to come," the horrible voice growled. "Look for no pity here, wretched woman."

Defiance shone in Sarah Winchester's eyes. It seemed this was not the first spirit to upbraid her. "Tell us your name," Sarah demanded.

An earsplitting howl was her only answer. Madame Rose writhed, her jaws snapping at the air. The table bucked again, and a terrified Rose Kennedy covered her face with her hands. Several candles blew out as an inexplicable thunder rolled through the room.

Patrick clutched Marissa close to protect her. An armoire tilted once, twice, then crashed onto the floor only inches from the table. Gerald Balfour screamed like a woman, the whites of his eyes showing.

"Reveal yourself!" Madame Rose shrieked in her own voice. Then she breathed deeply, and a pasty white rope of ectoplasm spilled from her lips and across the table.

Gerald Balfour slapped a hand over his own mouth and lurched backward, racing for the door.

Madame Rose tilted her head back as more ectoplasm foamed up around her neck.

Marissa covered her nose.

Margaret Murray leaned closer to study the pile of ectoplasm. "Is it a face? Can you see?"

Eleanor Balfour leaned over, too, but the Man with the Cold only hooted into his handkerchief.

Marissa heard Patrick's teeth chattering in her ear and, despite her fear, she was able to enjoy the fact that he would not mock her hobbies quite so quickly anymore.

"Take her! Rape her! Rape her now!" It was the horrible voice again, enraged and rasping.

Marissa covered her ears to block the stream of profanities that filled the room, along with a stench of rotten meat. As Madame Rose undulated, dripping, ectoplasmic fingers reached out from her lap. To everyone's astonishment, the corporeal hand lengthened across the table, stretching and quivering like the outer-dimensional handshake of an unspeakable monstrosity. Then the giant slime hand splashed onto the table in a spewing finale—soaking coats, dresses, and faces with cold, clinging ectoplasm. Madame Rose collapsed onto the table, exhausted.

There was a moment of held breath.

Then excited questions from the guests: "What did it mean?" "Who do you think it was?" "It pointed at you."

"Marvelous! Absolutely marvelous!" gushed Margaret Murray. Patrick and Marissa clapped more out of relief than anything else.

Madame Rose leaned back in her chair and nodded serenely as the applause died down to a single pair of clapping hands. Madame Rose glanced up through her tangled locks, as did Rose Kennedy and Eleanor Balfour. The clapping continued. Marissa knew she did not like the Man with the Cold, and this confirmed it. What was wrong with the man?

"The best. Just the best ever," the Man with the Cold crowed, and continued clapping.

Madame Rose bowed her head. "Thank you, Monsieur."

"Quite impressive. Really," he said, as his hands finally stilled.

Again, Madam Rose inclined her head graciously. "The spirits were quite anxious. We're not always so lucky."

"Indeed." The Man with the Cold glanced at his fellow attendees, then back at Madame Rose. "So, can we eat it?"

Madame Rose hesitated. "I'm sorry?"

The Man with the Cold leaned over the table, drew a finger through the thick mound of ectoplasm, and before eight sets of astonished eyes, popped the finger into his mouth and sucked it clean.

Rose Kennedy gasped. Patrick Newlove's jaw dropped, and Madame Rose straightened in her chair with alarm. "That is not edible."

"Ugh, how disgusting." Eleanor Balfour turned away with peacock offense.

The Man with the Cold winced and nodded in agreement, then swallowed with effort.

Margaret Murray spoke for the group. "How rude!"

The Man with the Cold blew his nose like a trumpet and stood up without warning, circling the table. "You produce fine ectoplasm, Madame Rose. The finest ever. Especially the floating hand; very good. I wager you'd make some fine muffins from that corn flour and baking soda."

"What are you talking about?" Madame Rose snapped. The Man with the Cold now stood by her chair, and the medium stiffened. "Get away from me. Why are you standing there?"

"This won't hurt a bit," the Man with the Cold said, then knelt down and reached under her chair.

Madame Rose leaped to her feet. "Get out!"

"Scoundrel!" Eleanor Balfour shouted.

"Just a minute. Yes. Ah! There we go." The Man with the Cold was halfway under Madame Rose's chair.

The table jumped in the air. The attendees screamed in unison.

The Man with the Cold upturned the chair with a dramatic flourish, unveiling a system of pulleys and wires connected to finger rings along the armrests. "Behold, ladies and gentlemen, how crudely you've been deceived."

Margaret Murray gasped, and Eleanor Balfour stood up stiffly.

"Get out, you bastard," Madame Rose shrieked. "Who the hell do you think you are?"

The Man with the Cold answered by flinging his white wig across the room and wiping the makeup wrinkles from his face.

"Oh my Lord, it's Houdini," Patrick Newlove exclaimed.

Madame Rose stood while Rose Kennedy and Margaret Murray giggled like schoolgirls. They flocked to Houdini, who raised his arms like a welcoming father.

Then Madam Rose rallied. "So how did I eject the ectoplasm onto the table, Houdini?"

Houdini autographed Rose Kennedy's program as he answered. "Pastry tubing in your brassiere, Madame, operated by contracting your abdominal muscles. But we all have special talents." Houdini crossed the room and ripped the curtains away from the wall, revealing a thirteen-year-old boy holding a fire puffer. Stationed beside the boy was a table containing a bowl of rotting meat mixed with excrement, bells of various sizes, and a drilled conch shell for voice amplification.

"*Bonjour, monsieur,*" Houdini said.

The boy looked to Madame Rose. "Do I still get my dollar, miss?"

"Shut up!" Madame Rose hissed.

Houdini turned back to her. "I once toured the vaudeville circuit with a belly dancer from Arabia, and she could do the most amazing things: pick up sticks, shoot quarters, drink with a straw, all with her . . ." Houdini looked at his watch. "Heavens, is that the time?" He turned and swept the adoring séance attendees toward the door. "My dear friends, how I wish this night could last forever, but I do have a bit of business to conduct with Madame Rose, so if we could all just proceed to the foyer, I'm certain the gentleman who took your tickets will reimburse your five dollars. Thank you so much. And remember, this fall *Terror Island* hits the big screen. Tell your friends. I'm sure you'll enjoy it. It's quite exciting, and all the stunts are real."

WHEN THE LAST of the guests had been shuffled out, Houdini turned to Madame Rose. "You should know better than to practice fraud in my town."

"Really? And what have you accomplished, Houdini? It's your word against mine. There was no press here, and my séances are sold out until February. You're just jealous."

"Jealous?" Houdini turned to the thirteen-year-old still cowering in the curtains. "Run along, boy."

"Yes, sir."

"And if I catch you at another séance, I'll box your ears."

"Yes, Mr. Houdini, sir."

When the door closed again, Houdini stepped closer to Madame Rose. "The papers follow my every move; the entire world is waiting for me to proclaim a séance the genuine article. And you? You're a dime-store fad."

"So, what is it you want, Harry Houdini?" Madame Rose leaned deliberately forward so that one strap of her dress fell off her shoulder. "Some special arrangement, perhaps? They say you're not quite as loyal to your wife as you claim . . ."

Houdini took Madame Rose's arm in a viselike grip.

And at that moment, horse hooves echoed on the pavement outside. Madame Rose's head whipped around, her eyes widening.

"Who's in the carriage?" Houdini demanded, sensing her terror.

"Please go," she whispered.

"Choose," Houdini said. "The police, or your friend in the carriage."

"I can't," she pleaded, trying to tear herself from Houdini's grip.

A carriage door slammed outside. Houdini heard footsteps enter the theater lobby.

Madame Rose turned to Houdini, desperate. "They can't see you. You don't understand."

Houdini shook her. "Who is it?"

"You don't understand; he'll kill us both." Her eyes flashed to the door of the séance parlor.

"Tell me."

The floorboards squeaked under the newcomer's weight. The knob rattled as the door groaned open, then Morris entered. He was dressed in an ill-fitting charcoal gray suit.

Madame Rose stood, alone and shaking, in the middle of the room. The curtains flapped as the wind blew in from outside.

Morris scowled at the window as Madame Rose quickly grabbed her purse and shawl. "I'm ready, Morris."

He ignored her and lurched toward the window. He stuck his head out and peered down at the black carriage and its two horses snorting steam in the cold.

"I said I'm ready," Madame Rose repeated sharply.

Morris pulled his head back in, not seeing Houdini perched on the ledge and pressed to the wall, holding his breath.

Morris closed the window and locked it reflexively, then escorted Madame Rose from the parlor. He shut the door behind them.

HOUDINI WATCHED FROM the ledge as they exited the building. Madame Rose slid into the carriage, aided by the white-gloved hand of a gentleman whose face was concealed by a low top hat. Morris took his seat on the bench and whistled the horses into motion. And for a second, Houdini thought he saw the flash of blue glass through the carriage window as it circled around in the street and slowly rolled into the fog.

25

THE TOWERING GOLD doors gave way to the cavernous lair of William Randolph Hearst. The publisher stood before a wall-sized window, the sprawl of the city unfolding behind him. With a lit cigar clamped in his teeth, billowing smoke, he appeared to be some sort of demigod, straddling New York City much as the Colossus did the harbor of Rhodes.

"Come in, gentlemen."

Houdini and Doyle exchanged glances as they crossed the threshold.

Hearst's invitation worried Houdini. He had specifically requested Doyle's presence, but Doyle was supposed to have been in America anonymously. Letters had been forwarded to Houdini's Harlem brownstone, to his Hoboken studio, and to the Penn Hotel. Every effort was made to suggest a specific agenda as opposed to a simple meet-and-greet.

Further muddying the waters was the presence of Barnabus Wilkie Tyson, the promoter extraordinaire and current man of the hour. Houdini knew Tyson could sniff out celebrities like a foxhound.

Houdini noted the somewhat leisurely fashion in which Tyson

rose from his chair to greet the new guests. It was not the standard forced casualness of sycophants in the presence of celebrities, but a deliberate form of disrespect. Houdini took an immediate dislike to the man.

But ignoring an invitation from Hearst was just not an option. William Randolph Hearst *was* New York City. Everyone paid homage to the man—even the mayor and the chief of police. For they knew it was through Hearst's lens that not just the city, but the whole nation viewed itself. He was a frequent guest at the White House, regardless of whether the occupant was a Democrat or Republican; the desire for favorable press knew no party affiliation. With a single word, Hearst could move stock markets in Tokyo and Berlin, annihilate hallowed reputations, and sway public opinion to match his own. In this age of party bosses and political machines, Hearst fit in perfectly. Business and politics operated with the same methodology as organized crime, and in that environment, Hearst was the kingpin.

The office reeked of stale cigar smoke, which had seeped into the mahogany shelves and desks, and the leather chairs imported from Paris. Red velvet curtains hung from the rafters in luxurious splendor.

Hearst eyed Doyle. "Why have you been hiding this man, Houdini? Shame on you." Hearst shook Doyle's hand. "Sir Arthur, New York City welcomes you."

"That's very kind, Mr. Hearst," Doyle answered.

"And I speak for her, sir; be assured of that." Hearst's smile was thin. "Have you met Barnabus? Quite the impresario of late."

"Thank you, Mr. Hearst," Tyson said unctuously. His smile was openmouthed and accompanied by an unpleasant breathy growl. He gestured to a coffee table and some assembled chairs. "Scotch, Sir Arthur? Wine? What's your pleasure?"

"Nothing, thank you." Doyle took a seat next to Houdini. They exchanged another look; Houdini shrugged at the presence of Tyson.

Hearst gestured to a room-sized humidor in the corner of the office. "Cigar? I've some marvelous Monte Cristos. They go wonderfully with a glass of port."

"I came armed with my own tobacco, Mr. Hearst." Doyle presented his pipe and tin.

"Call me William, please. Houdini? What would the Great One like?"

"You know me. One drink and I'm talking to the furniture."

Tyson growled a laugh as he returned with his own sloshing glass of scotch. As he sat, all the air escaped the cushions with a rush.

Hearst did not sit; he preferred to circle. "Barnabus has impressed me of late. He's got your appetite for publicity, Houdini, and knows how to use it. Who knows? Someday he may give you a run for your money."

"No, Houdini's still the master of promotion," Tyson said diplomatically.

Houdini chuckled and crossed his legs.

"Barnabus has built quite an interesting roster of clients. He's chosen very strategically, and Hearst Incorporated has taken an interest in a few of them for the stage and the motion pictures. But it's a delicate time. The public needs time to get to know these people through our newspapers and magazines, through public speaking events and the like. There's money to be made." Hearst nodded to Tyson. "But I don't have to tell you this, Houdini."

"No, indeed." He looked over to Doyle again with a questioning arch of his brow.

Hearst had stopped circling and paused behind Houdini's chair. "I heard you had an interesting meeting with the psychic seer Madame Rose."

Houdini looked directly at Barnabus Tyson as he answered. "Yes, we had a gay old chat."

Tyson wore a lazy look of defiance as he sipped his drink.

"I was told there may have been a misunderstanding," Hearst went on.

"There was, William. There most certainly was. You see, Madame Rose appears to be under the impression that she is some kind of channel for spirit voices from the Great Beyond, whereas I had the distinct impression that she was a craven fraud and shameless thief. And I believe it was upon this point that our paths diverged."

"What business is it of yours, I might ask?" Tyson growled.

"You might ask that, but I don't suggest you do," Houdini snapped.

"Gentlemen, gentlemen; come," Hearst chided. "It's too easy to get your goat, Houdini." Hearst began to pace again, trying his best to seem amiable. "You can't say I haven't spent some ink on your medium-busting exploits, my friend."

"And?" Houdini never felt he had to thank anyone for the publicity he generated.

Hearst's smile faded. "This is a special case. We've invested some time and energy into Madame Rose, and would hate to see all that go up in flames. Besides, we're easing her out of the medium business and into acting. Move her into the pictures, that sort of thing. So she needn't disturb your sensibilities any longer."

"What if I went out and told the world how you busted out of those handcuffs, eh?" Tyson offered, unhelpfully.

Houdini leveled Tyson with a look of contempt. "My good man, I dare you to try. In fact, I insist that you try. But I feel compelled to remind you just who I am. You may have gotten used to being a big fish in a little pond, but that tends to overinflate one's sense of one's position in the world. I am Houdini. There is only one. Irritate me, as you're beginning to, and you'll earn yourself a most daunting enemy."

"Barnabus misspoke, Houdini. Be merciful." Hearst placed a hand on his shoulder. "What are your plans?"

"My plans for what?"

"For Madame Rose, of course."

"I plan to tell the truth."

Tyson sat up and crushed his cigar in the ashtray. "I don't have to sit through this," he snarled.

"No, you don't. And don't let me keep you." Houdini winked at Tyson.

Clearly seeking to change the subject, Doyle motioned to the floor-to-ceiling window. "Quite the view."

"Best in the city," Hearst answered proudly. Then he stepped away from Houdini's chair and strode over to the window, his face a mask of concern. "She is my garden, you know. I control the knowledge that feeds her, and weed out her enemies. Water her roots with money. But no matter how many fences one builds . . ." Hearst sighed. After a moment he turned back to Doyle and Houdini. "There is a perverse murderer loose in my city, Sir Arthur. He was caught briefly, but escaped from Bellevue's asylum for the criminally insane—escaped with the aid of accomplices, I'm told."

Houdini raised an eyebrow.

"Finding this madman and bringing him to justice . . . Well, frankly speaking, it's become my obsession," Hearst continued.

Tyson nodded to himself, solemnly.

"A few banner headlines and you'll feel better," Houdini said.

Hearst turned to Houdini with a frown. "Your cynicism wounds me. These crimes are horrendous, and the victims are missionaries, of all things—citizens striving to save the most unfortunate souls in the city. And the killer is apparently an occultist. A vile organism. Lovecraft's his name."

Houdini's sip of water went down the wrong pipe. He coughed, breaking Hearst's train of thought.

"The story has taken many strange turns. The strangest of all places you, Sir Arthur, at the residence of the accused." Doyle seemed about to answer, but Hearst cut him off. "You're outraged, I'm sure. And I don't blame you. It's nonsense, of course. But as you well know, once the public starts to pick up the scent of a story, even the most outrageous rumors have a way of transforming into fact." Hearst shook his head, regretfully. "It's just the unfortunate reality of the news business."

"I haven't been following the story," Doyle said tersely, and puffed on his pipe.

"Yes, well, I'm sure your business here, whatever it is, is very important and very distracting. But I should warn you that being associated with something of this nature—even falsely—could harm your reputation. It's certainly the last thing your fledgling Spiritualist Movement needs right now."

"The Movement can take care of itself, I'm certain," Doyle responded tightly.

But Hearst knew how to play his cards. "Sooner or later, I may be pressed to come forward with this information, unsubstantiated as it may be. The story becomes its own animal, you see. And the public hungers for new information. At some point, I may need more wood to feed the fire."

"Is that a threat?" Doyle demanded.

"But there may be," Hearst went on, sidestepping Doyle's question, "a way to spin this information into a positive." Hearst crossed to his desk. "Yes, I do believe events transpire in the order they do for a reason—a divine reason." He plucked up a newspaper, then returned to the coffee table and leaned closer to Doyle. "What do you say, Sir Arthur? Let's make some news." Hearst laid down the *Daily Journal,* revealing a headline that read:

SHERLOCK HOLMES HUNTS OCCULT KILLER

Doyle said with disinterest, "Make some news, eh? Beats reporting it, I imagine."

Hearst smiled coldly. "Tomorrow's headline. When the safety of the greatest city in the world is threatened, then one must call upon the greatest detective in the world to protect her."

Doyle raised his eyebrows and put a match to his pipe. "Is it the custom in America to report the news before it's happened?"

Hearst frowned. "It's disappointing to find you acting so cavalierly about such a serious matter."

"And you find this to be a serious approach, do you?" Doyle responded.

Tyson curled his lip. "Arthur, you're new to these shores." He turned to Houdini. "Have you explained to him how things work in New York City?"

"It's 'Sir' Arthur, you charmless pup," Houdini answered. "And you're not fit to kiss his boots."

Hearst sighed. "I must say, I'm surprised. There's no better currency in the world than good publicity. I thought you would leap at the opportunity, considering the bruising you've been taking in the British press, Sir Arthur."

"You were wrong. I'll neither lend my name, nor the name of Sherlock Holmes, to a false investigation. And if you attempt to do so without my consent, I'll publicly rebuke you in the *New York Times.*"

"Well, I can always go with the first story. Perhaps that's the better angle anyway. I've a police detective for a witness, and you can't find a better source without paying. 'No' is not a word I'm accustomed to hearing."

"No." Doyle stood up and offered his hand to Hearst. "There. That wasn't so bad, was it? Thank you for the view, Mr. Hearst." And Doyle headed for the door.

Houdini rose as well. "You run that story, they'll laugh you out of town," he said.

"Perhaps. Or maybe you can keep your opinions to yourself for once, and we won't have any problems at all."

The muscles in Houdini's jaw tightened.

Hearst turned to Doyle as he was leaving. "It's refreshing to see someone so unmoved by what others think of him."

Doyle hesitated.

"My hat's off to you. If you find any ghosts or goblins or faeries during your stay here in New York, I do hope you'll tell me. I'm thinking of running a children's section in my Sunday *Journal*. Your Spiritualist reports would fit in splendidly."

Doyle was about to respond, but Houdini put a hand on his arm, stopping him.

In the silence, Tyson slunk over and spoke in a hushed tone. "I hate to see things end like this, gentlemen." He handed them an engraved invitation. "Consider it a peace offering from Madame Rose. It's a costume ball, seeing as Halloween is coming. It is this Saturday night at her estate. She said you, Houdini, would find it particularly diverting."

"Did she?" Houdini said, fingering the invitation. "I'll check my date book."

"We'll have a few drinks and put all this unpleasantness behind us."

Sensing, like Houdini, both an opportunity and a trap, Doyle shook Tyson's hand. "Please inform Madame Rose that I look forward to meeting her."

26

MADAME ROSE REMOVED her earrings and placed them on the top of her bureau as she gazed at herself in the mirror. Her purple silk nightgown was concealed beneath a paisley robe. The material flowed over her body like water. Her eyes went to the bed, as reflected in the mirror, then she noticed a figure standing in her doorway, cloaked in shadow. Madame Rose went still. He entered her room, quiet as the shadows that concealed him, and did not stop until he was close enough that she could feel his breath on her neck. Unconsciously, she grasped the marble bureau top tight enough that her knuckles went white.

"Darian," she whispered in a small voice.

His fingertips grazed the points of her hipbones and softly caressed the smoothness of her belly.

"Darian," she said again, warning him.

His thumb and forefinger pulled at the flimsy belt of her robe, and Madame Rose's breath went shallow as she shrank inside herself. The robe fell open. His left hand reached around and cupped her right breast, crushing the other with his forearm.

"Darian." Her voice was sharp.

His other hand clasped her groin, feeling every hidden part of her beneath the silk.

"No, Darian, we can't. We can't," Madame Rose insisted.

He bit and sucked on the white of her shoulders and the back of her neck, paying no heed to her words. She struggled beneath his advances, feeling herself softening and weakening.

"Please . . . please, no," she begged.

He pushed her, painfully, until her breasts pressed on the cold marble of the bureau top. Suddenly her nightgown was about her waist, and the roughness of his hands on her buttocks shocked her into action.

"Stop it! Darian, stop it!" She whipped around to face him.

Then his hand was in her mouth, gripping her bottom jaw as he slammed her head backwards against the mirror. Madame Rose heard the glass crack as his other hand grasped her neck. His breathing was fierce. She thought she could hear his teeth grind as his thumb pressed on her throat. *So easy,* she could almost hear him think.

Then he suddenly released her and stormed out of her bedroom, the walls ringing with the slam of the door.

Madame Rose wrapped the robe tightly around herself with shaking hands as she sank to the floor, her heart racing.

FOUR HOURS LATER, though she lay in her bed, she was still wide-awake. She feared to sleep. All she could hear was the thud of her heart in her eardrums. The floorboards of the corridor outside her bedroom door groaned under the weight of a man.

He was outside.

Madame Rose shut her eyes tightly. In the past weeks she'd begun to fear Darian in an entirely new way. And she feared for him. Feared his silences. His distance. The feverish gleam in his eye. It was a look she knew and remembered all too well.

Candlelight filtered in under her bedroom door. Madame Rose waited, feeling the ache in her muscles from the hours of tensed expectancy. But gradually the light on her carpet faded to blackness. Darian had walked past her door. She thought she heard him on the stairs. His heels clicked in the distance; he was wearing his boots. Madame Rose checked the clock again. It was 2:25 in the morning.

Resigned to sleeplessness, she sat up and tucked her hair behind her ears. She slid her feet with their perfectly manicured toes into slippers and threw a robe around her shoulders.

From the landing on the second floor she could see the front door click softly shut. Madame Rose descended swiftly, the lightness of her frame causing little complaint from the stairs. She slipped out the front door, and immediately questioned her mission. The October winds were fierce, raising gooseflesh on her arms and legs. Her teeth chattered. She could hear the trees creaking, bent to the will of the front that moved in from the west. Dark clouds churned overhead, blocking out the moon. The wind whistled across the sloping hills of the estate and moaned over the green cliffs that loomed above the Willow Grove Cemetery.

Madame Rose caught a glimpse of lantern light vanishing around the southern portion of the mansion, and she followed, slippers padding over the huge, circular gravel drive. She slunk behind the tall shrubs sculpted in geometric shapes, and peered around the wall. The large marble pool was covered until next summer, and lawn furniture was turned upside down and stacked by the back wall of the house near the enormous piles of firewood.

However, the normally latched door to the gardener's shed banged open in the angry winds. Madame Rose thought she saw firelight briefly flicker behind the dirty window. Wishing herself back in the warmth and safety of her bed, she dashed across the wet lawn up to the shed, pulling open the door.

The scent of earth and cobwebs filled her nose. The gardener kept his tools in an orderly fashion; rakes, shovels, and spades stood at attention along the walls. The only disarray was where a wheelbarrow had been tossed aside and a three-by-three section of the floor removed, revealing a large steel ring affixed to the ground. Pulling with both hands, Madame Rose wrenched the trapdoor open, revealing a ladder leading down into a secret abyss. And as she bent over and peered into the gloom, the ghost of Darian's lantern light flickered like a distant beacon.

Madame Rose felt sick at the thought of entering the hole, yet fear had always been an attraction for her. Terror was her aphrodisiac, and she had tested its limits since she was a small child—thanks in large measure to the family she was born into. The early childhood ghost stories and bloody tales of goblins and stolen children not only caused her nightmares, but stimulated her sex and heart and mind in a way that would dictate the whole course of her life to come.

And since she had been a young teenager, she had chosen men who made her afraid as her sexual partners.

Yet Darian was the boundary she had thought she'd never cross. But in a way, they'd been slowly circling like satellite moons, drawn by an irresistible gravity into a slow, elliptical dance that was doomed to end in fatal collision.

It was why she was climbing down the ladder into the fetid stillness of an underground corridor.

It was why she loathed and thrilled at his mystery and cruel moods, running away but always returning, praying his vicious ways would end and conversely hoping they never would.

It was why every fiber of her being tingled beneath her sheer silk gown and desire filled her as the corridor reached out into charnal blackness.

It was why her mind recalled not Darian's caresses of hours before, but the feel of his hand clutched around her throat.

Madame Rose walked in near-total blackness, grazed her fingers along the dirt wall for direction. A thrum from somewhere deep in the tunnels began to gradually take the form of a chanting voice, and the sound of it pulled her forward.

The tunnel pitched downward and curved, first right, then left, then right again, until she began to lose track of the path she'd taken. Then the tunnel moved downward at a steeper incline, prompting her to almost jog to keep up with the pitch. Her heart was like a clenched fist jabbing at the back of her sternum.

Moment by moment, another sound—a discordant hum—began to fill the corridor, drowning out the chanting voice.

Madame Rose felt the hum throb in her temples. It was some-how an alien sound, coming from both inside and out.

Seeking to orient herself, she looked up at the low ceiling and barely made out the shadowy forms of tree roots reaching down through the dirt like tentacles. Sweat broke out across her back when she realized she was beneath the Willow Grove Ceme-tery—beneath even the graves. Her legs weakened. She couldn't go on, and she couldn't turn back. She was frozen and shivering in the dark tunnel, hearing sounds she imagined to be the moaning sobs of the dead. She felt them, just beyond the reach of her hand, watching her, studying her.

Then a root touched her shoulder and she screamed. It felt like a skeletal finger, and she whirled about, disoriented. She began to run, totally blind, her cries a feeble counterpoint to the warbling hum in her temples, which only deepened and vi-brated.

The chanting echoed through the tunnels, and Madame Rose could now identify Darian as the speaker. His tone was hateful and exultant. He chewed the words of a foreign, yet beautiful, tongue into a bitter paste of bile.

A divot in the path turned Madame Rose's ankle and she sprawled face-first, bloodying her lip and knocking what little wind there was from her lungs. Then she realized that there was light coming down the corridor.

Two church doors, painted black, waited at the end of the corridor. A candelabra flickered before them, set onto a small stone ledge projecting from the wall. The doors seemed to breathe with the pulsing of voices, and the discordant hum, which she could still feel in her molars and bones and stomach. She climbed to her feet, one bare from the loss of a slipper, and stumbled toward the church doors. The humming grew more intense than ever—so loud, so impossible, this deep beneath the ground.

Darian's voice rose in pitch, and her heart ached because he sounded so in command, so filled with meaning. Maybe things could be different. Maybe there was a path out of darkness.

Madame Rose could see the dirt under her nails as she pressed her hands against the doors.

They opened.

And there was Darian at the altar, his smile dazzling, his eyes ecstatic and gleaming, his skin whiter than chalk.

There was an ancient tome in his hands, and from this he read a curious language, his lips twisting and contorting to fit the wonderful and strange new words.

Seeing her, a keening laughter rose to his lips, but the strange words continued to roll from them, caught up as he was in an electrified trance.

Tears of joy rolled down Madame Rose's cheeks. She'd never seen him so blissfully and frighteningly alive, and she wondered to herself what blessed flock had the honor of this inspired sermon.

She spun around to see them, to celebrate with them. And they, in turn, swarmed toward her: a bobbing, ragged collection of ruby eyes and reaching, bandaged hands. Madame Rose's mouth opened to scream, but no sound came. The beings squealed like pigs at the slaughter, and she could now see that they were the source, too, of the nauseating hum that rattled in her bones.

Those piercing, ugly squeals mixed with Darian's words, overwhelmed her senses. Her eyes rolled back into her skull as consciousness seeped away. And all was peaceful and quiet and dark.

27

BY THE TIME Doyle and Lovecraft made it inside the converted Chinese Theatre, which was now the home of the New York Rescue Society, they were soaked to the bone. The rain drummed on the roof as they shook freezing water from their coats. It had been a long night prowling missions and churches, searching for witnesses and information. Once they were able to compile names and descriptions and locations, all seemed to lead to this building. The air was stale and filled with the cacophony of nearly forty snoring tramps. The combined odor of rancid breath and sour socks was overpowering.

The building was long and cylindrical, with benches serving as beds laid out on both sides and a long aisle in the center. More bodies were strewn on the floor, and Doyle and Lovecraft walked carefully so as to avoid stepping on the sleepers. Bare lightbulbs swung overhead. The walls were painted with questions written in all capitals, like: HOW LONG SINCE YOU WROTE TO MOTHER? and THE LORD WILL PROVIDE. CALL UPON HIM WHILE HE IS NEAR.

"I'm afraid we're all filled up," spoke a stern voice from the back. It belonged to a tall, clean-shaven fellow with white combed-back hair wearing a white shirt and suspenders. His nose was hawkish and his face angular. Doyle took note of the revolver tucked in his belt.

"We're not looking for beds," Doyle said, opening his hands to show he carried no weapons.

"Fine. That's plenty far." Lovecraft and Doyle were only halfway down the aisle when the man spoke. "If you've no need of beds, you've no point being here. So get on your way."

"We'd like to speak with you—" Doyle began.

"What you journalists don't seem to understand is that we are grieving. Privacy is all we want. We've lost family, and this is neither the time nor the—"

"We're not reporters and we're not police," Doyle said, cutting him off. "You might say we're investigators, and this case has come to our attention. Ten minutes is all we ask."

Minutes later, Doyle and Lovecraft sat with the man, who introduced himself as Joe. They were joined by his wife, Judith—an elegant, weary woman in simple clothes. There was such a weight of sadness on her it seemed an effort for her to walk. She was a gracious host, however, and made hot tea to warm bodies chilled by the storm. But her nervousness was evident as she fiddled absently with a porcelain butterfly brooch.

For simplicity's sake, Doyle conceived names for himself and Lovecraft, and a back-story, which neither Joe nor Judith seemed to question. Troubles weren't in short supply at the New York Rescue Society, and if strangers wanted to help, who were they to argue?

"So, is everyone accounted for?" Doyle asked gently.

Joe and Judith exchanged a look of exasperation. "All that can be," Joe replied.

"There are others?" Doyle pressed.

"Wayward children," Judith said weakly.

"Damned criminals," Joe growled. His wife nodded, agreeing but obviously disapproving of her husband's language. "But what can we do?" Joe asked Doyle as if accused. "We've no extra hands. I've a brood upstairs to look after. I can't chase them to Hell and back, can I? We've already lost one trying to track them down. Dexter." Joe frowned, as if still surprised by the depth of his grief. Judith only sighed and gathered up Doyle's empty teacup.

"More, sir?" she asked.

"No, no, that's fine." Doyle leaned in to Joe. "I know it's difficult, but do any of your children or any of those who work for the mission," Doyle dipped his hand in his pocket and brought out the coin pendant, "wear anything like this?"

The coin spun slowly in the candlelight.

"That's Matthew's pin," Judith said instantly.

"Matthew? Where is he?" Doyle asked.

"I just said—" Joe started, angrily.

"No. Tonight, I mean. With the rain. There must be certain areas of retreat in a storm like this. Somewhere the tramps would go."

Joe nodded, understanding. "Well, if not here or the mission on Twenty-third and Lex . . ." He turned to Judith.

"Then the train tunnels," she concluded.

"Which ones?" Doyle demanded.

"I'd start with the City Hall station," Joe answered.

28

"PARIS," ABIGAIL SAID, between sips from the wine bottle. "And I'd be a dancer." She threw out her arms and twirled in a circle, her laughter echoing off the tiled walls of the City Hall station—a gothic labyrinth of arched ceilings, shadowy stairwells, and spidery chandeliers. One could walk for days and not retrace one's steps, thanks to all the dividing, merging, and subdividing levels and passages. At this late hour, the station was a quiet sanctuary from the driving rain.

"Boring," Matthew said as he tried to grab the wine bottle from Abigail's hands. "Besides, you can't dance."

"I can," Abigail pouted. "See?" She stood on her toes like a ballerina, until her legs buckled and she fell.

It was Matthew's turn to laugh. Abigail tilted the wine bottle and slowly poured its contents on the floor in revenge.

"Hey!" Matthew shouted, reaching for the bottle.

"Say you're sorry."

"I'm sorry."

Abigail kept pouring.

"I said it," Matthew yelled, slurring his "s."

"Mean it," Abigail instructed.

"I mean it," he exclaimed, grabbing her in an embrace and bearing her down to the floor.

She wriggled beneath him. "Your breath stinks." She waved a hand in front of her nose as Matthew tried to kiss her.

Matthew nipped her nose with his lips. "What about Hong Kong? We'll steal away on a freighter."

"Do I look Chinese to you?" Abigail asked. Matthew laughed as she kissed him.

"As long as I'm with you, I don't care where we go," Matthew said.

"And what about the others?" But Abigail immediately regretted asking, for Matthew's expression changed in an instant.

"Aren't we allowed our own lives, for God's sake?" He climbed off her, sat up, and swigged the remaining wine from the bottle.

"I know," Abigail said, also sitting up.

"If you want to be a baby all your life, go on, then! Let them tell you what to do." Matthew's temper could get hot when he drank, and Abigail spotted a tantrum on the way. She tried to soothe him by stroking his hair, but he shoved her off. "I don't know why I waste my time with you. You never change."

"That's not true," Abigail said. "I want to go with you."

Matthew staggered to his feet. "Forget it. I want my own life."

"Don't leave," Abigail pleaded.

Matthew scowled. "Don't follow me. Go back to Mummy and Daddy. I'll find a real woman." His emphasis on the word "real" made Abigail wince.

Matthew lurched off into another passageway. Abigail could hear him muttering, and knew his guilty anger would subside when he sobered up. But for now she was alone, and Abigail hated to be alone. She tilted her top hat down over her ears and blinked at the flickering chandeliers. She slid down the wall and sat by the puddle of wine, arms locked around her knees. She could hear the pounding of the rain on the streets above, and the sound made her indefinably sad. Tears trickled down her cheeks, but she paid them little heed. They always came in these moments when she was alone. They were tears Matthew had never seen, and never would if she had anything to say about it. They were her secret, a private sorrow that had been with her as long as she could remember. She closed her eyes and rested her forehead on her knees, trying to sleep, letting the distant raindrops lull her, when a tremulous squeal echoed in the tunnels.

Abigail lifted her head and peered down both ends of the long corridor. "Matthew?"

ELSEWHERE, JUST BELOW street level, four shadows reached across the stone floor of City Hall station.

Houdini removed his hat and shook off the rain.

Doyle stepped past him, trying to get a sense of his environment.

Marie shut her umbrella and scanned the tunnel archways. "Somet'ing wrong here," she said.

Lovecraft brought up the rear, lugging a battered satchel, which clanged loudly with every step.

Marie covered her face with a trembling hand.

Doyle approached, worried. "Marie, what is it?"

"I don't know," she whispered. "Feel like I can't breathe."

"Claustrophobia, perhaps?" Houdini asked.

"No," Marie answered. "Somet'ing in the air."

Doyle turned to Lovecraft. "It's time."

Lovecraft set his satchel on the ground. He unhooked the latches and opened it, revealing a set of quasiscientific instruments—a mobile workshop of demonological research. Most of the devices had no obvious purpose, but Lovecraft fingered each with a surgeon's deliberateness, clearly weighing their usefulness. He removed his black fedora and slung a pair of bulbous goggles around his neck. Then he worked his arm into a gauntlet that appeared carved from a large animal bone, and tightened it to his wrist and elbow with leather straps and buckles. Symbols were etched into the gauntlet and multicolored wires had been threaded through the bones like veins. They reached from the jade hand-shield into a control unit, which was a small steam engine shaped like the end of a fishing rod. Lovecraft fixed the goggles over his eyes and rapidly spun the reel on the control unit. With accompanying sparks, tiny pistons started moving up and down. A hum shuddered through the gauntlet as power flowed along the bundled wires, causing the snakelike symbols to glow.

Doyle watched in mild astonishment as ghostly mathematical symbols appeared in the air like flickering fireflies around Lovecraft, emanating from the transistorized gauntlet. As the reel spun on its own power, Lovecraft rotated a red dial on the steam-powered unit with his free hand and watched closely as some of the phantom numerals blinked out, only to be replaced with different floating formulae. "Fascinating," Lovecraft muttered to himself.

"Is that thing dangerous?" Houdini asked, taking a wise step back as greenish light enveloped Lovecraft.

Doyle cleared his throat, "Howard?"

Lovecraft shushed him.

Doyle tried again. "What is that instrument doing?"

Lovecraft spoke quickly and quietly, as if not to disrupt the operation of his tool. "It's an Eltdown Shard, which Duvall modified. The symbols you see belong to the Great Race of Yith."

Houdini whispered to Doyle: "Does that answer your question?"

Doyle frowned. "But, Howard, what's it doing?"

Visibly irritated, Lovecraft glanced away from the floating symbols. "I'm forming a small ether-bridge, obviously, but I need a moment to finish, so be silent."

As Lovecraft walked away, Doyle and Houdini returned to Marie, who was huddled against a column, shivering.

"Can you explain what you feel?" Doyle asked her.

"Cold. Worse than ice. Inside me." Marie wrapped a shawl about her neck. "Normally, I can feel the breath of the spirits around me, but not here. There's just a void here."

"I've got something," Lovecraft cried. He pulled the goggles down around his neck. His face was moist from the heat of the instrument. "There's interference, but I'm definitely picking up a sub-aural chatter."

"A what?" Houdini spoke for the rest of them.

"It's confirming a relatively new theory of mine, quite exciting actually, on the wave-band thickness that an extra-dimensional signal structure would have to travel on to achieve coherence on our material plane."

Three sets of eyes just stared at Lovecraft.

He sighed. "Perhaps I can simplify. It's been posited, for example, that whales signal to one another on a far deeper frequency than we do in our day-to-day conversations. And why is that? Because water carries sound differently than the far thinner atmosphere between our bodies. Now, imagine the consistency of an extra-dimensional universe of, say, sixteen dimensions as opposed to our four. When a life-form accustomed to vibrational signaling in that environment suddenly comes to our world, then I theorize the trace of their heavier frequencies would linger on the air like a footprint. A recording."

"And translated into the king's English, Howard?" Doyle asked.

Lovecraft smiled grimly. "It means we're not alone down here." He pointed at the blinking, changing formulae in the green mist surrounding the gauntlet. "I'm picking up five or six energy signatures within three hundred yards."

Doyle studied the symbols, unable to make heads or tails of them. "How do we know they're not vagrants or the police?" he asked.

"The way they're talking, Arthur. It's definitely not human."

At that moment, from somewhere deep in the bowels of the tunnel system, a tremulous squeal arose that chilled their collective hearts.

"The stairs!" Doyle shouted, already ahead of the others. Marie and Houdini followed, trailed by Lovecraft, who was still lugging his equipment.

"Can we track them, Howard?" Houdini shouted as he took the steps three at a time down toward the deeper platforms.

"I can try," Lovecraft stammered, attempting to free himself from the gauntlet as he ran. He stuffed it back into the suitcase and extracted another tool, this one resembling a battery-operated eggbeater with the handgrip of a pistol. It, too, seemed to be a hybrid of enhanced technology built about a primitive relic. As Lovecraft squeezed the trigger, the battery pack spit sparks and the eggbeater portion—fashioned of wooden tribal fetishes—began to turn and beads trapped inside the wood rattled together. "They're close," Lovecraft said.

As he ran, Doyle gripped the knob of his walking stick, pressed a hidden button, and freed a long blade from its sheath.

Houdini, the fastest of them by far, had taken the lead, when Lovecraft suddenly called, "Wait!"

The others stopped, and turned.

Lovecraft stood at an intersection and studied his instrument. When he pointed his device down the north tunnel, the fetishes slowed their turning considerably. When he pointed it down the south tunnel, they sped up. He looked up at the others. "This way."

"That thing can sense them?" Doyle asked, looking down the south passage.

"Yes, it can. They're demons."

"According to whom?"

Lovecraft held up the spinning fetishes. "According to the Mad Arab Abd al-Azrad. This is his demon rattle, discovered in the Nameless City. A design improved upon, with the benefits of technology, by Duvall and myself."

"Demons," Houdini groused. "I hate demons."

Doyle stepped aside and gestured to Lovecraft. "Lead the way."

Lovecraft set off in front, looking paler than usual. Steam rose off the instrument as Lovecraft and the Arcanum spread out onto the first-level train platform. The fetishes whirled and the beads inside rattled loudly. Sparks spit from the battery pack. Lovecraft held the instrument out at arm's length, then the entire contraption blew to pieces, raining wood and steel across the floor. And then there was silence.

Doyle looked at the smoking pieces of the demon rattle on the ground, and contemplated an evil purer than anything even imagined by the Mad Arab Abd al-Azrad, author of the *Necronomicon*.

Slowly, Lovecraft turned back to the others. "In there."

*   *   *

ABIGAIL EMERGED FROM one of the pedestrian corridors onto a platform some one hundred feet below street level. Still the storm winds moaned from the mouth of the tunnels, even this far down.

"Matthew?" she called, then looked back at the long corridor she'd just traversed. As if in answer, another flurry of squeals erupted from somewhere nearby, freezing her blood. "Matthew!" she called again, stepping closer to the edge of the platform. "Matt—?"

A hand burst from the darkness below and grabbed her ankle. Abigail screamed as a laughing Matthew rose from the pit.

"Why did you do that?" she cried, close to tears, picking herself up off the dirty stone floor. "I hate you!"

Matthew climbed out of his hiding place. "You're such a girl sometimes."

Abigail caught Matthew solidly on the jaw with her fist, knocking him down.

"Why'd you make those sounds?" Abigail demanded.

"What sounds? I came down here and waited." Matthew rubbed his jaw and stood up. "It was probably just the wind."

Suddenly, another squeal erupted from the pedestrian passageway across the tracks, and a strange, birdlike shadow spilled across the platform.

Matthew swallowed. "Jesus."

Abigail gripped the back of Matthew's jacket, but he shook her off. "Go," he whispered.

"No."

Matthew whirled around, more serious than she'd ever seen. "Go. Now!"

Abigail turned to run, but several robed bodies flowed into the passage in front of her. Their heads bobbed grotesquely as they squealed in unison and surged toward her. Abigail saw their ruby eyes and sticklike noses, and felt her legs weaken.

"Abby!" Matthew shouted, spinning her around.

Three more of the creatures appeared on the opposite platform. These carried blades. They waited, watching. Their breath wheezed, and their ruby eyes did not blink.

Matthew took Abigail's coat and pulled her toward the edge of the platform. "Get ready to jump."

"Why? What are they?" she demanded, close to a panic.

"I don't know," Matthew answered. "But I think they're the ones who killed Martha. We'll lose them on the tracks." He tried to sound confident, but failed.

The creatures behind them wailed, freeing shining hooks from their tattered sleeves.

"Now!" Matthew barked, swinging Abigail over the edge of the platform and dropping her onto the tracks.

She landed in a puddle, and rats scuttled away from her. Matthew landed beside her. "Move!"

It was like a nightmare. Abigail's legs felt rubbery, and she couldn't run fast enough. She glanced back and saw the creatures flow across the platforms and spill onto the tracks.

Matthew turned to face them, and Abigail clutched at his arm. "Matthew, no!"

Rotted scaffolding clung to the tunnel walls, forgotten pieces of an abandoned construction site. The floor on both sides of the tracks was littered with nails and wood.

"It'll give you time," he said, his voice rough with fear. He picked up a two-by-four from the dusty ground and swung it menacingly.

Abigail backed up a few steps. "Please, Matthew—"

"Don't look back. Just run and don't look back." Matthew cut the air with his makeshift club.

Tears streamed down Abigail's cheeks. "You can't. Please come with me!"

The creatures swayed and squealed, studying their prey.

"Go!" he roared. He snarled at the creatures, readjusting his grip on the wood.

Then, with fluid precision belied by their awkward gait, they struck together, hooks biting savagely into flesh.

Abigail screamed and charged.

Matthew twisted in agony, one sickle blade embedded in his chest, the other caught under his ribs. He gazed up at Abigail, his eyes pleading, his lips wet with blood. "I love you. Go!"

Abigail stood frozen as the creatures continued to attack Matthew. They ripped his jacket away as two more hooks rose in the air and fell wetly into his flesh. But when one of them swiveled in Abigail's direction, a jolt of fear shook her from her trance. She stumbled backwards as it raised a blade, slick with Matthew's blood, then she turned and fled.

She tried to run over the uneven surface of the tracks, but the creatures were fast. Three of them broke off from the others and sped after Abigail, their robes flowing behind them. They moved far too fast, slowly but surely cutting her off. She heard the rustling of robes to her right and left, and the burbling squeal of a creature rising up behind her. She drove her legs to their limit but the darkness only swallowed her deeper and deeper down its endless throat. There was a stench of decay on the air, a wafting charnel odor. She couldn't run anymore. They had her.

With a sob, Abigail stopped running. Her body shook beneath the heavy man's coat she wore. Her eyes were filled with tears as she gazed at the creatures. Their arms were overly long, and the sickles they carried scraped the ground. As one of them scuttled toward her, she lashed out reflexively with a cry. This prompted a round of tremulous squeals, sounding not unlike laughter. The creatures were playing with her, darting in and out of the circle of her reach, squealing gleefully as she beat her fists futilely at the air. But in the next moment, the play was done and the hooks rose together. The creatures howled, and then a blinding burst of fire and smoke threw them back.

Abigail's ears rang from the blast, and she felt warm, muscular arms enfold her. If this was death, she thought, then someone must have taken pity on her.

DOYLE CLUTCHED A torch in one hand, banishing the shadows. His sword was clenched in the other. When one of the demons raised its sickle, he fought it back with his sword, hacking its bony arm deeply above one elbow.

Bellows of confusion tore through the demon ranks.

Then Lovecraft emerged out of the darkness, hurling

makeshift torches in a semicircle about the demons. "This won't hold them long," he warned.

Away from the battle, Houdini set the bewildered Abigail down on the ground. His hand touched her cheek. "You're safe."

"Marie," Doyle shouted.

The voodoo queen's smile was strange and frightening. Her eyes shone. She began clicking her teeth together, uttering a high-pitched, piercing cry. In her clenched fists were small animal bones that she shook like dice, in time with her bizarre call.

More demons had gathered, spreading out to attack.

Marie continued toward them, still uttering her cry.

Lovecraft grabbed Doyle's arm. "For God's sake, what's she doing?"

Doyle was about to pull Marie back, when he sensed movement around them. "Fall back!" He shoved Lovecraft into the shadows and waved his sword at Houdini. "Fall back!"

"Why? What's happening?" Lovecraft demanded, his voice frantic.

"The walls," Doyle answered.

A veritable waterfall of rats was boiling forth from the walls. Writhing bodies wormed out of cracks and fell from the arched ceiling, their slick black fur gleaming in the torchlight. They squirmed free of holes in the ground and wriggled out from under the train tracks. The tunnel shook with the collective squeak and chitter as the rats surged forth, creating a vermin barrier between the Arcanum and the demon horde.

The demonic squeals of rage were lost in the tumult, but just before the torches were doused by the sheer volume of rats, Doyle saw the demons turn and retreat, their robes weighted down with dozens of small, clinging bodies.

29

WHEN THE RAIN finally abated, the city smelled fresh and the buildings shimmered. The sky slowly awakened in a palette of bruised blues.

After arranging for a Dodge sedan to pick them up, Houdini then sent an anonymous tip, through his assistant Franz Kukol, to the police at Fourth Ward, detailing the whereabouts of Matthew's body. Now their only hope was to return the woman they had rescued, who said her name was Abigail, to her guardians at the New York Rescue Mission before her shock transformed into a dangerous catatonia.

The ride was silent, and their mood grim. What they'd seen that evening confirmed many of their worst fears but provided few new answers.

Houdini was holding Abigail to his chest as she stared out the window. Her eyes were at half-mast, but she was neither awake nor asleep.

Doyle rested his head in his hands, still struggling to conceive of newer, better strategies, growing ever more conscious of the horrifying consequences should they fail to catch up with the killers.

Marie was sound asleep, utterly spent.

Lovecraft, Doyle noticed, seemed to find it difficult to take his eyes off Abigail, but his gaze wasn't probing like a scientist's. Instead, there was something open in Lovecraft's expression. His lips were slightly parted. Doyle wondered if he saw the same beauty in the oily blond ringlets hanging about Abigail's cheeks, and in her delicate features, puckered for now in a child's frown.

Then suddenly, Abigail's green eyes flew wide. She glared at Lovecraft, looking both feral and terrified. He dropped his gaze to his shoes, looking stricken—and didn't look up again until Abigail drifted back into semiconsciousness.

Though it was only half-past seven in the morning, Orchard Street was bustling with wagons filled with crates of lettuce, carrots, and potatoes. Wheelbarrows spilled over with raw chickens and eggs. Dodge trucks, open at the back, offered barrels of apples and fresh-squeezed cider. Shoppers swarmed, and goods were stuffed in brown bags amid the incessant din of market day. Laundry hung from fire escapes and windowsills, like flags of victory.

Kukol, who was driving, beeped the horn to clear a path. But the pedestrians, on principle, still refused to give ground to automobiles, so they crawled along at a snail's pace. And it wasn't only the market traffic that caused the delay. Bells clanged in the distance, and Kukol thrust his head out the window. There was a small cone of smoke rising above the roofs.

"Franz, what's the problem?" Houdini asked from the backseat.

"Fire," Kukol responded.

After the traumas of the evening, nothing so minor could stir them. Soon an artery gave way and traffic again flowed down Orchard Street, and through the Bowery, toward Chinatown. On Canal, Kukol found himself driving side by side with fire trucks heavy with unsmiling volunteers. The bells were now a constant clamor.

Doyle shifted uneasily in his seat.

"Franz, stop the car," Houdini ordered.

Kukol applied the brakes and Houdini detached Abigail's

arms from around his neck and leaped out onto the sidewalk. Doyle followed and said to Lovecraft, "Keep her here, you understand?"

Lovecraft nodded.

Doyle and Houdini ducked down an alley. Above them, a noxious cloud of billowing black smoke hovered over the buildings. They cut through a playground and stepped onto Doyers Street, where a crowd had gathered and a snarl of fire trucks blocked an intersection. Houdini and Doyle ducked between the trucks, onlookers, police, and volunteers, until they stood before their target.

The Chinese Theatre, home to the New York Rescue Society, was in flames, engulfed in a laughing, wind-frenzied inferno. The fire licked greedily at the sky, caught on sheets of gusting wind. Golds and oranges, yellows and reds shimmered as the flames roared up the walls and exploded out of windows.

"No," was all Doyle could muster.

Charred bodies, frozen in positions of agony, lined the sidewalks at the feet of the bucket-wielding firefighters. Police pushed back gawking neighbors. Doyers Street was choked to capacity with emergency vehicles. Panicked screams could still be heard inside the building despite the roar of the flames. The heat scalded skin fifty feet away, but still the firefighters continued pushing closer. It was hopeless, though. The Mission House was a hissing oven.

Doyle pulled at Houdini's sleeve. "Hurry. We can't let her see this."

Houdini nodded, and just then Doyle spotted a familiar face in the crowd. Detective Mullin was looking right at him, from some fifty feet away, his cheeks smeared with soot. His eyes narrowed to slits as he reached into his jacket for his pistol. "Hold!"

Doyle shoved Houdini through the crowd and into the maze of fire trucks and wagons.

Mullin used his elbows and gun to clear a path, spilling water buckets from the hands of the firefighters, and knocking gawkers onto the sidewalk.

Houdini and Doyle emerged onto the other side of Doyers

Street and waved for Kukol. "Start the car! Start it!" Houdini shouted.

Mullin burst through the crowd, just in time to see Doyle dive into the back of a speeding Dodge sedan.

JULIE KARCHER, THE Houdinis' personal assistant and Bess's lifelong friend, opened the door as Doyle charged through, carrying an unconscious Abigail. The Arcanum followed behind him.

Bess led them into a warm den on the first floor of their Harlem mansion. A fire crackled in the fireplace.

"Are you all right?" Bess asked.

Houdini kissed her on the forehead. "She's been through a trauma," he answered. "We'll rest here and move her tonight. It will be safer then anyway."

Julie Karcher bustled by them, knowing better than to ask too many questions. "There's soup on the stove, and I'll get some tea with lemon."

"And extra blankets, Julie. Use the ones on the third floor," Bess added.

"Right away."

Bess turned to her husband, her face stern. "Just what are you involved in?"

"It's Arthur's fault," Houdini answered.

"Are you in danger?"

"Of course not."

"You are a terrible liar." And Bess punched him lightly in the stomach.

Houdini sighed. "This is serious business, my darling."

"But why—"

Houdini shook his head. "I can't tell you that, love."

"Very well," Bess said solemnly, as Houdini went to join Doyle in the corridor.

"Everything all right?" Doyle asked him.

Houdini gazed back at his wife with undisguised adoration. "She'll look after the girl. She'll be safe here. Why don't you and the others take rooms upstairs? We'll sleep through the day, then get back to work."

"I fear we may have lost more today than we can even realize," Doyle said. "I know you put no stock in Lovecraft's theories . . ."

"I'm open to a great deal more than you give me credit for, Arthur." Houdini checked his pocket watch. "So, in eight hours we're back on the case. Where to then, Detective?"

"The morgue," was Doyle's grim reply.

30

THE STEEL SLAB erupted from the wall, exposing two bloated, purplish legs and a frosty bottle of milk between them. Ray Bozeman picked up the milk and poured some into his coffee. Then he returned the bottle to its place and studied the dead man's legs a moment. For no particular reason, Ray plucked a curled black hair from one of the frozen thighs. Then he took another deep sip of coffee and slammed the freezer door.

Ray's desk was covered with a mountain of paperwork. There were forms and more forms. It had been a busy night. The fire in Chatham Square had forced St. John's morgue to split duties with St. Luke's, all the way up on 116th Street. Twenty-five charred bodies in total, not to mention another victim of the Occult Killer found in the subway tunnels of the City Hall station.

Ray yawned and grabbed the first form off the pile. Simultaneously, a slender hand reached around from behind him and cupped a handkerchief over his mouth. Ray stiffened and struggled for all of three seconds before he slid off his chair and onto the floor.

*　*　*

MARIE STUFFED THE chloroform-soaked handkerchief into Ray Bozeman's shirt pocket, took his keys from his belt, and went to the back door of the morgue, where she opened the doors for the rest of the Arcanum.

ST. JOHN'S HOSPITAL on the Lower East Side was a dreary place, catering as it did to the neediest, sickest, and poorest segment of Manhattan's population. And it was ideally suited for the Arcanum's purposes this evening because it was also woefully understaffed, thus ensuring them privacy.

Doyle quickly found the freezers. In the center of the room, which was lit by hanging electric lightbulbs, were metal tables, thankfully empty. Beside the tables were buckets, and stands of operating equipment. The left side of the room held cabinets of cleansers, soaps, and chemicals, and two sinks side by side. To the far right was a large freezer whose engine banged noisily. The freezer had forty metal doors. On each, a clipboard dangled by a nail.

They fanned out across the morgue, checking the body descriptions on the clipboards.

Lovecraft wrinkled his nose. "They're all burned." He turned to the others. "You can smell it on the air."

"Stay focused," Doyle advised him, squinting to read the small writing on the clipboards.

"He's here," Marie said, backing away.

Doyle double-checked the file sheet. "All right. Stand back. This won't be pleasant." He pulled the handle, hard. The steel platform rolled out fast on its tracks and stopped with a clang.

Houdini shut his eyes and turned away, muttering, "Christ."

Marie crossed herself and backed up against the wall.

Lovecraft leaned in, fascinated. "What happened to his face?"

Doyle's experience as a field doctor in the Boer War aided him here. "Rats," he said.

"Ah," Lovecraft responded.

"Let's get him onto the table," Doyle said. He removed his suit jacket and unbuttoned his shirtsleeves.

Moments later, Doyle set his medical kit on the autopsy

table. He gazed at Matthew's butchered body. While most of his curly, blondish hair was still intact, the boy's face had been chewed away by rats, leaving a deep red, sinewy mask, punctuated by the white bones of his skull. The neck, too, had been gnawed to a gaping, stringy morass of flesh and shredded muscle. His chest was largely unmarred, but his abdomen was open, with his intestines piled sloppily on top. No doubt some clumsy medical technician had taken the organs off the ground and attempted to stuff them back into the body. Matthew's legs were also riddled with rat bites, though there was one large puncture wound on the right hip.

Doyle opened his satchel and brought out his magnifying glass. He scanned the body, searching for clues.

"Anything?" Lovecraft asked.

"This carnage speaks for itself," Doyle answered. He straightened and sighed with frustration. "Let's turn him over."

Reluctantly, Houdini took Matthew's cold feet as Doyle held the boy's shoulders. "One, two, three . . ."

They rolled him over.

"*Mon Dieu,*" Marie exclaimed.

"What in Heaven . . . ?" Doyle whispered.

Matthew's back was completely shredded. Skinned. Violently torn open between the shoulder blades. Doyle spoke aloud as he probed the injuries with a scalpel. "Trauma to the musculature of the upper ribs through the latissimus dorsi and the trapezius. The spine is missing from the fifth lumbar vertebra to the seventh cervical vertebra. What . . . what is this?" Doyle examined two nubs of thick muscle parallel to the shoulder blades. "Could be a torus, I suppose. Odd."

Houdini stepped forward. "What is it?"

Doyle passed his magnifying glass over the injuries. "Extraordinary thickness to the teres major and minor. Look, here, at the density of the infraspinatus. It's as if . . ."

". . . he's deformed," Lovecraft finished.

"How?" Houdini asked.

Doyle hesitated. "Without the spine, I can't say, exactly. A curvature, perhaps. The musculature compensated somehow—"

"You know that's not it at all," Lovecraft interrupted.

"Explain yourselves," Houdini demanded.

Doyle wiped the sweat off his brow. "Something congenital. A malformation—"

"Don't allow your logical mind to blur the truth, Arthur, difficult though it might be to absorb," Lovecraft scolded.

Doyle grew angry. "I'm a physician, and I understand anatomy. And this is not right." He searched for the words. "If I were to design a physiology that could . . . a musculature that would accommodate . . . ." He hesitated again.

"Flight," Lovecraft said firmly.

"Flight, very well, Howard, if you want to hear me say it. Yes. A musculature designed to accommodate flight." Doyle's shoulders sagged.

"So, you're . . . ?" Houdini looked at the body. "So, you're saying . . . ." He chuckled nervously. "What you're saying is this boy had *wings*? Is that what you're saying?"

"Not a boy," Lovecraft cautioned, "but a creature of the Mythos. Something that looks like us and has learned to behave as we do. But it is not us." Lovecraft turned to the others, a glint in his eyes. "Steel yourselves. For this is a revelation that our minds are ill equipped to endure."

"They're taking the wings," Doyle said with a tremor in his voice. He flashed back to his conversation with Archbishop Hayes and seized Lovecraft's arm. "That is the mechanism."

"What do you mean?" Lovecraft asked.

Doyle's voice was thick with emotion. "The cutting of the cord. The severing of the wings. The separation of the material and the spirit. God took his wings . . . ."

Lovecraft caught on. "And now the Devil wants them back."

Suddenly, Doyle wheeled around to the freezers and began pulling open the doors. Charred-black bodies rolled out into the air.

"Doyle, what are you doing?" Houdini ran over to pull him back, but Doyle shook him off and continued throwing open doors and yanking out the body trays. The stench of burned flesh permeated the room.

"Why didn't I see it?" Doyle muttered. "Examine them," he said louder. "All of them."

Twelve bodies in all were exposed. Houdini pinched his nose for the smell and bent over, feeling his stomach turn.

Marie and Lovecraft spread out across the room, turning the corpses over by their shriveled, petrified arms, gazing at their backs, searching for injuries.

Doyle's voice shook. "My God, what evil is this?"

"It's her. Arthur!" Lovecraft said.

Doyle ran over.

"It's her. What's-her-name." Lovecraft pointed.

Doyle gazed down at the mangled, charred corpse of a woman. Her skull and face were blackened from the fire, the hair burned away, her features melted into a gluey clump.

"Judith. Wasn't that her name?" Lovecraft asked.

Doyle could make out no distinguishing features. "How do we know it's her?"

"The brooch," Lovecraft answered. His finger pointed to the corpse's throat where Judith's porcelain butterfly brooch had seared into the flesh. "Now, look." Somewhat ungracefully, Lovecraft wrenched the body onto its side so Doyle could see a gaping hole where Judith's spine used to be.

"And her husband, too. Joe," Doyle said softly.

"Yes. And I'd wager many others at the uptown morgue," Lovecraft replied. "We've found the Lost Tribe of Enoch."

Doyle was unreachable. "What evil is this?" he whispered again.

31

LOVECRAFT SCRIBBLED NOTES in his journal while, around him, Houdini's brownstone thumped and creaked with activity. He shut his burning eyes briefly, but there was no time to sleep. If these were the End Days, Lovecraft was determined to see every minute through. And though his will was strong, his body faltered. He felt his heart flutter weakly against his bony chest. His hands shook, and his stomach burned.

They'd returned from the morgue hours before and postponed their trip to Crow's Head in order to tell Abigail the terrible news about the fate of the Rescue Society. Or rather, Doyle and Houdini had; Lovecraft had stood in the hallway and listened. He'd been impressed with their sensitivity. Lovecraft, himself, wouldn't have thought to shield Abigail from any of the gruesome details. Still, it would have been almost a relief if the girl had reacted—to anything. Instead, she took the news with an unnatural calm. The only words she spoke were: "I'll have a rest now."

That was hours ago. Lovecraft could hear Houdini and Doyle in the kitchen, debating the fate of the girl—weighing the pros and cons of dragging her into an adventure that might cost her her life. On the other hand, where to take her if not Crow's Head?

Lovecraft sat back in his chair and stretched, then winced at the freakish wallpaper in Houdini's guest bedroom. He assumed the room was reserved for the visits of small nieces and nephews, thus explaining the undersized furniture and disturbing circus motifs. But it did nothing to curb Lovecraft's distaste. The blankets, rugs, and walls were awash with cartwheeling midgets, unicycling monkeys, trumpet-playing elephants, and sinister ringmasters.

Lovecraft preferred a padded cell.

Then he heard voices outside his room. It was Houdini and Julie Karcher.

". . . Just wanted you to know, sir, she's taken the silverware."

"And put it where?" Houdini asked.

"In her coat pockets. I hear it clinking when she walks."

"Then let the poor waif keep it. We'll buy more silver."

"Yes, I figured, sir. But I just wanted you to know."

"Thank you, Julie."

Lovecraft turned back to his journal and accidentally tipped the inkwell with his elbow. A black puddle washed over the desk. "Blast it." He could not find a towel, and so he went to the second-floor hallway and crossed into the bathroom. It was double the size of Lovecraft's room. In fact, it was larger than his old apartment and was the only bathroom he'd ever seen with a full-sized sofa and set of chairs in it. There was also a claw-toed bathtub big enough for three. Lovecraft entered the walk-in closet, searched in vain for the light, then bumped into a shelf and was buried beneath an avalanche of several dozen towels. He resurfaced to hear the bathtub faucets squeak open and water patter into the tub. The closet door was nearly shut, but there was still a wide crack that let in light. Lovecraft inched his shoe out of the light and wormed his way into the back of the closet, unsure of what to do.

Voices came from the bathroom:

"Now, you just put your clothes on that chair, and I'll wash them up first thing. I put your towels and a robe on the sink, and some warm milk beside the tub." Julie Karcher sounded more nervous than usual.

Lovecraft could see shadows and movement through the crack in the door, but nothing more.

"Do you need anything else, my dear?"

There was no answer.

"Well, if you do, just holler, and I'll come running, okay? Just keep putting your finger in there to make sure it doesn't get too hot, now."

The bathroom door creaked shut. Lovecraft fought off a flash of panic. He thought of running, but instead just sat there, frozen. Through the crack in the door, he saw Abigail cross over to the tub.

Almost without conscious volition, he crawled across the fallen towels and pressed his face to the narrow seam of light along the door's hinges.

Abigail sat on the edge of the tub, still wearing her filthy coat. The ever-present top hat sat on the floor. Her hair was a tangle of greasy blond ringlets. She gazed into space as her hand stirred the water. Steam rose from the bath. She turned and stood up a little sleepily, then her hand went to her forehead and she faltered, falling to her hands and knees.

Lovecraft almost sprang up to help her, but then held back when he realized she was crying. She was collapsed on the floor, her eyes open and unblinking, letting tears stream unheeded off her nose and lips and face. Lovecraft shifted in indecision, but gradually she rose to a sitting position and stood again. She locked the bathroom door and set a chair under the knob. Then her coat fell to the floor.

Abigail wore a long sweater, which hung to her knees, and scruffy, dark red boots. She brushed the tears off her cheeks absently and pulled the sweater over her head, getting her arms briefly tangled.

Lovecraft's neck grew hot, and he was certain Abigail could hear his heart pounding. He tried to breathe as shallowly as possible.

Under the sweater was a dirty man's dress shirt, which was

missing both the collar and cuffs, and the bottoms of a man's long underwear.

She untied her boots and kicked them off, rubbing her toes through socks that might once have been green but were now dingy and filled with holes.

Abigail then pulled the long underwear down around her ankles and stepped out of them. She still wore a slip that hung down about to mid-calf. Her dirty fingers undid the buttons of the shirt and it, too, dropped onto the pile.

She was now wearing just a slip and a strange corset as she went to the tub and turned off the faucets. She had become little more than a phantom in the steam, which now filled the bathroom.

Lovecraft perspired, and the silence roared in his ears. He squinted to see her through the steam. She would sharpen into view, then fade into a shadow again as she crossed from the closet to the sink.

But even the steam couldn't hide the gleam of scissors in Abigail's hand and, for a terrible moment, Lovecraft thought she would turn them on herself. But instead she just flipped the strings of her slip from her shoulders and allowed it to slide to the floor.

Lovecraft bit his lip. Abigail was now naked from the waist down, and it was the first time in Lovecraft's life he'd ever been in the same room with a nude woman. He wasn't sure if he could handle the cumulative effects. Sensations flooded his mind, and he could not swallow.

But what distracted him most was the way Abigail attacked the corset with the scissors, pulling off bits that seemed to have been pinned on. In fact, it seemed to be less a corset than a collection of bandages, which gradually unraveled under Abigail's attacks.

This activity pushed Abigail farther from the closet and into the mist. Lovecraft could not see what was happening. Then something upset the water and Lovecraft could barely make out the form of Abigail through tufts of dispersing white steam, bending over in the tub, now pouring hand-cups of water over her bare arms and her small, white breasts. She knelt and slowly eased herself into the hot water. There was a curious *whump, whump* sound, like wet canvas shifting, then Abigail stretched out her arms as two dark shapes unfolded behind her.

Lovecraft's eyes widened and he gasped.

There was a splash of water, and Lovecraft kicked his way into the back of the closet as the door flew open.

ON THE FOURTH floor, Houdini was just tying the rope of his bathrobe when an earsplitting scream shot through the house. He ran out into the hall.

Doyle was already out there, clad only in an undershirt, suspenders, and slacks, his glasses still perched on the bridge of his nose as he peered about in confusion.

Bess was not far behind them.

"Where is she?" Houdini demanded.

"Second floor," Bess answered. "Julie, come quickly!"

Julie and Marie were waiting on the third floor in their robes, and quickly joined them.

"I made a bath for her, I can't imagine—"

Julie was interrupted by a crash and a slamming door.

Houdini and Doyle reached the landing of the second floor simultaneously. Lovecraft stood stiffly against the wall next to the bathroom, pale as a sheet.

Houdini could read his stricken expression. "What happened?" he barked.

"She ran that way," Lovecraft answered, pointing.

"Your shirt is soaked through, Howard," Doyle said. "And your glasses are fogged. What were you doing in there?"

Houdini pushed Lovecraft against the wall. "Were you spying?"

"This isn't my fault," Lovecraft stammered.

Houdini couldn't find words in his fury. He only thrust a warning finger under Lovecraft's nose before racing down the hall.

Doyle followed.

Houdini skidded to a stop at the door to the servants' stairwell. "This goes down to the kitchen, but it's locked at the bottom."

Doyle opened the door and gazed into the blackness of a spiral staircase. "Abigail?"

There was silence. Then they heard shuffling at the bottom, and a desperate scratching at wood.

"Abigail, what happened?" Houdini asked gently.

When no answer was forthcoming, Houdini started down. Doyle padded behind him, followed by Marie, holding a candle.

More furious scrabbling came from below.

Houdini peered around the corner.

"Don't come near me!" Abigail shrieked.

Her voice was high and panicked, her breathing labored, like an animal's. There was more scratching at the bottom of the stairs, a symptom of Abigail's frantic efforts to open the door.

"My dear girl, what happened?" Houdini continued.

Abigail sobbed deeply.

Houdini stepped closer. He could make out Abigail's outline, huddled in a tight ball at the bottom of the stairs. "It's all right—"

"Don't! Stay away from me. All of you," she cried.

Houdini knew something was wrong by the way Abigail moved, the way her body lifted with her breathing. In the darkness it was difficult to discern, but a prickly feeling crept up his back. The hairs on his arms stood up, and the floorboards creaked under his weight as he inched closer.

Abigail was wrapped tightly in something both thick and soft, which covered her body. Her sobs echoed painfully in the darkness.

Behind Houdini, Doyle drew a breath and said, "Marie, give me your candle." And as Marie complied, he added, "Prepare yourselves."

Abigail squirmed into a tighter ball.

Another stair groaned as Doyle passed Houdini and he crouched down beside Abigail, lowering the candle.

In the glow of the candlelight, Abigail's tearstained face rose up from between two enormous wings of silk-white feathers.

They twitched nervously even as they enfolded naked Abigail like a vast blanket. Her wet eyes pleaded for understanding, acceptance, forgiveness. No words were, or could be, spoken.

In that musty corner on the bottom floor of Houdini's Harlem brownstone in New York City, the barriers between realities shattered.

32

THE MORNING AFTER dawned crisp and clear, the sky brilliant with that rare blue clarity so unique to October in Manhattan.

A perfect day on its surface, except that Lovecraft was missing. Marie and Doyle searched both the brownstone and the surrounding streets, but the demonologist was nowhere to be found. Whether a permanent leave-taking or merely a temporary absence driven by his own embarrassment and shame, no one could surmise. Lovecraft was dependably unpredictable. But significant though it was, it came second on Doyle's list of concerns.

Abigail had spent most of the night huddled at the bottom of the stairs, shivering. Deciding a woman's touch was needed, Houdini and Doyle had left her in Julie and Bess's care. They exerted all their charms to lure her out, offering bribes of baked breads, fresh chicken soups, warm teas, and bricks of fudge. But it soon became apparent that the way to Abigail was not through her stomach.

Ultimately, it was Marie who succeeded where the others failed. The priestess sat on the second step of the stairwell with a pot of herbal tea and a candle, and told Abigail stories of her childhood. One, in particular, had the desired effect:

THE COOL POND *water ripples away from her naked legs. With a soft splash she submerges, eyes open, staring into the watery green darkness. Marie is thirteen years old. Her limbs are long, but still awkward and bony as childhood flirts with adolescence. She twirls up to the surface, face to the sun, eyes closed. She is safe here. This is her mother's swamp. Even the snakes fear the Voodoo Queen of New Orleans.*

The young Marie takes hold of the smooth branch of a live oak bent over the waters like an old woman's finger, and pulls herself up. She lays her naked body on the curve of the branch, and lets the sun roast her skin.

The birds are quiet.

The swamp is quiet.

Marie opens her eyes and turns to see a silver fox watching her from the shore of the pond. It pants but does not drink.

The fox follows Marie as she walks home, barefoot, through the swamp. She is shirtless, skirt tied low about her boyish hips.

"Go home," she tells the fox.

It hunkers down and lays its snout to the dirt submissively.

Marie approaches the fox, kneels down, and reaches out to stroke its silver fur. The fox allows this, worming closer to nuzzle at Marie's toes.

Marie wants the fox as a familiar. This must be a sign from the spirits. Her mother has many familiars: a snapping turtle, three tabby cats, and a flightless crow. And now that Marie is of child-bearing age, she, too, should follow in her mother's footsteps.

Her mother pays the fox no heed when Marie comes home with it curled about her bare shoulders like a stole.

"Clean a chicken for supper," is all she says.

Marie's feelings are hurt. She is a voodoo priestess and deserves respect.

The silver fox waits outside the chicken coop, ears pricked. Marie emerges with a tawny hen held by the neck. She takes the butcher knife from its nail on the coop wall, holds the hen against a stump with her hand and foot, and takes the head off with a clean chop. The fox watches, nose twitching.

"What you got there, girl?" Marie's uncle Toto has a sleepy eye and a slow mind. There's a machete in his fist, and sweat on his muscular chest. "Ain't that a pretty fox."

Marie avoids the leer of Toto's good eye and continues ripping feathers free. "You act like you never seen one," she answers.

The fox lies between Marie's feet, head on paws, watching Toto with bright green eyes.

"Prettiest I ever seen," Toto says again, his eyes on Marie.

That night, the Voodoo Queen does not allow her daughter to sleep with the silver fox.

"If he your familiar, he be back in the mornin'," she tells her daughter.

Marie is inconsolable. Tears wet her pillow. There is an inexplicable pain in her heart at being separated from the fox.

The fox sits on the porch, panting, as the Voodoo Queen shuts the front door in its face. The fox turns and pads down the porch stairs onto the lawn. It skirts under the moonlight and trots two miles into the forest, over a worn dirt path to a dimly lit cabin, deep in the swamp. The fox scratches at the door with a front paw.

Uncle Toto finally answers. "What you doin' here?"

The silver fox looks up at Toto with bright green eyes.

Toto stiffens. "How you do that?"

The fox tilts its head.

Toto hisses, "How you talkin' like that?"

MARIE'S HEAD LIFTS off her pillow. "Mama?" There is a curious scent of mint in the air. The curtains flutter in the hot wind. Marie turns on her back and kicks off the sheets to cool her skin.

Then she smells the reek of bourbon.

A hand slaps over her mouth. Her scream dies in her throat as Toto looms over her. His one good eye burns red.

"Ain't that a pretty fox?" he slurs. His other hand paws at her kicking legs. Marie scratches at him as he climbs onto the bed, smothering her under his weight. Toto fumbles at his drawstring pants.

Marie squeezes her eyes shut, wishing herself elsewhere. The bourbon fumes sting her nose. She can't breathe.

Then Uncle Toto screams. His weight lifts away, and Marie opens her eyes in time to see him burst into flames, his arms swinging like burning timbers. Marie looks about her bed and sees a crystalline dust scattered there: angelica root. That explains the smell of mint.

The Voodoo Queen herself stands in the doorway. She holds the silver fox by the scruff of its neck and it howls with a dozen voices—some laughing, some screaming, some weeping. It is unlike any sound Marie has ever heard, and one she'll never forget.

The fires catch on the fluttering curtains as Uncle Toto topples out the window and runs into the night, skin still burning.

The Voodoo Queen takes the fox's snout in her fist and hisses in his ear. "Your fight's wit' me, Devil. Leave my daughter alone." Then with a quick jerk, she cuts the fox's throat with a knife. It howls again in that terrible voice and breaks free of the Voodoo Queen's arms, scampering down the hall and out of the house.

Marie Laveau lunges into her mother's arms, sobbing.

MARIE UNFURLED A blanket and held it out with both hands. "You see, child? We can't always know what's best for us. We got to trust sometimes, even though it's hard."

After a long pause, a small voice rose up from the bottom of the stairwell. "Did you ever see the fox again?"

"That weren't no fox, Abigail, that was de Devil, hisself. An' that's his pleasure, that's his power. To corrupt, see?"

The steps creaked softly, and Abigail emerged from the darkness like a child of myth, her skin like porcelain, and her wings tucked tightly against her back. She crept into both Marie's embrace and the blanket, holding back tears.

"There, there, sweet miracle. It's all right. Ssh. Everythin's all right."

"WE ARE THE Arcanum." Doyle sat in the parlor on a walnut-backed chair, with Houdini standing beside him.

Abigail sat on the matching love seat, cupping a bowl of tea. Until her clothes were washed, she wore one of Bess's plush white bathrobes. Marie sat with her, a reassuring hand on her leg.

"You might call us Investigators of the Extraordinary," Doyle continued. "The four of us were brought together by a mystic we knew as Konstantin Duvall, a man of many secrets. His charge and our mission was the same: to act as both explorers and defenders of the unknown. For as Hamlet said: 'There are more things in heaven and earth, Horatio, than are dreamt of in your philosophy.' And you, Abigail, are living proof of that. More than anyone, Duvall knew that in such cases as these, there needed to be a secret society, with talents uniquely suited to the task, to ensure that these secrets did not fall into the wrong hands. In short, Abigail: You are our responsibility."

"You're wrong, old man. I'm not special." Abigail's voice was flat. "I'm a freak. Like those babies born with no arms, or two heads. That's why my parents gave me up."

"Is that what Judith told you?"

"She didn't have to. Anyway, it doesn't matter. I can take care of myself."

"I see. And how long did you live with Judith?"

"Forever, it seems."

Doyle paused, then said, "How old are you?"

Abigail shrugged.

"How long have you lived in New York?"

"Not long."

"And where were you before that?"

"Budapest."

"And before that?" Doyle continued.

"Nanking."

Houdini took over. "And which was your favorite?"

"None of them," Abigail said, dismissively. "Though, I liked the Buddhist caves of Mandalay."

LATER, WHEN ABIGAIL was sleeping, Doyle, Houdini, and Marie conferred in the first-floor hallway.

"Well traveled for a teenage orphan," Houdini said.

"Indeed. Not many can recommend the Hanging Gardens of Babylon as a pleasant spot to picnic."

"She thinks she's human," Marie said.

"That seems to be the case," Doyle agreed. "Somehow, across the oceans of time, Abigail's lost her origins."

"Perhaps Judith didn't want her knowin'. Didn't want her feelin' diff'rent," Marie said.

"Either way, it presents us with a unique dilemma. Considering what she's already been through, I'm hardly inclined to burden her further. And yet if she doesn't understand the role she plays in all of this, she'll have no reason to stay under our watch."

"She's a flight risk," Houdini agreed.

Doyle and Marie gave him a weary look.

Houdini smiled. "You know what I mean."

"You're right, though. For the moment she seems to trust us—and you in particular, Marie—but that could change at any moment. We need to keep a close eye on young Abigail."

"Now, I have only one question," Houdini said, "Where in the blue hell is Lovecraft?"

CROWLEY OPENED THE door to his Greenwich Village studio wearing only a loosely tied blue kimono. His face and hairless chest were damp with sweat. "Dear me, someone's left their babe at my door."

Lovecraft gazed at him from under the brim of his fedora. "If I can get the Book, you'll have it. Provided you help me stop them."

Crowley pursed his lips to keep from smiling. "Poor Howard." He opened his door wider and slung an arm over the demonologist's shoulder as he entered. "It can't be all that bad, can it?"

The poorly ventilated studio smelled sour, as though meat was rotting in a corner, yet it was also sweet with vanilla incense. Just like Crowley himself, with his repellent attraction.

"You timed your visit perfectly. I just finished my yoga practice and was boiling some water for tea."

Lovecraft looked around, seeing first a tall, black marble

carving of Baphomet—a demon with a bull's head, a female torso, and a goat's legs. It was a rendering made famous by Eliphas Levi. The exposed brick walls were partially covered with Crowley's watercolors: renderings of hallucinatory worlds and deformed self-portraits.

Crowley folded his meditation blankets and dropped them in the corner, beside a ceremonial plate used for conjuration. Headless mannequins wore the magical vestments of Crowley's numerous mystical associations, and beneath the studio's only window was an East Indian circular table—an altar—on top of which were all the accoutrements of a practicing sorcerer: the serpent crown, wand, sword, simple cup, and holy oil, as well as Crowley's own Book of Spells.

"You're wearing your heart on your sleeve, boy," Crowley warned as he plucked two dirty cups from the basin. "Lucky for you, this week I'm vegetarian." And he smiled.

Lovecraft was forced to stand because there wasn't a chair. He turned his hat in his hands. "No more riddles. I want straight answers."

"Is there any such thing?" Crowley answered.

"Who is he? Who is Darian?" Lovecraft demanded.

"He is a gifted young man who is drowning in deep waters."

"And how do you know this? Was he a student of yours?" Lovecraft pressed.

"Not only of mine," Crowley said smugly as he poured boiling water into the strainer, "but of Duvall's as well."

Lovecraft was horrified. "Duvall?"

"Darian was a prodigy. I haven't seen his like since your promising early years, before you chose the safe road."

Lovecraft winced.

"And it wasn't simply his scholarship and ambition that impressed me. He was also a telepath of rare ability. That combination heralds the arrival of a true magus. Naturally, he came to me once he tired of Duvall and his controlling ways."

"And?" Lovecraft took a small step forward.

"At first he showed promise. But in the end he was unwilling to shake loose the chains of his upbringing, and I tired of him." Crowley offered Lovecraft a cup of tea.

He took it. "I don't understand."

"Of course you don't," Crowley sneered. "The boy's full name is Darian Winthrop DeMarcus."

Lovecraft's voice lowered to a whisper. "The son of Thorton DeMarcus, the steel magnate?"

"You know him, do you?"

"Only from the archives. The DeMarcus family has one of the oldest and most feared Satanist bloodlines in the world," Lovecraft stammered. "But that was before I was . . ." His voice trailed off.

"Invited into the Arcanum?" Crowley finished. But was that a hint of envy or contempt in the sorcerer's voice?

"Yes. Thorton DeMarcus was one of their most feared adversaries."

"Present company excepting, I pray." And Crowley blew on his tea.

"He was behind those murders in Arkham, the witch cult."

"And the Boston exorcism, and the summoning of the Jinn. And, lest we forget, the scroll of Nyarlathotep," Crowley said, easily listing three of the Arcanum's most infamous investigations.

"Duvall killed him, didn't he?"

Crowley smiled.

"But Darian still came to him to study?"

"He kept his family name a secret; it's what I admired about the boy. So young, yet so calculating. He broke into Duvall's inner sanctum and used the old dog's vanity against him until he sucked him clean of secrets."

"Then you were deceived as well."

"Perhaps." Crowley sipped his tea. "Or perhaps the enemy of my enemy is my friend."

Lovecraft threw his tea to the floor, shattering the cup. He swung around and yanked a ceremonial dagger from a sheath nailed to the wall and turned it on Crowley. "Don't think I won't!"

Crowley's eyes widened, then he laughed. "So. There's fire in the boy yet."

"You set him on the path. You're one of the preeminent scholars on Enochian magic in the world. How else would Darian
know it was there in the Hall of Relics?"

"Nothing would give me greater satisfaction than being responsible for Duvall's death, but the boy beat me to it. His
agenda was clear from the start. He would acquire the Book of
Enoch from Duvall, and the means of using it from Aleister
Crowley." Crowley gazed off into space for a moment. "He really
is a creature after my own heart."

Lovecraft frowned. "So that's what this is? Revenge?"

"Don't you listen, you pup?" Despite the knife in Lovecraft's
hand, Crowley circled around the kitchen counter and backed
him into the wall by the sheer force of his presence. "Detach!
Use your intellect, not this . . ." he jabbed a sharp nail at Lovecraft's chest ". . . useless organ." In a swift move Crowley
snatched the dagger from Lovecraft's hand and pressed it to his
throat. "Revenge was an afterthought. This boy has ambition.
He's a purer strain than his father."

Lovecraft stood paralyzed under the press of both the steel
and Crowley's regard.

The sorcerer breathed hotly on his face. "He serves one master and one only: the true Lord of Darkness. He seeks to bring
about the end of the world, and possesses the means and the
will to do so." Crowley shoved off Lovecraft and crossed the
room. "You've become just like that oaf Doyle: despicably soft."

Lovecraft rubbed his throat. "I don't seek your approval,
Aleister, and I don't want it. This is a simple transaction: the
Book for Darian."

"And why are you so hot to bargain? Getting close, is he?
Some boys and girls getting the ol' chop-chop? How many are
left, eh? Go on, you can tell me. Tell Uncle Aleister how many
little birds are left."

"You can go to Hell," Lovecraft growled.

Crowley laughed. "You're dancing to his tune and you don't
even realize it. He's lured you right into his trap."

"How? There's no . . ." Lovecraft trailed off, blinking. "The
party. The invitation."

Crowley picked his nails with the knife blade.

"But that was Madame Rose. She was the . . ." Again Love-craft hesitated, remembering Crowley's earlier words. " 'A Rose by any other name' . . ."

"Dear Thorton didn't only father a son," Crowley said.

"She's his sister," Lovecraft deduced.

"Madame Rose is really Erica DeMarcus. And her gala Halloween celebration will be hosted at the DeMarcus family estate. So, you'll be walking into the mouth of the lion. He'll be waiting, and so will his forces."

"How do we stop him?"

"By giving him what he wants."

"But that's—"

"That's all the answer you need," Crowley spat. "Now leave."

Lovecraft started to go, then hesitated. "You ask for no assurances about the Book?"

Crowley turned his heavy-lidded gaze on the demonologist. "You've given me your word as a gentleman; that will suffice. I have ways of dealing with those who betray me." Then with a dismissive wave, he turned his back on Lovecraft.

Lovecraft opened the door and stepped into the hallway.

"Howard . . ." Crowley called after him.

Lovecraft turned.

Crowley stood facing his window at the opposite end of the studio. "There's yet another player in this game."

Lovecraft stepped toward the apartment, a question on his lips, but the door suddenly creaked on its hinges and, under its own power, slammed shut in his face.

33

"WHERE THE BLAZES were you?" Houdini demanded as Lovecraft entered the Harlem brownstone.

"At the library, doing research," he mumbled as he crossed into the parlor to warm his hands by the fire.

Doyle and Marie joined him there, with Houdini following.

"And?" Houdini insisted.

Lovecraft sighed. "Close the door."

Marie shut the French doors dividing the parlor from the first-floor hallway.

"You have a great deal of explaining to do, Howard," Doyle scolded.

"What the hell were you spying on Abigail for, you little pervert?" Houdini demanded.

"I wasn't—"

"You were in the closet."

"It was a mistake. I spilled the ink . . ." Lovecraft looked at their faces and saw only scorn. "Think what you want, then," he snapped. "It doesn't matter what I say, does it?" Lovecraft glared at Doyle. "Does it?"

"That's not what we're—"

"Yes, I'm convenient, aren't I? Useful in a pinch but never accepted. Never trusted."

Houdini waved him off. "Please."

"Where would you be without perverted, scheming, little Lovecraft, I wonder?" Lovecraft's eyes were dark and cruel.

"Your value to the Arcanum has never been questioned," Doyle said.

Lovecraft laughed dryly. "The Arcanum. That name has always meant more to you, Arthur, than it did to me. Duvall had knowledge I sought, that's all. Now that he's dead, I see little to keep me here."

Houdini swung around. "We won't be victims of your childish snits," he growled. He turned to Doyle. "Send him away, and the sooner the better."

But Doyle kept his gaze locked on Lovecraft. "We all miss Duvall—and none of us more than you, I'm certain."

Lovecraft turned, hiding his reaction.

"But this is the course he set for us," Doyle continued. "It was his dying wish. We honor him by putting past differences aside and uniting on this final quest. And I think I speak for all of us when I say the Arcanum would cease to exist without H. P. Lovecraft."

"It's true, Howard," Marie agreed.

Lovecraft rubbed his eyes, though he did not turn to face them. Then, still speaking to the window, he said, "Darian is Darian Winthrop DeMarcus, the only son of Thorton DeMarcus."

Houdini turned ashen. "DeMarcus?"

"How do you know?" Doyle demanded.

Lovecraft ignored him. "Madame Rose is his sister, Erica. The party is to be held at the DeMarcus Manor." Lovecraft stepped away from the window, turned, and slumped in one of the chairs by the fire. "They say there's an old system of tunnels beneath the house, connecting it to the local cemetery. Legend has it there's a church in those tunnels, a Satanic church where Thorton performed his Black Mass."

"So, the son avenges the father," Doyle mused.

"More than that," Houdini said. "He wants to finish what the father couldn't. We can't go to this party."

"Oh, yes, we will," Doyle countered. "In fact, Abigail's coming, too."

Lovecraft looked over at him.

Marie took Doyle's arm. "*C'est fou* to bring her, Art'ur."

"Precisely. One hopes it will be the last thing he expects. We'll lure him as he attempts to lure us. Force a misstep. Drag him kicking and screaming into the light."

"And then?" Lovecraft asked.

"And then . . ." Doyle's voice dropped ". . . we avenge Duvall, and destroy the DeMarcus bloodline once and for all."

HOUDINI'S SILVER GHOST Rolls-Royce rolled along a narrow road, lined with towering birch trees, their limbs knobbed and hooked overhead like dragon claws. The car's headlights barely cut through the darkness, giving the impression they were submariners in a deep ocean trench.

Inside the car, Lovecraft sat in the driver's seat, wearing a chauffeur's uniform, with a bushy moustache glued to his upper lip. His eyes kept darting to the rearview mirror, watching as Abigail sat stiffly beside Houdini in her Little Red Riding Hood costume.

"Eyes on the road, Howard," Doyle cautioned from the seat beside him.

Lovecraft glanced at Doyle, who was clad in a deerstalker cap and English cloak. The costume was topped off by a long, curving pipe clenched between the author's teeth.

"Subtle," Lovecraft offered.

"Anything but, and that's precisely the point," Doyle countered.

Through a clearing in the trees, Lovecraft spied a sprawling graveyard in the bowl of the valley. Thousands of headstones dotted the terrain like broken teeth, a withered field of desolation stretching to the gnarled trees of the distant woods.

"The Willow Grove Cemetery," Lovecraft said.

All eyes traveled from the graveyard at the bottom of the valley, up to the peak of the promontory where the DeMarcus Manor sat: a forty-room Tudor glowing with candlelight.

"I don't want to wear this cape," Abigail complained from the backseat. "It itches."

Doyle turned to address her. "Should anyone ask, what do you say?"

"I'm your niece from California," Abigail recited absently.

"Very good. And what are you never to do at any point this evening?"

"Leave your side," Abigail answered, sounding annoyed.

"That's correct. That's supremely important. Our objective here is to lure our enemies to us. And it's you they want, Abigail. Do you understand?"

"I'm not deaf," Abigail snapped.

"Be respectful, Abigail," Houdini chided.

"I don't have to listen to you; you're not my parents. I don't care how famous you think you are." And Abigail folded her arms.

Doyle shared a look with Houdini.

"Howard, are you up for this?" Houdini asked.

Lovecraft drove on in silence for a moment before answering. "Without the Book, Darian's powers are greatly diminished. If it's in that house, I'll find it."

Doyle freed a pocket watch from the inside of his cloak. "Regardless of our progress, we'll rendezvous at the main gates at ten-thirty."

Lovecraft checked his own pocket watch. "Ten-thirty; fine."

In the backseat, Houdini was gazing at Abigail. It was clear to all of them that just beneath her bluster lay a profound fear. Lovecraft knew how she felt. Who had ever been able to protect her? And why, at this hour, did she have any reason to trust the Arcanum?

He didn't know how to help her—though it seemed Houdini did. Suddenly, the magician freed a pink handkerchief from his breast pocket and sneezed theatrically, startling everyone in the car. Abigail turned to him, alarmed. Houdini crumpled the handkerchief in his fist, then handed it to Abigail.

"Hold this for me, won't you?" Houdini said, and placed it in her hand.

Abigail stared at it. "That's disgusting."

"It is not," Houdini said, hurt. "Open it up."

Brow furrowed, Abigail unfolded the pink handkerchief, revealing a tiny canary. Abigail's gasp of pleasure was genuine, and brought a smile to everyone's lips.

The canary tweeted and shivered.

"He's cold," Abigail said.

"It's a she, I think. Warm her with your hands." Houdini demonstrated, and Abigail cradled her hands protectively over the bird. Doyle looked back and Houdini gave him a wink.

"What shall you name her?" Doyle asked.

Abigail stroked the canary wings with her thumb. "Isabella," she said, with sudden certainty.

"Bravo," Doyle said, then turned back to face the road.

Abigail turned to Houdini. The words were on her lips but she had trouble speaking them. Houdini patted her knee and nodded. "I know; it's all right."

Abigail smiled and turned her attention back to Isabella.

"There's something you should know, gentlemen," Lovecraft stated, after some deliberation. "Darian's a telepath."

"And what am I to do with that information?" Houdini snapped.

"Just make sure your thoughts are your own," Lovecraft cautioned.

" 'He's in my mind,' " Doyle muttered under his breath before turning back to Houdini. "Duvall's last words."

Houdini frowned. "Well, thanks for the tip, Howard," he offered sarcastically.

Lovecraft tapped on the brakes as they reached the wrought-iron gateway to the DeMarcus mansion. The car idled as they surveyed the murky forest and the menacing gargoyles perched atop the spears of a high gate.

"From this point forward, be on your guard," Doyle counseled.

The Silver Ghost rolled up the drive. But the house was not the vampiric fortress any of them were expecting. The tuxedoed parking attendants and the tall torches lining the gravel road destroyed that illusion. In fact, the only off-kilter aspect was the structure's unsettling geometry. The house spilled out over the grounds as though an architect had run amok. Many incongruent additions had been applied over the Manor's three-hundred-year history, slowly bleeding grandeur away into chaos.

Expensive cars lined the wide circular drive, gleaming in silvers and blacks. It looked to be a well-attended event.

Parking attendants wearing devil masks opened the doors of the Rolls-Royce. Doyle, Houdini, and Abigail stepped into the cool night air.

Houdini handed a coin to one of the attendants. "My man will park the car."

"Yes, sir, Mr. Houdini," the attendant answered, clearly marveling at both the man and his automobile.

With a wary look, Lovecraft pulled away and drove to the farthest, most shadowed portion of the driveway, nearest to the sprawling lawns of the estate. He exited the car and circled around to the trunk to open it. With a sigh of relief, Marie emerged and crouched down behind the car. She handed Lovecraft his leather briefcase, and once they were certain no one was watching, they struck out across the grounds, toward a sheltering of trees.

A BUTLER WITH the eyes of a lizard, dressed as a Musketeer, complete with a curling wig, held the door open for Doyle, Houdini, and Abigail. Immediately they became entangled in fake cobwebs hung for effect. Thousands of candles flickered, as a string quartet played haunting melodies. Hundreds of costumed guests flowed through half a dozen rooms.

"Gentlemen!" Madame Rose breezed through the dining room. She was wearing a stunning strapless black dress, her raven hair spilling over her white shoulders. Her eyes shone brightly behind a black butterfly mask. "How thrilling to have such distinguished guests." Her smile flashed, and she shook their hands. There was an intensity to her, a coiled tension that set Doyle on his guard.

"Well, we were thrilled to be invited," Houdini said, carefully not mentioning the events that had brought them together.

Madame Rose pretended not to understand, and instead turned her attention to Doyle. "Is this a first, or do you do this every Halloween?"

He tipped his deerstalker cap. "Ah, you've missed the sly shading, Madame Rose. The costume of Sherlock Holmes, but . . ." Doyle opened his top coat and patted his belly ". . . sadly, Watson's body."

Madame Rose laughed—too loudly. Then she whirled on Houdini.

"And you. Where is your costume?"

Houdini held up his arms, revealing handcuffs, one set dangling from each wrist. "Why, Madame Rose, this evening I am none other than the Great Houdini."

"Of course. How silly of me not to notice."

Then, with certain predatory interest, she turned to Abigail, who shrank back behind Doyle and protected her canary with cupped hands.

"And who is this darling thing?"

"I'm his niece," Abigail answered from behind Doyle's coat sleeve.

"Cousins of my wife's in Los Angeles, of all places, sent her to keep an eye on me," Doyle explained with a wink. "Her name is Abigail."

"And look at this wickedly adorable ensemble. Little Red Riding Hood, isn't it? Oh, and you even have a picnic basket for Grandma. Perhaps we can find some cookies for you later, my sweet."

Madame Rose's manner seemed unnaturally forced. The shade of her skin, the fierceness of her gaze, the lines in her forehead all suggested a woman under enormous strain.

With the pleasantries over, Madame Rose vanished back into the crowd, saying, "Walter will take your coats. Do enjoy. And thank you so much for coming."

Meanwhile, the presence of celebrities had drawn more party-goers into the foyer. Doors opened from the kitchen and guests wandered in from the large, chalet-style living room. Being New Yorkers, however, no one pretended to recognize Houdini or Doyle. Proximity was the key.

Doyle clasped Abigail's hand, despite her resistance, and the three of them made their way into the living room, which was cleared of furniture, replaced with groaning tables of food. There were steaming bowls of cider, pumpkin pie, dripping caramel, buckets for apple bobbing, and freshly baked cakes brought in from Ferrara's in Brooklyn.

A waiter in a disturbing white mask that gave his face a look of solemn coldness brought a tray of martinis to the men, and a cider for Abigail.

"Compliments of the hostess," he said.

The olives, Doyle noted, had been painted in the likeness of jack-o'-lanterns.

"I must have truly arrived," bellowed Barnabus Tyson, looking oily in his Teddy Roosevelt costume. "Two sightings in one week."

"How lucky can we be?" Houdini asked Doyle as Tyson clasped their hands in his sweaty mitts.

With Tyson was the young district attorney, Paul Caleb, wearing a simple brown robe with a rope belt and a bald cap on his head, in the middle of a nest of straight black hair.

Before Tyson had the opportunity to leer and drool over Abigail, Doyle said, "My niece."

At that, Tyson lost interest. Instead, he asked, "Have either of you met Paul Caleb, the new D.A.? And this monk business ain't an act, so watch the cussing."

Caleb sighed, pretending not to notice.

Houdini offered his hand. "I haven't had the pleasure."

"Mr. Houdini." Caleb shook his hand in a firm grip. "I'm a huge fan. Really, the pleasure's mine."

Houdini smiled broadly and motioned to Doyle. "May I introduce my dear friend Sir Arthur Conan Doyle?"

Caleb hesitated only an instant. "Well, well. Mr. Doyle, creator of legends."

"You're too kind," Doyle answered.

"Tell me, Sir Arthur, just out of curiosity, and noticing your uniform this evening . . . does the creator ever confuse himself with his creation?"

Doyle considered his answer. "I trust we're all full of unexpected surprises."

"But does the writer possess his detective's supernatural powers of detection, eh?" Tyson added, punctuating his question with an unnecessary slap to Doyle's back.

Doyle took a step away. "Certainly not," he demurred.

"Rubbish, man," Houdini said between sips of his martini. "He's better."

"Nonsense. No more martinis for you, Houdini."

"Show them, Doyle; don't be an old hen," Houdini said cheerfully.

Caleb smiled. "Yes, please. That would be fascinating."

"Well, as I see there's no escape . . ." Doyle searched for a target, seeming to judge each possibility with a surgeon's precision, before settling on Tyson. After a few moments, Doyle said, "You just ate a caramel apple."

"How did you know that?"

Doyle pointed at Tyson's vest. "Because you're still wearing most of it."

Houdini grinned. Caleb applauded, and Tyson tried—without much success—to clean himself.

But even as Doyle had been surveying Tyson, he was still aware of the rest of the room. And he suddenly realized that he, too, was being watched.

The man stood by the window, dressed like a sheik, with a black head-cloth wrapped to cover his nose and mouth, revealing only dark eyes filled with a naked malice. The man held no food or drink, and no one spoke to him. But his look was so intense that Doyle averted his gaze, wondering if he'd intercepted a glance intended for another. But it took him only a second to realize the look was directed at him. Doyle's eyes swung back to the window, but the sheik was gone.

"Abigail?" Doyle whirled around, nearly spilling his martini.

"This is boring," she said.

But Doyle's mind was elsewhere. Reflexively, he drew her close, putting a protective arm around her shoulders as his eyes searched the party once more.

34

THE GAY YET muted roar of the party echoed across the grounds, but the glow of the candles and torches spread only so far. Most of the estate was cloaked in shadow—ideal for Marie and Lovecraft as they crept across the wide, sloping lawns and past a series of fountains enclosed by walls of trimmed pines. The only mark of their presence was the gentle clanking of Lovecraft's leather briefcase. They took cover briefly when voices sounded close by, but it was only the parking attendants sharing a cigarette and gossiping in nasal Brooklyn accents. Marie and Lovecraft crawled on all fours behind a wide pine tree, and waited until the attendants returned to their stations. Then they lunged to their feet and sprinted toward the dark northern portion of the mansion.

Marie saw no dogs, no security personnel. The grounds were devoid of life. No crickets chirped, no frogs buzzed. It was the house. Marie could feel its malignant energy, like a riptide beneath calm water. It infected everything. The trees were rotten at the core, and any bird nests within those branches were empty—and had been for decades. But a spiritual cancer of this magnitude could not blossom off a single event. No, this house—these grounds—were drenched in several centuries' worth of blood, cruelty, and despair.

Lovecraft's touch shocked her back to the moment. He pointed at a second-floor window. They stood at the side of the house, beside a rose trellis thick with ivy. Marie nodded, understanding. She took hold of the slats of the trellis and pulled herself aloft, wincing as her fingers caught on thorns and splinters impaled under the soft flesh of her palms. As she reached the second-story window, she chanced a look down. The lawn was fifty feet beneath her. Lovecraft looked frail and ineffectual as he slung the satchel around his shoulders and grabbed the trellis, shaking it so, it nearly dislodged Marie.

Marie hung on grimly. Below her, Lovecraft dangled and swung, his briefcase still clanking. His feet scrambled for purchase and the leaves rustled loudly under his desperate hands. Marie swallowed and prayed as Lovecraft lost his footing and slid down the trellis, only to save himself at the last minute. He nearly lost his satchel completely, almost spilling his demonological instruments all over the lawn. By the time his sweating, pale face lifted to meet hers, Marie was livid.

"Next time, jus' kill me," she hissed. "You got the grace of a dog wit' one leg."

Lovecraft could not respond; he was too busy gasping for air. Marie just shook her head and turned to the window. She tried prying, pushing, picking the lock, but finally she simply popped her elbow through the pane, reached in, and turned the lock. The window slid open. She wormed her way inside, then crouched down on a soft rug, surveying the terrain. White sheets covered the furniture like death shrouds. It was a spare bedroom—unused. Marie rose and pressed her ear to the door. Then, hearing nothing, she turned back to signal to Lovecraft.

He toppled through the window as quietly as a man in plate armor, then bumbled to his feet, stuffing strange tools back into his satchel.

"I'm fine; I'm fine," he whispered loudly.

"Just shut up and get over here, 'fore you get us killed," she hissed again.

The second floor of the mansion was as still as a tomb.

Sounds of the party echoed from the distant east wing. Most suspicious was the relative sterility of the art and furnishings. This was the home of several generations of madmen—a family of devout Satanists—and yet there were no incriminating images of any kind. No paintings, no talismans, no questionable mirrors, no fixtures or crystals, no furniture that suggested even the most innocuous symbolism. The house guarded its secrets. And for some reason, this bothered Marie more than if infant trophy heads had lined the walls. It suggested maturity, discipline, and a darker heart than she liked to contemplate.

THE HOMBURG FLOATED past a dozen pairs of disbelieving eyes and performed a loop-the-loop in front of Doyle. It then sailed across the wide dance floor, with Houdini trotting alongside like a proud papa. His hands waved through the air, inexplicably dictating the flight of the hat. Whispers of delight murmured amongst the party guests. The homburg hopped from head to head, leaving a trail of startled laughter in its wake before settling with a final soaring leap onto the balding dome of Paul Caleb.

Applause resounded. This sort of performance cost ten dollars and was standing room only on Broadway.

Houdini bowed low as the whistles, laughter, and applause continued.

Paul Caleb removed the homburg from his head and made a mock attempt to levitate the hat, to no avail.

"A drink. A drink for this man," Madame Rose shouted to the crowd as she pulled Houdini toward the bar. Her smile never faded but her voice dropped to a shaking whisper. "We have to talk. You're in terrible danger."

Houdini nodded to well-wishers, but answered her. "Where can we go?"

"Downstairs. To the wine cellar." Madame Rose dropped his arm and crossed into a hallway, where she pointed to another door. "You enter through the kitchen."

Across the room, Doyle smiled and sipped his Laphroaig, his eyes on Abigail, who sat against the wall, whispering to Isabella.

Then he felt a presence behind him, a heavy gaze on the back of his neck.

A measured voice said, "As a child, I adored Sherlock Holmes. I believe I've read every one of his stories."

Doyle turned around to face the sheik.

"You have your father's eyes, Darian," he replied.

"But not his weakness," Darian answered.

"He wasn't weak." Doyle sipped his drink. "Only mad."

Darian's eyes flashed. "Oh, I am certainly that."

"Which Holmes story was your favorite?" Doyle needed to buy some time as he strategized.

"There are so many to choose from. Something appropriate to the occasion, perhaps. Maybe *A Scandal in Bohemia*?" A mischievous gleam shone in Darian's eyes. " 'It is a capital mistake to theorize before one has data. Insensibly one begins to twist facts to suit theories, instead of theories to suit facts.' "

"Very good. Word for word. However . . ." Doyle stepped closer. " 'I think there are certain crimes which the law cannot touch, and which therefore, to some extent, justify private revenge.' "

"You'll learn quite soon about vengeance, Arthur. You and the young lady."

Doyle reached out and clasped Darian's wrist. "You'll taste your own blood before you harm a hair on her head."

Darian ripped his arm away. "I'll leave you with a final quote, from *Hound of the Baskervilles*. 'In a modest way, Watson, I have combated evil, but to take on the Father of Evil himself would, perhaps, be too ambitious a task.' " And he turned on one heel and left.

Doyle swung around to check on Abigail, and instead slammed into Houdini.

"Whoa. Easy, Doyle," Houdini cautioned.

"Darian's here."

Houdini stiffened. "Where is he?"

"He's dressed as a Bedouin. I think we've misjudged him. He may hold the advantage tonight."

"Madame Rose wants to talk."

"It's too dangerous."

Houdini opened his jacket, revealing a pearl-handled revolver stuck under his belt. "I can take care of myself."

"Then do it quickly, for I fear the trap's already sprung."

Houdini backed away, glancing from Abigail to Doyle. "Watch her."

"I will. Be careful, Houdini."

AS HOUDINI DUCKED through the crowd, Darian watched him. Watched and waited.

MARIE GENTLY SHUT the door to yet another bedroom, exasperated. "This gon' to take us all night," she whispered.

The third floor was vast. Lovecraft marveled at the forty-foot ceilings, the yawning length of the corridors, the enormous, gilded portraits of DeMarcus ancestors, their sinister eyes leering down at the intruders.

Lovecraft knelt on one of the many hundreds of priceless rugs and unlocked his satchel. He threw back the leather flap and dug around for a few moments. But what he ultimately produced caused Marie to wrinkle her nose.

"What you doin' wit' that t'ing, Howard?"

Lovecraft held out a withered, gray-brown, amputated left hand. The nails were long and chipped. An ax or sharp knife had chopped through the arm bone, leaving a grisly stub. Tendons, brittle as twigs, stretched to the swollen knuckles through the petrified fingers.

"The Hand of Glory," Lovecraft said reverently. "Chopped from the arm of some thief in the fifteenth century. If enchanted properly, it becomes quite a useful relic. It should find us our—"

The fingers of the corpse hand suddenly curled on their own, and Lovecraft dropped it in shock.

Marie threw herself against the wall. "It's alive!"

"No, it merely knows what we want." Lovecraft smiled as he studied the Hand of Glory writhing on the floor like a hairless tarantula. Then the hand flopped over onto its back, fingers

bent into a fist—all save the decayed forefinger, which pointed
toward a door at the end of the hall.

"My word, it doesn't always work this well."

"Get that t'ing away from me," Marie snapped.

Lovecraft plucked the Hand of Glory off the floor by its bone
stub and walked quickly in the direction of the door.

"It's guiding us," he assured Marie. "It knows what we seek."

Lovecraft and Marie, guided by the Hand of Glory, entered a
two-story library. Thorton DeMarcus's collection was impressive by any standard. Lovecraft would've liked to stay a month—
a year, even. Scores of walnut cases held a selection of titles
behind locked glass doors. Surrounding the balcony above were
even more cases, containing what looked to be first editions.

Four large fourteenth-century tapestries hung from each
wall, suspended between the cases, and there was an enormous
oak table in the center, easily five meters in length.

A candelabra containing four long tapers provided the only
light in the room.

And set in the middle of the table, beneath the candlelight,
was a simple codex. Neither scroll nor printed text, it consisted
of many hundreds of vellum leaves folded once over and connected with stitching. The dried leather enclosing it had long
since cracked and peeled, but there was no doubt what it was.
Before them sat the Book of Enoch.

Lovecraft licked his lips as he approached the table, freeing
his satchel from around his shoulder. He plunked the Hand of
Glory back into the bag as he set out a more delicate collection
of instruments: pen knife, metric ruler, a small vial of clear
fluid, a dropper, and vernier calipers. Then he removed his
glasses and replaced them with a gemologist's lens. He measured the thickness of the paper by pinching the vellum between the calipers, then with the eyedropper applied a tiny drop
of the clear fluid to a frayed corner of the page.

"We ain't got time for—"

"Quiet, for God's sake," he snapped.

His answer was a tremulous squeal.

Lovecraft looked up and pulled the lens from his eye.
"Marie?"

Marie was as still as a statue. "That wasn't me," she whispered.

With a collective screech, four demons surged from behind the four tapestries.

Lovecraft gathered up the Book of Enoch as he scrambled up onto the table, with Marie beside him.

The demons freed hooks from their sleeves and slashed at the air. Lovecraft felt the wind from the force of their swings.

Their ruby eyes reflected the candles' glow as they surrounded the table.

Lovecraft and Marie climbed to their feet, standing in the center of the massive table. Lovecraft clutched the Book to his breast.

"Do something," Lovecraft demanded.

"You're the demonologist, Howard," Marie retorted.

"Can't you call some rats?"

"There ain't nothin' livin' in this house."

A hook flew by, ripping Lovecraft's pants leg.

In that instant, Marie grabbed the candelabra from the table, spun it around, and flung it in the face of the nearest demon. The creature staggered back, squealing terribly, its hood in flames.

Marie took the opportunity to leap onto the closest ladder and pull herself up to the balcony.

The rest of the demons lunged at the table as Lovecraft followed Marie's lead, ungracefully throwing his body against the ladder. The strap of his satchel strangled him as skeletal hands pulled at his ankles.

Lovecraft screamed as he kicked at the squealing creatures beneath him, one arm wrapped around a ladder rung, the other grasping the Book.

Finally he was close enough for Marie to reach down and grab his collar, heaving him over the balcony rail.

Then they were both sprinting for the door, Marie in front, as the demons circled and squealed in frustration below.

35

SOMETHING TICKLED HOUDINI'S memory. A warning lost and forgotten.

The air hummed.

He stood at the bottom of the stairs to the wine cellar; a catacomb of tall shelves reaching out in all directions. He touched the air in front of him, almost expecting to feel a pane of glass between himself and the rest of the cellar. There was definitely something odd about the place.

He noticed the humming again.

He knew something was wrong, yet the danger slipped from his mind's grasp.

"You can't fool me," Houdini heard himself say.

"*Ehrich . . . vielleicht bin ich nicht . . . da wenn du zurruck . . . kommst . . .*"

Directly in front of Houdini, some thirty paces away, the pale, withered face of an old woman floated from the shadows, then retreated.

"Mother?" Houdini stepped forward, tentatively.

"*Get dock . . . in Gott's nahmen . . .*"

"Mother!" Houdini ran toward her, into the darkness.

"*. . . in Gott's nahmen . . .*"

Houdini emerged into an old storage area filled with milk crates and vegetable boxes. The train of a gray dress slid up the last few steps of a basement staircase.

"Mother, it's me," Houdini called.

"*. . . in Gott's nahmen . . .*"

Houdini took the stairs two at a time until he reached the landing of the first floor.

Only it was the first floor of his Harlem brownstone.

Houdini was home.

The door clicked shut behind him. There were no lights on, only moonlight spilling through the dining room windows and across the table.

Dinner rotted on the table. Flies crawled over a sour pork roast.

"*He's in my mind.*"

The words were low and intimate, the sharing of a sinister secret.

Houdini whirled. Out of the corner of his eye he saw someone cross into the kitchen.

"Julie?" Houdini crept down the hallway, his heart thumping. "Julie?" He pushed open the kitchen door.

"*He's in my mind.*"

A woman darted from the kitchen into the dining room through another swinging door across the way.

"Julie, are you all right?" Houdini could barely speak due to the wafting stench of rotting food. Maggots and silverfish swarmed over the sink, and the chunks of meat piled therein. It didn't look like food; it looked like—

"*He's in my mind.*"

She was behind him.

Houdini spun around to face Julie Karcher. She stood in the doorway, chewing on her fingers. Her lips and chin were bright with blood streaming from her chewed fingertips and down her forearms, staining the bunched sleeves of her blouse. But Julie just kept chewing. In her fear, she had not noticed that her nails were gone and that she'd begun to devour her own hands.

Houdini spoke with effort through the lump in his throat. "Julie, stop. Your fingers."

"He's in my mind," she said, then backed away through the swinging door as suddenly as she had come.

Houdini followed her. "Wait!"

Julie sat by the dining room window, staring out onto the street, biting on her forefinger. Skin squished under her teeth.

"Julie, where's Bess?"

Julie looked at Houdini for a moment, then said, "Sleeping."

Houdini backed slowly out of the dining room, then turned and launched himself up the stairs. "Bess! Bess!" He flew through the bedroom door.

Bess looked up at him with sleepy eyes. "Hi, peanut." She plopped her head back onto the pillow. "Come to bed." Bess's hand patted the space beside her, and Houdini saw she wasn't wearing her nightgown. "Come to bed, love."

Houdini removed his tie and jacket, let them drop to the floor. "Something is wrong with Julie."

"She's just overtired."

Houdini sat on the bed to remove his trousers. In T-shirt and boxers, he climbed under the covers and stared at the ceiling.

"I thought I saw Mother . . ."

Bess's hand reached around and caressed his chest. Her warm breasts pressed against his arm. She breathed in his ear.

Houdini turned around and kissed her, pulling her naked hips to his.

"Mmm, scratch first." Bess kicked the covers down, exposing her body. She rolled onto her belly. Houdini obligingly started at her neck and scratched downward.

"Shoulder blades," Bess murmured.

Houdini scratched her shoulder blades.

"Harder."

"Any harder and I'll give you red marks, peanut." Houdini stroked a hand across her curving backside.

"Cheater."

"Of course." Houdini smiled, resuming his ministrations.

He was allowed to look, though, and saw his handprint on Bess's buttock, dark in the moonlight. He touched it; it was blood.

"Bess?" Houdini sat up and turned to his wife. She wouldn't

answer. Her neck was bent in a strange position, her eyes lifeless. Her back was covered in blood. Clawed savagely, torn into
the flesh between her shoulder blades, were the words:

FEAR ME

Houdini wailed and he kicked himself off the bed, onto the
floor.

". . . *in Gott's nahmen . . .*"

Houdini spun around to see a tiny, withered woman in the
doorway, hair pulled tight in a bun, hands extended.

". . . *in Gott's nahmen . . .*"

But her face was that of Darian DeMarcus.

"No!" Houdini roared. He freed the ivory-handled pistol from
his trousers and fired—once, twice, three times.

The shots reverberated off the walls of the cavernous cellar.
What followed was a damning silence. Houdini wiped his forehead with a shaking hand; it was slick with sweat. There was a
stutter of high heels.

As the smoke cleared, Madame Rose stumbled out of the
shadows.

Houdini gazed at her with horror.

She wobbled, as though drunk, then took two steps forward.
She attempted to speak, but a gout of blood spilled out from between her lips instead, dribbling down her black dress.

The pistol fell from Houdini's hand.

"M-M-Madame?"

Madame Rose looked down at the clean, red hole in her left
breast just above the seam of her strapless gown. She looked
back up at Houdini with surprise, then her knees buckled and
her skull cracked against the cement floor.

"God!" Houdini dropped to his knees by her side. He cradled
her limp body. "Madame Rose?"

But her eyes stared vacantly into space.

DOYLE EXCHANGED A look with Paul Caleb as the gunshots
rang out, and both men surged toward the kitchen, followed by

a man in a Santa Claus suit. Tyson was not far behind them. But most people seemed to assume that the shots—and the scream that followed—were nothing more than another creative expression of the Halloween spirit.

But for the first time that evening, Abigail looked up from her seat and could not see Doyle.

Isabella chirped in her palm.

Abigail's eyes scanned the room, which now seemed filled with a growing unease. Most conversations resumed, yet there was a distracting sense of something amiss. Abigail's eyes searched every stranger's face until they fell upon the eyes of the sheik, who stood watching her.

Abigail rose from her chair.

The sheik approached her.

Abigail turned and ran into the opposite hallway. She crashed into a man in a gorilla suit, spilling his gin and tonic before careening off toward the stairwell. Her hand had just reached the banister when she saw a demon surging down the stairs toward her.

Abigail screamed and whirled, only to find herself grasped firmly in anonymous arms. A door to the outside opened nearby, and Abigail was borne kicking into the night.

DOYLE STOOD NEAR the bottom of the wine cellar stairs with Paul Caleb and the man dressed as Santa Claus.

Houdini was on his knees. Madame Rose—Erica DeMarcus—lay dead in his arms. Blood coated Houdini's hands and he looked up at Doyle desperately.

"Doyle? What did I do?" he asked.

Barnabus Tyson trundled down the stairs and gasped like a woman.

Doyle and Caleb both turned at the interruption, and saw other party guests staring down into the stairwell. "Close that door," Caleb ordered. "No one is to come down here."

Tyson knelt beside Houdini and took Madame Rose's lifeless hand in his own. "Dear Lord," he said, and tears came to his eyes.

Doyle could do nothing but walk to Houdini and help him to his feet.

"Harry . . ." Doyle's voice trailed off.

The man in the Santa suit absently pulled his beard and hat, revealing the bulldog mug of Detective Mullin.

A grim resolve set in Caleb's jaw as he stepped forward, registering Mullin's presence. "Detective, find a back route out of this house. There can be no witnesses, do you understand?"

"Yes, sir." Detective Mullin freed a set of handcuffs and snapped them around Houdini's wrists, removing the costume cuffs Houdini already wore. The escape artist never stirred.

"Mr. Houdini, sir, you're under arrest and the charge is murder," Mullin said.

Tyson looked up at Houdini with tearstained cheeks. "How could you?"

Houdini tried to explain. "I thought I saw . . ."

On instinct, Doyle stepped between Mullin and Houdini. "I don't think we can leap so readily to conclusions, Mr. Caleb."

"What? No hello fer me, Mr. Doyle?" Mullin growled.

"I assure you, there's an explanation," Doyle insisted.

"Let me guess. 'E's your pal, too, now, eh? Step aside, sir." Mullin elbowed Doyle out of the way as he took Houdini by the collar and marched him toward the back of the wine cellar.

"Watch him, Detective. We don't need him slipping out of those handcuffs," Caleb warned.

"I've an extra set in the car, sir," Mullin assured him before vanishing into the shadows with Houdini.

"The situation appears clear enough to me," Caleb said, turning back to Doyle. "We'll take Houdini out the back and try to keep everything under wraps until a thorough investigation can be done. I'm no more interested in dragging his name through the mud than you are, and the last thing we need here is reporters."

"I'm going with him."

Caleb barred Doyle with an arm. "I'm afraid that's impossible. If I were you, sir, I'd start working on my story. For you're beginning to take on a rather prominent role in a rather dirty business." Caleb pulled out a handkerchief and plucked the ivory-handled revolver off the floor. "Perhaps, once you have dropped off your niece, you can pay me a visit downtown."

"My—?"

Doyle launched up the stairs.

MARIE AND LOVECRAFT sprinted across the rolling lawn, circling around the driveway then curling back to the south end of the mansion where the party echoed louder and the windows gleamed with light.

Then there was a cry, cut off by silence.

"That was Abigail," Lovecraft exclaimed.

The two began to run, ascending a small rise. Before them unfurled a breathtaking view of Westchester—all the way to the distant shimmer of the New York skyline. And much closer, at the bottom of a steep, wooded hill, the ragged graves of the Willow Grove Cemetery.

Marie raised her voice as loud as she dared. "Abigail?"

No answer. The only sounds were the muted strains of the string quartet.

Beyond the covered pool and the slate patio sat a gazebo. At the edge of the manicured lawn was a gardener's shed. Its latched door banged loose in a growing wind.

"There," Marie pointed. "Come on!"

They reached the shed and pulled the door open. It smelled of mulch. It was dark and moist, cobwebbed. A wheelbarrow lay tilted on its side. Rakes and hoes hung on rusty nails. Large rusted clippers sat in buckets with balled-up gloves beside a hose coiled up like a sleeping rattler. In the center of the floor was a three foot by three foot moss-covered door. A heavy iron ring lay in the center. Two large plywood planks, the perfect size to conceal the door, had been tossed aside. But the giveaway to Abigail's trail was Isabella fluttering against the beams of the shed's ceiling, panicking to escape.

Marie seized the iron ring and pulled. The door moaned on its hinges, and wet, stale air wafted out of the hole.

Lovecraft paled. "It's the entrance to the tunnels."

Far below, they heard a muffled squealing.

Marie took the first step. "She's down there."

But Lovecraft just stood frozen.

"Howard, get the hell over here," Marie insisted as she vanished into the hole.

Lovecraft shook his head, suddenly overcome with terror.

"To hell with you, then," Marie's voice echoed up from the tunnel staircase.

"Marie?" Lovecraft stepped forward, then turned around, eyes wide with panic. "Marie, don't leave me alone."

But there was no answer. Lovecraft stared down into the hole. Then, with an agonized moan, he descended.

36

THE STAIRCASE LED Lovecraft and Marie about a hundred feet underground to a narrow, dank tunnel carved out of earth and living rock, all of it supported by aging wooden timbers. The ceiling was not even six feet high, and the passageway narrow, forcing Lovecraft and Marie to walk single file. They pulled torches from the wall and lit them, but the fire's light did little against the featureless darkness. Screams echoed in the distance. As they stumbled forward, they passed branching tunnels that led to even deeper and more secret places.

Lovecraft craned his neck, straining to remember their route as the tunnels forked, then forked again.

"Did we go right?" he said.

"Ssh!" Marie counseled, and stopped to listen.

But all they could hear was their own harsh breathing—until a ghostly wail split the dim light.

"*Va!*" Marie dragged Lovecraft forward.

The narrow passage forked in three directions, and Lovecraft panicked.

"It's a labyrinth. We'll never get out."

"I can see light," Marie responded.

They proceeded cautiously, aware that they were approaching the heart of the unknown.

"What's become of the others? If they got Abigail—"

A horrendous squeal cut through the tunnels. One of the creatures was close—too close. But whether it was in front or behind them, Lovecraft couldn't tell. Instead he buckled over, struggling to catch his breath.

"Go on," he gasped. "I can't."

"What you doin', Howard?"

Lovecraft grew paler as he fought to breathe. "I've pushed it too far. The exposure to the Mythos . . . it's too much." He trembled, but as he put out a hand to brace himself, he encountered something wet and slick. Lovecraft turned and regarded the slimy face of a dead woman. He jerked his hand away. The corpse's white hair was still knotted in a bun.

Corpses were everywhere, surrounding them—five and six bodies deep. Like the Roman catacombs, the bodies were piled into holes in the earthen walls. Most were decayed to skeletal remains, with hair and nails grown wispy-white and claw-long. They wore the disintegrating remains of Quaker clothes. The maidens still had scarves tied under their bony jaws.

Lovecraft bit his lip to keep from screaming, and Marie yanked him forward by his jacket sleeve.

"Abigail?" she called.

"Don't do that," Lovecraft begged.

But the earthen walls just absorbed the sound. Suddenly, Marie paused.

Lovecraft bumped into her. "What?"

Marie pointed to a set of black doors at the end of the corridor.

"The church," Lovecraft whispered.

"Oh, God, no!" Abigail's terrified voice rang out from the black doors.

The true import of the moment made Lovecraft weak with terror. But then all his differences, all his failings—all the otherness that separated him from his fellow man—fell away like a snake's shed skin. All that was left was a single, surging will to survive.

And the vessel for that survival was Abigail.

Lovecraft shoved past Marie and charged down the tunnel, his fears transmuted by rage and a primal instinct to defend. The black door loomed ahead of him; inhuman squeals screeched from behind it. Lovecraft screamed and bared his teeth as his shoulder connected with the door, buckling the aged planks.

The door shattered inward, and Lovecraft tumbled headfirst into Hell.

The scale and dimensions of the church were overwhelming, and every inch of it was meant as a visual mockery of the Christian Church. There was a short transept and a nave, flanked by double aisles and square chapels. There were enough pews for a congregation of two hundred—a chilling thought in itself—but that was subsumed by the cumulative effect. The mighty columns were adorned with early gothic carvings of disemboweled souls and copulating creatures. And the figures, who in any other cathedral would be Old Testament kings, were instead grotesque demons: hideous mixes of animals and people with slicing fangs and barbed tails. The floors were drenched in blood and gleamed in the light of flaming black candelabras. The air was thick and cloying from the thousands of black roses hanging from the ceilings, and the rotting, excoriated animals hung over the altar, their entrails dripping from an upside-down cross.

Eleven monstrous demons swathed in monklike robes and hoods wrestled Abigail onto the altar, her red cape half torn off her body. Her legs kicked impotently. They spread her thin arms open as she was forced face-first on the viscera-stained block. Shining steel scythes cut the air.

"Leave her be," Lovecraft bellowed as he scrambled to his feet and readjusted his grip on the torch. Three of the squealing creatures turned and flowed toward him. Lovecraft swung his torch in wild, soaring arcs. As tiny embers showered the room, the dried roses and brittle wooden figures adorning the columns burst into flame. Tendrils of fire lanced out in all directions. The flames reflected in the ruby eyes of four more creatures as they converged on Lovecraft.

"Back! Stay back!" Lovecraft jabbed with his torch. The

demons circled, gurgling to each other. The phlegm-coated sounds rolled deep in their lungs.

Several sickles sunk into a pew just inches from Lovecraft's arm and he instinctively wrenched the torch around and struck one of the beasts in the side of the head. Fire exploded, followed by squeals of rage and agony.

By now, the cathedral was an inferno.

An arm like a tree branch whacked the back of Lovecraft's head, toppling the demonologist from his feet. His torch flew in the other direction.

The legion was moving in for the kill, when a shriek spun them around.

Marie stood, barefoot, astride two pews, her eyes rolled back. She chanted unintelligible words as white smoke poured out from between her lips. Her body shuddered as she clawed the air with her hands.

Before the demons could advance, other forms filled the broken doorway of the church. Heads bobbed and torsos swayed as the firelight spilled over the corpses of the catacombs, stumbling forward on skeleton legs—hands reaching, mouths open in silent screams, eye sockets black and empty. Some were children in their now ragged Sunday best. A mother with patchy blond hair and most of her teeth cried weirdly, clutching her rotted infant's body to her lean breast.

Marie shrieked and moved her arms like a symphony conductor, white smoke still flooding out of her mouth.

The demons turned on the zombie intruders, lopping off heads and arms, flinging body parts across the transept.

But still they came—a marionette army. Some pulled themselves along the floor, their legs missing, grabbing at the demons' robes, biting at their hands with clicking jawbones.

The demons squealed and hacked, reducing the mother and her baby to a cloud of corpse dust, beheading a white-bearded pilgrim, and cutting a grandmother still wearing her yellow wedding gown in half.

Lovecraft sat up as the skull of a six-year-old girl landed in his lap. A piece of his mind broke off and he felt it go, like a loose tooth falling out—another small piece of his sanity swept away.

And from that point forward, Lovecraft knew he would always have a phobic terror of little girls with blond ponytails.

He screamed as Marie grabbed at his shirt and dragged him into one of the side aisles. Marie looked scarcely better than the animated corpses.

"Howard . . ." She fell into his arms, her lips gray, her eyes fluttering.

"Mr. Lovecraft," a voice called out.

Abigail waved both arms from the altar and pointed to a side door.

Lovecraft threw his satchel, with the Book of Enoch, over his shoulder, and dragged Marie to her feet.

"Marie, please walk!"

But she was spent, so Lovecraft took her in his arms and dragged her to the altar.

The demons were making short work of the corpses, and now came at Lovecraft en masse, a wall of grasping arms and swaying heads with sticklike noses. They squealed like pack animals. Lovecraft lunged for the door behind Abigail as a wall collapsed behind him. Fire, rock, and timbers came raining down, crushing several demons.

Lovecraft dove through the door, propelled by a gush of hot wind and billowing sparks.

DOYLE MUTTERED GRIMLY as the Silver Ghost surged into the tunnel of trees and toward the stone gates and the perched gargoyles that marked the head of the drive. The Rolls swerved to a stop and idled at the appointed meeting place, but though Doyle leaped out of the car and jogged to the road, there was no sign of the others. He checked his pocket-watch. It was 10:50.

He plunged into the woods, dried leaves crackling underfoot. His cries fell on a chilling silence, as if the estate had swallowed his companions whole. He cursed his willfulness, his flawed strategy. Darian had taken their measure and bested them with ease. Even knowing it was a trap, they'd taken the bait. Now here was the great Sir Arthur Conan Doyle blundering through the woods like a panicked child. Who was he to presume he could fill Duvall's shoes? Maybe he wasn't as inured to the criticisms of the press and the British public as he thought. Perhaps it was pride that had thrust him back into the game, and to what end? To watch the others die as Duvall had? Houdini, an accused murderer? Sweat streamed down his face and into his moustache as he stumbled out into the clearing on the southern side of the mansion. Green hills rose and dipped before dropping steeply to the Willow Grove Cemetery some two hundred feet below.

Branches snapped to his left.

Doyle lunged behind a tree. He heard something large push through the bushes. Whoever it was, it snorted and spit into the grass, and Doyle detected the scent of ammonia—a scent he'd encountered recently. He peeked around the trunk and spotted Morris only a few steps away, carrying a Winchester shotgun. He was dressed as an Italian opera clown, with a white and black face and a circus tent for a gown. Morris's misshapen head swiveled, studying every shadow. A cigarette pack crinkled in his grip. He lit a match on his tooth and sucked in smoke. Doyle was about to sneak away but his shoe caught a twig and it snapped.

Morris turned and aimed.

Doyle dove forward, tearing through the brambles. Wood chips exploded in his face as a shell tore into a tree. Between his thundering footsteps, he heard two more shots and the impact of bursting shells.

Morris stormed after him, much faster than he looked. He gained on Doyle with every stride. Doyle darted left, ducking under a fallen tree, then cut right. Morris just obliterated the tree, plunging straight through it.

Doyle reached the edge of the forest, which opened onto a clearing. The gardener's shed sat fifty feet in front of him. Even from this vantage point, he could see black smoke seeping from the edges of the window and leaking out the front door. Doyle ran to the shed and threw open the door. He saw the hole in the earthen floor, the aged pine door, and instantly knew.

Something slammed him from behind, and Doyle pitched forward into the far wall, tools raining down around him. Morris loomed above him, flicking the rifle open to reload it. Doyle found a shovel and swung it, knocking the gun from Morris's hands. He swung again, and the shovel snapped in two across Morris's forearm. The giant instead took Doyle by the collar, lifted his two-hundred-plus pounds effortlessly, and bashed him to the wall. Doyle's hands clawed at the orderly's face as Morris wrenched and hurled him into the other wall, which collapsed. There was a deafening crunch, and Doyle landed on the grass.

He looked up in time to see Morris ducking through a huge hole in the side of the shed. Doyle attempted to stand, but Morris hammered a fist into his jaw. Morris then hefted him to his feet and threw him into the side of the shed. Doyle landed, gasping, stars bursting behind his eyes. He pawed frantically through the grass and found the wooden handle of a pair of rusted hedge clippers. When Morris reached for him again, Doyle pulled the clippers open, locked them over Morris's fingers, and snapped them closed.

Morris howled and ripped his hand away, minus the halves of three fingers. Blood spurted from the stumps and the giant lumbered back, horrified.

Doyle lunged to his feet and limped off across the clearing, hearing Morris's cries of agony fade in the distance.

37

MARIE AND ABIGAIL were lost. The ceiling of the tunnel looked like a black ocean of flowing smoke. The fire was spreading. There was no sign of Lovecraft; Marie could only assume he was dead, lost in the tumult of their escape. She would mourn the eccentric demonologist if she managed to survive herself. The fire had already consumed much of the breathable air. Marie's lungs burned, and she could tell Abigail had inhaled too much smoke. Her face was dark with soot, her breathing labored. And they had no protection from the demons save for a long wooden stake that Marie had salvaged from one of the splintered pews.

Worse still, her efforts in the cathedral had backfired—not only exhausting her, but also adding an unexpected new gauntlet to run.

For the bodies of the dead still walked the tunnels and they, too, were now on fire.

The corpse of an old woman, gray hair in flames, flailed at them as she surged from the shadows. Marie fended her off with the stake, and the old lady plunged into the earthen wall, burst into pieces, and clattered into a pile of smoldering bones.

Abigail tugged anxiously on Marie's wrist. They'd lost all sense of direction in the smoky haze.

"This way," Abigail suggested.

"We been dat way," Marie countered.

Squeals resounded from the tunnel Marie had chosen, and ruby eyes gleamed just beyond the flames.

"Hurry, Marie!" Abigail ran down her chosen tunnel.

By now, they could not even see the walls, the smoke was so thick. The fire roared through the tunnels—snapping timbers, igniting corpses, fouling the air.

Then, just as Marie sucked in what she feared would be her last breath, her foot slammed into stone. Pain shot up her leg, and she tumbled into a wide, circular crypt. The taller ceiling drew the smoke up from the floor. Marie collapsed, dragging herself forward on all fours, coughing violently.

ABIGAIL TRIED TO help Marie to her feet, but could not. Instead she crossed the floor of the tomb until her hands found a solid monolith of stone set into the wall—the doorway sealing off the dead from the living. She screamed and scratched at the stone in futility as her strength ebbed.

ELSEWHERE IN THE underground labyrinth, Lovecraft gasped for air. His labored breaths made him light-headed, and he ran only because stopping meant dying. He had no idea where he was; no energy to think with as the flames roared around him. He fell to one knee and just barely found the will to stand again.

A toddler, cloaked in fire, staggered from the shadows, still clutching a ragged teddy bear, bouncing crazily off the walls before careening down another tunnel.

Lovecraft laughed at the absurdity—a high, manic sound.

Then the demons squealed, close by.

He didn't want to die at their hands. It was better to suffocate in the smoke than be pulled apart by a mob of demons, or burned alive like a heretic. Though he realized with some irony that the situation was fitting: to die in a grave. Why bother his aunts with a funeral now? He was already buried, and there would be no need for a coffin once he was cremated.

He fell to the tunnel floor suddenly, utterly spent. He would not—could not—function any longer. The dirt was cold. He was thankful for that. A hum filled his ears, drowning out the crackle of the flames, and Lovecraft wondered what visions would overtake him in the moments before death. As his consciousness swirled, the ragged hem of a worn brown robe swept into his field of view.

Lovecraft looked up, seeing first the glint of a scythe. Then his gaze traveled higher, to the long wood beak and, finally, those jeweled eyes.

The creature didn't see him.

Another flowed out of the fire and joined its companion. They gurgled at each other, heads bobbing like crows. Then one of them turned and, for a moment, the back of its robes parted, and Lovecraft dug his fingers into the mud walls to keep from screaming.

For behind the ragged robes, Lovecraft saw the feathery tips of bloodstained white wings.

As the demons flowed back into the fire, Lovecraft felt small comfort in the chilling notion that, as he died, the world died with him.

THE CHAIN LOCK flew to pieces and the steel gates tore off their hinges as the Silver Ghost crashed through into the Willow Grove Cemetery. The car finally plowed to a stop after upsetting two headstones. Doyle kicked open the driver's door and ran onto the field. The moon had broken through the clouds to provide a hazy illumination.

"Howard! Marie!" Doyle was losing strength and resolve, the full weight of his sixty-plus years pressing down on him.

"Marie!"

He stopped, and turned in a circle. All he could see around him were silent headstones and the occasional white block of a mausoleum. Crows squawked in the distance, their calls carried on the wind. Doyle turned back to the car, when the crows cawed a second time, making him hesitate. Crows were diurnal. Doyle stopped to listen, head tilted.

There it was again, but now it didn't sound like a crow at all. He began to run. Graves flashed past him as crow calls transformed into shrill cries of terror—

"Arthur!"

Doyle surged toward a mausoleum. "Marie?"

His call was answered from inside the crypt, weakly. "Arthur!"

Now he could see the smoke, trailing from the tiny cracks in the door. "Marie?" he called again.

There was no answer. He banged at the door with his fists; he dug his fingers into the narrow groove, tearing skin, but nothing gave. Doyle even tried flinging his battered body against it, but in vain.

He pounded some more. "Marie, answer me!"

More black smoke escaped from the tomb. It seemed to be growing thicker.

Doyle backed up and forced himself to think logically.

"Secret tunnels," he muttered as he assessed the mausoleum. His fingers searched the borders of the slab and found rounded grooves, not too different from tracks. At the top corners of the slab were holes, and when he probed at these, Doyle felt steel. So, somewhere, there was a catch to open this door.

He began to look around. A rectangular grave some thirty feet distant boasted a marble statue of a blindfolded woman holding a sword. Doyle noticed that the sword pointed directly to a gravestone in the shape of a cross. He walked over to the cross, which was not buried in the ground, but rather set into a steel square. Odder still was a curious engraving, which read: TURN TO HIM FOR HE IS NEAR

" 'For He is near,' " Doyle repeated.

He grasped the arms of the cross and lifted it from its sheathe. Then, grunting from its weight, he turned the cross upside down and set it back into the steel square.

Something clicked, and the mausoleum slab rolled ponderously open. Abigail and Marie flopped out of the opening and onto the grass.

Doyle rushed to their sides.

"Marie? Marie!" He slapped her cheeks and checked her pulse, which was too weak to detect. Then he took a deep breath, tipped her neck back, and pressed his mouth to hers, blowing air deeply into her lungs.

Out of the corner of his eye, he was aware of Abigail coughing raggedly and crawling away from the mausoleum.

Doyle pressed his fingers again to Marie's neck and continued to work, forcing air into her lungs. Finally, Marie's chest lifted, she breathed.

Her slender hand caressed Doyle's cheek, sliding around to the back of his neck as she kissed him. After a long moment, their lips parted. Marie's finger brushed a tear from Doyle's cheek, then she was overcome with a violent jag of coughing.

Abigail said quietly from behind him, "Mister Lovecraft is still back there."

Doyle stood up and regarded the column of black smoke still billowing from the tomb.

"No, Arthur. Don't," Marie said.

Doyle tore off his topcoat and threw his deerstalker cap to the ground, then took in a great gulp of air and plunged into the crypt.

His eyes stung from the smoke, and tears flowed down his cheeks. Visibility was nil, though the glow of the flames provided a ghostly light. The corpses—at least those who remained in their graves—shimmered like coals. Aging support timbers groaned, and Doyle heard one of them collapse up ahead—a sound that didn't bode well for the rest of the tunnel system.

"Lovecraft!" he shouted, but there was no answer. He waited another few seconds, but heard nothing save the crackle of the flames. He plowed deeper into the tunnels, shielding his face from the patchy fires dotting the ground. He climbed over a collapsed timber and dove away just as another buckled to his right. His path out of the tunnels was slowly vanishing.

He wiped the sweat from his eyes. "Lovecraft, can you hear me?"

"What? Can't a man die in peace around here?"

Doyle whirled. Lovecraft sat propped against the wall, his

arm slung around the skeleton of an old lady, his satchel still clutched in his lap.

"What are you doing in my dream?" Lovecraft asked, but Doyle just yanked him to his feet.

"Shut up and save your air."

Suddenly, the tunnel shook, and clods of dirt rained down. Doyle fell to his knees as the ceiling broke open, only twenty feet in front of him. A tsunami of black dirt and corpses washed into the passage, and the timber supports began snapping all around them. Lovecraft curled around his satchel as dirt showered down from all sides.

Doyle grabbed both Lovecraft and satchel, and literally tossed them through the hole of the tunnel roof.

A wail crescendoed behind them as the demons massed.

As Doyle lunged after Lovecraft, the last of the pillars gave out and an avalanche of black dirt poured down around them.

"Move, Howard! Don't look back," Doyle roared as they scrabbled free of the dirt.

Marie and Abigail were waiting by the mausoleum, but there was no relief in their eyes.

"Arthur—!" Marie began.

"Don't stop," he commanded. "Run, damn it!"

Doyle shoved both her and Lovecraft ahead. "Run, Abigail!"

Eleven demons—engulfed in flames—burst from the mausoleum in a beautiful and horrifying eruption of light. They soared after their quarry, breaking into packs, weaving around headstones, propelled by an unseen force—leaving a thick and dancing trail of sparks in the air.

Doyle knew they had lost, and made the decision to sacrifice himself for Abigail's sake, as Matthew had before him.

But just beyond a thicket of trees, one last hope revealed itself.

A small, white chapel lay at the edge of the cemetery.

"Quickly, head for the church," Doyle shouted.

Marie and Abigail obeyed, half dragging Lovecraft between them.

The demons soared closer. Doyle could hear the wind whip their flowing robes, feel the hot breath of the fire.

They screeched like circling hawks.

Marie reached the door to the chapel first. She yanked on the handle, but the door was locked.

Lovecraft used his satchel to shatter a small stained-glass window beside the door, then boosted Abigail through. Next came Marie, assisted by Abigail from the other side.

"Hurry!" Doyle shouted as he turned on the demons with nothing more than balled fists.

Lovecraft straddled the windowsill. "Arthur, don't be daft," he said. And then he, too, vanished inside.

Once the others were safely through, Doyle turned away from his pursuers and launched himself through the window just as six hooked blades sank into the chapel walls.

The chapel had the comforting smell of an empty barn. There was a single aisle, and there the Arcanum gathered. Doyle threw his arms around Marie and Abigail as they all knelt on the cold stone floor. Squeals resounded outside, and they could see the blurred orange glow of the demons as they passed before the windows.

All eyes went to the door and the slender wooden bar that locked it.

"That'll never hold," Lovecraft said.

Doyle stood up and dragged a pew against the doors. He tipped another onto its side and crashed it down atop the first, barricading them inside.

Glass shattered as a sickle smashed a window, but still the reaching demons continued to circle, as if unsure of what to do.

Then, as Doyle knelt down beside the others again, he saw the simple steel cross above the altar, and understood.

"This is a holy place," he whispered.

"They can't hurt us here," Lovecraft realized.

Doyle lay down along one of the pews and allowed himself to breathe again, to rest. For the moment, they were all safe.

Gradually, the squeals of the demons receded and their glow faded, until the chapel was completely dark—save for a beam of moonlight. Doyle sat on the cold stones, watching, until the sky lightened to a crepuscular blue and dawn broke over the Willow Grove Cemetery.

38

HOUDINI SAT, HIS hands handcuffed in front of him, in a tiny jail cell in the basement of Police Headquarters, just one block south of Bleecker Street on Bowery.

They'd brought him in at two A.M. through an alley off St. Patrick's Avenue, and shuttled him inside with Mullin's coat over his face. They immediately locked him in a secure room in the basement, where no one else but Mullin was permitted access.

Throughout the proceedings, Houdini was passive, dazed.

Detective Mullin sat outside the cell on a hard-backed chair, still half-clad in his Santa costume. An Enfield .38 lay, cocked and loaded, in his lap. Houdini's reputation was formidable, and Mullin was prepared to shoot if escape seemed imminent. But now Houdini looked like a beaten man. A bewildered man. Mullin's only other worthwhile observation of the evening was that Houdini was far shorter than he'd expected.

The sounds of footsteps on the metal stairs beyond the door brought Mullin back to the present. He readied his pistol and shot a glance at Houdini, who remained immobile.

Paul Caleb entered the room, still looking polished save for

two purplish rings beneath his hazel eyes—the only signs of his
fatigue. He'd abandoned his monk robes for his standard attire.

Mullin lowered his .38.

"Detective."

"Mr. Caleb, sir."

"Has he said anything?"

"No, sir. Just been sittin' like that."

Caleb gazed at Houdini.

"Give us a moment, will you?"

Anxious for the break but aware of his duties, he offered the
.38 to Caleb.

"That won't be necessary."

"Yes, sir. I'll be just outside, then," Mullin said, and left.

WHEN THE DOOR had closed behind him, Caleb took Mullin's
chair, turned it around, and sat down close to the cell door.

At this, Houdini lifted his head, clasped his fingers, and
rested his chin on his fists—still not looking at Caleb.

"Would you like to tell me what happened, Harry?" Caleb
asked, softly.

"Houdini," the escape artist mumbled.

"I'm sorry?"

Houdini closed his eyes, "No one calls me Harry." He
pinched the bridge of his nose a moment, then ran his cuffed
hands through his wiry hair. "Not even my wife."

"I see." Caleb bit his bottom lip thoughtfully.

Houdini leaned back so his shoulders touched the wall, and
gazed off into space.

"I'm afraid the 'Handcuff King' died tonight, when you shot
that woman," Caleb said. "Your fame, your celebrity—they're all
gone. To me, you're just a suspect in a crime. A very guilty suspect. So, I'll call you Harry if I choose. Because that's what you
are to me, just another Tom, Dick, or Harry. I don't mean to
sound cruel, but that is the reality of the situation we find ourselves in. And it's a taste of what's to come. And while I'm not
here to save your reputation, I am very eager to save your life."
Caleb leaned over the back of the chair. "That is, if you let me."

Houdini looked at Caleb for the first time. His eyes were red and exhausted, his cheeks hollow and gaunt.

"Now, I know there's more to this murder than a vendetta over a séance," Caleb continued. "And I know that others are involved. I may be new to this job, Harry, but that doesn't make me an innocent."

Fear showed in Houdini's eyes, though he struggled to contain it.

"I see a conspiracy, my friend—a vast and chilling conspiracy. Moreover, I believe that Madame Rose saw the same conspiracy and was killed for it. I see a cancer of occultism spreading across this city, and I see the spilling of innocent blood in our streets thanks to ritual murders committed by occultists who seem to have very powerful friends indeed. And I believe you are a part of this conspiracy." Caleb allowed his words to sink in before continuing. "For too long, the law enforcers of this city have turned a blind eye to the moral decay, the decadence, afflicting the power elite. Well, no longer."

Houdini turned his face away.

"Give up your friends, Harry," Caleb insisted. "Save your soul, man. Break open this cabal. Lead me to them, and I promise you mercy."

Houdini clenched his fists and bent over to rest his elbows on his knees. He rubbed at his tired eyes.

"This silence doesn't serve you, Harry. We can play this by the book, if you like. Call your lawyer, but I'm telling you the moment that happens, you're front-page news all the way to Tokyo. And you're savvy enough to know what even a whiff of scandal can do to a career. So my way is the only way, and you damn well know it."

"I want to speak to my wife," was all Houdini said.

"Of course you do." Caleb stood up and turned the chair back around, placing it against the wall. "And if I do that for you, what do I get in return?"

"You'll have your answer. After I speak with my wife," Houdini growled.

"So be it." Caleb nodded as he unlocked the door.

Mullin straightened and crushed his cigarette under his shoe as Caleb shut the door behind him. He waved the smoke away, turning back to the cell, but Caleb stopped him.

"Listen, Detective, I know we didn't exactly get off on the right foot. I doubted you, I'll admit that."

Mullin scratched at the roll of stubbly flesh under his chin.

"But this is the sort of case that makes legends out of men like us. And now I'm counting on you. Don't let me down." Caleb went so far as to clap Mullin's shoulder. "We can do great things."

"If you say so, sir," Mullin replied, unmoved.

Caleb stood there a moment, nodding and smiling, then abruptly backed away. "Yes, well, carry on, Detective."

"Yes, Mr. Caleb, sir." And Mullin reentered the basement, leaving Caleb in a cloud of stale smoke.

BESS HOUDINI SAT in the library at Crow's Head with her hands folded in her lap. Sunlight streamed in through the windows, giving the room a golden glow. She was dressed conservatively, her hair tightly pinned beneath a boxy, flowered hat, waist cinched tight in a beige dress with an ankle-length hem. For the past hour she had sat immobile as the night's adventures were recounted, including the revelation of her husband's twenty-year involvement in a secret investigative society—something she'd always suspected but had never had confirmed.

Doyle and Lovecraft sat across from her, as bruised and battered as prisoners of war. Doyle was just finishing the story:

"They won't let us see him. My sense is they'll hold him in an effort to flush us out. And I fear this was Darian's goal from the start: to pin the murders on the Arcanum. Perhaps as insurance in case his mission failed, or simply as revenge for his father's death. In either case, knowing your husband, the enormity of his guilt may cloud his judgment. But he must not give in to despair. That's what Darian wants. Houdini is not responsible for the death of Erica DeMarcus. She was murdered by her brother because she knew too much. Now, obviously, proving this will require unconventional means. But in the meantime, he needs you to give him strength." Doyle sighed deeply. "I'm so sorry, Bess. Is there anything we can do for you?"

Bess cleared her throat. "A drink, perhaps?"

"Of course." Doyle rose. "Coffee? Tea?"

"Whiskey."

"Right away."

After a few moments, Doyle returned with a full glass, and Bess downed it in a gulp. She closed her eyes as the liquor burned down her throat, and then her face relaxed. She stood up and brushed off her skirt.

"You're a real shit, Arthur Conan Doyle."

Doyle nodded, not disagreeing.

Bess checked her lipstick in her compact. "Give me the message to bring to him." She snapped the compact shut. "And what are your plans to stop this Darian?"

Doyle ran a hand over his head. "We're working on that."

"Well, you'll need reinforcements," Bess said with all the assurance of a field commander. "I know just the folks."

WITH THE FRANTIC rush for survival over, Doyle quickly felt his aches and pains return. His suspenders hung about his legs and his shirtsleeves were rolled up to his elbows. Even shaving and a sponge bath were torture. His lower back throbbed. He stopped midway down the hallway of the dusty third floor as his bruised ribs stabbed forks of agony across his midsection. It was then he heard the water running beyond a crack in the door just across from him. He could make out a flash of wet skin.

Marie stepped out of the bathroom, clad only in a thin robe. Her wet hair was tucked behind her ears, and hung down her back. She turned to Doyle with pursed lips, as if expecting some comment. Her eyebrows arched in a question, and Doyle winced—ostensibly at the pain in his back.

"I think I've finally gotten too old for this," he joked, as he stretched the sore muscles.

"Let me." Marie said, turning him around. Her strong hands pressed deeply into his flesh, and he tensed at the sudden pain.

"Relax," she said. The heels of her palms swept up his vertebrae, then her fingers clenched around his shoulders. He let his forehead droop as Marie's thumbs probed at the edge of his trousers, working the knots out of his muscles.

But even as his body relaxed, Doyle felt the heat rise across his neck and burn up into his cheeks. He was too aware of his own breathing, and the tension that weighted the air between them. Marie's hands opened over his ribs, and where her fingertips massaged, the rest of her caressed. He could feel the warmth of her breath through his shirt, and her fingers slowly crept from his ribs to his forearms, climbing up to his biceps.

He turned and found her very close. Her chin lifted. He took her by the shoulders. "Marie . . ." he whispered.

Her wet hair dampened his shirt as she rested her head there. "We never have the luck, do we?"

His arms enfolded her, his chin resting on the top of her head. "I love my wife."

"It's natural to love more than one person."

"Jean showed a great deal of courage by giving her blessing to this voyage. I can't repay that kindness with betrayal. We've been through too much together these past few years. The war took so much from us. My son . . ." His voice trailed off.

Marie lifted her head, then pressed both hands to his chest as if in benediction.

"I'm sorry," he offered.

Marie put her finger to his lips. "The next life."

"The next life," he answered.

LOVECRAFT WANTED TO die. There had been moments in the preceding days and weeks where he'd fought it off, but not anymore. Now he really wanted to die. His head ached fiercely, and his hair was caked with dried blood. A front tooth was loose. He could move it back and forth with his tongue, which horrified him—for he'd had nightmares since he was little about losing his teeth. He could not sleep due to the swelling migraine behind his eyes—a consequence, he presumed, of having swallowed enormous quantities of corpse dust. The stitched-up gash at the base of his skull, caused by God knows what, burned and itched.

And that was just his head.

He sat up on the cot, clad only in his torn, dirty trousers. His bony torso was wrapped in gauze bandages. Every breath, no matter how shallow, inflamed his scorched lungs. The frequent coughing fits brought tears to his eyes.

A mewling through the wall distracted him. Annoyed, Lovecraft grabbed his candle, wrapped a blanket over his shoulders, and padded into the hallway.

Abigail's room, next to his, was the source of the sound.

Lovecraft peered inside and saw her hunched over at the roll-top desk, crying.

Lovecraft backed up a few steps, and coughed.

Abigail turned reddened eyes to him and stood. She opened her door all the way and glared at him.

"Why are you always staring at me?" she demanded, the tears drying on her cheeks. "What do you want?"

"I'm not sure," Lovecraft answered honestly.

"Well, stop it."

"I can't."

"Why?" Despite her anger, a trace of curiosity kept Abigail frozen.

"I'm sorry," Lovecraft stammered, "About what happened. Earlier."

Abigail shrugged. "It doesn't matter. I've met all kinds of perverts. There was a man in Paris who used to steal my dirty britches."

"I wasn't . . . I'm not a . . . It was simply . . ." Then Lovecraft just sighed and turned to go.

Abigail watched him shuffle away for a moment before asking, "So what did you want, anyway?"

Lovecraft stopped moving, but didn't turn around. "I understand," he said.

"Understand what?"

"Your loneliness," he answered softly. "More than the others ever could."

Abigail's eyes gleamed with distrust. "I don't know what you're talking about."

"Yes you do. I've felt it, too. Ever since I was a boy, I've been different. I was shunned by other children. I didn't understand their games; I couldn't kick or throw balls. I found their discourse obtuse and primitive. Truly, I believed that I was from some distant planet, that I'd somehow been orphaned on a world of violent monkeys." He flushed, uncomfortable with revealing such private thoughts.

Yet Abigail was listening, so Lovecraft continued.

"They wanted no part of me and, as a result, I wanted no part of them. And my world would have been quite empty had I not discovered books. It was like seeing one's true home through windows of paper and words. I could only touch it through my thoughts, yet I knew I had found the place where I truly belonged—in worlds where carpets flew and magical swords decided the destiny of kings. And look at you. Up until a few days ago, you were just a theory, a supposition built on fanciful platforms of science and myth. And, now, here you are."

The intensity of his gaze must have been unnerving, but Abigail didn't flinch.

"Abigail, you are another orphan like me, from those lands behind the words and behind the paper—a manifestation from the ether, born out of the wishes of children and desperate men. And you must realize that your being here makes a dull, gray world suddenly quite remarkable."

Abigail took a single step toward Lovecraft, and a thunderous gong suddenly shook the walls of Crow's Head.

"Howard?" he heard Doyle shout.

"I'm upstairs," he called back.

"We're under attack." Doyle's voice rose from below.

Still wrapped in his blanket, Lovecraft shuttled Abigail down the wide central staircase as the gong continued to sound. Its source was an eighteenth-century grandfather clock, modified by Duvall into an occult alarm.

Doyle came to meet them, clutching a cavalry sabre in one fist and a Colt .45 in the other.

"Marie, I need light," he said.

Marie padded from the grand parlor in her bathrobe, holding two gas lanterns.

"They've breached the inner fence," Doyle said to Lovecraft as he picked through a ring of keys. He unlocked a heavy door and swung it open, revealing a small but deadly armory.

"Keep her away from the windows," Doyle ordered Marie as he flung a .22 Winchester rifle at her. She caught it one-handed, then clasped her other hand over Abigail's arm and pulled her into the parlor.

"Howard." Doyle threw a chambered tommy gun into Lovecraft's hands. The demonologist dropped his blanket to heft the weapon.

"Shoot first," Doyle recommended as he stuffed the .45 in his pants pocket.

Leaving Marie and Abigail in the grand parlor, Lovecraft and Doyle doused the rest of the lights, then crept through the kitchen to the servants' quarters, where there was a hidden door in the wall of one of the bedrooms. They stepped through, and onto the Crow's Head grounds.

A cold wind gusted dried leaves across the lawns. Beyond a row of maple trees, they saw the black, ivy-wrapped gates. Nothing seemed amiss, but still they heard the muffled gonging of Duvall's alarm. They stuck close to the shadows of the hedges, traveling slowly around to the front of the house.

"An animal, maybe? A raccoon?" Lovecraft whispered.

"Duvall's enchantment was set to act on invaders only. They're here, Howard; we just can't see them," Doyle answered.

They turned the corner and were now facing the circular gravel drive and the roman fountain, when a flock of white doves erupted from the nearest maple and fluttered away.

A disembodied voice suddenly hissed, *"We mean no harm."*

Doyle whirled around as a man with slicked-back white hair, wearing a white tuxedo, walked calmly across the grass.

"Hold!" Doyle commanded as he pulled out his .45.

"Drop your weapons," the phantom voice hissed again.

"Lovecraft."

"We mean you no harm."

"Be still."

"*Arthur.*"

The voices came from everywhere and nowhere at once.

Something heavy fell onto Lovecraft's shoulders. He screamed, and fired his tommy gun wildly into the air.

A black cat sprang, hissing, from Lovecraft's shoulder and sped into the hedges.

The man in the white tuxedo vanished as Doyle fired into the air.

"Show yourselves," he shouted.

Lovecraft turned and reared back. "Arthur?"

A woman, clad all in black, clung to the wall of the house, as if defying gravity. She hissed at Lovecraft, narrowing feline eyes, then scampered up the wall to the roof.

"*Don't fear us,*" the ghostly voice said.

At that moment, the guns flew out of their hands and suspended, ten feet above their heads.

Doyle held tightly to his sword, gazing at the .45. "What magic is this?"

Lovecraft looked over his shoulder. "Behind us!"

Doyle turned to see a hooded behemoth approaching.

"*Be still.*"

"*Drop your weapons,*" the phantom voice persisted.

"Identify yourself, or I'll run you through," Doyle warned the oncoming figure.

But it just kept coming. Doyle's sabre sliced the air, though the blade stopped in midair, clasped between two giant hands.

The hood fell back, revealing a powerful man with a bald head, a thick moustache, and a pirate's earring. The giant broke the sabre in half with bare hands.

"That's enough, Otto," a firm voice said.

The giant dropped the sabre and backed away.

Lovecraft and Doyle turned to the man in the white tuxedo, whom, they now realized, hovered four feet above the gravel drive. The autumn wind whipped the tails of his tuxedo jacket.

"Greetings to our brothers the Arcanum. We come to you in your time of need, and on behalf of our dear president, Harry Houdini. I am Sebastian Aloysius. We are—"

"The American Society of Magicians," Doyle finished, with more than an edge of distrust.

LESS THAN TWENTY minutes later, the players assembled before the fire in the enormous library. Sebastian Aloysius introduced the Arcanum to the A.S.M.'s current board of directors.

"You've met Purrilla, Cat Lady of India." Sebastian gestured to the spooky-eyed lady in the black satin suit, curled by the fire.

"Then there is Dr. Faustus, Master of the Hypnotic Eye."

Faustus was an erudite, gray-bearded gentleman in his fifties, bejeweled like a gypsy king with talismans and rings.

"And you've met Otto, of course, the strongest man in the world."

The behemoth lifted a small hatbox off the seat beside him and stood, offering the box to Lovecraft.

"I've stopped more than fifty cannonballs with my stomach," he boasted.

"How nice for you," Lovecraft replied, weakly.

"For you, friend." Otto held out the box.

Lovecraft hesitated. "Thank you."

Otto placed the small hatbox on Lovecraft's lap, and the demonologist raised his eyebrows. "It's heavier than I expected."

Otto grinned. "Is good gift."

Lovecraft untied the bow, opened the hatbox, and gazed in horror at a human head. Then the head opened its eyes, and Lovecraft screamed.

The American Society of Magicians cackled at his reaction.

"Get it off me!" Lovecraft shrieked.

A small hand reached out of the hatbox and wagged a finger under Lovecraft's nose. The hand was followed by a slippered foot, and then another. Slowly, an entire human being untangled himself from the hatbox and hopped onto the carpet.

"And Popo," Sebastian finished. "The greatest acrobat in all of China."

In one bound, Popo sprang onto Otto's broad shoulders and curled up comfortably.

Sebastian himself needed no introduction. Doyle knew him as one of the finest illusionists in the world. He also was a notorious con man and charlatan. Years ago, the childless Houdinis practically adopted Sebastian, and Houdini himself had taken the young man on as an apprentice.

In return, Sebastian had turned Houdini against the Arcanum, feeding his paranoia and inflating an already dangerously large ego. Houdini needed praise more than food, and it was this that made him vulnerable to people like Sebastian. Houdini's imprimatur brought legitimacy to any association, and that was what Doyle believed Sebastian's aim to be—to practice his former hobbies under an umbrella of respectability. Despite Houdini's insistence, Doyle was not convinced the man had entirely rejected his earlier lifestyle. On the contrary, Sebastian's newfound talents would make him a thief to be reckoned with, and it was this reputation that kept the A.S.M. on the periphery of the occult world. But Houdini continued to let the group call him president, despite his complete ignorance of their activities.

Seeming to read Doyle's mind, Sebastian said, "No strings, Arthur. Let us join forces. What you see here is only a fraction of our might. Say the word, and in half a day I'll assemble an army at your doorstep. And not just of pickpockets and jugglers, mind, but of engineers, technicians, marksmen, whatever you wish."

"Forgive me, Sebastian, but I'm an old man, and tired. Perhaps that makes me cynical, but after all we've been through, why should I trust you?"

"We're none of us angels," Sebastian answered, clearly missing the irony. "I don't presume to know what's in your heart, nor should you presume to know mine. But if it puts you at ease, here is my reason: I do this for the only father I've ever known. And let's leave it at that."

There was an uneasy silence.

"Then, if that is the case," Doyle rose from his chair, "on behalf of the Arcanum, I accept your generous offer."

The two shook hands.

"Have you a plan?" Sebastian asked.

"Forming, yes. And your talents will aid us quite well."

39

PAUL CALEB OPENED the door for Bess Houdini. "Perhaps you can talk some sense into him."

At the sight of her husband, Bess felt her resolve crumble. "Oh no."

Houdini stood. "I'm sorry," he said. "I'm so sorry."

Bess reached through the bars of his cell. Houdini took her gloved hands in his, and kissed them repeatedly as she fought back tears and swept back the hair that had fallen over his tired eyes.

"What did they do to you?" she whispered.

Detective Mullin blinked sleepily and looked over at Caleb, who stood in the doorway to the stairwell. The D.A. gestured for Mullin to give them privacy. Mullin got up and stepped past Caleb.

"Think I'll have a smoke," Mullin muttered.

"Yes, do that," Caleb answered. After a moment, he closed the door, leaving the Houdinis alone.

Houdini kissed Bess through the bars, then lost his composure. He slid slowly to the floor, sobbing. Bess kneeled before him, her hands clasped with his.

"What have I done?" Houdini managed, between sobs. "What have I done?"

"My love, listen—"

"Don't call me that."

"Houdini—"

"Don't . . ." Houdini tore away from her and half collapsed to the ground, his eyes wild, ". . . call me that!"

Bess fought to sound soothing, but her voice shook. "Arthur said—"

"To hell with Arthur!" Houdini scrambled to his feet. "I did it. I did what they say."

Tears fell from Bess's eyes as she rose to join him. "Now, you listen—"

"No."

Bess slapped him through the bars. "Stop it," she declared, then clasped her hands to either side of his head so he couldn't look away. "Remember Duvall's last words. That's what Arthur said: 'Remember Duvall's last words.' "

" 'He's in my mind,' " Houdini whispered.

"Arthur will fix this," Bess insisted.

"How?" Houdini demanded.

"Did Duvall throw himself in the path of that car?"

"I don't—"

"Did he?" she demanded.

"That's not—"

"Did you hate this woman?" Bess asked sharply.

"No. I—"

"Did you want her dead?"

"No, of course not."

"Then why did you kill her?"

"I didn't."

"I know. And if you didn't, then someone else did."

Houdini tugged at his hair. "What would you have me do?"

"You're Harry Houdini," she growled. "Look at these bars."

"No."

"Yes!" Her eyes flashed. "What other choice is there?"

"That is no choice," he hissed. "It's suicide. The world would know in hours. Then Arthur would be next, the others—"

"Then let Sebastian come and get you out."

"No."

"Then, what? What will you do?"

Houdini's eyes squeezed shut. "If I sacrifice myself, he can't go after the others."

Bess could see Houdini summoning his resolve, and it horrified her. She knew the look. "Please, my love. There has to be another way."

"No. I can't endanger the others. I won't. There is too much at stake."

As Bess opened her mouth to protest, the stairwell door opened. Paul Caleb entered.

"It's time, Mrs. Houdini. I'm sorry."

Bess hastily wiped her tears away. Houdini clasped her hands tightly through the bars. He kissed her gloves.

"I love you more than life," he breathed.

Bess touched his cheek, then backed away. She rushed past Caleb and into the stairwell.

AS THE DOOR closed behind her, Caleb approached Houdini. "Well, Harry? I've been more than patient. What shall it be?"

Houdini's gaze burned into Caleb's. "I won't lie to save myself."

Caleb frowned. "You've accomplished too much, my friend, to throw it all away now. It's not worth it. You may even have a career to salvage. What better tonic for a fading icon than a little infamy to spice things up? Do the right thing."

Houdini took the bars in his fists. "Perhaps my actions in the past have left the impression that I would sacrifice my loved ones for my reputation, but let me set the record straight. You want to nail someone to your cross of righteousness?" Houdini held out his wrists. "Do your worst."

DOYLE ENTERED THE burgundy salon on the second floor, formerly the sanctum of Konstantin Duvall, and shut the door softly so as not to disturb Lovecraft. The latter paced the room, deep in thought.

"I need time," Lovecraft complained.

John Dee's obsidian mirror sat on one of the desks, propped up so it faced the center of the room. Every spare surface was cluttered with books, scrolls, and manuals, as well as a cow bell, a triangle, and a flute.

"Time is precisely what we don't have," Doyle retorted.

"It responds to certain vibrations, I can tell you that much. Observe." Lovecraft took the triangle from the arm of the chair and held it out about three inches from the surface of the mirror. He flicked it with his fingernail, and the gentle chime wavered on the air for several seconds.

"What—"

"Ssh!" Lovecraft snapped. "Look." He pointed to the mirror.

Doyle stepped closer. As the chime faded, a ripple—almost invisible to the human eye—shivered briefly in the center of the mirror.

"What was that?" Doyle whispered.

"It's a window," Lovecraft said.

"A window? To where? And what is on the other side?"

"For John Dee and Edward Kelly, it was a way to speak to angels. I suspect it depends on the frequency of sound one uses. It might also be used to contact . . ." Lovecraft hesitated ". . . other things."

Doyle didn't like the sound of that. "What do you mean, 'other things'?" Then he spied a tall cabinet of solid oak wedged at the back of the study. It was secured by a dozen locks, requiring as many keys, but also with glyphs of warning in seven separate magical languages seared directly into the wood.

Its doors stood open.

"Howard, that's Duvall's vault."

"I know."

"You were instructed never to go in there."

"Was I?"

Doyle suddenly recognized the nature of the books surrounding them—likewise forbidden.

"Have you completely lost your senses?" Doyle exclaimed.

"Not yet," Lovecraft replied.

"These are the books of the Cult of Cthulhu."

"I know what they are."

"And you risk more than madness breaking their seal. Do you truly intend to open a portal to the Deep Ones and their kind?"

Lovecraft spun on Doyle, his eyes fierce. "Darian seeks ancient knowledge. Well, I intend to give him what he wants."

"At what cost to yourself?"

"Leave me now," Lovecraft responded, turning back to the mirror.

"Howard—"

"We can't let him succeed, Arthur." Lovecraft's voice was dispassionate, certain. "No matter the cost."

Doyle weighed the words, then nodded briskly, stirred by Lovecraft's willingness to sacrifice himself for something.

As Doyle left the study, Lovecraft called after him, "Lock the door. And barricade it. Whatever you may hear, do not come in. Is that understood?"

Doyle paused, then nodded again. "As you wish."

"Thank you."

Doyle threw one last look at Lovecraft before shutting the door.

It took Otto on one side, and three men on the other, to heft the walnut armoire up the stairs from the library to barricade the front of Duvall's study. The armoire covered not only the door but a great deal of the wall, and that was how Doyle wanted it.

Otto was posted as guard, with stern orders to ignore everything he heard inside the study. The same orders were given to the several new arrivals from the A.S.M., who were scattered about Crow's Head in a flurry of activity and construction.

The cacophony of saws and hammers filled the house, accompanied by a cloud of sawdust. The bottom floor of the manor swarmed with dwarves, sword swallowers, and other carnival folk, and was strewn with piles of manila rope, wire rope, turnbuckles, shackles, hooks, clips, chain hoists, and anchors.

By three A.M., the bulk of the carpentry was completed, and the workers stole a few hours of sleep.

*   *   *

OTTO SLEPT AS well, seated upright on one of the velvet dining room chairs that had been set before the armoire. An empty jug of Chianti hung from his finger. His nose made a painful digging sound as he snored loudly.

Then a shout like a rifle report snapped his eyes open. He blinked several times, trying to remember where he was.

Another horrendous gasp echoed from behind the portal—followed by a breathless, gulping laughter that lasted a full thirty seconds and was neither funny nor joyful.

Less than a minute went by before the next shocked cry.

As Otto waited for the next outburst, the silence became menacing. It was deep and long and pure. Though Otto could not quite put into words what was most disturbing, he felt that the silence was somehow conscious, somehow primordially intelligent.

The next scream was even worse. This time, there were words in it: unintelligible, guttural.

Then more silence.

Otto writhed in dreadful anticipation. The longer the silence held, the more he wished for it to end. And the more he feared the next terrible sound. He looked at his pocket watch, then placed it back carefully in his vest pocket as a wail worse than all the rest erupted from the study. It was indescribably sad, and lasted an infinity of seconds. Begging, pitiless.

Otto threw himself against the armoire, attempting to remove it, when Doyle appeared at the end of the corridor.

"Leave it," he ordered.

"Is not right," Otto shouted back.

After the terrible wailing came a frantic, constant stream of whispering, as if Lovecraft were spilling all the secrets of the world to a friend and his time was short. His voice grew hysterical, breaking several times, then soaring into higher and higher registers—until it sounded like he was sobbing and talking at the same time. Like he couldn't stop. Like his mouth had run away from his mind and he couldn't catch up.

Abigail suddenly burst from her room and ran toward the armoire. Doyle caught her, and held her back.

"No! Let me go," she wailed.

"Please, Abigail. It's necessary."

"But something terrible is happening."

"There's nothing we can do. Abigail." Doyle turned her around and took her firmly by the shoulders. "This is for us. For you. If we go in now, we risk killing him. Do you want that?"

Abigail's eyes were filled with confusion and panic.

"Listen to me." Doyle took her hands in his. "There's no more qualified man in the world to swim these waters than H. P. Lovecraft. If we can keep him in our hearts, I wager he'll find his way back. Can you do that? Can you conjure him in your mind?"

Abigail nodded tremulously, and Doyle kissed her on the forehead.

"Then, that will be his beacon."

The workers, too, had nervously converged before the barred study door. They huddled there, unblinking. Some held their ears to block out the screams and the relentless, freakish chatter. But worse were the drawn-out, swollen silences that conjured in each of them an unutterable dread.

AT LONG LAST dawn broke—to an eerie stillness.

Doyle and Marie stood beside the armoire with Sebastian, Otto, and Dr. Faustus. They had all aged that night. The evidence was in their eyes and hollowed cheeks, in the pallor of their skin. Doyle had seen such results before, an exposure to the Mythos, he called it—like a sunburn of the soul. And indirect though this exposure was, it forever changed a person. So what would be the condition of the person at the epicenter?

"Proceed," Doyle said grimly.

Otto took hold of the bottom of the armoire, and pushed it several feet across the floor, exposing the door to Duvall's study.

Doyle fit the key in the lock and turned the knob. Just before opening the door, he said, "Let me go first."

Marie and the others nodded and stepped back.

Doyle advanced into the study and shut the door.

The room was in shambles: chairs toppled, shelves swept clean, scrolls and tomes tossed haphazardly about. At first, there was no sign of Lovecraft at all, and Doyle had the suspicion that the obsidian mirror had somehow swallowed the demonologist—shoes and all.

But then he spied a limp hand behind the rolltop desk.

"Howard?"

The hand didn't move.

Doyle circled, to find Lovecraft slumped brokenly against the desk.

"Howard!"

Doyle dropped to his knees and took the man in his arms. Lovecraft's clothes were soaked with sweat, and his glasses were cracked and hung from one ear. A sour-smelling paste was congealed on his lips. His skin was so pale, it seemed faintly blue. Doyle pulled back his eyelids and checked his pupils, which were fixed and dilated.

"Christ," he muttered. He felt for a pulse and, to his great relief, found one, faint as the beat of a butterfly wing. He snapped a vial of smelling salts under Lovecraft's nose, and the man's head jerked back. But Doyle persisted, until Lovecraft pushed him away.

What followed was a full-blown seizure.

Lovecraft kicked and thrashed in a panic, while Doyle held him down as best he could.

"Howard? Howard, it's me. It's Arthur."

Lovecraft scrambled to his feet, eyes staring blankly, then turned and pitched noisily over the desk. The impact seemed to knock some sense back into him.

Doyle hovered as Lovecraft attempted to stand, more gingerly this time.

"I'm blind," he said.

Doyle took Lovecraft's hand and placed it on his arm so he could guide him.

"What day is it?" Lovecraft asked.

"Monday. You were only in here for a night."

"Can you see my journal anywhere?"

"No. And I think we should get you into a bath. You're ice-cold."

"I should get these thoughts down before they fly off . . ."

"I think you've done enough for one day," Doyle said firmly as he led him toward the door.

"I wonder if I'm blind for good?"

"If I were a betting man, I'd say it's temporary, attributable to shock. Not unlike the reports one reads of war survivors and their periodic episodes of psychosis."

"Really? How interesting," Lovecraft replied.

40

THE ARCHBISHOP OF New York strode quickly down the aisle of St. Patrick's Cathedral in the full regalia of his office: red robes, vestments, and skullcap. His hurry was precipitated by an early-morning telephone call from Sir Arthur Conan Doyle regarding an urgent matter of the gravest consequence.

The archbishop's brow furrowed as Doyle and Marie entered the cathedral, each holding one of Abigail's hands. Behind them came Bess Houdini, on the arm of Sebastian Aloysius.

Hayes frowned slightly as he saw the charms around Marie's neck: a mix of Christian, Neo-Pagan, and Voodoo talismans. He turned to Doyle, questioning.

"Your Eminence, I thank you for this audience," was all Doyle said.

"Yes. This is most unorthodox. Normally I do morning Mass, but I was quite alarmed by your call, Sir Arthur. Though I must say it was rather vague."

Doyle gestured to Marie. "This is Marie Laveau, of New Orleans."

Hayes blanched. "The Voodoo Queen?"

Marie bowed respectfully. "*Bonjour*, Monsieur Archbishop."

"The one and only," Doyle said, then introduced the others. "Mrs. Bess Houdini, and Sebastian Aloysius, acting chairman of the American Society of Magicians."

Hayes smiled broadly at Bess. "Yes, Mrs. Houdini. Welcome."

"Your Eminence." She shook his hand gravely.

Hayes then shook Sebastian's hand, still looking confused. "This is quite an unexpected group, I must say."

Doyle took Hayes's elbow and Abigail's hand, and led them away from the others.

"We've much ground to cover and very little time, Your Eminence, so please, forgive me if I'm abrupt. But this morning I place in your hands perhaps the gravest responsibility ever conferred upon a man of your office."

"No need to overstate your case, Arthur. I'm listening," Hayes reminded him.

"Excuse my bluntness, but I may even be understating the case."

Hayes scowled. "What exactly is going on here?"

"Your Eminence, do you recall our last discussion?"

"What? About Spiritualism?"

"I'm referring to the Book of Enoch."

"Ah, yes, the Apocrypha. What of it?"

"That day, we talked about the Fall—and both the literal and figurative consequences of Lucifer's banishment from the spiritual plane."

"Yes. And?"

"I asked you if you believed in angels."

"And I said I did."

"And I asked you who protects them."

"And I answered they don't need protecting. Now, it's a very busy day for me, and I don't—"

"Your Eminence, we have nowhere else to turn." And Doyle pulled Abigail from behind him and presented her to the Archbishop. "This is Abigail."

Hayes smiled, eyes creased with confusion. "Welcome, child."

Abigail's gaze questioned Doyle, and he gave a slight nod in reply.

With that, Abigail turned and walked slowly down the aisle of the near-empty cathedral, toward the altar and the choir stalls. Her eyes were fixed on the enormous iron and gold crucifix looming above her. She let her coat fall from her shoulders as she stopped at the altar steps.

"What is happening?" Hayes demanded. Doyle just brought a finger to his lips, then directed the archbishop's eyes back to Abigail.

Abigail stood at the foot of the stairs, her back to them, slowly undoing the buttons of her collarless man's dress shirt. She pulled the shirt open, then let it fall to the floor.

Hayes clapped a hand over his mouth and backed away, but Doyle held him, making him look.

Abigail turned shyly to the others as she knelt before the steps, cupping her breasts. Her long, feathered wings unfolded from her slender back, trembling, reaching and testing the air like silken fingers.

"Dear God," Hayes whispered, his hands at his lips, pressed together in prayer.

"She is the only survivor of the Lost Tribe of Enoch. She and her kind have been hunted down and murdered as part of a conspiracy that threatens the very heavens. We beg you for sanctuary."

DARIAN DEMARCUS, NAKED and smeared in his own blood, lay sprawled on the stone floor of the private meditation temple concealed beneath his bedroom floor. The glass of the blue eye monocle was cool on his chest. The wounds were self-inflicted, carved with a straight razor on the undersides of both arms. There were more cuts on his calves and stomach. He used pain as a tool for focus, for discipline, yet for all the cutting, he could not chase off the rising anxiety. He was not in control; things were slipping away. It was as though he'd played host to leeches who sucked his blood while feeding him the illusion of nourishment.

The Arcanum had regained the Book of Enoch. Yet, infuriating as that was, it was not the killing blow they had assumed it would be. Darian had sucked its secrets clean, and set his plan in motion long before the Arcanum blundered onto the scene. And Darian was not without his revenge. Framing the Arcanum for the Occult Murders was both elegant and cruel. It ensured Darian's position as the unchallenged player in the game. Even Crowley would soon be forced into submission. And if not, he, too, would be devoured.

These thoughts reassured him, and he felt his doubts recede. So what if he had miscalculated just a touch, and confused his priorities. So what if ambition had clouded his judgment. Certainly, vanquishing Duvall and the Arcanum and uncovering the secrets of Enoch were sufficient accomplishments to claim victory. The world was his for the taking. The secrets of the Hall of Relics, the legacy of Konstantin Duvall, belonged to him now. He would determine the fates of kings; he would dictate the flow of history. With such power at his fingertips, nothing could be denied him, no mystical association could challenge him.

Hunting down the last member of the Lost Tribe, however, was proving troublesome. If he wanted, he could have her—but perhaps this was not the time. Yet if it wasn't Darian's decision to make, then whose was it? Beyond that final cut, beyond harvesting the last pair of wings, the future became very uncertain. Look at what he had achieved to date. So why give it up to an uncertain future?

Suddenly, his doubts crashed back. It was true that he'd heard The Voice from the start, but so what? Surely it was only a manifestation of his desires, not some entity unto itself.

Then why had The Voice left him?

Why, unless The Voice had gotten what it wished and no longer needed him?

But that was absurd, impossible.

IT IS TWO years earlier. Darian's skin is slick with cold sweat despite the roaring fire. He sucks on the reed of his hookah and feels the smoke caress his mouth. He pours cognac down his throat. But his heart won't quit racing, and the anxiety has made his life unbearable.

Erica's eyes dart nervously at him as her high heels click on the hardwood floors. Her perfume is pungent, like an oil slick on the air. Her disgust for him is masked only by her fear; but he is losing even her. If she leaves him he will die. He tells her this to make her cry and she begs him not to torture her. But still, he's losing control of her, of his body, of everything.

Erica shuts the door behind her. Darian hears her carriage roll down the drive. His eyes flick to the portrait of his father looming above the fireplace. A gnawing rage rises in his throat as he studies his father's stern features: the wide-set jaw with its bristling black beard; the long nose and its flaring nostrils; the wrinkles like knife gashes; the squinting black eyes.

"Konstantin."

Even in his drugged haze, Darian is shocked enough to scramble off the sofa as he searches for The Voice.

"Who's there?" he cries.

There is a hum in the air, a sizzle of electric whispers.

"Find it."

The Voice is crisp and sexless. It is in the room.

Darian laughs, then cups his mouth. He muses on a life in straitjackets, chewing cockroaches in some cell.

"Avenge him."

Darian screams and falls to the floor. He stares again at his father's portrait. "Go away!"

"Avenge him," The Voice commands again.

"Avenge . . ." Darian crawls across the floor, shivering as he realizes that The Voice is not in his head.

"Find the Book," it orders.

"Which book?" Darian gasps.

"The Book of Enoch," The Voice answers.

NOW THE THOUGHT that he might have been deceived was too much for him. He doubled over and wretched clear bile onto the floor. He stared at the symbols drawn on the ceiling in his own excrement. Was it The Voice who filled him with false promises? Had he become so obsessed that he could not see some other agenda at work? Now Darian could almost feel the hook in the soft tissue of his cheek.

His hours of ritual chanting had borne no fruit, no communion with The Voice that only days ago had whispered sweet encouragement. This new emptiness filled him with dread. Darian DeMarcus was no child's puppet.

He repeated this to himself as cold perspiration trailed across his cheeks and back. It was a sweat toxic with drugs: ether, peyote, heroin, cocaine, and hashish—a methodology straight from the syllabus of Aleister Crowley. But the harder Darian pushed to regain The Voice, the more damning the silence became.

Things were breaking down, his logical mind giving way to drug-induced visions and his deepest, unspoken fears. His thoughts splintered into fractals and trapezoids. Language dissipated. A flood of bloody images swept away the clinging vestiges of his identity, the cardboard desires and smiling dolls of his personality. His shattering mind visualized magic symbols of protection to ward off the madness of Hell, and he glued his concentration to those images like a shipwreck survivor to his life preserver.

Just then, a tremendous crash, like an explosion, shook the house, and wrenched Darian back to the moment. He sat up with a gasp, waving away the twisting leviathans of the ink-black ocean of his mind. Candles flickered, but the bulb in the electric lamp was dead. The room was dark. The effort to summon his thoughts was akin to sculpting statues from wet spaghetti, but somehow Darian managed to struggle to his feet.

Something had just happened in his father's house.

Darian snatched his silk robe off the floor, put it on, and tied it around his waist. He ran a shaking hand through his hair, then climbed the spiral staircase to the hidden door in his closet and reentered his bedroom. The lights were out there, too.

A furious scratching on the ceiling directed his attention upward. It sounded like there was an animal on the roof. A large animal.

Darian wiped the sweat from his neck as he staggered into the corridor. "Morris?" he shouted.

More skittering sounded above his head. There were animals scrabbling on the roof or wriggling inside the walls. His heart drummed too fast, and he willed it to slow down. But still his breathing grew faster and more labored.

Thunder ripped across the sky, along with a sudden rain that pounded the windows and pelted the roof. Lightning filtered through the corridor, illuminating yet another portrait of Thorton DeMarcus, his fiery gaze locked on his trembling son.

"Papa?"

At this, lightning turned the house into a carnival of shadows and another crack of thunder shook the walls.

The portrait of Thorton DeMarcus seemed to grow and swell, his downturned lips curled in a sneer.

"*Murderer . . .*" said a hollow voice.

"I didn't," Darian babbled like a child, backing away.

"*Sister . . .*"

"It was her fault," Darian cried. "You always take her side!"

Then a blood-choked shriek ripped up the stairwell.

Erica.

The silence that followed was chilling. Darian froze, then licked his dry lips with a drier tongue.

"M-Morris?" he whispered.

A door slammed downstairs. More lightning flared, then more, thunder shaking the chandeliers. "Morris?" Darian's voice was hoarse with panic. The rain drummed around him like a thousand fists. A thousand demons, waiting to get in. He lunged into a bedroom and ran to the window, ripping the curtains back. The rain and darkness made it impossible to see, but as a splintering fork of lightning turned the world briefly into day, Darian saw a lone figure standing at the edge of the field. A figure in robes.

Then another sound rattled the house that was neither rain nor thunder.

Darian leaped back from the window. What in the Devil's name? It sounded like the beating of . . .

Darian's fingers dug into his temples.

"Stay away!" he barked.

Something moved in the attic, something with sharp claws. Darian ran back into the corridor. More creatures scratched the walls and skittered over the roof.

Darian roared with defiance, and was answered in kind.

Windows banged of their own accord. Doors slammed. Darian raced toward the stairwell, spun around the banister, and collided with Morris. The blow knocked him flat on his back.

Morris loomed over him, wet with rain. The hand with its missing fingers was heavily bandaged; in the other he clutched his Winchester shotgun. "Miss Erica is in the house," he said thickly, as if his tongue was too big for his mouth.

"Don't say that," Darian moaned, but in answer, Erica's voice lilted from the east wing.

"Darian?"

Morris looked befuddled. He turned to Darian, questioning. "Don't you want to see Miss Erica?" he asked.

Darian climbed to his feet and shoved past Morris, continuing down the stairs. On one of the landings, he stole a wide cutlass off a set of Arabian armor.

MORRIS WAS ABOUT to follow, when door hinges squeaked open behind him. A pair of emerald green eyes blinked in the darkness, like a cat's. Morris stumbled toward the door instead.

AS DARIAN REACHED the ground floor, he found that the front doors of the DeMarcus Manor had been blown off their hinges and lay on the ground, still smoking. Wind and rain blew into the foyer, making the floors treacherously slick. Still, it offered an escape, and Darian was about to flee into the yard, when some fifty yards away something that glowed began lurching toward the house.

The approaching phantom was well over six feet tall and its cloak billowed in the wind. It walked slowly and steadily despite the driving rain, and glowed with a sickly green luminescence. More lightning seared the heavens, but still he could not see the being's face. Although . . .

Darian thought he recognized the cloak.

He backed away from the hole where his doors used to be, panic adding an electric jolt to the chemicals already sizzling in his bloodstream. The solidness of objects became less dependable. The walls bled; the floor stretched like rubber. Darian squeezed his eyes shut, but could still see.

"Darian?" Erica's voice sounded from the next room.

"Go away," he gasped.

A woman's shadow crossed the floor about twenty feet from where Darian stood. He darted away from the shadow and plunged reflexively through the doors to the old wing—a place he normally feared to go.

The old wing was a hundred years older than the rest of the house, attached to the new wing by a gigantic corridor, a statuary with forty-foot windows looking out on the fountain gardens. Darian hated the corridor, having feared it since childhood. He was halfway down the towering hall before he noticed the blood, and froze. A trail of bloody bootprints showed up black on the old wing's tile floor, glowing intermittently in the lightning flashes. Darian felt numb. There was a ringing in his ears.

Erica's childlike voice sounded from behind him. *"Darian?"*

He whirled around.

"No!" He backed away, slipping in the bloody footprints. He scrambled back on hands and feet across a slick of blood, screaming, as Erica DeMarcus pushed her way into the corridor.

She was bathed in blood and still wearing the black dress from the party.

"Don't punish me," she pleaded.

"Pet," Darian stuttered as he climbed to his feet, "pet, I'm sorry," stumbling back from the bloody wraith of his sister.

"Don't punish me!" Her voice whined, high-pitched, like a windup toy.

"You were going to tell on me," Darian protested. "Why couldn't you let me be?"

She staggered toward him, seemingly having no control of her own limbs.

"No. Stay away!"

"Why, Darian?" she said.

"Because you wouldn't love me," he admitted, finally confessing the deeper truth. "You betrayed me. I was your brother. You were supposed to be loyal to me, and instead you tried to hurt me. So I hurt you."

"You killed me," she said.

Darian slapped his hands over his ears. Between the rain pounding on the windows and the jarring thunder, he could not think. "Stop it, Erica. You're not real. You're dead. I killed you!"

Darian lunged at her, but even as he reached out, she was torn in two by giant, unseen hands. Her torso thumped against the windows, trailing blood down the glass as it fell. Her legs slapped noisily into the wall, then collapsed in a sticky heap.

Darian's knees hit the ground to the wail of his own voice and the rise of the thunder. He lurched away from the image of his slaughtered sister, only to find the phantom from the field standing at the end of the corridor, rainwater streaming from its cloak.

Darian raised his hands beseechingly.

"I warned you, Darian." The phantom walked toward him, its voice seeming to boom from the very heavens. *"I warned you the price you would pay . . ."*

Darian could summon only a hiss as the revelation struck him. "Duvall?"

The phantom continued forward as Darian shielded his eyes. *". . . were you to steal the Book . . ."* it continued.

"Leave me alone!"

"Now you will answer for your unspeakable crimes . . ."

Darian thrashed his head back and forth. "Get out!"

The phantom towered above him.

"You will answer to your victims . . ."

And then the dreaded sound began again, above the storm, above the thunder—beating wings. The walls trembled from the din. Duvall's voice rose above the noise. *"And the cost is your broken soul!"*

With that, bloated forms plunged down from the roof, on unfurling chains, jerking to a halt before the wide windows of the corridor. Lightning exploded again, revealing bodies swinging on hooks, slapping at the glass with ill-attached wings, smearing it with blood. One after another they fell, wrapped in dirty bandages. Body after body plummeted from the sky, to the crack of thunder, bloody pendulums painting the windows red, dancing on their chains to the chorus of Darian DeMarcus's screams.

All around the house, a din of chimes, like church bells, rang out discordantly.

Duvall's cloak fell away, and Darian found himself staring into the dark void of John Dee's obsidian mirror. The chimes activated the mirror, causing its surface first to ripple, and then produce inexplicable images.

An alien landscape unfurled before Darian's horrified eyes—a primitive world of strange, shiny dwellings, surrounded by jagged mountain peaks beneath an orange sky with four moons.

The images honed in on a triangular cyclopean temple in the heart of the alien city—taller and wider by far than any Egyptian pyramid. Darian heard a frenzied chanting on the hot winds as the mirror sucked him into the blackness of the temple.

Within was a canyon of tenebrous shadows. And in that wet and horrible darkness something breathed, and the swollen echo resounded through the temple's endless, endless halls.

The light shunned the unknowable life-form hidden within the murk. At first, all Darian could sense was the creature's size—it was grossly, ludicrously huge—and yet proportioned vaguely like a man with yellow, blistered skin.

But as his eyes adjusted, he could see fleshy pieces of tiny men dribbling from the massive hooks of its crablike mouth. The goliath shifted out of the shadows into the light . . .

But the rest was unrecordable, because Darian's mind went white.

His eyes rolled back as his heart spasmed and stopped beating, and he crumpled forward onto the stones of the statuary hall.

Duvall's phantom stood over the prostrate Darian—both still. In this frozen tableau, only the bloody angels swung outside the window.

The storm quieted its fury.

The rain eased.

*   *   *

UPSTAIRS, MORRIS STOOD in the darkness of a large ball-room, shotgun aimed at the curtains. A purring sounded behind him. He whirled, to see a lithe woman crouched on top of a table. She raised her hands in a gesture of piety. Morris lumbered toward her, lured by his childhood love of strangling cats. But as he got close, something glimmered in the cat-lady's hands. She blew into her palms, and Morris was enveloped in a choking dust. It burned like embers beneath his eyelids and like acid in his throat. His mouth filled with spit, and clear fluid drained out his nose as he gagged—while behind him, the curtains parted and a figure emerged. A hand grasped Morris's testicles, another clasped his burning throat. And, for the first time in his life, Morris was lifted bodily into the air.

He screamed as the giant threw him through one of the ball-room windows. He shut his eyes as his face burst through the wood and glass and his enormous body followed, clearing the window and pitched down. He felt the cold winds and biting ice rain on his cheeks, and when he opened his eyes, he could see the ground spinning up to meet him. The fall seemed to last a long time. Then, finally, Morris collided with the cement patio.

After that, there was only pain, and darkness—then nothing whatsoever.

BACK ON THE first floor, all was quiet.

Then there were footsteps like skittering mice.

Two A.S.M. magicians, dressed in black, darted out from the shadows and knelt over the torso of Erica DeMarcus. Together, they lifted her from the pool of corn syrup.

The phantom Duvall pulled back his hood, revealing Popo the acrobat crouched on a small platform near the head of the deftly engineered marionette. Lovecraft crouched atop another platform at the midsection, and a dwarf named Bruce finished up the triad by operating the legs.

Lovecraft was outfitted like a space explorer between the obsidian mirror and the hand-cranked Dictaphone slung over his shoulder with its recording horn. Not to mention the green-glowing halogen—his spirit illumination.

Doyle entered the corridor. "Did we get it?" he asked Lovecraft.

"I think so," Lovecraft replied, patting the Dictaphone.

Angel bodies—really mummy-wrapped potato sacks dipped
in syrup—were lowered to the ground from squeaking winches.

Sebastian Aloysius burst through the doorway. "Magnificent,
eh? Better than *Prince of Blood!*"

Doyle raised an eyebrow. "Are the grounds secured?" he
asked.

"Of course," Sebastian answered, sounding hurt at the lack of
praise.

"What about the orderly from Bellevue?"

Otto stepped in behind Sebastian, wiping his hands. "He fell
out window."

"It's a wonderful victory, Arthur," Sebastian insisted. "We
should be celebrating."

Something crunched beneath Doyle's shoe as he gazed down
at the body of Darian DeMarcus. "Forgive me if I don't feel
much like celebrating." He lifted his shoe and saw Darian's blue
eye monocle shattered into pieces.

Lovecraft unfolded from his crouch as the Duvall marionette
was disassembled by the A.S.M. crew. The demonologist then
fixed the bone gauntlet—the Eltdown Shard—over his arm and
spun the reel of the control unit. Once again, tiny pistons
worked up a head of steam, and spectral symbols formed in the
ether surrounding it. Lovecraft studied the ghostly equations.

"Anything?" Doyle asked.

"Nothing." Lovecraft stopped spinning the reel and removed
his goggles. "The grounds are clean."

"Then we should send word to the others."

41

ABIGAIL GAZED DOWN at the Vanderbilt Mansion from her lofty perch in one of the towers of St. Patrick's. The night was cold, and the sky clear with stars but for a sliver of moon. Abigail heard the wind moan in the long corridors of the church. Below, tiny people hunched their shoulders against the chill, and pulled their collars tighter. All those people. She tried to count them, but she quickly gave up. There were too many, moving too fast—on foot, by trolley, horse, and car. Hundreds. Thousands. Husbands and wives on nighttime strolls, children pulling their grandparents into toy stores. Businessmen leaving work, pausing to check their pocket watches to see how late they'd be for dinner if they stopped off for a drink with the fellows. Even the people who walked by themselves had someplace to go. A brother to write to. A mother and father in the country. A lover waiting. All of them had families. All of them were born of mothers. All of them but her.

Abigail thought about these people's lives as she absently dragged the knuckles of her fist over the wall, scraping the skin. She thought of Mr. Houdini's wife, and the way she concealed her tears. What was it like to be loved that way, to have someone willing to sacrifice everything for you? Mr. Lovecraft had sacrificed for her, and all she'd been to him was mean. As she was to them all—and to her family before that. Family. She'd never called them that to their faces, though Judith had longed for it. Abigail had cursed them instead. Had run away. Stolen. Lied. She'd never let anyone love her. Instead, she'd blamed them for her sadness, for her anger, for her otherness. For their otherness. Her isolation. None of the people below had an inkling how lucky they were, no understanding of why Abigail would trade places with any single one of them in a heartbeat. They did not count the smell of their living rooms or the sound of their mothers' slippers as they climbed the stairs among their treasures. She dreamed of the color of their bedsheets, and their end-of-the-day conversations around the dinner table. "How was work, dear?" and "What did you learn in school today, Margaret?" She even envied the orphans, who could at least turn to the stranger in the bed beside them and say, "We're the same, you and I." Abigail envied every last stupid one.

She looked out on the world from an invisible box with no key. And it wasn't that she was incapable of love, she reminded herself. It's just her love injured with equal impunity. Ask Matthew. Or the Rescue Society. Or the Arcanum. They were all decent people who volunteered to help her, and suffered because of it. And this night was no different. Somewhere out there, the Arcanum risked their lives for her. And for what? If Abigail were gone, who would miss her? No one. She was simply a burden, and if she were removed from the equation, their lives could resume. And in a moment of clarity, Abigail came to a decision. She could finally, after all this time, do something right.

BESS HOUDINI SAT on the steps of the altar, gazing at the cathedral ceiling while Archbishop Hayes sat in the first pew, hands clasped in prayer but eyes focused intently on the two A.S.M. magicians. They tinkered with the controls of a boxy, two-way radio that stood on four unsturdy wooden legs. The radio squawked, then hissed with static. Half-formed words occasionally surfaced from the noise as the men searched in vain for the signal.

The shorter magician—a stout Irishman in his fifties—flicked a switch on the box and spoke into a microphone. "This is Smedley. Do you read? Over."

The larger magician—a sweaty chap with an enormous belly—looked up from the wires and hollered, "A little to the left, Bob!"

Bob, the red-bearded antenna man, had climbed to the highest point of the cathedral with mountaineering ropes, and now swung from the rafters on a makeshift rope seat, trying to hold up a twenty-pound steel antenna six feet long.

"I'll try," Bob replied gamely, and leaned back in his rope seat, making adjustments. The antenna wobbled.

A clear voice suddenly erupted from the radio. "This is Arthur Conan Doyle. Do you copy?"

Gasps of relief and praise and thanks encircled the group. Bess clasped hands with Archbishop Hayes as Smedley flicked the switch and spoke into the microphone. "This is Smedley, Mr. Doyle. Is everyone well there? Over."

It was quiet for several moments. And for a second Bess feared the worst. Then Doyle's voice rang out even louder.

"Mission accomplished. We're coming home. Over."

The magicians clapped hands over the radio as Archbishop Hayes rose to his feet, kissing his rosary. "Praise God."

Bess wiped away tears of relief as Hayes took her arm. "Let's go tell Abigail the good news, shall we?" he said.

It was not easy to reach the room Abigail had chosen to call her own, two hundred steps up the tower stairs. And when they knocked on the door and called her name, she did not answer. The archbishop's brow furrowed. He opened the door. "Abigail?"

The room was empty, the window open wide.

"Oh dear Lord," Hayes breathed.

Bess wheeled around. "Abigail?" She raced down the stairs, calling her name, and was out of breath by the time she reached the main body of the church.

Concerned, the magicians ran to help her, but Bess shook them off.

"Abigail's gone. Smedley, Bob, alert the others. Go!" They

broke into a run, Smedley grabbing his gas lantern off the floor as he went.

OUTSIDE, THEY SKIDDED to a halt. Smedley held the lantern up, cupped his hand over the light, and began to transmit a series of coded signals.

Atop one of the Vanderbilt Twin Houses, Johnny Spades—a master of playing card prestidigitation—read the code and instantly snatched up his two-way radio, spinning the crank.

The cord had been unspooled that afternoon and run across the rooftop of the Vanderbilt House, across Fifth Avenue, and south for several blocks to the arched roof of Delmonico's on the corner of Forty-fourth and Fifth. There, the other end of the two-way phone buzzed. Chi-Chi, a tuxedoed dummy, answered the phone with a lit cigarette dangling from his wooden lips. He was hand-operated by the famous, and more than slightly eccentric, Carlos the Brazilian Puppeteer.

"*Alo?*" Chi-Chi answered.

Johnny Spades's voice burst from the receiver. "Put down that stinking puppet. Abigail is missing!" Johnny Spades exclaimed.

With a suction pop, Carlos extended his ship-captain's spyglass and scanned the streets. While Carlos did that, Chi-Chi looked over the edge of Delmonico's roof to help with the search.

"I don' see not'ing," Chi-Chi whined.

"I've got her," Carlos said. "She's headed for Grand Central."

Through the lens, Abigail could be seen walking quickly down the sidewalk, her arms folded against the cold, her head tucked low. Carlos then panned his spyglass up a brick wall to a nearby rooftop, where several ragged creatures watched Abigail with gleaming ruby eyes.

Carlos lowered the glass, blinking twice. "What the hell?"

But when Carlos examined the rooftop again, the creatures were gone. He swung the lens left, then right. He found them again in the alley, but they weren't there for long. He gasped as one of the creatures scrambled up the adjoining wall like a skinny spider. The spyglass dropped from his hands as he grabbed for the phone.

"I think she's being followed," Carlos reported.

Johnny Spades relayed this message via lantern signals to Smedley and Bess, who was now waiting with them outside the church.

Smedley grimaced as he translated the code. "She's being followed," he said to Bess.

Immediately, Bess broke into a run.

"Mrs. Houdini," Smedley called, then took off after her, his gas lantern swinging.

GRAND CENTRAL TERMINAL was an enormous, split-level structure composed of mighty columns and eighty-foot windows, swallowing up four city blocks and two avenues, interrupting Park Avenue at Forty-second Street. And below its high ceilings and ornate lobbies lay thirty-two miles of tracks, connecting the city to the rest of the nation.

As soon as Bess entered the station, she was swept into a press of bodies—the tail end of rush hour. Hundreds of people in anonymous suits of gray, black, and brown swarmed around her. It was impossible to see for all the bodies, so Bess took the stairs to a balcony, where she could look out over the entire station. After fruitless minutes of searching, she despaired of finding Abigail, but at that instant she spotted her quarry at the far end of the building, entering a line of ticketed passengers. Bess watched Abigail's top hat disappear into a stairwell to the lower train platforms.

AT FIVE-FOOT-FOUR, all Smedley could see was an ocean of neckties. He elbowed his way through the crowd, then he heard a piercing voice call out from somewhere in the bowels of the station: "All aboard!"

ABIGAIL FELT A growing panic, jostled by the flowing current of bodies along the train platform. The air was warm and smoky. On platform after platform, steam rose and engines churned. The trains muscled against the platform like bulls in the gate.

"Abigail!"

Abigail whirled around, to see Bess Houdini descending the stairs.

Abigail ducked hastily onto the Empire State Express.

SMEDLEY JOGGED ALONG a neighboring platform, dodging columns, his eyes on the Empire State Express. The whistle blew, deafeningly loud. Smedley covered his ears. Bess Houdini still walked quickly alongside the train, peering into the passenger windows as rods and pistons began moving and the train rolled slowly from the platform.

"Mrs. Houdini!" Smedley called.

Bess turned to Smedley, eyes frantic. "Get help!" she replied, then darted through one of the train doorways at the last possible instant.

Smedley ran a worried hand over his head and stared after the train. As the Empire State Express retreated into the stygian tunnel, a curdling squeal rose in its wake, mocking the steam whistle of the engine. The sound came from above him. Smedley peered into the nest of steel beams soaring above the tracks.

At first he thought they were rats because of the way their red eyes shined, but then he realized they were far too big. But they didn't move like men, either, the way they flowed across the beams like swift-moving snakes, chasing the Empire State.

Smedley watched in horror as the creatures dropped at the last minute from the ceiling beams and onto the steel roof of the train.

42

As SMEDLEY COMPLETED his gas lantern SOS from the corner of Forty-second Street, Carlos the Puppeteer turned his lantern south and began his own set of signals, cupping and uncupping the illuminated glass bowl.

That signal was received by Gilda the Geek, atop the Metropolitan Life Building on Madison and Twenty-third. She dropped her salami and orange juice, lifted her own gas lantern, and repeated the call.

It was relayed to Buttons the Juggling Clown on the roof of Clinton Hall, between the Bowery and Broadway, just as he was relieving himself on a gargoyle. But still Buttons repeated the signal, hoping that his comrades were paying attention.

Balthazar the Magnificent was the smallest magician on record, at a paltry twenty-two pounds. He was also three feet tall in heels. As he paced the roof of Police Headquarters, one block south of Bleecker Street, Balthazar noticed a tiny light, blinking on and off in a sequence of fours. Reading the simple message, Balthazar sprung onto the ledge of the four-story building, wrapped himself around a gutter pipe, and slid all the way down to the sidewalk. Then he dashed across the street and into an alley where the Rat Man waited.

The Rat Man crouched in the shadows as he listened to Balthazar's hurried instructions. Then the Rat Man touched his pencil lead to his tongue, and scribbled a note that he rolled like a cigarette into a tiny scroll. He freed a wriggling mouse from his shirt pocket and whispered in its twitching ear, then tucked the note into its very small string collar and placed the mouse on the ground.

The mouse skittered across the street, narrowly avoiding being crushed under an approaching police wagon. Instead, it darted between policemen's shoes and scampered up the four steps to the front door.

The mouse ran through booking and processing, down the stairs, through the detectives' offices, around administration, down another flight of stairs, and past a row of lockers and jail cells, to another longer stairwell. It descended rapidly, then squirmed under the locked door at its base. Beyond was a small, colorless room with a single cell.

DETECTIVE MULLIN SLUMPED on a chair outside the cell, grumbling in his sleep. The Enfield lay in his lap, still loaded.

Houdini sat against the wall on his cot, staring off into space, devoid of hope. It took him several moments to even hear the squeak at his feet or feel the press of a small body against his ankle. In fact, he blinked at the mouse for several more seconds before leaning down and offering his finger. The mouse skittered up his arm and onto his shoulder.

"Tame little thing, aren't you?" Houdini said softly.

The mouse stood up on its tiny hind legs, revealing the scroll stuck into his string collar.

Houdini frowned and gently slid the scroll from its sheath. He glanced at the creature sideways as he unrolled the paper and read. His body shook as he crumpled the paper in his fist.

*   *   *

MINUTES LATER, DETECTIVE Mullin awoke from a nightmare with a jolt. He blinked rapidly and smoothed his moustache, but what brought him to his senses faster was what he
saw in the cell before him.

Harry Houdini's body swung from the ceiling, hanged by the
neck with his cot blanket. The copper piping groaned from the
strain.

Mullin ran to the cell door and threw it open. Houdini's lips
were blue. His eyes bulged, and his neck lolled brokenly over
his chest.

"Jesus, Mary, and Joseph," Mullin whispered as he wrapped
his arms around Houdini's waist and tried to lift the magician up.

That was when Houdini opened his eyes.

SUDDENLY, HOUDINI'S LEGS came up, his thighs clenching
around Mullin's head. Spittle flew from Mullin's lips as he beat
against his captor's hold. Unperturbed, Houdini locked his fists
over the copper piping and tightened his grip until Mullin's
body went slack as he plummeted to the floor, unconscious.

Houdini swung from the pipe by one hand as he freed his
neck from the noose, then dropped to the floor. He freed the
ring of keys from Mullin's belt and took the Enfield from the
table by the chair. Then he opened the stairwell door and
dashed up the stairs.

There were men talking in the locker room, so Houdini went
up another flight, to the administration offices. Here, there
were only two men at their desks, on opposite sides of the large
room. Houdini crawled, low to the floor, until he found an office overlooking the Bowery and the front stoop of Police Headquarters, now one story below him.

The scene outside was typical Lower East Side chaos. Bells
rang incessantly. Police carriages, motorcycles, and Model-T
ambulances crowded the block as police corralled dozens of
drunks and dancing girls into Headquarters—the remnants of a
Chatham Square Dance Hall knife fight earlier in the evening.
Amid the shoving, screaming, and arguing, there was a sharp

sound of breaking glass, and something landed, hard, on an ambulance roof.

POLICE AND BYSTANDERS caught a glimpse of a fast-moving figure in a tattered linen shirt bounding in single strides across carriage and car rooftops. The officers grappling with the Chatham drunks could only watch, confused, as the figure—who bore a striking resemblance to the Great Houdini—leaped to the ground and slung a leg over one of the police motorcycles, a high-powered 36-inch V-Twin Scout.

The Indian's two-cylinder engine coughed, then roared as the motorcycle's hard-tail swung in circles before firing forward like a pistol shot. Houdini swerved between trucks, horses, and fist-waving prostitutes. More police trucks rolled to a halt, blocking Houdini's route, skidding him out. Houdini idled, feet on the ground, eyeing the gauntlet of police officers growing wise behind him, filling the street. He revved the engine in warning and turned the cycle to face them. The few officers unencumbered by drunks freed their truncheons and assembled in a line, shouting orders, which Houdini could not hear over the growl of the motorcycle.

Suddenly, Houdini turned the throttle and the Scout spit toward the officers, popping a wheelie as it blew past Police Headquarters and the disorderly mob, tore a right turn zipping down Prince Street, before flying onto West. Houdini opened the throttle and the Scout's speed climbed to forty, fifty, sixty miles per hour. The Hudson River sparkled to his left as he blew past the Gansevoort Market and London Terrace on his right. Houdini hunkered down, face in the wind, legs tucked up tight as he passed the Weehawken Ferry.

THE EMPIRE STATE Express surged out of an underground tunnel and rattled over the city streets on elevated tracks.

Inside, Abigail kept moving to the front of the train, always one step ahead of the conductor checking tickets. She would linger in the loud and windy spaces between cars, where small bridges spanned the couplers, then at the first sight of the conductor's cap she'd move ahead.

In one of the more crowded cars, filled with standing passengers, someone grabbed her arm.

Abigail tried to pull away, but Bess Houdini held her fast. "What in the name of St. Peter do you think you're doing?"

"Leave me be," Abigail snapped, pulling her arm away.

"We're trying to help you, Abigail."

"I don't want your help; I want to be left alone. Why can't you people understand that? If I leave this place, you can all go back to your lives."

"It isn't safe," Bess insisted, lowering her voice.

Abigail scowled. "I was taking care of myself while your ancestors were wearing animal skins."

"Tickets," the conductor said from behind them, and Abigail flinched guiltily.

Bess calmly opened her purse. "Two, please, sir."

Abigail continued to glower at her rescuer.

The conductor punched two tickets and handed them to Bess, who then pulled Abigail deeper into the crowd.

"Now, let's find some seats, shall we?" Bess said.

UP AT THE front of the train, the engineer perched on a high, padded seat on the right-hand side of the cab. He cocked his head out the window, affording himself an unobstructed view of the tracks ahead. His left hand pulled down on the long throttle lever, as the train rumbled along at forty miles per hour.

Then the engineer turned to glance at the back of the train. Normally, at this stage of the journey, he'd have received a "reduce speed" or a "proceed" signal via lantern from one of the two brakemen in the caboose. But no such signal was forthcoming. The engineer frowned.

To be on the safe side, he pulled down on the air-brake lever, slowing their course until he could find out what the problem was.

*   *   *

THE TRAIN'S CABOOSE lay far behind the engine cab, separated from it by thirteen passenger cars. Three unused lanterns sat atop the coal stove. In the back of the room, which also served as the crew's living quarters, was a cupola, from which the brakeman could keep an eye on the train and maintain the signals. But now it lay empty.

Instead, ragged brown robes slid over the chalky face of one of the brakemen, his sooty gray uniform spattered with blood. The other brakeman sat in the corner, his hands cupping his intestines. He looked sleepy and was still breathing, but just barely. Several soft, trembling squeals flitted across the caboose as eleven jewel-eyed demons swayed with the motion of the train, sickles gleaming.

43

HOUDINI'S SILVER GHOST sped through the Hudson River Valley, uplifting tornadoes of leaves as it passed.

Doyle was unaccustomed to American roads. So despite the press of time and Abigail's disappearance, he dedicated most of his concentration on not veering left into the lane of oncoming cars.

He was aware that Lovecraft was locking his arms and pushing against the dashboard. And as Doyle took a particularly sharp turn and once again merged into the wrong lane, Lovecraft shrieked.

"Right side! Right side!" he shouted as Doyle wrenched the wheel back.

"Americans always have to do things their way," Doyle groused.

"I'm gettin' sick back here," Marie complained, her hand over her eyes.

After receiving Smedley's message, Sebastian had volunteered to finish tidying up at the DeMarcus Manor so that the Arcanum would be free to follow Abigail and Bess. Throughout the crisis, Sebastian had performed magnificently—not only keeping all his promises, but also exhibiting enormous courage and selflessness. And Doyle realized that he owed the man his thanks, and also a debt. Without the aid of the American Society of Magicians, Darian's madness might have consumed all of the city—not to mention the world. And where he had once been suspicious, Doyle now had to admit the A.S.M. was an impressive body, deserving of trust and, perhaps, responsibility. Even if this victory was to be theirs, the sun was setting on the age of the Arcanum. Soon another secret society must take up the mantle, and carry on the mission and charter of Montalvo Konstantin Duvall. Meaning that Sebastian Aloysius and the A.S.M. might find themselves the inheritors of a more daunting legacy than they had anticipated.

"Do we know where the train is headed?" Doyle asked, pulled back to the present by the realization that he had absolutely no idea where he was going.

"It runs through Poughkeepsie, but I don't know the way," said Lovecraft. "Just head for the river. I know the tracks run parallel."

"Is there a road to the river?" Doyle asked.

"Do I look like a cartographer?" Lovecraft replied tartly.

"Bloody hell," Doyle growled as he swerved off the pavement and onto a dirt road that appeared to wind through woods and over hills into the heart of the valley.

DETECTIVE MULLIN SQUEEZED the small piece of paper between his stubby fingers and read the message again:

Bess in Danger/Empire State Express

His Model-T police cruiser strained at thirty-five miles per hour up Second Avenue, past Jefferson Park, where he eventually hooked a left onto 125th Street. The Alhambra Theatre flashed by on the right-hand side, then he swung right at Nicholas Park, honking his horn to clear the pedestrians and slower carriages from the road.

His actions were violating every police protocol, but his instincts drove him on. Something was going on here. Mullin had

a nagging suspicion the real players in this dark opera were
about to take the stage.

LEAVING MANHATTAN ISLAND behind, Houdini surged onto
the semipaved roads of Spuyten Duyvil, looking up at the high
arches of High and Washington Bridges. He sped north through
Bronxville to Yonkers, where the air was thick with the chemical
smells of the many carpet factories. The Scout fishtailed as
Houdini steered onto a dirt country road parallel to the railroad
tracks along the Hudson River. The cycle bucked and lurched
over the road's holes and divits. At a clearing in the brush, Houdini swerved onto an embankment. The back tire spewed dirt
into the air as the Scout groaned and muscled up onto the railroad tracks. With a train whistle fading in the distance, Houdini
poured on the speed, hot on the trail of the Empire State Express.

BESS GAZED AT Abigail, who was asleep beside her, face
pressed to the window and breath steaming the glass as moonlit
valleys flowed by outside. She noticed a leather pouch hung
about Abigail's neck with a string of what looked like human
hair. Bess reached for it, but Abigail shifted, removing it from
reach. Instead, Bess watched her raspberry tea slosh in its cup
as she tried to determine how to return Abigail safely to New
York. She could attempt to wrestle her off the train at the next
stop, wherever that might be, but doubted the likelihood of success. Abigail seemed surprisingly stubborn once she had fixed
her mind on something. Bess then wondered if she might not
enlist the train conductor's help, but that would open up a
litany of questions to which she had no sufficient answers. That
left the option of simply following Abigail until she could find a
way to contact Arthur.

Bess felt a sudden panic. Unlike some wives, she had grown
so accustomed to fearing for her husband's life that it was like a
switch had been turned off in her brain. It was as if the relentless pace of his existence and the danger of his stunts had

become the norm. But prison . . . Prison was all too real, and the stakes far graver. Up until now, Bess had always believed her husband capable of anything—for it had been a trust he had borne in proof time and time again. He had always risen, as predictably as the sun, to whatever challenge presented itself.

SEVERAL CARS AHEAD, the conductor ducked his head into the engine room and shouted, "We're behind schedule!"

The engineer swung around, his gaze angry. "That's because I ain't gotten a signal since we left the station. Get back there and find out just what in the Sam Hill is goin' on, will ya? Otherwise, I'm stopping at Tarrytown till we sort this out. An' if they're drinkin' on the job again, I'll hide their asses myself."

The conductor needed no further instruction. He ducked out of the engine room as the engineer applied the air brake, and a scream of protest rose from the engine. But the Empire State Express slowed its approach to the Tarrytown station near the shores of the Tappan Zee.

ABIGAIL BOLTED AWAKE. "Why are we stopping?"

"Perhaps someone needs to get off," Bess answered.

The conductor entered the car from the front, wearing a concerned expression. He passed Bess and Abigail as the train surged into a tunnel, and the entire car went black save for the flash of track sparks.

Abigail jumped to her feet. "What's happening?"

"Sit down," Bess said soothingly. "It's only—"

A curdling squeal echoed down the car, and a flash through the windows revealed a trio of demons flowing down the aisle, their ruby eyes glinting, sickles biting into anything in their path. Bess watched in horror as the conductor caught a blade under the ribs and was flung forward like a rag doll, to land atop a family of five.

Abigail scrambled over Bess and toppled into the aisle.

"Abigail!" Bess screamed, then cursed herself for revealing

the name. For amidst the screams of the passengers came squeals of discovery as the demons located their prey.

ABIGAIL KNOCKED OVER a waiter as she ran, sending wine-glasses tumbling. As she reached the car door, she looked back and saw creatures following, heard the screams of frightened passengers. She pushed open the door and darted into the windy gap between cars. Abigail could see the train tracks flashing by beneath her, and the steam whistle shrieked as it announced the Empire State's arrival at the Tarrytown station. Abigail lunged across the pedestrian bridge above the couplers and stumbled into the next passenger car, the train whistle blurring into the howling of her pursuers as they burst through the door behind her.

And still Abigail kept running, until she came to the engine cab and slammed into the iron instrument panel. This close to the engines, the noise was deafening.

The engineer scowled at her. "Get back to yer seat."

Abigail touched a hand to her bleeding forehead. She opened her mouth to speak, but couldn't find the words.

Something about her expression must have alerted the engineer, for he leaned toward her. "What's the matter?"

His answer came in the form of a long neck, which swiveled around the doorway, topped off by a lean head in a sackcloth hood, with rubies in place of eyes.

The engineer cast his eyes from the creature to Abigail and back again. He released the air brake and climbed off his chair, placing himself between them.

"What the Christ is going—?" he began, then the demon raised its blade. Abigail saw the sickle bite deep into the engineer's gut. Something splashed on the floor. Then a wet, red hook lifted, and the engineer fell into a corner of the cab.

"Water," the engineer begged.

The creature then reached for Abigail, who sprang onto the engineer's chair and scuttled out the open window, out of reach of those long fingers.

Wind screamed in her ears and tugged at her oversized coat. She looked down at the tracks flashing past beneath her. Should she slip, she would fall beneath the train and be ground into chopped meat.

With shaking hands, she reached along the outer wall of the cab and grabbed a maintenance railing as the demon lunged after her. Half of its lithe body dangled from the cab, arms swinging for Abigail as she leaped onto the rounded neck of the K-4 engine—the vibrating, superheated, 242-ton power core. She slid her small feet along the narrow ledge, fists affixed to the steel railing, standing over the chewing cylinders and valve chest, the crisscrossing rods, links, and reversing gears. Her hat flew off her head, bouncing off the body of the demon that followed her onto the engine. Its robes rattled in the wind as it gurgled, uncertain, jewel eyes glancing down, bandaged feet sliding, cautiously, on the ledge.

INSIDE THE ENGINEER'S cab, two more demons studied the complex tubing of the instrument panel. Their heads swayed as wet purrs sounded off the iron walls. Then one took hold of the throttle lever, which was currently pointing up, slowing the train down to less than thirty miles per hour. With a squeal, the demon pulled the lever back down, and the engines kicked in protest. Valves shuddered and cylinders trembled as superheated steam was introduced from the steam dome into the boiler, forcing the pistons through the piston rods, which, in turn, pushed and pulled the valve rods, freeing more steam.

With fresh plumes of exhaust rising from the chimney, the Empire State Express began speeding up.

EVEN AT SIXTY miles per hour, Houdini feared he would not catch the train. The landscape on either side of him, the rising highlands, he knew as the approach to Tarrytown. The railroad tracks turned away from the river and headed west. Houdini knew the Empire State would have to circle through Irvington before the Tarrytown stop. His only hope of catching up would be a direct route through the rolling countryside. So, taking a deep breath, Houdini opened the throttle and soared off the tracks, passing over a rocky embankment, landing ugly on his front wheel in a river valley pasture with only mud roads. Houdini toppled from the Scout and struck the ground some twenty feet away, landing on his back. The Scout wheezed on its side as its wheels spun. Favoring his ribs, Houdini ran to the cycle, righted it, straddled the seat, and tore across the field.

Cresting a promontory twenty minutes later, surrounded on all sides by lush valleys and cornfields, Houdini caught sight of the Empire State Express and the spires of the tallest church in Tarrytown. The train tracks plunged through the heart of the village, and from his high vantage, Houdini could see the thick puffs of steam as the train started to move faster.

Houdini surged straight into the cornfields. The Scout's wheels battered and bounced off the dried mud, spitting chunks of dirt and loosening wheel bolts, while Houdini propped himself above the seat, knees bending to absorb each impact. Then the cornfields parted, and Houdini roared onto the main road.

Thanks to the shortcut, he had arrived in Tarrytown in advance of the train. The Scout flew down a residential street, engines whining and straining. The whistle of the train pierced the air.

Gradually, the estates of Tarrytown gave way to the village center—to restaurants, drugstores, and clothiers, all closed for the evening. Between the buildings, Houdini could see the Empire State building up speed, blasting past the train station at fifty miles per hour and climbing.

Knowing the area, Houdini realized that he would have one shot—and one shot only—to overtake the locomotive. He throttled the motorcycle for one final, all-out surge.

The few pedestrians still on the streets dove for safety as the Indian V-Twin rocketed for the cobblestone bridge spanning the train tracks. The Empire State had already passed halfway under the bridge. Houdini had mere seconds to act.

He steered the cycle onto the bridge, turned his body toward the train, tucked his legs under him, feet on the seat, fingers grazing the handlebars. He knelt down into a crouch, measuring the distance with his eyes, and dove from the motorcycle. The world's greatest magician cleared the bridge wall—arms waving to control the trajectory of his flight—soared through the night air, and plunged thirty feet down onto the last passenger car.

His body spun on impact and rolled wildly left. In the blink of an eye, Houdini was dangling off the side, one hand attached to the maintenance railing, the rest of his body pitched above the rushing ground.

THE SILVER GHOST skidded to a stop on the dirt shoulder of a hilly road in the Hudson Highlands. Doyle, Lovecraft, and Marie spilled out of the car and raced to the edge of the lookout. From the crest, they could see the waters of the Hudson and, to the south, the distant lights of Tarrytown. Then a whistle blew, and the Empire State Express snaked around a wooded corner, its headlight gleaming fiercely.

Lovecraft suddenly pointed. "Look!"

All eyes went to the third-to-last passenger car, where a man in a tattered linen shirt was battling the winds, running the length of the roof, and diving to the next car.

"That's Herry," Marie exclaimed.

"He's mad," Lovecraft said as Houdini made another perilous leap.

"Yes, he is," Doyle said, a small smile on his lips. "And thank God for it." He turned to the others as the train vanished around another bend. "Back to the car. We'll catch them in the hills."

44

ABIGAIL HUGGED THE rounded top of the engine car. Tarry-town was nothing more than points of light now, lost in the distance. An occasional punch of wind landed in the depths of her coat, threatening to fling her off the train. So, she wormed free of the garment and it flew away, cartwheeling across the train roof.

Unfortunately, she couldn't shed the demon quite as easily. With a squeal of rage, it locked its hand around her ankle. Abigail tried to kick it away, but the demon pulled at her with unexpected strength, slowly dragging her closer. At the last instant, she wrapped her arms around the bronze bell set between the chimneys, clinging tightly. But far from deterring the creature, this only encouraged the demon to use her as a ladder, climbing up her body and onto the roof of the cab.

She couldn't leap clear; the land dropped away sharply to either side of the tracks. And the train was moving too quickly.

The demon freed its sickle and clumsily swung at her. The blade clanged loudly off the bell. Keeping her grip on the bell, Abigail let her body swing down along the side of the train, then hooked the railing with her foot and used that to scamper up the other side of the bell. The demon was not so agile, and seemed reluctant to follow.

Abigail, however, had run out of train. Gouts of steam erupted from the chimney stack only a few feet from her head. The heat was unbearable, and the sound deafening as the train screamed down the tracks at ever-increasing speeds.

Abigail looked up at the stars. Though it went against all she had trained herself to believe, flight was an option. But to do so was an admission of her inhumanity. It threatened to burst wide a psychological dam, holding back two thousand years of abandonment and shame. Her wings were a reminder of what had been lost. The sky was not her escape but her prison. If she was to die, she would die human.

The demon raised its sickle again, and Abigail moved her hand just in time to prevent it from being hacked off. But the demon continued to target her handhold, forcing Abigail to switch hands and then, finally, to release the bell altogether. There was nothing to hold on to anymore. She was backed up against the chimney, hotter than any furnace. At the next burst of wind, she'd be thrown off the train.

The glowing eyes of another demon peered over the engine roof. It was less hesitant than its fellow, pulling itself onto the maintenance railing then climbing onto the roof.

Abigail could see more demons lining up on the narrow ledge outside the engineer's cab, their robes whipping about like curtains in a storm, their keening squeals a victory cry. One by one, they advanced on her.

When the next set of gem eyes broke the plane, whatever crumbs of hope Abigail had left blew away in the winds. It writhed onto the roof, its robes like a cape of living shadow. It called to her like it knew her, gurgling in that spit-clogged voice, reaching out with long-bandaged fingers.

Abigail felt despair fill her. She'd done all she could to avoid them, but it seemed they wanted her to die more than she wanted to live. Because what was she, after all? She was neither human nor angel. She was the last of the Lost Tribe, an affront to God—as much a disappointment as the abominations of the

Flood. And Abigail was tired. She stared at the approaching demons and imagined the killing blow, hoping that it would be fast and painless.

The closest demon reared back, and its sickle cut across the silver moon. Abigail could see the engineer's blood still dripping off the steel. But as the creature leaned forward to strike, something pulled its robes, and the demon flew off the train and into the path of an oncoming telephone pole. Flesh met wood pillar with a sickening thud, and the demon fell away into the brush.

Houdini dragged himself up the side of the train and into the demon's place. He took Abigail's hands and locked them around the bell once more. "Hang on, sweetheart."

Then Houdini spun around, balancing on his fingertips, and swept a leg into the knee joint of the next approaching demon, snapping its leg like kindling. It squealed and flopped backwards, inadvertently knocking the third demon from its feet. The wind did the rest. The third demon slid over the side, somersaulting over a dozen jagged boulders before vanishing over the side of the hill.

The demon with the broken leg sat up and took hold of Houdini's shirt, yanking him forward. Houdini collided with the rear chimney, scalding his hands. The demon pulled Houdini down on top of it and they wrestled, rolling perilously back and forth near the edges. Houdini coughed and gagged as the demon stuck its fingers in his mouth, perhaps trying to tear out his soul. His stomach recoiled at the taste of its rotted hands. The keening demon scrambled on top of Houdini and dug its sharp nails into the flesh of his neck, pressing, strangling. Houdini clawed at the creature's face, snatching one of its gem eyes and ripping it free. The demon wailed as the gem eye dangled from living veins and fabric strings.

Then Houdini curled into a ball, wedged his feet under the demon's ribs, and launched it into the air. The demon's robes snagged in a passing oak, and Abigail watched the body snap into a dozen shapes around the massive branches.

*   *   *

THE SILVER GHOST fishtailed out of the forest and onto a narrow strip of dirt road that ran parallel to the railroad tracks and the Empire State Express. The left-side wheels of the Rolls bumped over loose rocks, grazing the edges of a long trench that ran between the tracks and the road.

The train howled and burped smoke like an Abyssal dragon.

The driver's door of the Silver Ghost swung open as Doyle pressed the accelerator to the floor, measuring the distance between the train and the car.

"What are you doing?" Lovecraft exclaimed.

"Howard, take the wheel," Doyle commanded.

"Good God." Lovecraft nervously grasped the wheel as Doyle turned to face the train, hands braced to either side of the car door.

"Arthur, *non!*" Marie pulled at his jacket, but he shook her off. He could see the frightened faces of the passengers pressed to the windows, beating with their fists for release. He knew the time had come to act.

Long weeds whacked the tips of his shoes as Doyle looked down into the rock-strewn trench as it flew by. The train was slowly passing them.

Then Lovecraft gestured frantically to him; the train was entering a tunnel, and the road they were on ended in a wall.

Realizing he could wait no longer, Doyle turned back to the train. A passenger car was pulling level with the Rolls, the hollow of the doorway steps as close as it would get.

Doyle stood up in the doorway of the Silver Ghost as Lovecraft slid into the driver's seat. The car swerved, nearly pitching Doyle out, but he held fast. The wind whipped his jacket as he leaped for the passenger stairwell. He landed hard, knocking the air from his lungs, then slid down the stairs—stunned—and grabbed the edge of the railing just in time. His body bucked off the gravel on the side of the tracks. The ground tore at his clothes and stripped his skin. His legs bounced along the side of the train, slipping closer to the chewing wheels, as his arms pulled with all their strength.

Then slender hands wrapped around his wrists, and Bess Houdini appeared. "Arthur!"

The extra leverage gave Doyle the strength he needed to pull himself onto the steps. There he collapsed, panting, while Bess draped her body over his in relief.

LOVECRAFT SLAMMED BOTH feet on all three pedals as the Empire State Express vanished into the tunnel and the stone wall rushed up to meet him. The wheels locked, kicking up a cloud of dirt, and the car twisted and threatened to roll over as Lovecraft fought the wheel. Then the Rolls-Royce came to a squealing halt mere inches from the wall.

Lovecraft wiped the sweat from his brow, and sat back, exhausted. But Marie slapped his shoulder as she squirmed into the front seat.

"What you waitin' for, Howard? Turn us around!"

AS THE EMPIRE State Express reemerged from the tunnel, Houdini lifted his head. He had been crouched protectively over Abigail, but now he saw the roof of the engine car was awash in demons. They advanced in small steps, using their numbers to shield them against the wind.

Houdini pulled Abigail to her feet, surveying the sweeping cornfields to the right and the woods up ahead.

A sickle hissed within inches of their faces, then another. Houdini yanked Abigail behind him, knowing that he couldn't fight them all.

They wailed at him like a single organism: a wall of fluttering black with dozens of gleaming eyes.

Houdini turned and hugged Abigail tightly. "Close your eyes," he told her, "and relax your body into mine. I'll hold you."

As Abigail sagged into Houdini's arms, he scooped her up, one arm under her knees and the other wrapped around her waist. He dodged a sickle, and it clanged off the chimney stack. Three more blades rose up as Houdini pulled Abigail close, then jumped off the train.

A cloud of dirt burst from the side of the hill as they landed, their bodies flopping and tumbling into a swaying sea of cornstalks.

Houdini flew like a cannonball through the first several rows of stalks, crumpling, finally, into a bruised and battered heap. He tried to climb to his knees, but toppled back onto the ground—spent. When he called Abigail's name, a fork of pain cut off the word. He looked down at his left arm lying weird and crooked on the dirt—dislocated. Wincing, he gripped his left biceps and jammed his shoulder back into its socket.

DOYLE PULLED BESS through train cars teeming with hysterical passengers. The sound of breaking glass occasionally punctuated the panicked screams, as some desperate souls attempted to dive out the window to safety. Bloody bodies lined the floor, marking the demons' path.

The number of wounded increased as they arrived at the door to the engine car. In front of the door lay a bespectacled man, clutching his slashed face. He grabbed at Doyle's pant leg.

"Some kind of monsters . . . don't go in there."

Doyle turned to Bess. "Stay here."

"Please be careful, Arthur. They're not human."

"Yes, I know."

Bess knelt down to tend to the wounded man as Doyle forced open the door, letting in the screech and howl of the winds. He shut the door behind him and clung to the rails of the small bridge above the couplers. The last door lay straight ahead. He crossed to it and wrenched the handle. The door slid open. Soot and steam filled the car, and it smelled heavily of blood. And no wonder, for there was a wide swath of it on the floor, and the engineer lay curled there—dead—though his stomach still hiccupped blood.

Doyle took a step forward, then ducked as a sickle sparked off the steel door. A demon lunged from the shadows, forcing Doyle back through the door, and together they plunged onto the wire bridge.

Under the force of their landing, one of the bolts of the bridge sheared off and the structure tilted wildly, one side dropping three feet onto the couplers. Doyle's head dangled above the crushing couplers and the sawing wheels. The bridge shook at a dangerous, pitched incline. The creature flopped down atop him, its blade inching toward his throat.

As Doyle struggled to push it away, he spied the couplers beside him. Their curving jaws hooked together like the fingers of two hands, and were fastened by two pins attached to lifting rods. Doyle managed to free one hand and wrapped his fingers around the coupler pin as the blade inched closer to his flesh. Then he ripped the pin out, and the couplers detached. The wire walkway slammed onto the tracks, spitting sparks, bucking the demon violently off Doyle.

Doyle clung desperately to the walkway as it thrashed about. The demon had managed to swing its arm around and catch the tail end of the bridge; it squealed with rage and pain as sparks flew in its face. Behind it, the last passenger car faded into the darkness. As the demon held on to the wire walkway, its body bucking off the stones, Doyle pulled himself up and into the engine car, leaving the demon still wailing behind him. He climbed to the engineer's chair, regarding the tangled forest of instruments, rods, hissing cranks, and dials in consternation.

Using his limited knowledge of the function of the Walscharts gear and his more general understanding of the principles of steam locomotion, Doyle took hold of the throttle lever and slowly eased it upward, cutting the flow of steam, then activated the air brake. The engine car jolted and slowed, wheels screeching on the tracks. Doyle turned. Within seconds the rest of the train surged out of the shadows to meet the engine car. Doyle applied the throttle and released some of the pressure off the air brake to avoid a more catastrophic collision.

The demon hanging off the walkway swung its head around, its gem eyes gleaming as the engine car slowed to meet the passenger cars. The demon wailed as it burst like a melon between the train couplers, their curved halves colliding and relinking through the mass of crushed demon.

Doyle sat on the engineer's chair, shoulders sagging with exhaustion as he wiped the soot from his eyes and face with the back of his hand and the Empire State Express groaned its way to a halt.

*   *   *

HOUDINI PROBED ABIGAIL'S knee, pressing at the joints until she cried out.

"You tore something in the fall," he explained.

Abigail nodded, wincing.

"Can you stand?"

"I don't know." She struggled to rise. He did his best to help, but when she put weight on the knee she gasped and shook her head.

"I need you brave now, Abigail, okay? We still have to make it to the woods."

Abigail bit her lip and nodded.

Houdini threw her arm over his shoulder and swept the cornstalks aside, making slow progress over the uneven ground. "That's it. Good girl. You're doing fine."

But Abigail's knee injury grew more painful by the step. Each time she moved, it felt like a nail was driven into her kneecap. She faltered, then her ankle twisted and she tumbled to the ground.

Houdini bent over to catch his breath.

"We have to keep going, sweetheart."

Abigail just nodded, shutting her eyes against the pain.

AS HOUDINI ONCE again examined Abigail's knee, a wail sounded on the wind. Haunting. Sad.

Houdini froze, gesturing for silence.

After a pause, the wailing rose again, sharper this time. And other voices joined the chorus, until the sky was filled with predatory squeals.

Houdini said a prayer as he lifted his eyes to the heavens, but nothing prepared him for the sight that greeted him.

They looked like vultures, stark against the moon, but only because they flew so high. As they drifted down over the cornfield in elegant circles, all doubts were erased as to their true nature. Broken, bloody wings beat, holding aloft hideous corpses. Eight sets of bloody wings unfurled from eight rotting backs. Eight sets of bone jaws fell open, and the demons squealed, a macabre choir of dead souls on the hour of their triumph, gem eyes set into their white skulls. Some flesh still stuck to the bodies in rotting patches like barnacles.

Somewhere deep in his memory, Houdini heard Lovecraft's warning voice regarding creatures of the Mythos and the human psyche, so he tore his gaze away before the shock set in. But their cries were inescapable.

Houdini again pulled Abigail into his arms and sprinted for the forest.

Their pursuers swarmed and dove.

Though Houdini could not turn around, he could hear the thump of wings in the air growing louder by the second.

"Hang on," Houdini shouted, then dove down as a sickle sliced over their heads, shearing the corn. A noisome body swooped past then peeled away, back into the sky.

Houdini swung Abigail up in his arms again and staggered toward the woods, the air around them thick with squeals and the beating of broken wings.

45

STUNNED PASSENGERS POURED off the Empire State Express and into a shallow ravine bordering lush pastures just a few miles outside of Poughkeepsie. Fire wagons and medical trucks were just arriving with first aid and blankets for the wounded, while local farmers hung lanterns on tree branches so the doctors could work, diagnosing injuries and separating the dead from the living.

Doyle guided Bess down a dirt road, away from the train. "We can't be seen here."

"What about Abigail?" she asked.

"She's with Houdini. At least, that's my hope."

"He's here?"

"He was on the roof of the train, trying to save Abigail."

Bess held her gloved hand to her lips, unsure whether to be relieved or newly afraid. "Then where are they now?"

Doyle shook his head. "I don't know."

Bess had maintained admirable steadiness throughout the preceding ordeal, but now she was spent. She sagged visibly.

Then a roaring filled their ears, and the Silver Ghost soared out of the darkness, with Lovecraft at the wheel. He slammed the brakes and the car spun a 180-degree turn, uplifting a cloud of dust and severing saplings.

As the car braked before them, Doyle could hear the familiar sound of Lovecraft and Marie arguing.

". . . almost run dem over!"

"Do you think it's easy driving with you squawking at me, woman?"

"It's by God's will alone that we alive!"

"I'm a scientist, not a mechanic!"

Doyle opened the driver's-side door. Marie slithered into the backseat while Lovecraft slid over to the passenger side. Bess climbed into the back with Marie, who was still slapping Lovecraft on the back of the head.

"Talk to me like I'm some whore?"

"Marie, please," Doyle interjected.

Lovecraft spun around. "Put your hands on me once more and I'll not be responsible!"

"Howard—" Doyle tried again.

"Don't threaten me, demon child!" Marie wagged a finger.

"Hold!" Doyle shouted, quieting the car. He took Lovecraft's satchel off the floor and pushed it into his stomach. "Find them!"

Doyle released the emergency hand-brake, shoved his left foot against the low-speed pedal, then turned the car around, facing away from the train. As he bumped his way down the rutted dirt road, he released his left foot and let the car into high gear. The Silver Ghost rumbled through an alley of trees.

AS THE CAR passed a particularly majestic maple, a match flared, illuminating the face of Detective Mullin, smoke pouring from his nostrils as he puffed a small cigar. Upon sighting the Arcanum, he slipped his finger through the loop of wire controlling the choke on his parked Model-T, and spun the hand crank affixed by the driver's-side door. The engine roared to life. He climbed up onto the trembling running board and into the car, releasing the throttle before the engine stalled. The Model-T lurched onto the road after the Arcanum.

THE INTERIOR OF the Silver Ghost was illuminated with a greenish glow from the spectral, floating equations of the Eltdown Shard. Lovecraft turned the reel as the tiny pistons chugged, feeding energy to the magical bone. Numbers flickered in and out of existence, and Lovecraft struggled to comprehend the curious, contradictory messages.

"They're close, I . . ." He trailed off, confused.

"Yes? What?" Doyle demanded.

The headlights illuminated farmers in groups of twos and threes, shotguns over their shoulders, still in their robes and pajamas, heading for the train. Word was spreading.

Lovecraft suddenly stiffened. "Left. Turn left."

There was no road, so Doyle turned into a space between the trees, then accelerated up a slight dirt rise and across a pasture. The Silver Ghost jolted as the wheels ground over dirt toward another forest.

FOLLOWING WITH HIS headlights off, Mullin attempted the same maneuver with terrible results. The top-heavy Model-T rolled up the small rise, then teetered on its left side, the wheels leaving the ground. Mullin slammed the gas, but it was too late. He dove out of the car as it rolled over onto its side, then, finally, back onto the road, completely upside down. Mullin cursed and flung his cigar at the Model-T as its engine sputtered and died. He turned and jogged after the Silver Ghost, whose lights were fading in the distance.

THE ROLLS HAD reached the edge of the woods. They couldn't drive farther, but Lovecraft had caught the scent. "Everybody out, quickly!"

Doyle assisted Bess as Lovecraft, holding out his gauntleted forearm, plunged along the edge of the woods. "They're close!" he said, then wheeled around and stopped. Doyle and Marie joined him. All was quiet save for their combined breathing as the demonologist studied the glowing numbers flashing in the air.

"Howard?"

Lovecraft motioned Doyle to silence. "They're here." He peered into the gloom of the woods. "I don't understand. They should be right here."

Doyle frowned. "Then the readings are wrong."

"They're not wrong."

Marie touched both their arms and pointed up.

All eyes turned skyward to the shadows blotting the stars, soaring in a circle over the trees.

HOUDINI CARRIED ABIGAIL into the shelter of the woods. But it was hard to navigate in the patchy moonlight, and soon a root caught his foot and he flopped forward, pitching Abigail onto the ground. Houdini tried to rise, grunting, but suddenly Abigail froze against him and clapped an urgent hand over his mouth.

You could drown in the silence. Houdini could hear the blood rushing in his temples, could hear the thump of his heart in his chest.

Then branches over their heads snapped, and leaves rustled, startling a flock of birds into motion. Shadows plunged into the trees from above, and debris showered down. Gurgles and squeals wailed through the woods, and those cries were answered by more, until the combined effect was like a symphony of disharmonic dread.

Suddenly, branches snapped at their left—lower down this time—and bodies burst through the darkness. Houdini launched at them from the forest floor, only to find himself nose to nose with Doyle.

"Arthur!"

Doyle threw his arms around Houdini, but Houdini was more intent on reaching Bess. He flung his arms around his wife and showered her damp face with kisses.

In the meantime, Lovecraft and Marie went to Abigail, wrapping protective arms around her and helping her walk.

The reunion was brief, however, as large bodies scrambled down through the trees, driving the Arcanum into the center of a small clearing. The starry sky formed a sparkling bowl over their heads. The treetops shook. Autumn leaves spiraled away as the demons descended into the thicket, and the air, which was normally alive with the chirp of crickets, was now quiet as a graveyard.

"You are resilient; I'll grant you that," said a voice from the border of the woods.

Houdini and Doyle whirled around. It was a voice both recognized.

Paul Caleb stepped into the light of the sliver moon. He was dressed in a gray suit, an enigmatic smile on his lips, "My compliments on a contest well fought."

"Caleb?" Houdini managed.

"Houdini. Shouldn't you be in jail?"

Houdini turned to Doyle. "What the hell is going on?"

"Something tells me Darian DeMarcus served another master, whether he knew it or not," Doyle said. "The single entity who desired the Book more than any man ever could."

"Remember me, Marie?" Caleb asked as he unbuttoned his collar, loosened his tie, and showed off a pink scar on his throat. "My little love bite." The D.A. then let his tongue hang out, imitating a panting dog.

Marie breathed in, "The silver fox?"

"*Mon Dieu, aidez-moi, Marie, aidez-moi, s'il-vous-plaît.*" Caleb's voice was that of an old Creole woman.

Marie's dagger flashed, but Lovecraft held her back.

"We made good use of her, I assure you." Caleb winked at Marie.

"Don't listen, any of you," Doyle warned. "He's the Lord of Lies."

From a pocket in the folds of her skirt, Marie retrieved one half of a clamshell. She tilted it in her hand like a bowl. Then, without attracting Caleb's notice, she took Houdini's hand and pricked his thumb with her dagger.

Houdini stood impassive as Marie squeezed his thumb, catching the blood in the shell.

"AM I?" CALEB asked Doyle. "That is convenient. Or is the truth so searing that we turn away from it? Marie Laveau Glampion has danced with demons all her days, made herself powerful on their backs, knowing full well the consequences of such a bargain. We cannot lie," Caleb said, his face losing some of its expressiveness, as if controlled remotely by some hidden puppeteer. His voice took on a grating edge, like steel scraping steel. "We know the desires and instincts that rule men's souls, Arthur, for we *are* those desires and instincts. Think of us not as an entity, but as an idea whose time has come." Caleb's smile faded as he held out a hand. "Come now, Abigail."

Doyle stepped in front of her, and Lovecraft pulled her back. The demons chattered in the trees.

LOVECRAFT GLANCED OVER and saw what Marie was doing, and he, too, secretly offered his hand. She pricked his thumb, and let her shell catch the blood.

CALEB FOLDED HIS hands behind his back, annoyed. "What is it you think you're protecting? A little girl? A downy angel? No, you're protecting a system that has failed, a symbol of power run amok. You have been programmed to hate yourselves since the dawn of time, all of you. And why? Because you were told to distrust your most natural and basic instincts, the urges awakened at the birth of every child. To survive. To thrive. To seek. To fight. Yet these primordial elements of self were twisted into sins. And why? To answer that question we must consider who is threatened by such virtues." Caleb pointed a finger to the heavens. "The answer is simple: God. For if mankind were to cast off its shackles and realize its true destiny, God would cease to exist. And then *we* would be God. All of us, ruling together. History is written by the winners, don't you see? We have been maligned as the Lord of Lies, when we are the champion of men!"

"Within that logic one might conclude that war is in fact peace," Doyle retorted.

"The bloody, tearing, ripping struggle of birth? The child's scalded hand at its first touch of fire? The frightening fears and transformations of adolescence? The rending and defilement of virginity? The slow, devouring pull of old age? Without violence, Arthur, there is no transformation. The peace you imagine is paralysis. It's death."

At that moment, Doyle felt a sharp pain in his thumb, as Marie surreptitiously took her blood offering.

"Perhaps," Doyle answered, "but it's a sort of death we're willing to sacrifice for."

Caleb shrugged. "So be it."

The demons burst from the trees and swooped into the clearing, sickles slicing the air.

Doyle and Houdini whirled around, forcing the others down onto their knees.

The demons hovered over the circle, creating a terrible wind with the beating of their stolen wings.

In the circle, Marie put the shell on the ground, then cut her own palm and made a fist, spilling yet more blood. She scattered ground herbs into the mixture with her other hand. "I need more time," she whispered to Doyle.

Houdini freed Mullin's stolen Enfield .38 from his pocket and checked to see that it was loaded.

Lovecraft fished the Book of Enoch from his satchel and threw it on the ground.

"What are you doing?" Houdini hissed.

Lovecraft opened the codex and studied a bookmarked page. "This isn't just a piece of the Bible, it's a tome of formidable magic. If I translate correctly, I may be able to bind these things," Lovecraft answered.

"So that leaves us," Houdini said to Doyle.

Doyle grinned fiercely back.

Together, they burst from the circle, taking the demons by storm. Doyle drew the sword from his cane, slashing at one creature after another. Houdini, in turn, squeezed off three rounds, which found their mark in a burst of bones and wings.

Lovecraft stood and turned to the demons, thrusting his right hand to the sky. *"La mayyitan ma qadirun yatabaqa sarmadi fa itha yaji ash-shuthath al-mautu qad yantahi!"*

One of the demons wailed and broke off from the others, hands clawing at its gem eyes. It flew into a tree, then dropped, broken, to the ground.

Houdini fired three more rounds into the largest grouping of demons. However, one of the demons surged around, away from the others, then circled back, slashing at Houdini from behind and knocking him violently to the ground.

"Houdini!" Doyle yelled as he fought his way backwards, away from the sickles of two hovering demons.

But as the demon attacking Houdini tried to fly back to safety, Houdini lunged upward and grabbed its leg, dragging it kicking and screaming back to earth, where he laid into it with his fists. There was a wide cut across his back, but Houdini clearly didn't notice. The demon squealed beneath the flurry of blows. Houdini felt knuckles pop as his fists met more skeleton than flesh, but his fury overmatched the demon, which wiggled helplessly like a broken bird.

Hoo-hoo-hoo. Hoo-hoo.

At first, the sound was swallowed in the squeals and grunts of combat.

Hoo-hoo-hoo. Hoo-hoo.

Marie pressed the clamshell into the dirt and knelt before it. She raised her arms and began to chant, willing a slender thread of the immaterial from the brownish, gritty mixture.

His foe temporarily vanquished, Houdini staggered away from the stunned demon and put his back to Doyle's. There was a temporary respite as the demons circled above them.

All the while, Paul Caleb waited, watching, hands in his pockets. His head tilted at the new sounds.

The demons seemed curious, too, halting their attack as they tried to determine the source of this new distraction.

"What is that?" Houdini asked Doyle in a whisper.

"Owls," Doyle responded with a grin.

Marie's hands danced above the shell, molding an inexplicable smoke that rose up from the vessel.

A demon's arms flew up in defense as a thick, feathered body plunged out of the trees and soared past its head, then darted back into the high canopy, screeching.

The cries were everywhere now, building to a crescendo.

"Konstantin!" Marie screamed to the sky.

More than two dozen huge owls came plummeting through the autumn leaves on massive wings, their talons extended. They wheeled and dived, ripping at the squealing demons.

Doyle, Houdini, and Lovecraft watched as two barn owls bit and clawed a demon's fragile wings. Feathers and blood rained across the clearing, and still the owls continued to come. The sky was a solid wall of bodies. The demons were lost in the mayhem—a swooping, devouring blanket of claws and beaks.

It was in this maelstrom that Caleb broke through the Arcanum's ranks and grabbed Abigail by the neck, baring his white teeth. "You'll still be mine!"

At that, Abigail ripped the pouch from her neck and cast it into Caleb's face in a cloud of sparkling dust. Caleb coughed and retreated, wiping his eyes as Abigail fell back into Lovecraft's arms. Then Caleb stared at his hands and saw the tiny crystals. He turned to Marie.

"Angelica root," he said, then burst into flames, howling in rage as his arms flailed and his borrowed flesh blistered and blackened. The fire caught on the wings of the plunging owls and licked at the shrieking, slapping demons, some of whom tried to escape into the sky, but the owls followed, unrelentingly savage.

And while the battle still raged higher above their heads, Caleb stumbled about the clearing until the inferno that was his borrowed body died down. He coughed up bits of scorched lung as he turned his melted eyes again on the Arcanum, his skull singed bald, cheeks dripping skin.

"We'll remember that, Marie," Caleb mumbled through swollen, still-sizzling lips.

"You've lost," Doyle told him.

The creature that had been Caleb managed to stretch its ruined mouth into a grin. "Have I?"

Lovecraft stepped protectively in front of Abigail. "You've no power here; Darian proved that. The Laveau legend is true. You're a corruptor, that's all."

"Have you heard nothing we've said?" Caleb chuckled as he gagged a black gruel onto his hand. "You presume us weak because we come to you in the form of a man. But as we've said before, there is great power in all of us, if only we channel that power into action." Caleb opened his charred suit jacket, and produced a Mauser. He fired three shots at Lovecraft.

IT HAPPENED TOO quickly to register. Before he knew what had happened, Lovecraft found himself on the ground. He felt himself over for blood and wounds, but found nothing. And then he noticed the others gathered over Abigail.

Caleb seemed stunned as well, the muzzle of his pistol still smoking in his grip.

Doyle opened Abigail's blouse. Deep red blood pumped from a hole in her chest and over her white skin.

Houdini cradled her head in his lap, tears welling in his eyes.

"Did I—?" Abigail tried to speak, but instead found herself fighting to breathe as blood flooded her mouth.

Lovecraft rose and joined the crowd leaning over Abigail. His face creased in an uncharacteristic display of emotion, and Marie touched him lightly on the back.

"Yes, Howard's fine, Abigail," Doyle answered her. "You saved him."

"I did?" Her eyes were wide with pleasure.

"Ssh; be still." Doyle placed a hand on her cheek.

Abigail's fists suddenly clenched Doyle's lapels as she struggled for breath, and he held her through the panic, tucking her head against his chest.

Marie covered her mouth, tears streaming down her cheeks.

Houdini pulled Bess into a tight embrace.

In the meantime, Caleb wheezed, "Now step aside."

Lovecraft lunged to his feet. "You stay away from her!"

Caleb held up his hands. "I'm taking what is mine. I'm taking back what was stolen from me. You of all seekers should realize this."

"No," Lovecraft protested. "Not her wings."

"Oh yes, her wings, dear boy. Claiming them opens a fissure between worlds. It shatters the false barriers that have kept us from Him all this time. Stand with us as we enter a new reality."

Caleb offered his hand as a sudden wind kicked up in the clearing. Clouds churned overhead in a sky empty of both demons and owls.

The Arcanum bowed their heads over Abigail as she took her final breath. Only Lovecraft turned his eyes skyward.

Meteors—or at least what seemed to be meteors—criss-crossed in the sky above the swirling clouds. First there were two, then four, then twelve, then twenty. After a time, Lovecraft lost count of their flaming tails.

A deep rumble of thunder sounded on the horizon.

Then beads of light, resembling fireflies, began appearing all across the clearing, swirling in tight loops, rising from the ground like bubbles from champagne.

At this, Caleb's eyes narrowed.

By now, the entire Arcanum was paying attention. There was a buzz on the air, as if a live field of electricity surrounded them.

And it came from Abigail's skin.

It was a bluish sheath of energy crackling with life. It became uncomfortable touching her, and Doyle had to lay the dying angel back onto the grass as the muscles in his hands and arms reacted to the small shocks.

The forest came alive with blinking lights. Frogs croaked and crickets chirped, suddenly awakened to the curious events of the evening. Farm hounds barked in the distance as sleeping birds started calling sharply from the treetops. Locusts hummed and foxes yapped.

Lovecraft heard Caleb mutter, "Don't you dare."

As the noise of the forest rose to a frenzied pitch, a wave of light composed of billions of tiny nimbuses swept through the clearing then out across the forest. It enveloped the Arcanum, rolling past Caleb, burning all eyes with its brightness.

In the white intensity of the light, colors and textures disappeared.

Lovecraft held his forearm over his eyes, attempting to see what was happening. He could hear Caleb's protests behind him.

"You can't do this. You betrayer. You coward!" Caleb's voice was strained, hysterical. "Face me! We dare you. Bastard! Lying dog! We hate you. We hate you!"

Lovecraft covered his ears to keep them from bleeding as Caleb's voice rose to the shrieking pitch of all the damned. One voice became hundreds of thousands. Only the light around him kept Lovecraft from slipping into the Abyssal sea of those agonized voices.

DOYLE, ON THE other hand, could not see. He could not tell if his eyes were closed or opened, so bright and all-encompassing was the light. It was hot but not burning, bright but not blinding, and somewhere within it Abigail's body lifted off the ground. Doyle could not touch her, but he felt her rise up and heard her say, "What is happening?"

And he heard himself answer, "I think you're going home."

And that was all that was said. For many moments, there was only white light and silence. Doyle could not feel the Arcanum, but somehow he knew they were close. And not only that, but he felt the closeness of many others. Somehow the essence of thousands was dissolved in the light, and was with him through those endless moments of resonant stillness. He felt the presence of the dead, and though he could not isolate any one name or any one touch, he knew Kingsley was there, and his mother and father, and his ancestors. He was flooded with warmth as the light began to fade. Gradually, the shape of the clearing resolved itself, and the muted chirps of the crickets began again.

And the Arcanum found themselves kneeling over an empty patch of matted grass.

Abigail was gone.

Most of their faces were wet with tears and sweat. The only one not crying was the only one who couldn't, because his tear ducts had been burned away. Caleb swayed in the cool breeze, steam still rising off his charred skin.

Doyle stood and turned to face Caleb. He did not speak, but simply stuffed his hands in his pockets and raised his eyebrows.

With that, Caleb exploded into a flock of large crows. They cawed, bitterly, and flapped away.

Doyle walked over to Lovecraft and helped him to his feet. "Are you well?"

Lovecraft nodded.

Something heavy moved in the bushes.

Doyle and Houdini crossed to the edge of the woods. They lifted the branches away, revealing a flustered and sweat-soaked Detective Mullin, lying on his back, still stunned from what he had just witnessed.

"Good evening, Detective," Doyle said.

Mullin just blinked. His lips were moving, but no sound came out.

Doyle knelt down. "Come to think of it, you're just the man I wanted to see."

46

MULLIN CRANKED THE handle of the Dictaphone, spinning the wax cylinder as Darian DeMarcus's scratchy voice spooled from the recording horn and into the office.

"You were going to tell on me! Why couldn't you just let me be?"

Mullin's red hair was slicked back against his scalp and he was dressed in a sharp-looking Cassimere suit with Oxford dress shoes and a Bat Wing bow tie. His felt fedora sat on the table beside the Dictaphone. As he kept spinning the cylinder, his eyes fell on McDuff, the chief of police, seated in an expensive leather chair. McDuff pulled on his close-cropped beard as he listened to Darian's screams.

"I was your brother. You were supposed to be loyal to me, and instead you tried to hurt me."

Next, Mullin's eyes fell on Captain Bartleby of Fourth Ward, who seemed more interested in the pricey hourglass on the coffee table than anything Darian had to say.

"Stop it, Erica. You're not real."

Across from Mullin, glowering hotly, was Barnabus Wilkie Tyson. He chomped on an unlit cigar as the Dictaphone warbled on.

"You're dead!"

Finally, Mullin's eyes fell on William Randolph Hearst, standing behind one of the lounge chairs, arms folded across his chest, his demeanor grim.

"I killed you."

Mullin released the handle and the cylinder stopped spinning. "Shall I play it again?"

Chief McDuff shifted in his seat. "If you don't mind—"

"That won't be necessary, Detective," Hearst interrupted. "I'll be hearing that voice in my nightmares. Obviously, a deranged and dangerous individual. Certainly fits the profile of the Occult Killer to a tee."

"And this all checks out, Shaughnessy?" Chief McDuff asked, scratching his beard.

"It does, sir," Mullin answered. "Papers of the estate identify 'em as brother and sister. The DeMarcus family had a history of this sort of Devil worship. Motives appear to be related to some kind of ritual scenario. The sister—Madame Rose or Miss DeMarcus, however you want to call her—found out about these crimes, but before she could contact the authorities, she was murdered by her brother. This fellow in the recording here."

"And what happened after this recording?" Tyson growled.

"Overdosed. He was a drug fiend. Thought he was seein' phantoms and what have you."

Tyson scoffed, but offered no rebuttal.

"But how'd you get the recording, Shaughnessy?" McDuff asked, still confused.

"A good investigator doesn't give up his sources. Isn't that right, Detective?" Hearst asked.

Mullin nodded. "Yes, sir, Mr. Hearst. That's my feeling about it."

McDuff scratched his head and leaned back in the chair. "And there's no sign of Mr. Caleb?"

"None, sir," Mullin answered. "He's skipped town."

"Astonishing," McDuff said.

"There was something about Paul Caleb that never felt quite

right, I must say," Hearst added, then clapped his hands together. "Well, gentlemen, it's been good of you to come."

The men all stood. Tyson didn't bother shaking hands. He
sneered at Mullin, popped his cigar into his pocket, and
stomped across the office, slamming the door behind him.

Hearst ignored him, shaking hands with the captain and the
chief of police. Mullin did the same, turning to Hearst, who, instead, took his arm.

"Stay a moment, won't you, Detective?" Hearst asked.

The chief and the captain took their hats and wandered over
to the door, looking back at Mullin before shaking their heads.

Hearst gave Mullin a wry grin and went to his bar. He
dropped ice cubes into a highball glass. "Drink, Detective?"

"Bit early for me, sir."

Hearst poured himself a scotch, then turned around, raising
the glass to Mullin. "You're a member of the club now, Detective. Tell me, what are your plans?"

Mullin looked out at the blue sky and sprawling cityscape beyond Hearst's window. "Thinkin' of goin' into business for myself."

"Private investigation?"

"Something like that."

"Excellent. Perhaps I'll call on your services sometime. Discretion is a large part of the job, isn't it?"

"Can be, sir," Mullin answered as he plucked his fedora off
the table. He nodded to the publishing magnate. "Good day, Mr.
Hearst."

"Good day, Detective Mullin."

Mullin had crossed the office and put his hand on the door-
knob when Hearst called to him again.

"Oh, and Detective?"

Mullin turned. "Sir?"

Hearst smiled. "Tell Houdini he owes me one."

"I expect you'll see him before I do, sir," Mullin replied as he
stepped into the corridor and shut the door behind him.

*   *   *

GULLS CRIED OVERHEAD as Lovecraft, with a square object wrapped in cloth under his arm, pushed through cheering crowds who were greeting soldiers just returning off a military transport from Annapolis. A brass band filled the air with celebratory music from a makeshift grandstand off Pier 14. Trucks and taxis honked—though whether in welcome or in irritation at the bottleneck, Lovecraft couldn't tell.

He elbowed his way onto Pier 16, where porters shuttled carts of luggage onto the gangplank of the mighty *Mauretania*.

Lovecraft stopped.

Aleister Crowley stood on the dock in his camel-hair coat and English cap, some twenty feet away, throwing pieces of bread to a hovering group of seagulls. As was his custom, he spoke to Lovecraft without having seen him. "You need a better coat," he said.

It was cold. Lovecraft pulled his frayed collar around his throat. Then, sick with guilt, he thrust a cloth-wrapped object toward Crowley with both hands. "Take it."

Crowley deigned to look over. He sniffed, brushed his hands free of breadcrumbs, and strolled over to Lovecraft. He took the bundle, then threw back the cloth and ran a hand over the cracked leather binding of the Book of Enoch. He then rewrapped the codex and tucked it under one arm.

"I'm headed to Sicily, you know. I'm opening the Abbey of Thelema. When you tire of vaudeville acrobats and overrated novelists, you should join me there."

Lovecraft only stared at the Book.

Crowley smiled. "Well, there it is. Cheers, Lovecraft." The sorcerer turned on his heel, and wandered slowly into the gathering crowd of ticketed passengers.

Hours later, Lovecraft had wandered through Battery Park, past the ferries to Brooklyn and Jeanette Park. He had tried to sip a whiskey at Fraunces Tavern, but had recoiled at the taste, and instead walked north to the Jewish cemetery near Mariner's Temple and Chatham Square. He was sitting on a bench gazing at gravestones when a black carriage, drawn by two horses, pulled up to the cemetery gates. Lovecraft recognized the driver as Franz Kukol, Houdini's assistant.

Sure enough, the door opened and Houdini stuck his head out. "What a surprise to find you here." Houdini gestured with his thumb for Lovecraft to join him.

Lovecraft entered the carriage and sat down beside Marie and across from Doyle and Houdini.

"Hello, Howard," Doyle said as he dropped a large, square object wrapped in protective cloth into the demonologist's lap.

AT THAT VERY moment, Aleister Crowley laid the shrouded Book of Enoch on a table in his cabin. The Atlantic Ocean swelled outside his porthole. He removed the shroud and caressed the leather binding. Then, perching a pair of reading glasses on his nose, he opened to the first page. In an immaculate handwritten script, it read:

Once upon a time, Cinderella lived with her jealous step-mother and evil step sisters . . .

"Eh? What is this?" Crowley muttered. Then his face darkened. He examined the leather binding and found traces of glue. In a sudden fury, he tore at the book, ripping and slashing the leather binding until its true nature was revealed. The title read:

The Tales of Mother Goose

Crowley roared and threw the book across the stateroom. As it thudded off a wall and onto the floor, a note slid free from one of the pages. The sorcerer snatched it up, and read:

Dear Aleister,
By way of thanks for your helpful information, we offer you this gift: a 1729 first edition, the very first English translation of Perrault's Contes de ma mere l'oye, *or as you probably already discovered:* The Tales of Mother Goose. *Enjoy.*

Best regards,
Sir Arthur Conan Doyle

Crowley crumpled the note in his fist and squeezed until his nails drew blood. He bared his teeth and growled, "Doyle."

IN THE CARRIAGE, Lovecraft gazed at the Book of Enoch sitting in his lap, minus its ancient binding. Then he looked up at the others. "It wasn't what you might think."

"And what is that?" Doyle asked.

"I was never working for him, I . . ." Lovecraft shook his head, unable to explain. "Do your worst. I deserve it, I suppose. But know this: I value my membership in this association. I . . ."

"But, Howard, this was my plan from the very start," Doyle said.

Lovecraft looked up. "What?"

"I counted on Crowley making this bargain and you following through with it. I'm sorry if you feel misled."

"But you couldn't," Lovecraft stuttered. "The . . . the conversation . . ."

"From the moment I learned of Konstantin Duvall's death, I knew the path would inevitably lead to Aleister Crowley. The circumstances were simply too tempting. And what we know of Crowley proves he is a man who prefers indirect means of getting what he wants. He far prefers to use others for his dirty work than risk a frontal assault. Yet the circumstances seemed to eliminate him as a suspect. My conclusion: If Crowley wasn't the hunter, then he very well might be the prey. Why else would he send us the clue leading us to Madame Rose? Why aid the Arcanum in avenging the death of his sworn enemy, if not to save his own hide? Only a student of Duvall and Crowley would know the location of the Book of Enoch and the means of unlocking its mysteries. But Crowley's no fool. I knew he would whet your appetite with clues, but save the meal for when you struck your bargain. And I knew you'd accept it."

"Why? Because I'm the heartless demonologist? Incapable of feeling? The one you all distrust?" Lovecraft's jaw was tight with embarrassment and anger.

"No, Howard, for precisely the opposite reason. Because any rational, caring man in your position would've done the same.

Because when you saw Abigail, the stakes became clear to you. Because you cared for her, and for her you were willing to take a grave risk. And I respect that. Now, were I to seek out Crowley and ask for his help, the results would have been quite different. But the two of you share a unique bond, a bond I chose to exploit. So don't torture yourself. For, though I loathe to admit it, in this situation we needed Crowley's help."

"But how could you—?"

"Honestly, Howard," Doyle cut him off. "It's elementary."

Lovecraft sighed, shaking his head. When he looked down at the codex, however, a cloud passed over his eyes. "He won't forget this, you know. He'll want revenge."

"Yes, that's what I want, too," Doyle admitted. "Because that way he is in our control. I prefer an Aleister Crowley bent on revenge against the Arcanum rather than one scheming in the shadows, with nothing but time on his hands. Do you understand? For every action there is a reaction, and therefore, predictability. And that's what I want Crowley's behavior to be: predictable. This occupation offers great rewards and great dangers, and we must be willing to accept that." He leaned over and patted Lovecraft's knee. "You took on a great deal of responsibility and did splendidly, my boy. Duvall would be proud."

"Quite." Houdini winked. "Good show, H. P."

Marie elbowed Lovecraft in the ribs—the closest she would come to a compliment.

"Now, here's the real question, Art'ur," Marie said as she slid a long, white feather from her pocket. "What we gonna do wit' dis?"

Doyle examined the feather. "Interesting. A remiges feather. Of a wing, in other words. The calamus. The downy coat, obviously keratin. It's real, all right. Taken together with the extraordinary proportions, it suggests a creature with an eight-foot wingspan—a flying creature roughly the size of an adult human being." Doyle handed the angel feather to Lovecraft. "Here is the newest addition to the Arcanum's Hall of Relics. I leave it in your able hands, Mr. Curator."

Lovecraft spun the memento in his palm and smiled, remembering her face.

ABOUT THE AUTHOR

AT TWENTY-TWO, Thomas Wheeler sold his first screenplay to Twentieth Century Fox and for the past eight years has continued to work on major Hollywood features. Wheeler lives in Los Angeles with his wife, Christina, and their son, Luca. *The Arcanum* is his first novel.